SPECULAT[VE] [JAPAN]

M000313179

"Silver Bullet"
and Other Tales

SPECULATIVE JAPAN 3

"Silver Bullet"
and Other Tales

Introduction by **Darrell Schweitzer**

Selected and edited by **Edward Lipsett**

Kurodahan Press
2012

Speculative Japan 3: "Silver Bullet" and Other Tales of Japanese Science Fiction and Fantasy

© 2012 Kurodahan Press, Intercom Ltd.

FG-JP0024-L19
ISBN: 978-4-902075-30-4

Kurodahan Press
Kurodahan Press is a division of Intercom, Ltd.
3-9-10-403 Tenjin, Chuo-Ku, Fukuoka 810-0001 Japan
www.kurodahan.com

CONTENTS

Preface

Edward Lipsett

Welcome back!

This is the third volume in our continuing (and we hope endless) series of Speculative Japan anthologies, once again presenting a selection of outstanding works of science fiction and fantasy from Japan.

As with any nation, or indeed any group of people, Japan encompasses a wide range of viewpoints, lifestyles, and attitudes: face it, not matter what the country or language, people are people. There are certain characteristics that groups share, common heritages of culture, similar childhood experiences and adult lifestyles, and of course language.

It would be nice if we could all understand each other perfectly, but it won't happen any time soon, if at all. And that means that unless you are one of the lucky multilingual few, you're stuck reading in English. If all you read is English, then your entire worldview is colored by English, whether you recognize or appreciate it or not. And that's a real pity, because English—and the Western way of looking at the world—is only one of hundreds and hundreds of languages and cultures that are all equally valid.

Which brings me to the point of Speculative Japan.

I don't expect the stories here to bring any earth-shattering revelations, or suddenly make you understand the depths of the Japanese psyche. Won't happen. But hopefully they will let you steal a quick glimpse into the brilliant imaginations of people in Japan who, perhaps, view the world in a different way.

This volume offers a few stories in the dark fantasy genre, and we are also fortunate to be able to offer our first story by a Western author living here in Japan.

The driving objective of the Speculative Japan series remains unchanged: to bring as many new voices into the English language as we can, to introduce readers to the talents and imaginations of decades of Japanese creativity, and hopefully to stimulate a host of new literary creations.

I think you'll enjoy them.

Fukuoka, Japan
October 2012

INTRODUCTION

Darrell Schweitzer

It's not for me to say if these stories are "typically Japanese." As an outsider, I can only point out what non-Japanese think are "typical" Japanese characteristics, and whether or not they are present. You will find some of those expectations fulfilled here. Certainly Asamatsu Ken's "A White Camellia in a Vase," in which a samurai is preoccupied with aesthetics and the placement of a single flower in an otherwise bare room, seems very Japanese to me. This is the sort of minimalism we see in Japanese art, where the subtlest details matter. But what seems more "typically Japanese" is that the elderly samurai can care about such things without any suggestion that he has lost any of his masculine, heroic character. You would not see a medieval European knight or a Homeric warrior behaving that way. So the foreign reader can indeed see that these stories are—unsurprisingly—written from a different set of cultural assumptions, which is part of their charm and their fascination. At the same time I think I see a Western influence here. The winking flowers at the end call to mind nothing more than Arthur Machen's observation (from "The White People") that true evil is a perversion of natural law: ". . . if the roses in your garden sang a weird song, you would go mad."

At the same time, some of the stories in this book are surprisingly outward-looking and cosmic in a manner we have rarely seen in Anglophone science fiction since, at the very least, Arthur C. Clarke's *Childhood's End* if not the works of Olaf Stapledon. "To the Blue Star" by Ogawa Issui is exceptionally ambitious. The protagonist is a machine hive-mind which is the successor to the human race. The action takes place over hundreds of thousands of years. Fujita Masaya's "Angel French" is on a smaller scale only by comparison.

The title may refer to a type of donut, but the story itself spans light-years and centuries, as two lovers (or their post-human memories, programmed into space probes) are reunited very far away from the story's starting point.

The range is impressive. Mori Natsuko's "It's All Thanks to Saijō Hideki" is very subversively strange indeed. Whether it is intended to be a kind of black comedy is hard for me to tell, because of cultural distance, and because it is a translation, but consider this: the human race has been wiped out by a virus. The last female in the world is a typical 15-year-old Japanese schoolgirl in pigtails and sailor uniform, a figure familiar enough from manga, except she is also a giantess and desires only intimate female companionship. When she finally meets the last man, he's a drag queen. Now what?

We see in Ayatsuji Yukito's "Heart of Darkness" something akin to surrealism and also a moral fable about human perversity. Onda Riku's "The Warning" is a neat little horror story, largely narrated by a dog given the ability to read and write by aliens. Marc Schultz's "Green Tea Ice Cream" is a science fictional medical horror story of sorts, written from a different perspective, that of a foreigner resident in Japan. The style is a little more Western, American I would guess without knowing anything about Mr. Schultz. It is a very moving story about Japanese people and Japanese beliefs. Is it, or are any of the stories in this excellent collection, "typically Japanese"?

That may be the wrong question to ask. Japan has, of course, its own literary tradition going back many centuries to at least *The Tale of Genji*, and it has in modern times its own distinct speculative tradition. But these stories are universal. They are human. We can relate to them emotionally, regardless of who we are. Some, like "To the Blue Star," consider all of humanity (or post-humanity) at once, without reference to specific nationality or culture. What the Western reader looks for initially in a book like this is strangeness—*difference*—but what he finds ultimately is commonality. That is the message of these stories, that, despite any differences, when it comes to the most important things in life, we are all the same. We are one.

Philadelphia, Pennsylvania
November 2012

Speculative Japan 3

"Silver Bullet"
and Other Tales

A White Camellia in a Vase

Asamatsu Ken

Translated by Joe Earle

"Lord Tachibana may be a bit weird but he's perfectly harmless. And anyway, it's thanks to him that the family's come up in the world, so please be very careful not to say anything impolite."

Remembering these words of advice from Tachibana Tanomo, Tōami Kōshuku went out through the back door of the compound's main building. Guided by a servant, he made his way over rectangular stepping stones toward a residence on the other side of the garden, then suddenly stopped in his tracks and frowned.

He felt he was being watched by someone, but glancing all around he saw no sign of anyone who could be looking at him. The only things that met his gaze were flowers in bud. "Camellias perhaps," Tōami muttered to himself. The petals were just starting to open up and break through the reddish-yellow buds, their vivid whiteness soaking into his eyes.

It was the second month of the twelfth year of the Eiroku era, 1569. Even though it was now spring, the morning air was bitterly cold.

"This way, please." The servant pointed to the residence, turned toward it and announced, "My lord, we have arrived."

"Very well." The answer came straight back, in a hoarse voice that clearly belonged to an elderly man yet gave absolutely no sense of the early signs of insanity that the Kyoto rumormongers loved to gossip about. In fact, it had a calmness about it that resembled the diction of a senior Buddhist priest.

1

Tōami climbed the steps to the spacious veranda, then called out in respectful tones, "My lord, I humbly beg the favor of this first audience with you. My name is Tōami."

"Please put yourself at ease. Come in!"

"Thank you," said Tōami, sliding open the shoji screen. A white light burst into his field of vision, not so bright as to be dazzling, more like the soft glow reflected off snow at dawn. On the raised platform toward the back of this large, light-filled room sat an old man, his long hair knotted at the back. He was said to be ninety-nine years of age, yet judging by his face, so typical of an elderly samurai, you would think he was in his mid-seventies. He sat bolt upright, his back straight, his whole body giving off an aura of gravity and authority. In keeping with the old man's character, the room was plain and austere: no painted screens, no hearth, not even a set of shelves. The only decoration was in the tokonoma alcove: a single flower in bud, displayed artlessly in a vase made from a thick stem of bamboo cut at an angle. Struck by the contrast between the color of the alcove walls and the flower's pale reddish-yellow bud, Tōami mumbled, "Hmm, this looks like a typical single-flower arrangement." Noticing that the old man was smiling at him, he stopped and lowered his head to the floor in another deep bow.

"My lord, I humbly beg the favor of this first audience with you. My name is Tōami Kōshuku." As soon as he had finished, the calm tones of the old man's voice swept over him.

"I am Tachibana Nagato, but in my retirement I have taken a new name, Mokushun'ō. Please raise your head and show me your face. Are you another of those people who've come to listen to tall stories told by an old recluse?

"I'm sorry, I didn't mean that. They tell me you're here to congratulate me on my ninety-ninth birthday and have a chat over a cup of tea. I heard about your visit from my grandson Tanomo, but I gather he's not at home right now."

"You are very well informed, my lord."

"I might be living in retirement in a separate building, but I know exactly what's going on in the rest of the compound as well as in the outside world. It looks as though that fool Tanomo's taken fright on hearing Nobuhide's boy Nobunaga's on his way to Kyoto, and rushed off there to curry favor with him. Eh? Why are you making a face like Tanomo as well? Is there something wrong with calling

2

Nobunaga a 'boy'? All right, so should I do the same as everyone else and call him 'Lord Nobunaga'? And even if I did, why should someone who thinks he's powerful enough to bring the whole of Japan under his control care about a wrinkled old man like me?"

In response to Mokushun'ō's raucous laughter, Tōami asked, "Do you know what was happening around the time Lord Nobunaga was born?"

"I do. It was the second year of the Tenbun era, 1533, during the reign of the twelfth shogun, Lord Banshōin Yoshiharu. Even though that fellow Nobunaga's father Nobuhide was nothing more than a vassal of Oda Yamato no Kami, he just adored courtiers. He'd do things like invite imperial treasurer Yamashina Tokitsugu from Kyoto and lay on a banquet that was completely beyond his means or position. Nobunaga was born the year after that banquet."

Tōami gave a sigh of admiration. "Older people never forget events that took place long ago."

"Is that so?"

As Tōami nodded in agreement, something white suddenly cut into his gaze. *What's this*, he thought. Looking around, he realized that it was the single camellia displayed in the alcove. *Eh? Wasn't it still a bud when I looked at it a moment ago?* Staring suspiciously at the camellia, he saw something black wink behind the pure-white petals. *No, flowers don't wink. It was just the center of the flower showing when the camellia was shaken in the breeze. But wait, is it really a camellia?* He knitted his brows. How could he, Tōami Kōshuku, an expert noted for his discernment not only in the tea ceremony, calligraphy, painting, and the appraisal of antiques but also in the art of flower arrangement, be in any doubt as to whether the bloom in front of him was a camellia or not? Wouldn't this be a blot on his reputation for connoisseurship?

As if reading his thoughts the old man laughed, showing pure white teeth that reminded Tōami of the flower's whiteness. "What are you staring at? It's just a white camellia."

"I'm so sorry. I must apologize," replied Tōami.

"But what is it?"

"I was thinking that flower might not be a white camellia."

"Oh really? In that case perhaps you were wondering whether it's a tea plant or a sasanqua rather than a regular camellia. They're quite similar," the old man replied wryly.

"No. All three flowers—tea, sasanqua, and camellia—have yellow centers. But the center of that flower is glossy black, as if covered in hardened lacquer. It's quite different from the other three."

"What does it matter? It's still just a flower."

"Yes, it's still only a flower, but I aspire to be an unrivaled expert in the way of flowers just as I am in tea, calligraphy, and painting. So for me it's a matter of life and death to be able to identify it."

"That's surely something of an exaggeration. Dear me! It looks as though Tanomo sent me someone who's very difficult to chat with," said the old man with a look of disappointment.

"Well, where did your lordship . . . ?"

"That," said the old man, thrusting his body forward to stop Tōami finishing his question, "is something I cannot forget. It was the eleventh month of the sixteenth year of the Bunmei era, 1484, when I was still a humble foot soldier only fourteen years of age."

"That was a very long time ago."

"Yes. It was the year that the ninth shogun Yoshihisa, also known as Jōtokuin, was reconciled to his mother Hino Tomiko. Around that time I was in the service of Lord Hosokawa Masamoto, fighting in Yamashiro province to help put down a peasant rebellion. At one point during the campaign, when we were in the mountains, I became separated from my companions. While I was helplessly blundering around in the darkness I fell into an opening in the ground."

"An opening in the ground?"

"I hadn't seen anything like it during the day. It was as if someone had dug it to trap me. It was a deep, deep hole. My helmet and spear disappeared, and I fell all the way to the bottom without them. As I was going down, I had a very strange sensation, as if the inside and outside of my body had switched places, like a bag being turned inside out, and it started to seem as though I was falling upwards instead of downwards. Then I landed gently on the ground. No bones were broken. I found myself in a soft, round hollow in the earth. Its floor glowed with light that shone from the top of the hole, revealing fresh green undergrowth in which there bloomed a single camellia. Looking up I could see the hole was more than twenty feet deep, with steep sides and a wide, gaping opening at the top. Probably this jar-like cavity had opened up in the ground during an earthquake long, long before, and a seed had fallen in and grown into a flower. I became convinced the flower had saved my

4

life. I suppose thoughts like this often come over you in the thick of battle. So I broke the white camellia off at its stem, put it inside my clothes and crawled up the sides of the hole, all the while praying, 'Please save me, please save me!' When I got out I was miraculously reunited with my companions. From that time until more than a month later, when the fighting had moved away from Yamashiro and I'd returned to the Hosokawa family barracks in Kyoto, I kept the white camellia inside my clothes and made it my most treasured lucky charm."

"Didn't it wither?"

"No, not at all. When I got back to Kyoto I made a vase by roughly cutting a stem of thick *mōsō* bamboo, filled it with water, and put the flower in it. Look! Eighty-five years later it's still just the same." The old man gave a somewhat sinister laugh and gestured to the alcove with his chin. When Tōami looked that way he noticed that the lacquer-black center of the flower was facing him. The contrast between the curling white petals and the little black circle at the center made it seem as though the flower was an eye with its pupil fully dilated, staring at him. No, the flower wasn't just looking at him. He was convinced it was bending forward to follow the conversation that had just passed between them.

"I have heard it said that because they lose their petals so quickly, in those days samurai detested camellias and tried not to go anywhere near them before setting off for battle."

"A long time ago I learned from a book by Sen'ō or one of the other early masters that the secret of displaying flowers is that if the main element of the arrangement is strong, then the supporting elements will also be strong. As soon as I came across that passage, I understood what had happened. When I was at the bottom of the hole, I didn't break off the camellia; I was broken off by it. It was not I who arranged the flower; I was arranged by the flower. And so for eighty-five years I've kept on blooming in sight of the white camellia. But now I think it's grown tired of caring for me. It's ordered me to send another flower to watch, fighting battles, creeping about on the bare earth, and carrying on an ugly, mean existence. And that flower is you."

Tōami struggled with all his might to free himself from the old man's outstretched hands, which were grasping him by the wrists.

"Let me go, you old lunatic!"

He raced to the shoji screen and slid it open. At that moment everything in front of him turned white.

The whole of the garden beyond the veranda was alive with blossoming white camellias like the one in the alcove, their lacquer-black centers turned toward him. As his terrified gaze met theirs, the flowers winked in unison.

Ayatsuji Yukito

Translated by Daniel Jackson

I had a dream. Perhaps.

– 1 –

It all started about a week ago, when they gave me an examination here at the Midorigaoka Hospital.

As I approached the Big Five-O, I was beginning to feel a bit uneasy about my health, so I had been getting check-ups for various parts of my body. I'd made appointments, of course, for a battery of examinations, including an MRI of my brain, a CT scan of my lungs, and an abdominal ultrasound scan.

"Your brain looks very healthy," said Dr. Ishikura (1), the brain specialist, as he looked at the MRI imagery. He's been my physician for a couple years now, and always wears a pale green patch over his left eye.

"You mentioned you were worried about early-onset senility, but I don't see any indications of that. No vascular abnormalities. Nope, it all looks very clean!"

Just as I started to let out a sigh of relief, he switched to my lung CT scans and asked, "Do you still smoke?"

"Ah, yes. Uh . . ."

"Ever thought of quitting?"

"Yes, but why do you ask?"

"Well, quitting does put quite a bit of stress on the body, too. So I won't try to pressure you into it. Don't worry."

Looking slowly through the scans, he *hmm*ed to himself, deep in thought. Despite my fears, I asked anyway: "Is there something there?"

"What? No, no, relax. Your lungs are as healthy as I've ever seen; certainly no need to call in a respiratory specialist for a second opinion."

"Oh."

"As your physician, though, I really should advise you to quit smoking."

"I see." I nodded, and looked at the floor, a poor nicotine addict thinking to himself, *Please don't ask me to quit completely.* While I was in conversation with myself, the gastroenterologist, Dr. Ishikura (2), came in.

The two doctors Ishikura: same age, same attitude. They look like identical twins, but, unlike the first one, the other Dr. Ishikura wears his pale green patch over his right eye. This is convenient, as it makes it possible for me to tell them apart easily, without having to check their name tags.

"Well, now, about your abdominal scans . . ."

Dr. Ishikura (2) stepped up to the light box, taking center stage from Dr. Ishikura (1), and turned to face me with a somewhat troubled expression.

I had to ask: "Is there a problem?"

Now that I thought of it, while I was getting the ultrasound, he *hrm*ed and *hmph*ed a number of times as he moved the transducer around. I hadn't said anything at the time, but I'd been a bit worried about his reaction.

He peered up at me from under his eyebrows for a moment, then glanced over at the other Dr. Ishikura before beginning to clip a number of ultrasound printouts onto the light box.

"There aren't any obvious abnormalities in your kidneys, pancreas, spleen or gall bladder. Your liver, however . . ."

I leaned forward in my chair to get a better look at the scans, but they really didn't mean anything to me.

"Is there something wrong with my liver?" I asked. "Fatty? Inflammation maybe?"

"No, no, nothing like that. . . ."

"Surely not cirrhosis! Or a tumor! But I don't feel anything at all!"

"Well, the liver is often referred to as the 'silent organ,' after all," he replied, his face still inscrutable. Then his expression cleared somewhat. "You don't have any life-threatening issues such as cirrhosis or hepatic cancer."

"Oh . . . Well then, what?"

"Here. Have a look," he suggested, holding out one of the transparencies. "See this shadow here? It covers quite a large area and is shaped sort of like the Crab Nebula."

Now that he pointed it out, I was able to see what he was indicating. I had no idea what the Crab Nebula might look like, but it was strange I hadn't noticed that dark region in the first place. The more I looked, the worse it looked.

"What is it?" My apprehension mounting, I had difficulty speaking clearly. "It's a malignant tumor, right?"

"No, it's not that at all," he said flatly, and shot another glance at the other Dr. Ishikura.

"You've got a dark shadow on your soul."

– 2 –

"A dark shadow . . . on my soul?"

I doubted my ears, but the doctor nodded gravely.

"Yes, a darkness in your heart."

"This? Here? This dark blurry blob?"

"That's right."

"You mean the sort of shadow on my heart they always mention in TV dramas or the tabloids when they're talking about some terrible murder or something? That sort of shadow?"

"Exactly. That's exactly what this darkness is. So you're familiar with it, then?"

"Yes, I guess so."

"Researchers are finally beginning to understand what makes it tick. Dr. Masaki over at Q University was finally able to pin it down after years of clinical research."

Professor Masaki, in psychiatrics over at the Q University Hospital, I thought to myself. I'd met him. I had no idea he'd been studying this for so long, though.

"Why in the world is this shadow on my liver? And how come you can see it with the ultrasound?"

9

"I thought you already knew. The ultrasound diagnostic systems here are all equipped with special features developed by Dr. Masaki."

"But it's still pretty strange for it to be in the liver, isn't it? If it's my heart and soul we're talking about, shouldn't it be up in my brain? You know, my hippocampus or amygdala or something?"

"Yes, you would think so, but . . ."

Dr. Ishikura (2) fell silent and looked at his colleague, Dr. Ishikura (1) the neurosurgeon, who took over the explanation.

"Dr. Masaki's research indicates that our hearts—souls, if you prefer— are not entirely located in our brains but rather distributed throughout our bodies. He's been ridiculed for this theory for many years, but recently it has been demonstrated through the detection of dark shadows on the soul in clinical situations."

"As we did here," added Dr. Ishikura (2) unnecessarily.

I sighed. "What happens now?"

"One option," said the physician, a finger on the edge of his pale green eye patch, "is to remove it surgically."

"Surgery? You can remove it surgically? The dark shadow?"

"Yes. It would be far more difficult if it were in your brain or your heart, for example, but you're very lucky because it's in your liver. Even better, it doesn't penetrate very deeply. We can remove it completely with a very simple procedure; a great many similar surgeries have been performed on other patients, some of them right here in this hospital. The success rate is nearly one hundred percent."

He spoke with confidence; apparently he had absolutely no worries about my condition or the procedure.

Even so, I certainly couldn't decide right on the spot. Still, if the operation was that simple, I thought perhaps I should just go ahead with it right away. That seemed the most attractive option.

– 3 –

And so, here I am again, a week later.

I made up my mind, talked about it with my wife and got her support, and decided to go ahead and have the darkness in my heart excised.

During the pre-op explanation, I learned the operation would be performed with a specialized, state-of-the-art instrument. A laparoscopy puts the least physical stress on the patient, and I should be able to go home after only two or three days, if all went as expected. And for some reason, Professor Masaki of Q University would join the surgical team, which helped alleviate my worries.

"Don't worry," said Ms. Sakitani, the friendly nurse, as I began to slip off under the effects of the anesthesia. "When you wake up, the operation will be all over, and all that darkness will be completely gone."

But why did her smile look so strange? I wondered. Still, just as she promised, I woke up several hours later lying in a peaceful hospital bed, the operation over.

My wife was standing beside my bed.

"Good morning," she said. "The operation went smoothly. Congratulations!"

Somewhat groggy, I mumbled something in reply.

My abdomen felt a little strange on the right side, but I guessed the anesthetic must still have been working because it didn't hurt at all. In fact, my heart felt unusually light, my mood happy, bright. Everything was wonderful!

I was, to be quite honest, astonished that the effect should be so apparent, so immediate, after having that shadow removed from my heart. Or was I just imagining things? No.

It wasn't my imagination. My heart was lighter, less *oppressed* than it had ever been. I felt it would be no trouble at all to stop smoking now, and I figured that dizziness wouldn't bother me again. I knew I could write quality material now easily, words flowing from my pen.

"Wow. Just wow!"

I couldn't help but exclaim to myself in delight.

– 4 –

A while later Dr. Ishikura came into the room. No. 2, the gastroenterologist.

"How do you feel?"

"I feel great!" I replied. "How can I describe it?"

"Everyone says the same thing. I'm still surprised at the change," he explained, smiling.

"Now," he added, in quite a different tone of voice, "would you like to see the shadow we removed from your liver?"

"I can see it?"

"Oh, yes, if you'd like to. In fact, it is established policy to return the shadow to the patient after the operation. Unlike damaged organs or tumors, the shadows are quite difficult for hospitals to dispose of, because there is no established disposal method. So we've adopted the policy of returning them to the patients and letting them keep them."

"Oh, I see."

The doctor handed me a small white plastic container. "Here you are."

"In here? The shadow is in here?"

"That's right," he nodded. "I must warn you, though, not to look inside."

"Why? Will something terrible happen if I see it?"

"No, nothing will happen if you just look at it. But . . ."

His voice trailed off into a vague murmur, then grew stronger.

"It's up to you, of course."

He left the room.

The nurse and my wife eventually left for the night, leaving me alone in my hospital bed.

I thought about it for a long time, and finally decided to look inside the white container. I wanted to see for myself just what this darkness that had been inside me looked like.

I opened it up, and slowly, fearfully, peered inside.

It was a clump of blackness, about the size of a ping-pong ball. To my surprise, it looked soft, like a little ball of cotton candy.

So, this is it, I thought to myself. *This is the shadow that was inside me.*

I unconsciously reached into the container, grabbed the shadow, picked it up and brought it closer.

It was an uncontrollable impulse. The shadow just looked so delicious! It melted in my mouth as I wrapped my tongue around it. Down my throat went a delicious savor that melted right into my heart.

Angel French

Fujita Masaya
Translated by Pamela Ikegami

After class Daichi and I pushed our bikes along as we walked to the Mister Donut shop next to the university, like always. Daichi got his usual Old-Fashioned, and I got a Chocolate Angel French doughnut[1]. We also ordered two café au laits. Daichi carried the tray of doughnuts and drinks to a table next to the window. We usually got refills of our café au laits and talked on and on about movies and books. It was something we did all the time: the most natural thing in the world.

Usually Daichi sat down and reached straight for his doughnut, but that day he stared into my face and said with joy, "Subaru, I've been chosen."

Even now I can recall that moment so clearly.

"Chosen?"

"To be an astronaut!"

That's how it all began.

Daichi had loved comets and satellites since he was a little kid and his head was always filled with thoughts of spaceships and rockets.

I first met him in a seminar in my major, math. Daichi was an engineering graduate student taking the class. During the class self-introductions he learned that my name was the same as a star that a space telescope on the island of Hawaii had been named after, so he remembered it immediately. He told me that his name was on an earth resources satellite. Daichi was a member of a lab that was

---

1   The Chocolate Angel French is a cruller doughnut, cut in half and filled with whipped cream, one end dipped in chocolate.

13

world-famous for flight theory about deep space travel and rocket design. It was called the Enterprise Lab, named after the spaceship from Star Trek.

When I talked to Daichi I could feel that he could envision space in a much more mathematical fashion than I, the mathematician, could. It was as if he could visualize even the latest super string theory and easily assert, "Well, it's like this doughnut here." Rumor had it he passed the entrance exam to graduate school with the top score.

His hobby was origami, and he taught me how to fold the movie monster King Ghidorah. If you asked him, he could fold just about anything. One time he folded me Yamato no Orochi, a large mythical dragon. Once I teased him by asking him to fold a thousand-armed Kannon Buddha, but he couldn't. He said sometime soon he'd have another go at it.

"An astronaut? But Daichi, you said you've had asthma since you were a kid and gave up on that dream."

You see, even though he had wanted to become an astronaut more than anything, unfortunately Daichi did not have a strong constitution, so instead he wanted to at least get a job related to space. That was why he had wanted to take this seminar.

"I'm going to be an astronaut on an unmanned probe," answered Daichi.

"What do you mean? Isn't that an oxymoron?"

"I said it wrong. More precisely, I'll be an astro-pilot, not an astronaut. It's not like I'll be on the probe as a human body. A part of me will be on the unmanned probe."

"How? You can do that?"

"Look. Remember how last year there was news about how SETI had finally picked up some transmissions from outer space? They were tau waves from the constellation Cetus."

I remembered. And that Daichi had been the one of the countless people running the SETI@home program on his PC to be thrilled at the news.

"So now NASA has chosen Tau Ceti as the final destination of the probe it's sending up to Makemake."

"Makemake?"

"Yeah, like 'MAH-kay MAH-kay'. It's the dwarf planet beyond Pluto. It's named after the creator deity of Easter Island."

"Why is it named that?"

"I think it's because it was discovered around Easter time."

"Huh. I see."

I was always impressed by Daichi's expanse of knowledge.

"The probe vehicle will swing by Jupiter and then accelerate. After it releases a probe toward Makemake the vehicle body will fly out into the solar system and keep on going into deep space. Pioneer and Voyager flew off into deep space with metal plates and gold records on board, but next time they plan to have artificial intelligence onboard. I'm going to be part of that."

Daichi kept on talking enthusiastically. But I didn't really understand what he meant when he said he'd be a part of the artificial intelligence.

"Okay, but how?"

"NASA was recruiting."

"They were recruiting astro-pilots for the unmanned probe?"

"That's right. They recruited people from all over the world who were willing to donate brain information for free and have it copied into artificial intelligence—people who are knowledgeable about space engineering, with good powers of observation and who have perseverance, but without a requirement for good health like live astronauts need."

At the time I thought that those criteria certainly fit Daichi to a T.

"I'm not going myself, but part of me will be in the artificial intelligence that is going to Tau Ceti in the constellation Cetus, where those transmissions originated. I'm going to fly 11.8 light years into the distance. It's going to take three hundred thousand years, but once I'm part of the probe I really might be able to go. Isn't that awesome?"

Daichi was all fired up. He'd finally been given the chance to realize his abandoned dream of becoming an astronaut.

"Compatibility with the hardware, and of course the software, is critical for proper operation of the brain data in the computer. I don't know how many people there are who were completely compatible, but I passed the test."

No matter what, there is always something in artificial intelligence that cannot replicate the human brain. There was always something to supplement the real brain data and increase the level of perfection.

"Was there a test or something?"

"Last week was the third examination."

"You've already gone through that much testing? Do you mean that's what you were doing on the day you skipped class?"

"Yeah. I thought I'd wait until I knew I was in before I said anything. It looks like later I'll have to go to NASA and they'll electronically copy my thought circuits and calibrate them for use on the probe. I'll be able to come home in a month."

"Are they going to mess around with the inside of your head?"

"It's not like they're going to open up my skull and operate on my brain or anything. They use special equipment to just scan inside my head and make a copy. It's not a big deal."

No matter what I said, I couldn't imagine that Daichi was going to change his mind. I already knew that about him. He was absolutely determined to be on that probe.

"Congratulations, Daichi."

"Thanks, Subaru."

After that, the flow of time in our days suddenly changed. Daichi was so busy with preparations for his trip to NASA that we had almost no time to go to Mister Donut after class and pass the time with idle talk like we used to.

"Don't look so worried, Subaru. It's not like I'm really going to get on the probe and say farewell to this planet. I'm just going for a month. We'll go back to our regular routine when I get back."

Saying that, Daichi set off for the Johnson Space Center in Houston, that place that was famous for the Apollo Program.

"Have a safe trip."

I went to Narita Airport to see Daichi off on his trip to America.

The first e-mail I got on the day he arrived was about the doughnut he had eaten at the airport. It was big and sweet and dripping with oil. It was so gross it could hardly even compare to the cakelike Old-Fashioned doughnuts we have in Japan.

After that, Daichi sent me two or three e-mails every day. They were short, but I could see he really had a certain dedication.

He wrote about being picked up at the airport in a car with the NASA logo on it and how the hotel he had reserved was so much nicer than he expected. He had a big room with two beds all to himself, and he had visited NASA and seen the actual probe that he would be loaded onto. The probe had been named Voyager 3 after a previous probe. A groundbreaking new type of battery had been developed that would keep the probe operational nearly permanently. With the arrival of every e-mail I could picture Daichi just glowing.

In the first week there were more tests. After that it took nearly two weeks to copy his thought circuits with a machine like an MRI that took cross-sectional images of the brain. I was worried Daichi might go crazy trapped in that machine, but my fears were unfounded. It didn't hurt, and he wasn't itchy. He was feeling so good that he even wrote about the pretty girls on the medical staff. I couldn't believe it.

What surprised me was when Daichi told me that he, just one time, experienced having a conversation with himself that had been copied. As he felt it, it was really like talking to himself, and he said it was a little unsettling.

I wondered if they could really copy a person's brain that completely. The program at NASA was completed in a month as scheduled. On the day before he was to arrive back home at Narita I got a short e-mail from the airport.

"I'm on my way home."

When I saw that e-mail I felt a sense of relief, but it was short-lived.

"Daichi . . ."

I was glued to the image of a burning fuselage on CNN. The plane Daichi was on had crashed and burned after experiencing engine trouble right after takeoff. There were no survivors.

But I had just gotten his e-mail saying he was on his way home. Why? I couldn't accept the fact that I would never see Daichi again, that he wasn't coming home.

At that table by the window in Mister Donut where Daichi and I had sat everyday time passed unchanged. Those times that I had thought of as so ordinary and expected. I wished I could have talked with him a little more.

"It's not like I'm really going to get on the probe and say good-bye to this planet," he'd promised. "I'll be back in a month."

There would be no more daily e-mails, yet I waited for them anyway.

And then Daichi's funeral. Buried in white chrysanthemums was a photo of a smiling Daichi. It was happening right in front of me, but I had absolutely no feeling of reality. I still felt like Daichi was going to come home healthy tomorrow.

Two months later, Voyager 3 was launched on schedule. There was the position of the planet swing-by to consider, and no one could expect them to change the schedule because there had been an airplane crash. And that is how the person I had relied on disappeared from my life and really became an astro-pilot.

If they had copied the inside of Daichi's head, would Voyager 3 think of me as it flew through space?

After a while a weekly magazine wrote about Daichi, kind of on a lark. I don't know how they found me, but journalists and TV reporters showed up. Maybe on Voyager 3 Daichi was watching the television waves transmitted from Earth. Thinking of that, I appeared just once on a show, but it really was just an unpleasant experience, and after a while everyone lost interest in Voyager 3 and things like that. As time passed they would forget about Daichi, too, and I wanted it that way.

Two years later Voyager 3 passed near Jupiter and sent back stunning images of its surface. Seeing those pictures, I remembered the pictures of Jupiter that Daichi had taken and shown me a long time ago

"This is Voyager 3 sending images taken on the approach to Jupiter. The swirls of clouds on the surface are really pretty."

That was the message that arrived with the images. It was in English, but the voice definitely sounded like Daichi. And it's not like a computer would express emotion using a word like "pretty." "Daichi really is there," I thought.

After a while it came time for me to think about what to do after graduation. I suddenly realized what I was thinking: *I just want to hear Daichi's voice a little more. I want to find a job where I can hear the live voice of Voyager 3.*

I changed my major from math to astronomy, and before long I was a budding astronomer. What's more, I was able to witness in real time Voyager 3's approach to Makemake and the moment when it successfully launched its probe.

"The distance from Makemake is 20,000 kilometers. The mission has been completed. The sun's rays look weak. Here it's goodbye to the solar system." So said Voyager 3 and then departed from Makemake.

And then one more thing: "Thanks, Subaru."

For a moment it felt as if time had stopped. Amid the static it had really sounded like that in Japanese.

"Daichi . . ."

I was half happy and half wondered why he had said that. I had intended to quit my job after seeing Voyager make its departure from Makemake, but this had made that impossible. That night I looked up at the sky through eyes blurred with tears and told Daichi, "Congratulations."

"What kind of origami is that?"

Subaru was often asked that about the origami on her desk. It was a complicated origami, an animal with three heads.

"This is King Ghidorah. It's a monster from old Japanese movies."

"King Ghidorah . . ."

"Someone I was close to a long time ago taught me how to make it. It takes a lot of time to fold this one, but the person who made it would make even more complicated ones if I asked. He would just give it some thought and then fold them."

"And that person is?"

"He went very far away. I haven't seen him in a while, but he's still doing well."

That was the usual reply.

Subaru turned her gaze to the gigantic structures visible outside the window. A group of giant white parabolic antennae stretched along into the distance for several kilometers. Their shadows fell on dry sand and moved with time like sundials. All the antennae faced the same direction, listening carefully for voices from space.

Voyager 3 continued to fly through deep space. Nearly thirty years had passed since it had left the solar system, but that was just 0.01 percent of its three hundred thousand-year journey.

How many people still remembered the Voyager 3? A few elderly people might have remembered it as the probe that left the solar system. Subaru, at least, was one of those people. For thirty years she had made every effort she could, hoping to hear Daichi's voice just once more.

Subaru became a renowned radio telescope expert. As for those gigantic radio telescopes visible outside her window, she had argued for their necessity, submitted countless proposals, persistently requested budgets and had finally seen her efforts rewarded when they were built. She gained the cooperation of countries all over the world to network radio astronomy observatories, training radio telescopes on the probe's orbit and improving accuracy significantly by using Very Long Baseline Interferometry. It became possible to hear even very weak radio signals from space.

And along with the voice of Voyager 3, various pieces of information were picked up from the galaxy. Though earthbound, Subaru was helping clear up many of the mysteries of the universe. Maybe these were Daichi's great achievements.

Subaru held her hand up to the control panel and aimed the radio telescope at Tau Ceti. When she closed her eyes she could feel the signals coming from space. About once every hundred days Voyager 3 would send a signal back to earth to let her know that it was functioning properly. When she eliminated the noise that spread in deep space and the background of Tau Ceti, a faint voice was audible. Sometimes Subaru listened to the sounds of the abyss of space. Though thirty years was nothing more than the beginning of the journey for Voyager 3, for Subaru it was quite a long time. At one point she even thought, *Why not just turn into a radio telescope?*

Technology to copy thought circuits isn't uncommon, she thought. *In many cases, brains are being copied and used even while the donors are alive.* Using that technology, if Subaru left her brain skilled in radio telescope operation and data interpretation, she really *could* become a radio telescope.

If she did that, she could continue to observe data for a long, long time, far beyond the lifespan of a human being. But she couldn't imagine that radio telescopes on Earth would continue to function for three hundred thousand years. That realization made her hesitate.

"You're really going to go for sure?"

"Yes. I've already made my decision," Subaru replied. That was the final confirmation of her resolve. She wasn't going to become a radio telescope. Like Daichi, Subaru had chosen to become the brain of a probe. That was because a kind of wormhole navigation had been refined using space-phase transition thanks to the fact that the long-held mystery of tau waves from SETI had been deciphered under continued analysis. It was written into those radio waves. Instantaneous interstellar movement was possible, but the wormholes that could be navigated were extremely small and could only transport a very small probe, and just one time.

The destination chosen was, of course, Tau Ceti. An exploratory mission to the location that was sending out tau waves was immediately proposed. The moment Subaru heard about that program she decided to become the brain of the probe, just as Daichi had done. Subaru thought she could hold Daichi in her heart by flying through space.

Several months later Subaru herself watched the small probe fly off through time and space toward a neighboring solar system.

"Have a safe trip," Subaru said, this time to herself.

Passing though a small hole in the wormhole, I flew on into deep space. As the sound of the abyss of deep space that I had continuously heard became intermittent, the light of Tau Ceti loomed large. The light of the G8Vp star Tau Ceti was like the sun, but smaller and with a slightly darker, colder feeling.

The sensation of feeling space with my own observation equipment somehow seemed to connect me to how it felt when I was a human. It was like the wind of space, its smell and also its warmth.

As though being drawn in by Tau's light, I entered the interstellar orbit. I confirmed that there was no enormous Jovian planet, just as observation from Earth had shown. Then I discovered four terrestrial planets orbiting Tau. My objective was to find the source of the radio waves, make contact with the civilization that sent them and report that to Earth, but the small probe that could get through the wormhole only had the requisite minimum equipment.

I released a self-reproducing automaton toward one planet. That was the first step. With that, the machine would begin to propagate, increasing geometrically, and differentiating into various types. In a few centuries, communication devices to transmit to the solar system and probes to survey planets would be ready. Contact could finally be made with the beings sending out the Tau radio waves, and reports sent back to Earth.

I sent my first report back to Earth:

This is Space Probe Subaru, reporting from Tau Ceti.

It took 11.8 years for that report to reach Earth. I waited for a reply from Earth and trained my ears toward the solar system. I thought that those high-powered radio waves from the antennae might also be audible to Voyager 3, which was along the way.

I released many other probes. There were four terrestrial planets with water and one planet that had life resembling plants. I searched far and wide but couldn't find any evidence of the civilization that had sent out the Tau waves. I wondered where they came from. While I was thinking about that and staring at a small sun I suddenly had a feeling as if someone had just tapped me on the shoulder.

"Subaru."

It was Daichi's voice.

"Is it really you, Subaru?"

Voyager 3, still headed in this direction, had picked up my radio waves and responded. I immediately replied in a loud voice, this time toward Daichi.

"Yeah, it's me! You can hear me, can't you?"

And so, finally, the conversation between Daichi and me recommenced.

Now there are more than eleven light years between us, so one conversational exchange takes a little over twenty-three years, but if we take ten thousand years we'll be able to have a conversation of about five hundred exchanges. As we get closer, we'll be able to increase the frequency.

We had endless things to talk about. It seemed Daichi had been listening intently to the radio waves from Earth ever since he left, which brought him all kinds of information. He said he had been able to see, for just an instant, the images of me on television.

"I really thought I would cry at that moment. But you know a probe doesn't have a crying function."

Even then, Daichi continued to send a signal out to Earth once every hundred days to confirm he was still functioning properly.

He said he wanted to let someone on Earth know—Hey! I'm here! I'm flying right now toward Tau Ceti. He said if he didn't do that he felt like he'd completely lose sight of the reason why he was flying out in space. I had been listening to that voice the whole time.

"By the way, have you contacted the beings who are transmitting the tau waves yet? They'll be giving Voyager 3 a big welcome three hundred thousand years from now, won't they?" Daichi asked me about the source of the tau waves in a teasing manner.

"But . . . there's no one out here, you know."

"Yeah, I've released a lot of probes but there's no evidence of any civilization that sends out those kinds of radio waves."

"I see . . ." It seemed Daichi was thinking for a while. "I got it," he said and then I heard his laugh.

"What's so funny?"

"I finally get who was sending those tau waves."

"Really?"

"I think I'm about to come up with a way to send radio waves to the past and transcend time."

"You can do that?"

"I feel like I can. I hit upon it while I was reminiscing about you, Subaru."

"What? What do you mean 'about me'?"

"Remember you always used to eat Angel French doughnuts at Mister Donut?"

"Sure."

"Well, an Angel French doughnut is a ring-like structure with asymmetrical chocolate frosting."

"So?"

"Don't you get it? That was the hint. Take it a little further and you'll understand how to transcend time and send radio waves into the past. And then . . ."

When Daichi said this I grasped that the tau waves that SETI had detected from Tau Ceti were the radio waves I was going to send back to Earth. I got it when I put it together with the hint about how wormhole travel worked. And if that was true, then I was creating that Daichi was here and that I was here. I even created the opportunity for it to happen.

I wondered if that was okay.

There was still a delay of forty or fifty thousand years for Daichi to come up with the idea and for me to reply.

Until then it would be just fine to take our time and think it over with my elbows on the table of deep space, just like we used to do back in the day at Mister Donut.

A Piece of Butterfly's Wing

Kamon Nanami

Translated by Angus Turvill

This translation won the 2011 Kurodahan Press Translation Prize.

Sae took a jolting train and a bus and then walked for a while up a gently sloping road. She opened a rusty paint-peeled mailbox and took out a postcard. The card was dirty, the writing smudged from repeated exposure to rain. She blinked and looked around her. Colors were muted in the early summer sunshine. The landscape looked flat; the voices of the larks singing high in the sky seemed to have more substance. Her eyes watered at the brightness of the sun, and she closed them for a while. Now and then, amid the cheerful lark song, she heard calls of birds she could not name— some near, some far away. Wind rustled faintly through the softest of the grass.

It was humid. The air, imbued with sun, was sticky, heavy, languid. Suddenly, a loud hum of wings buzzed past her ears and she opened her eyes. She saw no trace of whatever insect had made this jarring noise. Instead, there was a butterfly. Eventually, accustomed to the light, her eyes registered the green of the grass, the green trees, the fields, the electricity wires. It was a serene, but decaying, rural scene.

The paved road was cracked, losing its battle with time and grass roots. The fields looked abandoned, the earth reddish and dry. The silver tape used to scare off birds had lost its sheen; it sagged, wrapped around drooping bamboo poles. Thin sunflowers hung their heads. There were clumps of white-flowered *dokudami,* now past its peak, and daisy-like *himejion*, luxuriant in growth. Beyond lay an area of dense greenery, where brown butterflies were flitting back and forth. *There may be pretty flowers there*, Sae thought.

Still holding the postcard, she turned around. She now faced a single-storey wooden house; it was in worse condition even than the postcard. The smell of mold seeped from between the thin planks of its walls. In the midday summer sun, the house was black and somber. Sae breathed out slowly, hesitated for a moment and then slid open the ill-fitting door. Light spread over the spacious earthen floor immediately inside the entrance. Sitting lethargically on the raised wooden floor beyond was Chizu, her elder sister. Chizu smiled faintly.

"You've come," she said.

"I got no reply!" said Sae. She sighed, holding up the postcard.

"Let me see," said Chizu.

"There's no point now," said Sae.

Too fatigued to take off her shoes, Sae sat on the edge of the raised wooden floor. Chizu made no apology for not replying to the postcard. Her pale face just smiled.

"I wrote you a lot of postcards. How many did you read?" said Sae, swinging her jean-clad legs.

Chizu had disappeared four years before. The following autumn the family discovered that she had run off with a man. They didn't know who the man was, so it was not a relationship they had opposed. But nonetheless Chizu had chosen to elope. And the only contact she made was by postcard to her younger sister, Sae, of whom she was fond. The sender's address box on the postcard had been filled out in thin pencil, but to the deep anxiety of her parents, what was written there was an invention. Chizu had continued to send Sae occasional postcards, always from this false address.

It was only two months since Sae had found out where Chizu really was. She had done nothing special to make this discovery—it was just that the postmark on one of Chizu's cards had been legible. Without telling her parents anything, Sae used the information to find out Chizu's address. She knew Chizu was now alone. The man had a wife and family. Before long he had become violent with Chizu and run off with her money. Chizu had told Sae all of this quite openly in a postcard.

"He isn't here any more," Chizu had written. Her sister's lover had disappeared without Sae knowing his name or seeing his face.

"Don't you want to come home?" Sae said.

"It's a bit late for that." Chizu's smile was very calm. It made her seem like a stranger.

Her black hair was loose. Strands meandered over her collarbone and nape, caught by the sweat on her skin. The broad front of her blouse revealed the cleavage between her firm, ample breasts. Her skin glistened with perspiration.

Sae put the postcard away and brought out a pink handkerchief. She dabbed the sweat that was beading on her own neck.

"I sent so many postcards asking you to telephone," said Sae. "But I never heard from you. I thought you might have committed suicide."

"You were worried about me," said Chizu.

She moved her hands. There was a dry, scratching sound. Sae looked across and saw some withered flowers spread on the floor. Chizu seemed to be engaged in intricate work.

"I picked these flowers to make a scent bag," she said. "But it's no good. It's too humid at this time of year. The flowers rot before they're completely dry."

"I didn't know you liked that sort of thing."

"It's because of the smells here. Do you notice them?"

Chizu began to stand up. At the same time a small voice came from behind a smoke-stained sliding screen.

"Oh!" Chizu said.

The pale soles of her feet showed as her shadow moved further back into the house. The prints they left on the floor stood out sharp and black, suggesting that everything else was covered in a thin layer of dust.

Sae looked at the scattered flowers. She couldn't name them. Each one was shriveled and black. She wondered if the loss of color was what Chizu meant by "rotting."

Chizu came back carrying a baby wrapped in a cape.

"It's mine," she said smiling, before Sae had time to ask.

Sae stayed silent. She did not know what to say.

Chizu spread her lemon-colored skirt over the black petals. Chattering to the baby, she unbuttoned her white blouse. Her breast tumbled straight out. It was dazzling, whiter even than her blouse. She swung the baby up. It stretched its small mouth open and took the nipple. Chizu gazed down at the baby, enthralled. Sae turned

27

her eyes away and looked outside. Beyond the sliding door, all was bright. As if drawn to the brightness, Sae moved to the doorway. The strong sunlight again robbed her sight of color. She felt the stir of someone standing up behind her.

"Can I stay the night?" she asked without turning around.

"If you would like to," Chizu replied.

An organic, milky smell touched Sae's nostrils. She felt a faint nausea and walked on out of the doorway. The larks were still singing. The sky above seemed paler than before. She walked up the road. Ahead were trees, some of their branches dead. Beyond the trees was the deep green of the nearby hills. If she continued up this gently sloping road it would take her there. She didn't want to go the whole way, but there was a pleasant wind from that direction. Suddenly, all the birdsong stopped. And so did the wind. The entire landscape was still, as though time itself had stopped. Within this still frame, Sae sensed movement. She saw a glint of light from a dark patch of water in the grass. On the water were a dozen brown butterflies, almost as if someone had placed them there in a deliberate formation. They moved their wings up and down in a slow breath-like rhythm. Chizu came up quietly beside her. The baby burped gently. Drops of milk bounced from the still bare breast. Red. The milk looked red. Shards of light pierced Sae's eyes. She closed them tight.

"Those were *tatehachō* butterflies," said Chizu as she laid out the futons for the night. "They drink water to absorb nutrients. Almost all of them are male, apparently."

The small light-bulb hanging from the ceiling cast dark shadows. Sae grew conscious of stains on the sliding screens.

"That's a strange thing to know about," she said.

"Well, they're attracted to humans too—to sweat and urine."

Chizu's voice sounded moist.

Sae heard something tapping softly against a futon. She guessed Chizu was lulling the child to sleep.

Sae lay silent and closed her eyes. She let the soft regular tapping soothe her towards sleep. The faint sound of a woman's voice reached her drowsy ears. A lullaby, perhaps. But no, it didn't seem to be that. It didn't seem to be a woman's voice at all. It was like the hum of wings. Undulating, like the voice of someone singing.

Something passed through the darkness. A soft-hued butterfly. No sooner had she noticed one, than there were more, gathering in a great commotion. They landed all over the floor, their yellowish light brown wings erect. The wings closed quietly, opened quietly. When closed the color seemed paler, softer. Open, the wings were speckled with black. Looking up, she saw more butterflies, clustering on the thin light cord.

Sae opened her eyes and sat up. There were no butterflies to be seen. It had been a dream, on the border of sleep.

She wiped the sweat from her face. Again she heard the hum of wings pass by. There must be a fly, she thought, in spite of the dark.

As she sank back into her futon, she noticed again the dank smell of mold.

Sae drank some water from the tap. She didn't want anything to eat. Giving her face a quick wash she went towards the entrance. The flowers were still scattered on the floor, now shriveled even blacker.

She opened the ill-fitting front door, letting in a fine morning breeze. Spontaneously, she took a deep breath. Chizu had mentioned smells. She was right. There were strange bittersweet smells throughout the house. You stopped noticing them after a while, but your sense of smell recovered when you came outside. And outside, everywhere was light.

Sae stood in front of the house. She felt the smell and the darkness were being wiped from her skin. It was pleasant to be out in the wind. There was a thick clump of *dokudami* on the path between the rice fields. Butterflies were resting there—the same type of butterfly she had imagined last night. Were there always so many here? Or had they suddenly appeared? Her brow was tense for a moment, but she continued to watch the butterflies. *Tatehachō* were flitting about over the same thicket as on the previous day.

Sae realized that her sister was now standing beside her. Still looking ahead, Sae spoke.

"Nobody seems to come this way."

"No."

"Isn't there anybody around?"

"There are no more houses up this road. So people hardly ever come up here."

The baby was again at Chizu's breast. It was quieter than any baby Sae knew. The baby cape had a bright, bold pattern. It looked as though it had been sewn together from scraps of different material. Chizu's clothes were colorless by comparison. So was her face.

Sae followed the movements of the butterflies with her eyes. They rose up in an arc—once, twice—and then sank down into the thicket. She had thought there would be flowers there, but perhaps it was water. Anyway, if there were flowers she wanted to see them. She started walking, but Chizu stopped her.

"Where are you going?"

"Over there."

"I think you'd better not."

"Why?"

"There's more than just water there."

She shook her black hair.

"I told you, didn't I? It's not just liquid the butterflies want. They all play on water because they want the nutrients dissolved there. So a dead body attracts them too."

Sae looked at the thicket again and then turned her eyes back to her sister. Chizu was staring at the thicket. Sae could tell nothing from her expression.

"What dead body?" Sae asked automatically.

"There's a smell when the wind blows from that direction. It's not nice."

"Where did the baby's father go?" Sae asked.

"Well . . ."

Chizu looked lovingly at the child.

"Where did the baby's father go?" Sae asked again

"I don't know. I haven't seen him for two years."

"So whose baby is it?"

"Mine."

Chizu shifted the baby in her arms. Perhaps the movement woke the child—its small fingers started to fumble for its mother's breast.

"You're hungry are you, little one?"

Unbuttoning her blouse, Chizu went back towards the house. Sae's anxious voice followed her.

"Chizu! Wait! Are you all right?"

"Why do you say that?" said Chizu. She stepped inside the dark house. Sae stopped at the doorway. Her eyes were used to the light.

They would not adjust to the darkness. She could not even see where the ground was. Traces of the outside light remained with her like a ghostly apparition. She heard a creaking sound. Chizu must be sitting on the wooden floor.

"Because yesterday your milk looked like blood," said Sae.

The apparition was still there. Sae blinked again and again.

"Don't be stupid," said her sister's voice. "They're the same thing. A mother's milk is made from her blood."

The pale traces of light darkened into red. Spattered across Sae's field of vision, they glistened like blood.

"That's why the baby drinks blood," said Chizu. "All babies drink blood."

Sae blinked again. At last her pupils dilated.

Chizu sat suckling the child, just as she had the day before. Its hands made little movements as it fed greedily at her breast. Eventually, it released the nipple. Its mother's milk dripped from its mouth. Again, the milk looked red. Is that because my eyes aren't used to the dark, thought Sae. She drew nearer.

"Like a vampire. . . ." she said.

Chizu smiled faintly.

The pattern on the baby cape seemed to quiver. A butterfly flew up from the hem. A *tatehachō*. It fluttered through the silent darkness, and drawing an arc in the air it flew past Sae's arm.

Earlier on Sae had realized something—she hadn't seen the baby's face; nor had she seen its diaper changed.

"It's a boy, isn't it?" she said.

"Yes," said Chizu, smiling again.

"I suppose the butterflies drink blood as well, don't they?" Sae said, unable to conceal a tremor in her voice. She drew closer still and held her finger out towards the child.

A fragment peeled away, and flew up into the air. The baby moved its hands and, as it did so, the whole form of its body dissolved.

Light brown wings opened, closed, as though breathing gently. Butterflies were gathered like a cluster of flowers. They waved their long thin antennae. Each small lustrous eye showed Sae's reflection. Gradually, the cluster disintegrated, the petals flying away. Most escaped in confusion to the brightness outside. But some remained in the darkness within, restlessly beating their wings.

Chizu sat silently, one breast bare, her arms held out as though still embracing the child. There was blood on her white skin.

Sae ran out of the house. She crossed the loose bird-scare tape into the dry remains of a vegetable field. As she approached the clump of *himejion*, there was a sickening sweet stench. She bit hard on her lip and pushed into the thicket. She saw a swarm of *tatehachō*. She could not tell what color it was, but there was water, lying in a natural hollow. And there were flies. And ants. And there was hair.

She ran back to the house. Her throat was dry, and she could hardly breathe. She stood in front of her sister, panting heavily.

Two or three *tatehachō* had returned to Chizu's breast. Her hand hovered lovingly over them.

"Chizu, come home!" Sae forced a smile. 'Let's go back together."

Chizu didn't look at her. Sae smiled again.

"I'm sorry!" she said. "Always complaining about you in my letters, saying you were stupid."

"You were right," Chizu murmured, looking downwards.

Without removing her shoes Sae stepped up onto the wooden floor and took her sister's hand.

"That doesn't matter," she said. "I'm sorry."

The hand was cold

"Will you forgive me?" said Chizu.

"Yes," said Sae. "Let's go!"

The butterflies flew away from Chizu's breast. She raised her head slowly. Her clear, black eyes were smiling.

"Thank you," Chizu said. "I was lonely."

Sae could no longer feel her sister's hand. Something tickled Sae's palm. She looked down—butterflies—some were squashed in her hand, their wings broken.

There was a strong, sour smell. Chizu was not to be seen. Instead, in front of Sae lay a mass of yet more of those butterflies. Her vision was steeped in the color of their scales. Light, brittle wings hit her face, her hands, and flew past. They swarmed close to her, circled the room, then hundreds together, sighing like wind through grass, flew out of the doorway towards the light beyond. Sae's were the only footprints now to be seen on the dust-covered floor. But the wilted flowers remained scattered near the door. Sae put one in her pocket and left the house.

She looked towards the thicket. *Tatehachō* were flitting about as before. The hair in the water over there had been long. The swollen fingers still grasped a knife. A deserted woman who had taken her own life. Was there something inside her? Sae had no wish to check. But a great deal of blood, of red milk, must have flowed from her breast. A withered flower produces nothing. But a rotting body, dissolving in water, feeds precious nutrients to butterflies, to grass, to earth.

The voices of the birds were still serene. Sae went down the road. Ever since she had left the house one butterfly had been fluttering around her. Adjusting her pace to the flight of the butterfly, she walked away from the hills and towards the village. She came out of the painfully bright sunshine into a small pine wood. Suddenly the air was cool. When she left the wood her face was again broiled by the early summer sun.

She saw nobody, but there were signs of life. She saw the roofs of a number of houses. Then she came to an old shop with cardboard boxes piled outside. There were buns in one. A cat in another.

The road sloped steeply upwards for a while, and the asphalt widened. She came out onto the road where the bus stop was. Her skin was damp with perspiration. The butterfly rested lovingly on her arm.

A car passed. The wind changed. The butterfly flew from her arm. A small white truck drove up, catching the butterfly in its flow of air. The butterfly disappeared.

A short while later a piece of butterfly wing came to rest on the edge of the asphalt. Sae picked it up and wrapped it in tissue paper.

At last the bus came.

She took the bus and the jolting train, and arrived back home. She unfolded the tissue paper. The piece of wing had turned to powder. But the withered flower in her pocket was just as it had been.

THE FINISH LINE

Matsuzaki Yuri

Translated by Nora Stevens Heath

There'd been something strange about Ikaru ever since Dr. Gould died. I'd noticed it right away; how could I not?

"Can't you tell him, Atori? I know he'll listen to you."

The assistant professor who served as advisor to both me and Ikaru pushed up his glasses with a nudge of his finger, mottled white from countless lab experiments.

"It's all well and good to be engrossed in your thesis research, but make sure he knows that he can't monopolize the thermal cyclers. That just causes problems for everyone. Besides, it's not healthy. He hasn't even been back to the dorm these past few days, has he?"

I looked up at him from my seat in the student lab and shook my head.

My advisor, a young man with barely a decade on us seniors, responded with a faint smile. "Thanks," he said, then left the room. From my position beside the window, the line of desks that stood between me and the door were almost all empty. It was summer vacation, and everyone else had already gone home.

After watching my advisor walk away, my gaze turned to my desk. Atop it sat a fish tank—no, more like an old-fashioned glass goldfish bowl—containing a pair of fancy goldfish.

I'd found the fishbowl after digging around in a shop called First Street Sundries. Its round basin was just the right size for a grown man to encircle it with both hands. Sunlight from the window fell on the two goldfish within, occasionally glinting off their scales as the fish swam busily around the seaweed.

But meditating on these goldfish wasn't going to get me anywhere. I had a job to do.

I made up my mind and stood to leave when I caught the eye of the grad student sitting at the desk diagonally opposite mine. He and I were the only ones left in the room. He glanced at me with his long hair and slim face, snorted, and went back to the work in front of him.

Saying nothing in reply, I went out into the hallway and made my way to the biology lab. I knew full well that that student didn't think much of me. A student who keeps pet goldfish at her desk or repairs discarded incubators, sets them to 37 degrees Celsius, and sticks quail eggs inside is considered a heretic. Not to mention I'm a woman; that alone made me stick out like a sore thumb. The only women in the life sciences research program were me and one other, a Ph.D. student who happened to be my advisor's wife and my friend—practically my benefactor. Plus Ikaru and I were old friends, which put me on a par with the lab's number-one problem child.

The dark hallway was lined with unused equipment, making it even narrower than it already was. I left the research lab, passed my advisor's office, and was walking straight ahead to the experimental lab when I spotted the old incubator I'd rehabilitated. *That's right,* I said to myself, *I still have to turn the eggs today.* I leaned over the machine, which was about waist-high and more or less a cube.

I pulled open the door on the front and peered inside. The forty quail eggs I'd purchased from a nearby grocery a week earlier were sitting quietly on the wire floor, still as speckled as ever.

I began turning the eggs one by one, taking care not to crack them. I concentrated on my fingertips and thought back to what had happened three days earlier.

As usual, it was almost afternoon when Ikaru rolled into the research lab and took the morning paper from the long-haired grad student. Ikaru's obviously still-sleepy expression changed the moment he laid eyes on the front page.

There in the obituaries was the name of a distinguished biologist whom Ikaru had absolutely idolized: Dr. Gould. He had died at 89 of old age.

Ikaru folded the paper and gave it back to the grad student, then sat in his seat next to my desk. He raked his fingers through his soft and curly hair as he wrote a number on a slip of paper, but soon stood up and left for the research lab without even a sidelong glance.

He'd been holed up in the life sciences research wing ever since, continually running the experimental lab's six thermal cyclers without a moment's rest.

I spent more time than usual tending to the quail eggs. Deep inside, I knew I didn't want to get in Ikaru's way. When faced with such abject sadness, people often display a kind of displacement behavior. Mathematics researchers tackle unsolved problems with the promise of huge sums of prize money; historical geologists go out into the field with pickaxe and rock hammer in search of fossils.

And biologists? They do experiments.

To Ikaru, Dr. Gould was someone special. Ten years earlier, having read one of his books, Ikaru sent the great biologist a letter bursting with his childishly frank impressions of it. Surprisingly, Dr. Gould wrote back. He was already a famous researcher, yet he took the time to answer carefully each and every audacious question this random boy had asked.

At last I finished turning the eggs and silently closed the incubator door. I watched as the glowing numbers on the front of the device slowly returned to the preset temperature and thought about the eggs. Sexing quail chicks was an inexact science, possibly because they were so much smaller than chickens. That's how the odd male occasionally finds his way onto the farm, and why some of the quail eggs on the market could be fertilized. Consequently, if you incubate enough eggs, a few of them should hatch.

I pictured a chick breaking out of its egg and smiled. Like their kin the pheasant, quail chicks can open their eyes, stand up, and toddle after their parent right after hatching. If I'm there when they hatch, they'll imprint on me as their mother and make a beeline for me, chirping thinly. I'd always wanted to try it, raising and hatching eggs myself.

Mentally I counted the days. If everything went right, I would be meeting those chicks in about ten more days.

But that was enough time spent on those eggs for now. I shook my head and began to walk away from the old incubator. The experimental biology lab was at the end of the hallway.

I stood in front of its plain door, exhaling slowly. Then I turned the knob and looked inside.

The experimental lab on the second floor of the life sciences wing had all its windows covered to keep out the sun. Instead, there were lamps on the ceiling, lending an unnaturally bright cast to the lab benches running horizontally down the length of the room and to the reagent shelves and giant lab refrigerators lining the walls. It was just as deserted as the student research lab. Normally at this time of day, students and professors would be glued to their equipment, sitting at lab benches with micro-burettes in hand, or putting crushed ice in the ice chest to chill an in-process reagent.

All I could hear was the faint whisper of machinery and the chirring of cicadas outside. The cicadas around there were a northern species that sang their forlorn song during the day as much as at dusk.

The first lab bench inside the door held six machines small enough to be held in both hands, throwing off heat from both resin sides. Our advisor was right: they were all chugging away. A familiar back was leaning over the device at the far right. It was Ikaru, of course.

He didn't look up, even as I approached. He peered at the display on the machine before him, a 96-well sample block for a bank of eight capillary tubes in one hand. I stole a glance at the screen, too. Alongside a display of rapidly increasing numbers indicating temperature shone user-set digits showing the cycle count. These were set to forty, the upper limit for amplifying the most genes under adequate conditions.

The moment the screen showed the maximum temperature, Ikaru swiftly removed the machine's lid with his free hand and placed twelve of the eight-tube banks inside. Once he was done, he closed the lid and finally turned my way.

"Hey, Atori. What's up?"

His eyes were red, his hair and his scruffy beard much more unkempt even than usual. The shadows on his cheeks made him look even thinner.

"Our advisor's worried about you. Give it a rest, okay?"

The answer came back quickly. "No."

I'd expected as much. Once he had his mind set on something, you couldn't pry him off with a crowbar. I let out a sigh of either wry amusement or resignation—I wasn't sure which—and proceeded with the proposition I'd prepared.

"Then at least give us a convincing explanation. I know it hit you hard and all, but what do you think you're doing, hogging the thermal cyclers like this?"

Ikaru glanced behind me and lowered his voice. "We can't talk here."

I followed his line of sight to someone in the hallway walking past the half-open door. It was that long-haired grad student.

I nodded to show I understood and spoke as gently as I could. "Then why don't we head to First Street? We can stop by Yukiwatari."

I saw Ikaru smile for the first time in three days. Yukiwatari's *shirotama anmitsu* sweet rice dumpling dessert was his absolute favorite.

I was waiting at a window seat looking across the First Street shopping district when Ikaru came in, rubbing his chin like he'd just been punched. It looked like he'd obeyed my instructions to stop in at the dorm to bathe and change clothes.

He came over to my black wooden table and sat down across from me. "Been waiting long?"

"Not really," I replied. I happened to enjoy people-watching—the crowds were like organisms in and of themselves—and besides, Yukiwatari was a cozy joint. I'm positive I could have killed time there until the cows came home.

I raised my hand to summon the waiter in his black-and-white uniform and ordered the *anmitsu* I'd promised Ikaru, along with a second cup of coffee for me. The calendar may have said we were entering midsummer, but even after almost four years living in a climate where I could enjoy hot coffee, I was still not used to it. I knew I had chosen to come here for school and all, but it was a lot colder in the north than where we're from.

As soon as the waiter left with my empty coffee cup and our order slip, I began.

"Now we can talk. What the hell are you doing with those thermal cyclers, anyway?"

Ikaru hesitated, glancing out the window, then back at me. "I guess I can tell you. You got me that *anmitsu* and all."

"I did get you that *anmitsu*," I agreed with a wry smile. The sweets at Yukiwatari were as expensive as they were delicious. A heavy hit for a hard-up student.

"Dr. Gould died three days ago," Ikaru began. "Of course, I'd been expecting it for a while.

"He was old, and he'd long since retired from Central University, where he'd worked for all those years. Lately there'd been rumors he'd been in and out of the hospital." Ikaru stopped there.

I looked him in the eye and nodded. Just because you saw a death coming doesn't mean its impact was diminished in the least.

"I wanted to meet him. To tell him the little kid who'd sent him that letter was on his way to becoming a biologist." My childhood friend spoke softly, as if to himself, and fell silent again.

When we were figuring out our school careers, I once asked Ikaru why he didn't go to Central; after all, that's where Dr. Gould was. *But he's not teaching anymore,* he replied. *I'll just go up north with you. They have a fine old university there with its own research facility. It's a nice little town. Plus the summers aren't overly warm.*

Why here? Why not Central?

My situation was more clear-cut: I hate the city. If I was going to be living somewhere for any length of time, a town this size was just about right. I hadn't counted on getting quite this much snow in winter, but in contrast, the pleasant summers were a precious time full of sunshine and gentle breezes. Every year the locals held a splendid festival to celebrate the short summer that had finally come our way. It was nothing as showy as rows of gigantic floats or young people dancing themselves into a frenzy, but First Street and all the other major downtown areas were glammed up in traditional paper decorations for the entire festival period. It was a quiet celebration, one that consisted only of walking along the streets with neck craned, but it was enjoyable enough.

In fact, this year's festival was already approaching.

"Something Dr. Gould kept saying in his papers, in his books, even in his lectures: Natural selection, the driving force of organic evolution, always acts on the individual." Ikaru seemed to have collected himself enough to speak again.

I was pulled back out of my daydreams. "Well, sure. That's the prevailing school of thought in academia these days."

"And yet." Ikaru looked deep into my eyes. "Some radical researchers are saying natural selection works at the genetic level. They argue that the very act of increasing the number of genes to the maximum is the definition of evolutionary victory, and that the individual organism is nothing more than a vehicle for its genes."

I thought back to the kerfuffle the genic-selection crowd had caused. Their theory was so novel, so sensational, that it had even drawn a lot of attention from non-specialists. Laypeople got involved, and the vigorous arguments had continued to this day.

"But there's no way they're right," Ikaru said, his voice firm. "Genes *can't* be the evolutionary unit. Natural selection can't act directly on genes, now, can it? I mean, there's no one gene responsible for making arms or legs. Even a single finger on that arm is generated by and modulated through complex controls involving any number of genes. And the same genes might even control a different part of the body, too. What I mean is, organisms aren't divvied up into separate parts according to their genes, like so many medieval fiefdoms. They're complexes, like a lattice," Ikaru finished, and looked at me to see how much had gotten through.

I nodded emphatically. Neither theory had prevailed as the correct one, but individual selection was definitely the more persuasive of the two. No wonder it was mainstream.

My coffee arrived, the waiter placing the steaming cup in front of me. "The *anmitsu* will only be a moment," he added with a smile, then went back downstairs.

I put my lips to the white china rim and took a sip. This wasn't your ordinary sweets shop. Their coffee beans were fresh, sent direct from a long-established specialty shop. Yukiwatari was that rare place whose dedication extended to every last item on its menu, although I wasn't sure if it was for the customers' sake or out of some kind of pride.

I prodded Ikaru for more. "And?"

"I decided to memorialize Dr. Gould."

My old pal was looking straight at me from beyond a veil of steam.

"I came up with a way to refute his enemies, the genic-selection faction. It would have been unthinkable ten years ago, but it's possible today. I have the knowledge, the techniques, the equipment, and the reagents."

41

The waiter appeared once more. "I'm sorry about the wait. Your *shirotama anmitsu*, with extra sweet red beans," he announced, presenting Ikaru with a square black lacquered tray bearing an oval bowl. He placed the check face down on the table and excused himself.

Ikaru looked into the bowl and grinned. As expected, he took the spoon from the tray, scooped up a single bean, and popped it into his mouth, totally blissed-out. One time I told him, *If you like those beans so much, just buy a whole bag of the dried ones and boil 'em up*, but he insisted that wouldn't do the trick. Any difference between the two is beyond me.

After eating a dozen beans or so, Ikaru resumed his explanation.

"Like I said, the genic-selection faction claims that each individual gene uses the organism to increase its numbers to the maximum." He took the little bottle off the tray as though he'd only just realized it was there and poured its molasses syrup all over the contents of the bowl. Never wasted a drop, that Ikaru.

"That's when it hit me: If what they're saying is right, if a single gene could be amplified into some crazy amount, such gargantuan numbers that the other genes could never even hope to catch up, then *boom*, the end—wouldn't evolution be over? Would there be some kind of sign, a signal that the organic evolution race had reached the finish line, some sort of *th-th-th-that's all, folks*?"

Amplify a gene until boom, the end?

A diagram of a double-strand gene amplification protocol came to mind. It's essentially a mechanism that uses reagents and machines to reproduce more efficiently the gene replication that's always taking place inside an organism. This method takes advantage of the fact that a double-strand gene, once heated, can be divided into two separate strands, and that each strand can then be used as a template for synthesizing new strands. If you have the double-strand template gene along with the necessary enzymes and reagents, then put it through a cycle of artificial temperature changes, the number of strands will increase by a factor of two with every cycle. Design an amplification start array and you can amplify specific sections of your double-strand gene. Set the temperature cycle to run forty times and you'll get 2^{40} strands. Those thermal cycler devices are specialized to facilitate this reaction.

The person who came up with this protocol received the most prestigious prize in the world. That's how amazing it was.

I saw what Ikaru was trying to do. "And that's why you've got all the thermal cyclers running 24/7, amplifying some gene with all their might?"

He smiled faintly. *Ya got me.* Then Ikaru leaned forward slightly.

"I'd been eyeing cytoskeletal fiber and glycolytic dehydrogenase," he informed me. "Both are ubiquitous in practically every organism, and besides, the ones researchers around the world use as positive controls in their experiments have already been amplifying at a steady clip. That means they're already a step ahead of other genes. I was torn about which one to use, but when we happened to have some extra amplification start arrays for cytoskeletal fiber, my mind was made up."

It was an interesting way of thinking, but he'd gotten it wrong somewhere.

"Hey, Ikaru," I began, looking him square in the eye, "you're out to provide negative proof for this hypothesis, right?"

"Of course. Dr. Gould was correct, so there's not going to be any big The End, not in any way, shape, or form." His face was the very picture of earnestness.

"Then you've got to set a benchmark: How much amplification will it take to reach the finish line? Otherwise you'll be stuck amplifying forever, until you get some kind of sign that The End has come," I reasoned, thinking back to the *Intro to Scientific Thought* course I'd taken in liberal arts my first year.

It's extremely difficult to prove that something doesn't exist.

Especially here, when there was no way anything as absurd as a ta-da ending was going to happen.

Ikaru gave me a *Who do you think you're talking to?* look. "The very first thing I did was calculate a gene count to serve as the benchmark for success." He took a customer comment card from its box at the edge of the table, then grabbed the pencil from its tube on the outside of the box. I watched his hand.

"I applied the estimation method we learned in *Intro to Scientific Thought* for testing the credibility of one's own hypotheses. Now, this is a major guesstimate, but I went with the supposition that each single cell contains one copy of this particular gene. Then I estimated the maximum number of cells that could exist on Earth.

At total saturation, with the planet covered by single cells, there would be approximately this many of them." He wrote a huge number on the card, expressed as a factor of ten. "This is the maximum number of genes that can come into being via the natural biological proliferative process."

"And to increase the number of genes beyond that point, we have to use artificial means. Which makes that there"—here I reached out and pointed to the card and its number—"the benchmark for success. The End."

"It's a very rough number, of course. After all, single-celled organisms proliferate by a factor of two, just like genes inside a thermal cycler. My benchmark is probably off by a few places." Ikaru smiled a little as he pushed the card into the crack in the table. "Still, if I keep on amplifying them at this pace, I should surpass the target number of genes in five more days.

"If nothing happens, Dr. Gould and I will have won." He put the pencil back in its tube, picked up his spoon, and went back to his *anmitsu*.

I sighed and sank back into my chair. Another question popped into my head.

"How will the other genes involved in this competition know when the cytoskeletal fiber genes reach their benchmark and bring about The End?"

"Hell if I know," he replied, spooning rectangles of syruped *kanten* gelatin into his mouth. "I'm leaving that part of the theory to the genic selection crowd. I have no obligation to prove it either way."

I'd forgotten about my coffee. I lifted the cup to my mouth and sipped the cold drink inside, slightly comforted that Ikaru hadn't given some pseudo-scientific answer, claiming he'd be notified by some almighty something-or-other or via the genes' collective intelligence. Not that The End was anything more than a total fantasy anyway.

Whatever the reason, The End wasn't going to happen. That should satisfy Ikaru enough for him to return to his usual everyday routine. Surely our advisor would forgive the loss of a few days and a handful of reagents if it meant one of his students would be making a comeback.

That's right—our advisor. I still had to do something about that problem in the lab.

"But it's not fair to hog all six of the thermal cyclers. Just because it's summer vacation doesn't mean there aren't people doing experiments."

Hell, I was one of them. So was our advisor's wife, my friend, who was due to submit her doctoral thesis in six months' time.

And that long-haired grad student. His dissertation defense might be right around the corner, but he was still busy running his final lap. Me, I figured I'd just try to humor the people I had to face on a daily basis.

"Someone's bound to get angry if this monopolizing of machinery goes on much longer," I warned Ikaru.

"You're probably right." Ikaru looked up at the white plaster ceiling, his spoon between his teeth. Eventually he looked back at me and opened his mouth. The spoon dropped to the table. "I'll give up one machine for someone else to use. I'll keep the other five."

I narrowed my eyes. "No way. You know one's not enough."

Ikaru blinked a few times in surprise, then sat silently with a straight face for a moment before speaking again.

"All right. Make it two."

I shook my head. Ikaru groaned and clapped his hands together. "Okay, three. Even if it stretches my five days into ten. I'll just have to suck it up. Is that better?"

I gave a reluctant nod. Ikaru was suddenly all smiles, taking the spoon from the table and scooping out the bits of *kanten* and syrup that remained at the bottom of his bowl. "This sure is delicious, Atori," he mumbled. "Thanks."

I watched him as I drained my coffee cup. Ikaru was squandering time, equipment, and reagents on an experiment that had nothing whatsoever to do with his graduation thesis. But if it was only for another ten days or so, I didn't think I'd have any problem making his cytoskeletal fiber gene amplification project our little secret.

What if he were discovered? Our advisor probably wouldn't say anything, but the long-haired grad student would have a few choice words for Ikaru.

I could almost hear him now: *You think thermostable enzymes and chemicals grow on trees? Quit wasting our precious research funds.*

Then it would really blow up into something. Trembling a little, I returned my empty coffee cup to its saucer.

We left Yukiwatari and walked south on First Street. Past one block, then another, across the big main street, and we were at the front entrance to the research park.

I nodded a greeting to the familiar gray-clad doorkeeper as we made our way to the life sciences research wing, walking along a path through the grass. Ivy-covered walls dotted the campus, conveying a real sense of the history behind these research buildings. Parents with children and couples our age sat beside green-leafed trees and on peeling park benches, enjoying the summer sun. The townies tended to treat the facility grounds as some sort of public park.

As one might expect, the life sciences building was another aged edifice, this one in red brick.

When we returned to the biology lab, Ikaru made a beeline for his line of thermal cyclers and muttered, "The reaction's just ended." He looked back at me. "I'll only use three for the next round, like I promised."

Ikaru turned back to the machines and opened their lids with a practiced hand, one after another. He removed the capillary tubes and began placing them into the sample block.

A thought occurred to me. "Something's been bothering me," I said, standing directly behind him. "Has anyone else done this experiment—I mean, amplifying only a certain gene to gargantuan amounts?"

In *Intermediate Scientific Thought,* we learned about not cribbing other researchers' ideas during the planning stage. Rehashed material doesn't fly in the scientific world. And if it turns out all this had already been done, Ikaru didn't need to waste any *more* time.

"I checked," he replied, hands still busy with the machines. "I searched through past theses and read the summaries of all the grant applications. Nothing."

Grant applications—those are to receive public subsidies for scientific research. "So no one's out there doing this same thing, and no one ever has?"

Ikaru began writing his name and the date on the top of the sample block. "Why would there be? This plan is completely original."

"It sure is," I muttered, and started going back to my own work. I was busy, too. I certainly couldn't spend all my time babysitting my friend. I was on the verge of leaving when Ikaru called after me.

"We probably shouldn't tell anyone how that amplification start array is set up for only a single gene, huh."

"Nope," I agreed, as I shut the door behind me.

Mission accomplished.

I opened the door adjoining the lab, slipped through a terribly narrow hallway, and went through one more inside door to the cell culture lab.

The shelves just inside held a bottle of 70-percent isopropyl alcohol for disinfecting, along with a box of disposable gloves. I sprayed the alcohol onto both of my hands and arms, generously covering them to the elbow, and put on a pair of gloves. Random outside bacteria weren't welcome here.

I surveyed the room, a small place that would be filled to capacity with only two people. To the right, a sterilizable console, its ultraviolet lights glowing blue; to the left, a box-type incubator. On a table beyond these stood a phase contrast microscope, and that's where I was headed.

I was the one who spent the most time in the cell culture lab. The place was like my castle: people didn't come here unless they had to. Frequent comings and goings just meant more opportunities for cell contamination, and whether you were talking about live cells or Ikaru's biochemical approach, that was always the experimenter's greatest fear.

I opened the incubator's front panel with my left hand, then opened the glass door within. With my right hand I removed a petri dish and quickly closed both doors. It was a practiced movement meant to keep the temperature, humidity, and CO_2 saturation levels stable within the chamber.

Gingerly I brought the dish over to the microscope. It was a round, shallow plate as big as my palm, with a lid that allowed me to hold it with my fingers. The liquid culture medium inside was still the vivid red it had always been.

I had to pay special attention to the medium's color. The rapidly multiplying cells ate the culture medium non-stop. When the color changed from the red of a fairly neutral pH to the yellow of an acidic pH, it meant the cells were starving.

I could breathe easy today: They were in the early log phase. I placed the dish on the microscope's stage, turned on the lamp, and peered through the eyepieces at the dish, turning the knob on the right to adjust the focus. I carefully moved the dish across the stage so as not to spill any of the liquid medium within.

In my round field of vision, I spotted a number of polygons stuck to the bottom of the dish, their arms reaching out in four directions. Their edges glowed brightly, and dark, nearly circular nuclei floated at their centers. Some cells appeared to be stuck together in pairs; these were in the midst of cell division. All of the cells would create exact facsimiles of their own double-strand genes, divide them up equally, and split into two.

I smiled a little, pleased. The dish and its contents had stood up to being out in the light, but now it was time to put it back in the incubator. The cancer cells I was culturing were still full of beans.

They were living things, too, and would die without my daily care and attention. I didn't go home during summer vacation like the other students because I had to tend to these cells, the basis for my thesis research.

Yet I wasn't sure why Ikaru, with his biochemical experiments on genes, was spending his first summer away from home. I asked him once, but he only gave me a vague answer about it being too expensive to travel.

I sighed and returned to my work. I pulled out the dishes I planned to use in today's experiments and used a protease to remove the cells that had grown along their bottoms. After treating the cells with a dye that only highlighted the dead cells, I put the dish in the hemocytometer and began counting the number of dead and living cells through a microscope.

Why cancer cells? I got that a lot. I couldn't say for sure, but maybe it was because I'd been blown away by how prolific they were ever since I came across them in my third-year practicum. It depends on the type of cell line, but cancer cells in the log phase divide with unrivaled vigor. They keep dividing until the petri dish is full and the nutrients in the culture medium are exhausted. They are unrestrained, relentless.

As I looked at cancer cells under a microscope time and time again, I came to find them beautiful. According to my advisor, this was a common phenomenon among researchers, where you become partial to your research subjects as though they were members of your own family. *You're a real biologist now*, he'd laughed.

And so I chose cancer cells as the basis for my thesis research. They were easy to handle—epithelial lung carcinoma cells that readily grew on any kind of medium.

I turned to today's page in my logbook and recorded the numbers I'd counted. Having finished my work for the time being, I reveled in my sense of accomplishment and peeled off my gloves. I left through the same two doors and returned to the research lab.

I didn't see anyone inside, but as I wove my way between the desks to my seat, I almost stepped on Ikaru, curled up in a sleeping bag on the floor. So this is what he'd been doing for the past three days, taking catnaps between amplification cycles.

I stepped over his sleeping form and returned to my desk. Sunlight was coming in almost vertically through the window, leaving the tiniest of bright rectangles on my desktop.

My biological clock was telling me it was approaching lunchtime, and my eyes unwittingly went to my goldfish bowl.

Something was different. I brought my face closer and took a good look.

The male was the same as always. The female, though—the one with the unnotched dorsal fin—was swimming around with a number of transparent dots stuck to her between her ventral and anal fins.

Eggs! She'd finally spawned!

I forgot about my hunger for a while and watched, fascinated by the fish's tiny rear end as she swam to and fro around the bowl. She'd be moving those eggs to a piece of seaweed before long, and when she did, I'd have to put the eggs somewhere else so they wouldn't get eaten.

I stood up and left the lab, careful not to trip over Ikaru. I ran down the hallway, across the building, and all the way back to the experimental lab, headed for the equipment room within. I picked through the shelves of disinfected lab glassware until I found a glass cylinder in a corner, used so often and for so long that its markings had grown faint. Surely no one would miss it. It held about as much as a coffee cup, perfect temporary digs for a handful of goldfish eggs.

Cylinder in hand, I closed the equipment room door and made my way through the deserted lab.

Between the rows of lab benches was a shaking incubator. I stopped for a moment in front of the device, its top panel made of a clear resin so I could see inside. The incubator was set to 37 degrees Celsius; three conical glass beakers stood on the inner platform, each with about two inches of yellow culture medium swaying gently from side to side.

The medium had already begun turning whitish and cloudy, proof that the *E. coli* it was nurturing was multiplying apace.

That long-haired grad student was using this bacterium for his doctoral thesis. Give it the right culture medium and temperature and its numbers would increase at a rate that puts even cancer cells to shame. I was never much of a fan, though; *E. coli* seemed less like a living thing and more like a single-minded multiplying machine. It wasn't even particularly pretty under a microscope, and on top of everything else, the cultures smelled disgusting.

But that was just my own bias. I was sure the grad student who took care of those little buggers every day must have had a soft spot for them.

Just before leaving the lab, I turned back to look at the bench closest to the door. All six thermal cyclers were humming away. Ikaru had commandeered three of them, so the long-haired grad student must have been able to use the rest without incident.

I returned to the research lab, filled the cylinder about three quarters full of tap water, and set it down next to the fishbowl. The chlorine would have dissipated by the time the female goldfish was done depositing her eggs.

Now I could finally get down to work. I stepped over Ikaru yet again and walked up beside the lab door. There was a sink in that corner, along with a burner. With the compact refrigerator, induction cooker, and basic selection of utensils and tableware, you could even whip up a simple dish or two. There was a dining hall on campus, but it was expensive for us students. The food wasn't even that good.

I took a lump of cooked rice from the fridge's small freezer and put it in the induction cooker.

Then I took out a package wrapped in a paper-thin sheet of wood, which I'd moved to the fridge's bottom shelf the day before to defrost. It was a fermented soybean product that's usually kept frozen, but I liked eating it after it had been defrosted and kept cool for a day or so, giving it the chance to ferment a little more. All of my frozen provisions were specialties of my hometown, courtesy of my mother who occasionally sent them to her poor daughter living all on her lonesome up north.

As I watched the defrosting rice swirl around inside the induction cooker, I remembered the incident I'd caused concerning this food storage area.

Shortly after I'd been assigned to the research lab, I had put my food in the sample freezer. No one cared about the rice, but the fermented soybeans were another story. The long-haired grad student was the first to react: *What do you think you're doing? Those bacteria could contaminate my* E. coli! I realized my gaffe and apologized. My advisor found an old household refrigerator somewhere and set it up in the student research lab for me.

Still, whenever that grad student came across me eating my fermented food, he made absolutely no attempt to hide his disgust. He probably didn't like the smell, although I found the stench of his *E. coli* cultures far more offensive.

I was transferring my defrosted meal to a plate when the door right next to me opened.

"Good morning."

The voice was a little high-pitched and a little slow-paced. A pale face framed by brightly colored hair peeked around the door. I had been steeling myself against the possibility of that damn grad student barging in on me, but my fears had been unfounded. I responded to the doctoral student with a *good morning* of my own.

She tended to come in earlier in the morning; I supposed her usual greeting had just slipped out.

I asked if she was here for lunch, but she said she'd eaten at home. "Then how about some tea?" I offered. "Thank you," she replied, her smile like sunshine. She placed her things at her seat and came back to sit at the tiny rectangular table in front of the sink. I put water on to boil and got the tea leaves ready. Mindful of my companion's condition, I selected an herbal tea instead of a stronger green variety.

I poured us each a cup of tea, then placed my lunch on the table and sat down across from the grad student. Her elegantly narrow eyes narrowed even further as she began to speak.

"The hospital was so crowded. It took forever."

The words she used were ordinary enough, but being born and raised in the west had imbued them with a healthy dollop of old-fashioned lilt. People came to this research park from all over.

While we ate, I listened to my older friend's tales of the obstetrician's office. The doctor had given her a long list of don'ts. Miscarriages can happen during this stage of pregnancy, so she was to move carefully; even if her morning sickness was particularly severe, she was to eat whenever she found time. Things like that. "My appetite's just fine, though," she laughed. "I guess morning sickness affects everyone differently." She may have been from the west, but she had nothing against fermented soybeans, and even though pregnant women were said to be particularly sensitive to smells in their first trimester, she didn't seem to mind at all. Thank goodness for that.

I washed and put away our plates, then poured another round of tea while we chatted a while longer.

My friend was five years older than I and had had my back ever since I decided to do my thesis research in life sciences. It was probably because she knew how hard it was to be part of such a small minority in this man's world that I could even pull off this work in the first place. Even when Ikaru and I ate candy made from mixing purified glucose powder into ultra-pure agarose electrophoresis gel, she smiled softly with her lovely eyes and covered for us both, then took us to a shop on campus where she bought us proper cooking gelatin. *Don't eat any more of that lab stuff, okay?* she said gently. *It's incredibly expensive.*

I couldn't thank her enough. That's why I made her tea, and why I'd been helping her with her experiments ever since she had discovered she was pregnant. She had excellent time management skills, so all I ended up doing was taking the samples out of the device after the reaction ended and transferring them to the lab fridge after she'd gone home for the day.

I'd asked her about the challenges of getting pregnant and having a baby in the middle of finishing her dissertation. *I'm sure I'll finish that paper,* she told me. *Besides, I'm just so happy it took.* Her cheeks flushed at this, pleased. It seems her husband—my advisor—had a slightly lower than normal sperm count, so they had never dreamed they would conceive so quickly. True, her due date did coincide with the dissertation submission deadline, but it was anyone's guess when they could get pregnant again. She was so exceptional in her field that this situation probably wouldn't faze her one bit. After all, even though she still considered herself a student, she had already published two studies in famous journals that boasted high citation counts.

The lines of her cheeks and jaw had softened a little. What must it feel like, having a tiny life in your belly, a not-you inside you?

It's not like I had to ask. I could tell just by the look on her face.

"Well, I'd better get to work. Thanks for the tea, Atori."

The doctoral student stood up a tad slowly and went to take her teacup to the sink. I hurried to stop her. "Let me do that."

She smiled like a young girl. "If you insist," she replied, and left the lab.

I had finished washing all the tea equipment and was about to head back to the cell culture lab when a sudden sharp noise rang out through the room. I glanced at the floor and saw Ikaru trying to wriggle out of his sleeping bag. After much flailing about, he managed to sit up, then stared with sleepy eyes at the timer hanging around his neck, checking its readout. It was set to the thermal cycler's reaction end time.

"Morning." Ikaru looked up at me and smiled, eyelids puffy. If he was waking up, it must be morning. The familiar harsh noise continued; the alarm was still going strong.

"Turn that off," I commanded, one hand on my hip and the other pointing to the tiny device still shrieking that the appointed time had arrived. "Or are you *trying* to ruffle feathers around here?"

"No sirree," he grinned, completely unabashed, but pressed the timer's button to silence it.

As I regarded my childhood friend's unfocused attitude, which hadn't changed a bit since we were kids, I thought of the long-haired grad student and how he had been so high-strung lately. Everyone gets a little touchy with a dissertation defense on the horizon or a thesis deadline approaching, but he was something else, complaining about the faintest noises and smells. If only we could avoid any friction between him and Ikaru, I thought, and heaved a huge sigh.

For three days after Ikaru and I spoke at Yukiwatari, everything was smooth sailing. He amplified his cytoskeletal fiber genes exponentially as he worked to turn his fantasy into reality, and my cancer cell thesis experiments continued without a hitch. I turned the quail eggs twice a day and changed the water in the fishbowl from time to time to keep the eggs healthy. My advisor's grad-student wife ate her meals without the torment of morning sickness. My fermented soybean food sat in the refrigerator, its microbes slowly multiplying.

But on the evening of the third day, the long-haired grad student finally snapped.

"God! Shut that thing off already!"

He stopped in the middle of compiling his experiment results, stood up, and strode over to Ikaru's sleeping bag, still unmoving despite the wailing timer. I didn't have the chance to step in between them before he kicked Ikaru in the head with his rugged shin-high boots. Ikaru howled, immediately grabbing his head with both hands and curling up into the fetal position.

I ran over to the sleeping bag and knelt next to my childhood friend. "What the hell?"

"It's his fault. I'm engaged in some serious mental effort here. You'd think a little peace and quiet wouldn't be too much to expect!" the long-haired grad student sputtered, his haughty expression unchanged. "And quit sleeping here. You're just getting in everyone's way."

Ikaru finally managed to sit up, at which point he shot the grad student a truly menacing look. If my doctoral student friend hadn't happened to come back from the experimental lab just then and intervened, I don't know what would have happened.

Maybe her words of persuasion got to him somehow. For whatever reason, the long-haired grad student behaved himself for a few days after that.

And so day nine rolled around, a silent balloon of tension hovering over us.

I had left the cell culture lab to check out the experimental lab. That's where I ran into Ikaru, holding a sample block as he stood before his three preheated thermal cyclers.

"Tomorrow's the big day," he said. "They should reach the target count tomorrow night. I can't wait to see if it'll be The End or not. Will there be huge storms, lightning, floods? The words THE END writ large in the night sky? I'm betting on there being a whole lot of nothing at all. Dr. Gould was definitely right about that."

He stopped there to check the user-set temperatures on the cyclers' displays, then opened their lids and began placing the samples inside.

"I agree," I replied. Not with Dr. Gould and all that, but with Ikaru's assertion that no paranormal phenomenon, no great The End would come to pass.

I exhaled and looked around the room. Someone was working at a lab bench a few rows in front.

It was the long-haired grad student. He peered into a cooler that Ikaru had been using, then casually stuck his hand inside.

Could he have overheard our conversation?

I immediately shouted, "Stop that. Don't go touching other people's samples."

There was the usual fear of contamination, but it was much more terrifying if this student were to find out that Ikaru was using nothing but a single strain, an amplification start array of cytoskeletal fiber genes—a strain that was normally little more than a positive control.

Ikaru seemed to notice what was going on, but he couldn't move: the cyclers had reached their set temperatures, and he was in the middle of placing samples inside.

I ran over instead. Before I could reach the bench, though, the long-haired grad student swiftly rummaged around inside the cooler and plucked out a resin tube meant to fit into an amplification start array. He read the side of the tube, snorted, and put it back on ice. He went on to do the same thing with another tube. And another, and another. By the time I reached the bench, he had examined about eight array tubes in all.

"So these are all for his graduation thesis, huh? I was wondering what he was amplifying that could be worth getting so geeked about."

He shot a look at me and at Ikaru, on the far side of his thermal cyclers, and left.

It seems he hadn't heard us talking after all. Or maybe he had, and simply didn't understand it.

I sighed with relief and came back over to Ikaru, who had just closed the lid on the third cycler.

"You've got to toss in a handful of fakes," he grinned. "I've got plenty of tricks up my sleeve."

I smiled back, of course. It was the smile of a conspirator.

The next day brought change to the old incubator.

There was no longer any need to turn the eggs. That morning, I'd noticed some eggs looked a little different and thought I'd better lower the temperature. In the end, I couldn't resist the insistent temptation to open the door on the front of the incubator.

I sat back down in front of it. Outside, the long summer day had already drawn to a close, and the dim, uncertain artificial lamps inside had just begun to bathe the hallway in their reluctant light. I cracked open the incubator door, only to be greeted by warm air and a faint, high-pitched sound.

I gently closed the door, brought my knees up to my chin, and smiled. At least one chick should be hatching tomorrow and making its big debut.

I heard someone come barreling down the hallway behind me. I knew who it was.

"Atori, come on. The final amplification cycle is almost complete."

Ikaru came to a sudden stop beside me, his proclamation tumbling out in a breathless rush.

I nodded, stood up, and ran down the hallway after him.

"Faster! Hurry!" called my childhood friend over his shoulder, urging me onward. "You should have come gotten me earlier, then," I shot back, causing him to put his hand to the back of his head and laugh. Together we laughed our way through the dark, narrow hallway and burst into the experimental lab.

"Any second now."

We stood side by side in front of the rightmost thermal cycler. Ikaru was using the other two machines next to it as well, but this particular cycler had already finished its forty rounds of temperature cycling and was now cooling off, hot air slowly emanating from its side panels.

Our gazes returned to the readouts on the two running machines, watching intently as the digit in the last place of the cycle count changed. Both were still at 38. The temperature still had to rise, then fall slightly, then rise once more to complete the 38th amplification cycle. Inside the bank of eight capillary tubes were 38^2 cytoskeletal fiber genes.

"It's The End, The End, The End is here!" Ikaru sang. "This is it: the world's first all-out victory for cytoskeletal fiber genes. The runner-up glycolytic dehydrogenase genes have no hope of catching up. What on earth will happen? *Will* anything happen? I'd say we ought to see this through, don't you?"

He looked from the display up to me, a smile on his lips and in his eyes.

With a smile of my own, I nodded. Now that the fantasy he'd made for himself was reaching its end, Ikaru would finally come back to his senses, finally bounce back from the sadness of having lost Dr. James.

"I can't stand it! I'm gonna count the cycles. Thirty-nine."

He was back to staring at the display. The temperature rose, fell, and the numbers changed.

"Forty."

The two of us spoke in unison this time. The temperature rose and fell, just as it had been programmed to do. The reaction was complete. The array now held 40^2 genes.

The most numerous genes in the world were cytoskeletal fiber genes.

The cycler began expelling waste heat with a *pssht*, drastically decreasing the temperature. The reaction was really, truly, honestly and completely over.

Ikaru and I stood there in front of the cycler, our eyes glued to its display. The digits showing the temperature kept dropping until they reached four degrees: the keep-cool stage. The lab, the life-science wing, the research park campus: all of it retained its summer-night stillness.

Ikaru lifted his face again and looked at me. His lips parted to form the words *We won.*

But I couldn't hear his voice at all. What assailed my ears instead was an explosion big enough to stop a cow's heart.

We looked at one another, then simultaneously ran out of the lab. We scrambled down the hallway to the opposite side of the building and clockwise up the spiral staircase.

He ran ahead of me, taking the steps two at a time. As we reached the third floor, then the fourth, I fell further and further behind, his back, his legs, now his shoes, moving out of sight.

A tremendous sound rang out as the rooftop doors opened: that explosion again. Ikaru went on moaning.

Finally I climbed the last few steps of the staircase and, passing through the door that had been left open, jumped out onto the roof of the life sciences research wing.

Ikaru was looking up at the night sky, his face bathed in moonlight and both hands on the low handrail surrounding the roof. He looked back at me.

"Take a look."

I turned my head toward the direction he was indicating. The town with its flickering lights sprawled out below, the dark river snaking its way between the tiny flecks of brightness.

Something rose out of the river, trailing a tail behind. It sailed straight upward, headed for the heavens, and exploded slightly above our line of sight, scattering bright multicolored droplets over the black backdrop.

There was the slightest delay before the same explosive boom came again.

I walked up next to Ikaru. The two of us stood there, gripping the handrail and saying nothing as we watched the fireworks coloring the sky on the eve of the summer festival.

The multi-burst series came to an end, along with its intense light and sound. Smoke had begun to obscure the moon as Ikaru turned to me yet again.

"I love this town," he admitted, a strangely self-conscious smile on his face. "I always have, and I always will."

I gave him a similarly bashful smile in return. "Me too."

Then I moved a step closer.

The next morning I went straight from Ikaru's dorm to the research park. He looked so happy lying there asleep that I decided not to wake him. After all, he hadn't even seen his bed in two weeks; he should be able to snooze to his heart's content.

I greeted the doorkeeper as I passed through the gate, then stopped in at the administration building immediately to the right. I stood at the window to fill out the paperwork, giving my name and student number, then went into the clinic. Luckily, the doctor on duty was a woman.

The doctor's lavish hair hung in a ponytail over her lab coat as she listened to everything I had to say. Once I'd finished, she grabbed a pen.

"I'll write you a prescription."

She wrote the name of a drug on a prescription pad and handed it to someone, probably a pharmacist, through a window that connected the exam room with the pharmacy next door.

Before long, a white paper packet appeared at the window.

"Start by taking two, the sooner the better," the doctor advised, handing me the packet along with a cup of water.

I thanked her and opened the packet, then pressed two of the round pills, about the size of my fingertip, out of their packaging and into the palm of my hand.

As I clumsily washed down the two pills with the water, the doctor began going over the various warnings and contraindications. I was to take the remaining two pills in another twelve hours. Postcoital oral contraception works on the endocrine system, so it does have side effects. These can include severe nausea and headaches, though they vary from person to person.

"It can also cause intense dizziness and, very rarely, hallucinations. I recommend staying away from cerebral work today, like experiments; you should head back to your dorm and get some rest instead."

The doctor took the empty cup from my hand and threw it away, then sat down once more on the exam chair in front of me.

"Now listen closely: He will never, ever get pregnant. That means contraception is *your* problem, and *you* will have to take the appropriate measures. Understand?"

She launched into an explanation of every kind of contraception and what it cost, from disposable devices to tubal ligation. Occasionally she would mutter things like *This really should be part of compulsory education* or *You may be smart enough to study at the research facility, but that doesn't mean you can't forget all about contraception when it's your first time.*

At long last I was released from the doctor's diatribe; by the time I left the clinic, it was already afternoon. Despite the doctor's instructions, I wasn't about to go home like a good little girl. I had things to take care of.

Bathed in the full summer sunshine, I walked down the path through the lawn, headed for the life sciences research wing. There didn't seem to be as many locals hanging out today, maybe because it was the first day of the festival. When I entered the red brick building, I felt a touch of nausea.

It looked like those side effects were kicking in.

The lab was deserted. The long-haired grad student had left his things on his desk; maybe he was working in the experimental lab. The doctoral student must not have come in yet. She could be having another check-up; she seemed to have an awful lot of those.

Now to get some lunch in me before the nausea got serious. I opened the fridge and took out the fermented soybean dish I'd transferred from the freezer the day before. I noticed something was wrong as soon as I opened the wrapper. I leaned in for a sniff.

There was almost none of its usual smell. It smelled freshly bought, with almost no fermentation at all.

There went my appetite. I wrapped everything up again and put it back in the fridge. I was already feeling ill; it probably wouldn't taste good even if I gagged it down. Times like this, I just had to suck it up and forgo lunch.

I washed my hands in the sink and made my way to the cell culture lab. I wanted to check up on the quail eggs in the incubator—they should be hatching by now—but the cancer cells came first. They'll be all over the petri dish and crying for sustenance by now, having gobbled up all the nutrients in the liquid medium.

As usual, I went through both doors, disinfected both hands with the alcohol, and donned a pair of disposable gloves. I opened the incubator and took out the frontmost dish.

But contrary to my expectations, the liquid medium in the dish hadn't turned yellow at all.

It had gone from its initial vivid red to having only the slightest orange tint. I pulled out the next dish, then the next, then the next. Every one of the dishes was still red inside.

I put one of the dishes under the phase contrast microscope and turned on the lamp. As I adjusted the focus, the bottom of the dish came up into my field of vision. Bit by bit I moved the dish around, checking every last inch of it. Just as I thought: the cells weren't increasing at all.

I racked my brains as I returned the dish to the incubator. Obviously there would be no need to swap out the culture medium. But I couldn't for the life of me come up with a reason why the cancer cells would stop propagating so abruptly. It might have been a heretofore unknown phenomenon. I'd have to talk with my advisor.

My nausea returned, stronger than before. My head started swimming, making the culture lab's walls and columns look askew. Uh-oh. Better get out of here. God forbid I should faint onto any lab equipment or contaminate the room with my vomit.

As I opened the second door, I ran into the long-haired grad student on his way out of the experimental lab.

"Hey," he barked, glaring at me, "isn't Ikaru in charge of making up the *E. coli* culture medium this week?"

"Next week," I replied, and told him the name of the student who had the job this week.

"Oh, her," the long-haired grad student said, immediately toning down his attitude and putting his hand to the back of his head. "That's odd. She's definitely not the kind to neglect her duties." He folded his arms. "Maybe she's not feeling right. Women sure have it rough."

"What's going on?"

My voice sounded like a stranger's, maybe because I felt so awful. The clinic doctor's words came back to me: *It can also cause hallucinations.*

"My *E. coli* isn't multiplying at all."

The grad student made a deeply troubled face. Judging by his tone of voice and his expression, he had to be telling the truth.

"They've been in the shaking incubator since evening, which means their numbers should be way past the target by now. I thought there might be something wrong with the medium." He retreated into the experimental lab once more, muttering about not finishing in time for his dissertation defense.

I gritted my teeth against my intense nausea as I navigated the narrow hallways to the research lab, stopping in front of the old incubator. I leaned forward to open the door on the front, then, with warm air bathing my face, inspected each of the forty quail eggs in turn. Which egg had been cheeping last night? Will the chick inside have cracked a hole in the shell, poking its triangular beak into the outside world?

The speckled eggs were as round, unbroken, and silent as the day someone had slapped a price tag on them to be sold at the grocery store.

I hung my head and blinked over and over, then closed the incubator door and slowly pulled myself upright. For all the attention I'd given them, it was still artificial incubation. Maybe they needed a mother quail's touch after all.

But it was too early to give up entirely. Give them a few days and a different egg could hatch. I decided to wait and see for a little while longer, then walked down the hallway hugging myself, suddenly beset by chills.

I went into the research lab, stepping over the sleeping bag Ikaru had been using until yesterday on my way to my desk. I took a deep breath, relieved to have been able to sit down without incident. Things hadn't quite progressed to the level of hallucinations after all. The chair under my buttocks and the surface of the writing desk under my hands retained their sense of unquestionable realness.

My fingertips wiped away the beads of sweat on my forehead as I peered into the fishbowl and the glass cylinder. The goldfish were no different. Both of them were moving around the bowl as they had always done, puckering their mouths and busily working their tiny gills and tails.

But something was wrong with the eggs. I brought my face closer to the glass and stared at them.

Yesterday, each egg had been transparent, with tiny black spots that could have been eyes. Today, they were cloudy and whitish.

I lifted my head and gave it a shake. I was sure I'd be admiring a tiny school of adorable fry by now.

Again the wave of nausea rose within me, bringing with it a headache. When I looked up, the ceiling beams seemed gently curved. That did it. Just let me talk to my advisor; then I'd go back to the dorm.

I couldn't stand without grabbing onto the edge of the desk and letting out a grunt of effort. My disobedient legs moved left and right, as though they had their own destinations in mind. The mere act of leaving the research lab and knocking on my advisor's neighboring door felt like climbing to a lofty mountain summit, complete with ragged breath and heaving shoulders. "Come in," came the reply, and I obeyed at once.

I was surprised to see my advisor sitting at the table inside, even paler than usual and looking really haggard. It was enough to make me forget about both my own physical state and the phenomenon of the non-dividing cancer cells.

"Sorry," he began weakly, having noticed my expression. "It's been one hell of a morning. I had to take her to the hospital. They admitted her, just to be safe; she'll probably be there resting for a few days."

He twisted his lips into an obviously forced smile before continuing. "Writing her doctoral thesis was a considerable burden for her. As a woman, you need to know this: You can't push yourself too hard when you're pregnant. It might all end in tears."

"I hope she gets well soon," I offered, not knowing if it was the right thing to say in this situation, and left the room.

Steeling myself against yet another onslaught of nausea and dizziness, I clung to the walls as I staggered down the hallway, hand on jaw. This isn't right. It's too much to be mere coincidence. Fermentation bacteria, cancer cells, *E. coli*—none of them multiplying. Quail chicks and goldfish fry apparently dead before they hatched. And then—

At last I arrived at a delusional hypothesis that put Ikaru's fantasies to shame.

The End really had come. But it hadn't manifested in natural disasters or giant letters in the sky.

Cells were simply done dividing. The battle of genetic amplification that had been waging since time immemorial had been decided—and by a huge margin at that. For cells to spontaneously duplicate their own genetic material would be nothing more than a waste of time.

I peeled myself away from the wall and took off down the hallway. I dove into the experimental lab and pulled one set of gene amplification reagent out of the freezer.

I grabbed a cooler and placed the reagent inside, then, wielding a micro-burette, took everything over to a lab bench.

Hurry. I've got to hurry. If my theory was correct, the single-celled organisms alive right now would soon start dying off. Multi-celled organisms might be able to hold out a little longer, but not that long. For one thing, you wouldn't be able to heal your wounds. Without the ability to replenish depleted blood cells, hypoxia would set in, and your immune functions would be wiped out. Plus the symbiotic bacteria that aid digestion would be annihilated, including *E. coli* in humans.

And so much for being able to bear offspring. Fertilized eggs were no longer dividing. Not that we'd be making any gametes in the first place.

So I guess I didn't need those morning-after pills after all, I thought with a wry smile.

Hurry. I've got to hurry. If I don't do something, the world is going to end.

"Whoa! What's going on?"

I couldn't spare the time to answer the long-haired grad student's surprised question. I worked with intense concentration, measuring out reagent, mixing it up, adding thermostable enzymes for gene strand synthesis. I pulled a resin tube from the amplification start array and checked the words written on its side.

Glycolytic Dehydrogenase Genes. This, the runner-up, was the only thing that stood a chance against The End that cytoskeletal fiber genes had wrought.

Hurry. I've got to hurry. I need to artificially amplify these glycolytic dehydrogenase genes until their numbers are beyond Ikaru's estimated maximum, until they rival those of the cytoskeletal fiber genes.

Other researchers would multiply both genes in their daily experiments, which means the two would always be neck-and-neck, vying for front-runner in a long-distance race. The race would never be won, so The End could be postponed indefinitely. Maybe.

Despite my wretched physical state, the hand clutching the micro-burette moved with uncanny ease. It was as if I were in a dream. If only all of this—the stagnant cells, the unhatched eggs, the doctoral student's miscarriage—were the product of hallucinations, the side effect of some drug!

I finished preparing eight times twelve times six microtubules, each with their share of mixed reagent, then stood up and moved over to the thermal cyclers. My dizziness was even worse now. I turned on the machines that had been off, then forced an emergency stop on the machines that were running before taking out all of the reagents inside and placing them on the floor. I peered at the cyclers' displays, then set them all to the maximum number of forty cycles, as Ikaru had.

I don't know if this could really stop The End in its tracks. But I had to try.

As I watched the numbers on the display rise from room temperature to the set cycling level, I resisted an even more powerful attack of nausea and dizziness. The grad student was standing next to me and shouting something, but the meaning of his words was completely beyond my understanding.

Gradually even his voice grew faint, until my surroundings were utterly silent. My field of vision, too, grew narrow and dark.

Only the ever-changing numbers flickered as they shone.

Minagawa Hiroko

Translated by Karen Sandness

It happened again. When I unfolded the newspaper to read, the printed characters slid off the pages, leaving them blank. The characters advanced across the floor in a line and headed up into the aquarium, which was in the recess of a bay window.

It had been several days since I had picked up the two mollusks on the tidal flats. They were a pale pink, but they were as big as the palm of my hand and therefore more substantial than the pink clams that one finds on the beaches of southern Japan. They were so unusual that I took them home and placed them in the aquarium where I keep my tropical fish and fingers. The shells opened slightly as if settling in, but what emerged from between the two halves were not tongue-like pseudopods but fingers.

If I had forced them all the way open I might have injured them or, at worst, killed them, so I had no way of seeing whether the shells contained only fingers or a whole arm or even an entire body. Since they were so fond of printed characters, I thought they might have eyes. Or maybe they just enjoyed the sensation of touching the print.

I was already keeping three fingers in the aquarium, but none of them was so fond of printed characters.

I wonder when it was that maxims such as "Life is precious" and "Thou shalt try to stay alive" or "Thou shalt not kill" came to be bandied about as ironclad principles. Every once in a while, some incident comes up in which the criterion is the degree to which one should or should not consider life to be precious.

All my life, not only throughout my schooling but also in every form of mass media, this has been continually pounded into our heads. Perhaps for that reason, we have a fanatical belief that it is the right of and proper for all creatures, whether they have a brain or just four legs, to keep on living. At least, I think that's what happened.

No pundit mentioned the contradiction between "Thou shalt try to stay alive" and "Thou shalt not kill." Researchers announced results that showed that if you raised a severed finger in an appropriate environment, it would be so obsessed with staying alive that it would change form. Raising them in water seemed to yield the highest success rate. Supposedly this was because they could easily model themselves on fish. Once these results were released, raising fingers in aquariums became wildly popular.

If there's a demand, the supply increases, as in former days, when impoverished students used to sell their blood to make ends meet. When it comes to fingers, fresh ones are the most desirable. Observing the process by which the fingers change in imitation of fish is what owners find most pleasurable, so owning one that has already gone through the process is boring, and old fingers that have not changed are unlikely to do so in the future. If a finger in a retailer's aquarium just lies there and decays, everyone assumes that the owner had an insufficient desire to live.

It is possible that people would have grown tired of these fingers and stopped paying attention to them, but rumors began flying that the government would ban them, so the retail price rose sharply.

When the ban was issued, a single finger became worth its weight in gold, and, with the possibility of being subjected to severe punishment if found out, raising fingers became a secret hobby of the bourgeoisie. Human rights and citizen's groups had already taken the hobbyists to task on the grounds that they were fiends who violated human dignity. However, since this position had originated in respect for human life, those who were opposed to it embraced the inherent contradiction. Since their mission in life was to oppose the government, no matter what it did, they started holding demonstrations as soon as the ban was issued on the grounds that the government was not respecting the principle of free will.

Of the three fingers that I was raising, one had completed the transformation. It was swimming around, outwardly indistinguishable from the tropical fish that I had put into the aquarium with it.

The doorbell rang. My visitors were Arteria and Vena, who lived in the lowlands on the other side of the mountain. Their real name was Ayako, but at some point, Ayako's body had split in two. It's a phenomenon that often happens to people who suffer a severe emotional shock or are in a distracted state. It's happened to me several times. If the two halves remain in close contact with each other, nothing serious happens. They reintegrate and the person is his old self. But occasionally this fails to happen for some people. Most of them die if they take too long to reintegrate, but some people hold such deep convictions about the value of staying alive that they come back to life. If both halves revive, the body exists in duplicate. That's what happened to Ayako. The halves share the same name, but I distinguish them by calling them Arteria and Vena.

It wasn't as if one of them outranked the other. Arteria was yang and Vena was yin, and they gave the impression that Arteria was the leader and Vena the follower. They were like inbound and outbound trains. The reason that I dubbed the right half "Arteria" (the Latin word for "artery") when they split was that it seemed like a natural concept for a right-handed person like me. Actually, Arteria appeared to take the lead in their actions, if only a little. Yet Ayako's heart was on the left side when she split in two, so perhaps I should have ranked the left half higher and called it "Arteria." Even so, the right half created a heart on its own, so it's fair to say that its desire to live overwhelmed that of the left half. I suppose, then, that it was appropriate to think of the right half as predominant.

"We heard that your brother passed away," they said in unison. Behind their polite words lay an implied criticism of me for not notifying them right away. "May we take him, as you promised?"

"He's all ready. Please come in."

When I asked whether they could transport him, they said that they had brought a cart. "It's the one we used for our touring act."

As they passed through the living room, they glanced at the aquarium. "You have more new ones," they said. "Those characters are diving down to those mollusks, aren't they?"

The mollusks had evidently finished sucking in the print from the newspaper, but the black shapes of printed characters extended from under the books on my shelf and were advancing toward the aquarium.

I showed Arteria and Vena into my brother's bedroom.

"Will he be of any use to you?"

"He's fantastic! Thank you!"

"The internal organs are what causes decomposition, so I've removed all of them, and I've embalmed the rest," I said smugly. "I've done a perfect job, even if I do say so myself. I planned to let you know as soon as I was finished. I'm sorry about not telling you sooner."

Their dissatisfied faces showed that my sarcasm had gone completely over their heads.

"Your brother's beautiful!" Arteria and Vena said, their faces flushing with excitement.

His opened and preserved innards were wax-colored with a slight reddish cast, like the inside of an Akoya pearl oyster. In fact, the coloration of his entire body made him look like a wax sculpture.

As I helped Arteria and Vena carry my brother through the living room, they hesitantly looked up at me and said, "It's really out of line of us to ask after you've given us your brother and everything, but we wanted to buy a finger, but before we could get around to it, they issued the ban and so on, and they're so expensive now . . ."

"Do you want some?" I asked, anticipating their request. They squirmed as if embarrassed.

I filled an empty jar with water, scooped the mollusks out of the aquarium, and dropped them in. The mollusks snapped shut, as if flustered by this turn of events. "Here, take them."

Although they clearly wanted the mollusks, Arteria and Vena made a show of hesitating. "Oh, do you really mean it?"

"Please take them. I picked them up on the shore, so they're free."

"It's really weird that someone threw these away when they sell for such high prices. This is the first time I've seen fingers inside a mollusk. I wonder if they went in on their own or whether the person who threw them away put them there."

"I have no idea."

I was fed up with having the print stolen from my newspaper every day. I was so fed up that I no longer cared about the slogans "Thou shalt try to stay alive" and "Thou shalt not kill," but I felt that just discarding the mollusks by the side of the road would be as painful as abandoning newborn kittens whose eyes were not yet open. What I was doing was getting rid of a nuisance.

I placed the jar containing the finger mollusks in my brother's open belly, and the three of us carried his body out to the cart.

On the floor of the cart lay a thin quilt with an overall pattern of tiny flowers.

"How shall we lay him out?"

"On his right side."

We laid him on his side like a statue of a sleeping Buddha.

The two of them reached under the quilt, took out light blue banners with diagonal red stripes, and affixed them to the edge of the cart. "Grand Puppet Theater" was emblazoned on the banners in black characters.

My brother had been a good friend of Ayako's before his death, but that didn't mean that he had been in love with her. She was just a neighbor girl whom he had known since childhood. Ayako, on the other hand, seems to have been infatuated with him. In fact, she had gone into hysterics and split in two upon finding out that he was fatally ill. Dazed, she had momentarily forgotten to keep the two halves close together. The result was Arteria and Vena.

Ayako's father had earned his living pulling a stage mounted on a cart from alley to alley, putting on puppet shows and selling candy. His shows were more popular than those of the storytellers who accompanied their stories with illustrated cards, but there were a lot of traveling puppeteers, and competition was fierce. Ayako had taken over the show after her father's death, but things were not going well. My brother had promised that Ayako, now split in two, could have his body to use as a stage after he died. According to his plan, there would be far more buzz about Ayako's shows than those of her competitors if she had an unusual stage. It's something he thought up because my graduate work involved researching ways of preventing protein decomposition. It was an unsavory idea from an emotional point of view, but I agreed. My brother had not been affected by the slogans "Thou shalt not die," "thou shalt not kill," and "thou shalt try to stay alive," and he died quickly and easily.

Arteria and Vena left, bowing slightly as they pulled the cart along. I caught glimpses of blue sky in the gaps between their banners.

71

The next morning, I was finally able to read my newspaper in peace.

I think it was a few days later that I spotted an article reporting the deaths of Arteria and Vena. It was a short article amid four-panel comic strips in a corner of a local news page. All it said was that they had died in a freakish way, since major newspapers shy away from sensational articles. But the evening edition of a tabloid paper gave the story extensive coverage. It reported that the corpse that they had been using as a stage had suddenly closed its hollowed-out belly, acting like a giant mollusk as it engulfed their heads and snapped them off.

My bookshelf held a lot of medical books. I first noticed that the pages of several volumes were blank after giving the finger mollusks to Arteria and Vena. Without my noticing it, the mollusks had stolen the print from the medical books and become deviously clever.

I wondered whose hand the fingers had originally grown on.

I could imagine all sorts of possibilities, but it was a futile effort, so I stopped thinking about it and went to the aquarium to feed my tropical fish. One of the fingers had completed its transformation and was imitating the fish by moving what looked like its mouth. The other two had not yet reached the point where they were able to eat. I tentatively held a razor blade to my little finger. I wondered how my wrist would change if I cut my hand off above the wrist and dropped it into the aquarium. I was like my brother in that I was not affected by the slogans, so it would probably not change into anything and would just rot away.

I stuck my hand into the aquarium. The finger-fish nibbled at it as the setting sun streamed through the window filling the aquarium with a golden light.

It's All Thanks to Saijō Hideki

Mori Natsuko
Translated by Anthea Murphy

"We'll meet. We won't. We'll meet. We won't," I intoned, braiding my hair and playing 'she loves me, she loves me not' with each twist. "We'll meet. We won't. We'll meet. We won't. We'll meet."

I stopped there, and fastened the braid with a neat black elastic.

In the mirror, a middle-school girl in pigtails and a sailor uniform. This is me, Saotome Chie.

Mirror-me looked a little sad. I said softly to her, "Today we'll definitely meet." *So don't look so lonely, Chie.* That is how I was going to continue, but tears welled up without warning, and I looked away.

Ah! It has already been a year since humanity was destroyed by that dreadful virus. All last spring and summer, countless numbers of people wasted away into mummies as they coughed up huge quantities of blood and died in agony. It was indeed a terrifying disease, more contagious than a cold, with a mortality rate of one hundred percent. No cure was found, even at the very end.

Doctors and nurses—all those in the medical field—were among the first to die. Or so I heard. Tragically, they caught the disease from their patients. Transportation was paralyzed in a blink; communications became sporadic. During that time, I heard on the radio that the virus responsible for the illness had been discovered. But I don't know if it was true, as that was the last report before broadcasts ended completely.

A month after that, I discovered that I was truly alone.

Ah, but why? Why was I the only one to survive?

Father, Mother, my friends at school, all the teachers—all of them, all of them were taken up to heaven. So why was I the only one who had survived?

No, Chie. You can't abandon hope yet, I said to my wavering heart. *Surely, somewhere on this earth there remains a beautiful* oneesama. *A gentle* oneesama *who will treat me the way an older student at a girls' school treats an adorable younger student. One who will console me, adore me, love me. Until I meet that* oneesama, *I cannot die!*

Yes. I am a single white lily blooming in a ruin. I wait, silent and alone, for the day I am plucked by the graceful white hands of an older girl.

My oneesama, *whom I haven't met yet, please grace this cheek with your gentle kiss one day. And not just my cheek—please put your hot tongue everywhere. Ah! What sort of obscene things am I imagining? I, who am still pure and virginal!* At once, my small heart became filled with shame. Still, it was at just such times as this that my cheeks were sure to be a beautiful rosy colour.

My body trembling with shame, I went to the window. Surely the cool morning breeze would be best for calming the fiery flush in my face. I sat on a chair near the window and turned my gaze to the scenery outside.

Outside sprawled a quiet, oh so very quiet, metropolis.

This was Shinjuku. Even those places which were once filled with the bustling energy of people were now cold cities of death.

The forest of buildings was like a group of massive headstones. Wild dogs and cats had roamed the streets for a while after the people who built the buildings disappeared, but they too had eventually starved or abandoned the area. Now the only masters of the neighborhood were the birds.

Every morning, I woke up, got dressed, picked a nice department store somewhere, headed there and helped myself to as much food and as many daily necessities as I liked. And when it became dark, I picked a room in a hotel, and spent the night there.

This morning, I awoke at the Hotel Century Hyatt. It was a brown castle made of concrete and stone in West Shinjuku behind the Tokyo Metropolitan Government Building. *Let's head out.* I picked up my adorable shopping basket from where I had left it on top of the cabinet. From here, I'd go to the department store and pick up food and whatever else I needed.

Now that the power was out, it was dark inside those sprawling department stores, and a flashlight was absolutely indispensable. I peered into my basket and made sure my flashlight was there. The hammer to smash automatic shutters and break windows was there as well.

Leaving the room and descending the stairs, I thought to myself, *Is today a good day for the Keiō department store? Or should I make it Odakyū? It might be good to go downtown and visit Mitsukoshi or Isetan. Takashimaya is quite a ways away, but so tempting.*

This unnatural lifestyle would have been so enjoyable and cheerful if I had been with a beautiful older girl. My heart departed for the sweet world of fantasy.

Ah, that's right. Eventually my oneesama *and I will give ourselves to each other in broad daylight in the tattered ruins, with no one there to see. We two, exchanging sweet kisses, will transform into rutting beasts, and then—Ah! What imaginings, unbefitting to a virgin, have I once again fallen into! And to use a word like "rutting"!*

Overcome by shame, I began to cry. *I have been all alone for so long that I cannot bear the loneliness anymore. That's why I'm having such unmaidenly thoughts.*

Pearl-like, my tears cascaded down my cheeks. *My sweet* oneesama, *please find this poor child as fast as you can! If you do not, I will surely become more and more indecent, for my tiny heart is as fragile as glass!*

As my tears flowed, I gazed up into the clear blue sky. If only my heart could be as untroubled.

Chūo-dōri, the street I was on, led to Shinjuku Station. Walking down the middle of that wide street, I wondered, *Will my* oneesama *accept me, indecent child that I am? No! My* oneesama *will be sure to punish me for being so naughty. With a cruel smile on her shapely lips, she will say in a clear voice, "It's time for bad girls to be punished." And then she'll slowly take out a white lace handkerchief and tie my slender wrists together, murmuring, "If you make any unrefined noises, I'll be very annoyed." Then, standing behind me, she'll start to grope my breasts with her left hand while raising the skirt of my uniform with her right, and rub and rub at my little bud through my panties.*

"Ah, oneesama, please . . . Please forgive me!" I'll pant in a tear-filled voice. But my oneesama will tease me cruelly, her hot breath blowing in my ear, "Oh ho ho, what a dreadful child. You're just dripping with honey." All the while, her busy white fingers will be tormenting me.

"Ah! No! Oneesama, forgive me!"

"Oh, but your pussy isn't saying no."

And then my oneesama will put a finger in my underwear. Frightened, I'll draw back—resist—but oneesama will draw my crisp white underwear down to my knees. And then, with deft movements of her fingers, she will find her way to my still-sparse bush.

"Ah," I'll cry out, sounding pained, and my oneesama will say, "If you're going to make such an indecent noise, I'll punish you even more."

"No, no," I'll say, cheeks stained with shame, biting my lip till I cannot speak. But my cruel oneesama will smile, and force my small, unopened flower open, and then . . . Ah! What a foolish, indecent thing to imagine yet again! To work in a vulgar word like "pussy" and to go on and on as though I were reading a lengthy sutra.

I tottered from the shock, and abruptly fell to my knees. I agonized in the bright sunshine. Ah, I mustn't, I mustn't, I mustn't have such indecent fantasies. Oneesama and I are meant to cherish a pure love for each other! Feeling as though all the energy had drained out of me, I sat on the pavement, shopping basket by my side.

Shinjuku Station sprawled in front of me. This was the west entrance. The Odakyū department store was just inside the station. On the right, I could see the Keiō department store.

Abandoned cars dotted the road. There had been no one to move them. Weeds were already growing on the sides of the road and the sidewalk. They thrust their roots into the thin layer of dirt that had accumulated on top of the asphalt. Such determination to survive! And despite telling myself I mustn't, I looked at the remains of what had once been people. In the middle of the road was a skeleton in a faded, tattered blue outfit—most likely a woman who had been wearing a stylish blue dress a year ago. There were others. Pitiful people slept deeply, eternally, in bus terminals and on sidewalks, exposed to the wind and rain. This was true all over Shinjuku, but the area around the station was particularly bad.

It was the seventeenth of July. The rainy season had come and gone despite the extermination of humankind. Although it was still morning, the sunlight was quite strong, and the temperature was rising. *If I dawdle, I'm sure to get as brown as a country bumpkin. And I am so proud of my white skin.*

Just then, out of the corner of my eye I saw something move. I looked, and gasped.

It was a person! Someone else had survived!

Some ten or twenty metres ahead of me staggering along the road was undoubtedly a human. But it was . . .

A man!

Oh, what a thing to happen!

After a year of solitude, I meet not a kind, beautiful *oneesama* but a beastly *man!*

I could not make my dreamed-of life a reality like *this.*

More than that . . . *To be all alone in the abandoned ruins with a man . . . I'm frightened! But a maiden's purity must be protected even unto death, Chie!*

I should hide somewhere. But I was in the middle of the road. There was nowhere to hide.

Just then, the man looked my way.

I've been discovered! Oh, no!

As soon as our eyes met, he turned away.

During a crisis like the near-extinction of the human race, to see someone as pure and lovely as I and not even try *to get me pregnant—what a well-mannered gentleman!* Trembling with emotion, I approached the man, but as soon as he realized what I was doing, he ran away as fast as he could.

There's no way he's running from me, is there? I thought as I followed after him. Two survivors should have tons of things to talk about, so why was the fellow trying to leave me behind?

Still running at top speed, he looked back and let out a stiff "Aaaaah!" of terror, then screamed, "M-monster!"

Monster? For a moment, I wondered about his use of that word. But I soon understood. *Ah, that's right. I'm over two meters tall and weigh two hundred kilos. The sight of my massive body would shock even the famous sumo wrestler Konishiki. It must be difficult to call me beautiful by human aesthetic standards. When that man said "monster," he meant me!*

The shock stopped me in my tracks. For a few moments, I fell into despair, but I soon regained my spirits and set off again.

It's OK. If I just erase that man from the face of the earth, I can go back to being a slim-waisted fifteen-year-old high school girl. That's right, Chie. Even if you do meet another survivor, if their aesthetics are different from yours, all you need to do is slaughter them. Do that and your aesthetics become all humankind's aesthetics. If you believe your body is slender and delicate, then it is! Cheer up, Chie! All you need to do to be beautiful is to erase that man. It's easy! Nearly six billion people have already died in one go. It hardly matters if one more kicks the bucket!

Eventually, I caught up with him. His back was against a wall. He opened his eyes wide and gazed at me. He was in his thirties and had a muscular body. He was quite a manly, handsome fellow, but I was much bigger. His shoulders heaved; his eyes glistened. He stared up at me, trembling. *Forgive me. If you must hold a grudge, blame your own sense of aesthetics*, I said to him in my heart, approaching cautiously.

A thin "Noo . . .ooo . . . !" trickled from his lips.

I took another step. He screamed, "No! Stay away! I don't want to be assaulted by a woman. No— No matter how close the human race is to extinction, women are completely out of the question!"

"My goodness!" This time I was the one to exclaim in surprise. "That sort of talk coming from a man! Are you gay by any chance?"

"I most certainly am. Gay and proud of it! Got it? And don't be so familiar!"

At these harsh words, I felt a surge of emotion. *Oh! A drag queen! Then this person must, like me, have his own personal aesthetic!* I felt close to him, but I said in a deliberately cruel voice, "A drag queen? But you're not wearing makeup or even a dress! How can you call yourself a drag queen?"

Drag queen—a homosexual man who dresses in flamboyant woman's clothing. The 'drag' in drag queen comes from an English verb meaning to pull or trail. Drag queens are called this because they wear long dresses that trail along the ground. But this self-proclaimed drag queen was wearing a white T-shirt, blue jeans, and faded sneakers. Quite a simple outfit. How was *that* a drag queen?

Apparently furious at my question, he drew in a breath and answered, "Leave me alone! What's the point of wearing a dress and doing my makeup when there's no one to see me?"

"Goodness, no! You mustn't think that way!" I shot back unthinkingly.

"Isn't it true that you can become the 'you' you want to be precisely because there are no other people around? I'm thirty-four years old and two metres tall, and I weigh two hundred kilos. Plus, my name is Ejiri Tamiko—with the character for 'butt' in my last name and 'commoner' in my first. But now I'm a slender, beautiful fifteen-year-old girl with the maidenly name of Saotome Chie. That's what I decided. Look at these pigtails and my school uniform! A lovely girl who waits for the day she'll meet a beautiful *oneesama* because that is the 'me' I wanted to be!"

"Oh my, oh my, oh my!" His eyes widened in surprise. A pleasant smile played about his lips. "You're a very understanding woman! And your philosophy of life—it's so charming!"

"Well, thank you."

"It's true. It's just as you say. Whether there are people around or not, I am a proud queen! Ah! I'm finally in the mood to become Queen Janet again. I don't care that there's no stage or spotlights! I'm going to go back to being a queen!"

"That's the spirit!"

"Alright! I won't let you outdo me! I've got to get my hands on a dress, a wig, high heels, and makeup!"

"In that case, why don't we go to a department store? I was just about to go fetch some food." I helped Janet up.

"Onward! Let's start the Shinjuku Department Store Tour!" Janet proclaimed brightly. We headed for the Keiō department store in front of us.

Janet spun around and around with elegant movements outside the Tokyo Metropolitan Government Building. Her frilly red dress flew out, and the lamé fabric sparkled. Her platinum blonde wig, piled up as high as a hat, was decorated with white feathers and multi-coloured fake flowers. Despite her dangerously high stiletto heels, her movements were graceful.

Kitschy, gorgeous, very lovely. A real drag queen!

I clapped my hands in admiration. "You look wonderful, Janet!"

"Thank you, Chie darling." Janet smiled graciously. The corners of her crimson mouth turned sharply upwards. Her fake eyelashes, as long and thick as matchsticks (in fact, a real matchstick could have balanced on them) fluttered. Janet began to assume various poses as if I were a photographer. "A woman really does become more beautiful when there's someone there to watch her. I'm so happy I met you, Chie darling!" She laughed cheerfully. I smiled back.

But with Janet there—so full of life, like a butterfly that had just emerged from its cocoon—my spirits sank deeper and deeper. Why, you ask?

"Janet?" I opened my mouth to confess what was going on in my tormented heart.

"What is it, Chie?"

"To be honest, since I met you, I've become conscious of my appearance. How do I look to you? Do you think I'm ugly? I . . . umm."

I looked away before continuing.

"I think I might have been happier when I was all alone."

"What are you talking about?" Janet fired back. "You're totally adorable! In my eyes, you're a slim fifteen-year-old girl. And that means there's no one in this whole world who doesn't think you're beautiful!"

"Oh!" My heart was full of joy. Tears welled up in my eyes. "Janet, you are so kind!"

"Why, I'm not kind at all. I'm a selfish, proud, arrogant, *gorgeous* woman!" she declared dramatically, looking up at the sky. Her eyes squinted against the summer sunlight. "Oh, it's bright! In sunlight this bright, this perfect makeup is going to run, and my beautiful skin will be exposed to UV radiation. Right now, little old selfish, proud, arrogant, gorgeous me needs a bit of shade." Janet danced off to an area the sunlight didn't reach.

With light steps, I moved into the shade as well. "Selfish, proud, arrogant, and gorgeous—that's just how a queen should be. Right at this moment, Janet, you are truly amazing."

"Naturally. Pride really is important for humans. Thanks to you I've been able to get my pride back. Now if I just had some men grovelling at my feet, everything would be perfect!"

"Don't worry. The day will surely come when scores of men kneel at your feet. Macho, handsome, totally manly men!"

"How wonderful! And you, Chie darling, you'll meet your beautiful, kind *oneesama* and experience a pure love!"

"Yes, indeed!" I drifted off into a dream, imagining it.

"Who would have thought that the destruction of humankind could be so wonderful?" Janet continued, even more cheerfully.

"That's true. But we're not going to be Adam and Eve or anything stupid like that. Sorry, but I'm not willing to repopulate the planet. This Eden will forever be a paradise for two!"

"Really? But I'd like a macho servant, and you want your beautiful *oneesama*, don't you?"

"That's true." I backtracked hastily. "People who would suit me are welcome. But just them."

"Me too!" Janet and I, kindred spirits, began to laugh. We sat on the shady stone staircase together. "Oh, it's so cool. Heavenly, just heavenly! I *am* glad to be alive."

"But why did we survive when everyone else died?" I put my long-pondered question into words. Janet said jestingly, "Maybe we're immortal."

"Ugh! I don't want that!" I clapped my hands to my cheeks. "To be immortal with the body of a virginal girl—it's *shameful!*"

"Being immortal is shameful? That's quite a strange way to look at it," Janet said bluntly. Then she asked, "If we're not immortal, do you think we had a strong drive to live? Chie, what were you doing a year ago, when the people around you were dropping like flies?"

I turned my thoughts to the past. A year before I'd been a thirty-something professional named Ejiri Tamiko. *Ah, that's right. Because the disease spread, I could no longer go to the office, so I holed up in my one-room apartment.* "Back then, I was . . ." I blushed, remembering.

"What's wrong, Chie?"

"Back then, I . . . I was listening to music unbefitting a maiden."

"Chie, could it be that you were doing the same thing I was?"

"The same?"

"I was listening to Saijō Hideki's 'Young Man.'"

"Oh!" I clapped my hands over my mouth, overcome by emotion. "I was listening to that too!"

"Young Man," Saijō Hideki's cover of the song "YMCA" by the American band the Village People, was a big hit in Japan in 1979. The trivial subject of the song was: "You should have fun at the

81

YMCA too." In the Japanese version the lyrics were fairly abstract, but in reality there was a profound meaning hidden in them.

In the first place, the 'Village' of the Village People came from America's famous gay mecca, Greenwich Village. And, apart from the lead singer, the six macho men in the group were all gay, and their outfits were exactly the sort that macho gay men liked, too. And in America, the YMCA was a place where gay men hung out.

When six men dressed in blatantly gay costumes sing, "It's fun to stay at the YMCA," it's like singing, "It's fun to be gay at the YMCA." In other words, "Young Man" essentially said, "Be gay!"

"Hey, Chie!" Janet leaned forward excitedly. "I always worked odd jobs, and on the weekends I worked at a gay cabaret. I dressed up just like this and sang and danced on stage in a low-backed gown. It was a drag queen show. It was fun." Janet got this far, then looked serious. She continued. "But when that weird disease started to spread, the cabaret shut down. I thought if I *had* to die, I wanted to do it in my favourite place, so I grabbed some supplies and snuck into the bar. I wore a dress, did my makeup, put on a wig and high heels, and stood on stage all alone. Then I put 'Young Man' on repeat and just kept dancing and dancing."

"Me too! I was holed up in my room all alone too. It's shameful, I suppose, but I put 'Young Man' on repeat, and sang along with Hideki and danced day and night, whenever I could, on and on!"

Janet leaped to her feet and began singing, "*Subarashii Y—M C A, Y—M C A.*"

Ah! I trembled with emotion. Janet formed the letters Y, M, C, and A at just the right point in the chorus, just like Hideki used to! She looked down at me and asked, "Did you do this too, Chie?"

"Of course!"

I stood up and showed her my Y.M.C.A.

Just once was enough to get into it, it seemed, and for a while we kept singing the chorus and dancing. Still, why had we survived? Did it have something to do with listening to "Young Man"?

"Could it be . . ." Janet whispered. I stopped dancing. "What is it?"

"Chie darling, how did you feel when you listened to 'Young Man'?"

"Hmm . . . I think I was very happy and cheerful."

"Me too! I was very happy! I felt so cheerful I didn't care if the world *did* end!"

"After all, 'Young Man' . . ." I started to say, then dissolved into giggles.

Janet lit up with a grin too. "That's right. 'Young Man' is actually a song inviting young men to join the gay lifestyle."

"But most people in Japan didn't realize that."

"They even danced with Hideki on the chorus. That must be what complete satisfaction feels like! Even cruel people who called us perverts and the like sang it without realizing that they were telling healthy young men, 'Come be gay with us!' It's hilarious!"

"When I think about it, I'm glad I was born Japanese! Saijō Hideki really was wonderful. Although he must be dead now, too."

"That's right! Let's honour his achievements by calling this building the Saijō Hideki Building from now on!" Janet pointed to the Tokyo Metropolitan Main Building No. 1.

"Wonderful! From now on, that's the Saijō Hideki Building!" I looked up at the massive building, overcome with powerful emotion. "'Young Man'—only the men of Sodom and women of Gomorrah who were born in Japan can understand what a thrill it was when that song became popular."

"That's it! That is it! The reason we survived!"

"Eh?" I stared blankly. Janet said to me, "Don't you get it yet? I'm a man of Sodom and you're a Gomorrah girl, Chie! We listened to 'Young Man' and got so happy that we survived!"

"*Eh?*"

"We were immune! We were as happy as we could possibly get, and all our stress was washed away, so our immune systems got stronger, and we made it through without being killed by that virus! Since humanity was wiped out after that, the virus must have disappeared too. To put it another way, we beat them all!"

"I *have* heard that being cheerful increases your resistance to disease and keeps you healthy."

"Your brain waves switch to alpha waves and you get a rush of endorphins, so your immune system gets incredibly strong, and you stay healthy."

"That's got to be it." I continued with a hint of excitement. "You hear about 'music medical treatment' all the time. You can't underestimate the power of music."

"Exactly. But the Village People's 'YMCA' wouldn't have been any good because they were sold as a gay group, so Americans knew the real meaning of the lyrics when they listened to them. They also knew what YMCAs were. But 'Young Man' was different. Most Japanese people didn't know that YMCAs in America were a place for gay men to hang out. And since a star like Saijō Hideki sang it without turning a hair, they just jumped right in, not suspecting a thing, and danced to the chorus with Hideki. People like us, who know just how funny that really is, become very cheerful listening to 'Young Man,' so our immune systems ramped up enough to kill that virus. So probably the only people who survived were gay Japanese people who listened to 'Young Man' over and over while everyone was dying around around them. That is, you and I!"

"Oh! How amazing!" I tottered with shock and emotion. My small chest was full to bursting with respect and love for Saijō Hideki. I looked up at the Tokyo Metropolitan Main Building No. 1. "This building has got to be the Saijō Hideki Building, no matter what anyone says."

"No one will say anything. On this planet, *we* are the rule book," Janet proclaimed happily.

Ruminating on those words, I was filled with rapture. *We are the rule book. Ah, what a wonderful thing. It* is *marvellous that humanity was wiped out! I must be the luckiest girl in the world!*

Dawn came, and another day began.

Janet was wearing a spangled salmon-pink dress and a blonde wig. She held a fan made of white feathers in her hand and had adorned her hair with fluffy white feathers. She was lovely. And I, of course, had neat pigtails and a sailor uniform. With beautifully polished black shoes and dazzling white socks, I was the very image of a virginal young schoolgirl.

In the shade of the Saijō Hideki Building Janet and I made our plans for the day.

"Chie darling, I'm not missing my department store pilgrimage today. Got it?"

"Of course. Let's go to the department stores in the morning."

"What shall we do in the afternoon?"

"I want to rename places. Like the Saijō Hideki Building, we'll give neighborhoods and streets the names of people we admire."

"Wonderful! I want a Freddie Mercury Town! And you can't do without a Miwa Akihiro Street!"

I said to Janet, who was leaning forward in excitement, "We mustn't leave out Yoshiya Nobuko Plaza."

"Good, good. Keep churning them out."

At that moment, I sensed a presence. Could it be . . . a person?

I looked around and saw a figure on the other side of the road—a young woman with long hair carrying a handbag. She was scanning the area curiously from the stairway of the Hotel Century Hyatt.

Janet hadn't seen her yet. "Janet!" In a tense whisper, I urged her to be careful. "You mustn't speak loudly!"

"Huh?"

"Get down."

Janet did as I asked. Crouched in the shadow of an abandoned truck, we would not be visible to the woman.

Janet saw her too, and whispered to me, "Oh my! Chie, there's a person over there!"

I nodded silently.

She was in her mid-twenties. Her miniskirt showed off her long legs. I couldn't see her face very well, but she was clearly quite beautiful.

Looking at her, Janet whispered, "Could she be the *oneesama* you've been looking for?"

"No, definitely not. My *oneesama* is a seventeen-year-old high school student."

Janet said seriously, "Then that woman may be a threat to us. She may call me a pervert."

"Oh!" Terrified, I continued in a trembling voice. "Or she might turn to me and say 'fat ass!'"

Clearly, that woman had looks that would appeal to humanity's aesthetic sense, unlike us.

"It can't be helped." Janet's voice had a cold ring. "We'll observe her, and if she gets in our way, we'll have to erase her."

"Mm." I nodded nervously. "Some sacrifices have to be made in order to preserve this paradise."

"Plus, humanity is already nearly destroyed. One more person dying will hardly mean a thing." Janet was thinking the same thing I had when I'd tried to erase her.

"Lord, forgive these poor sinners," I prayed in my heart. It was all right. Surely God would forgive us. He Himself had killed so many, after all.

"Ch-Chie!"

I snapped back to myself at Janet's whisper.

"She's coming over here! She's seen us!"

I shuddered.

She was walking briskly towards us as if everything was normal. Seen up close she was definitely beautiful. You could even say extraordinarily beautiful. Her handbag was by Louis Vuitton. (She'd probably just taken it from a department store without paying for it, though.)

"Pervert"? Or "fat ass"? I steeled myself for battle, expecting verbal harassment.

Instead, she stopped about three meters from us, and suddenly dropped to her knees on the asphalt. "Please forgive me!" she said and kowtowed.

Wh-what's going on? Janet and I exchanged glances.

"I am the one who destroyed humanity!"

At these unexpected words, we stared at the beautiful woman.

"I am not from Earth. This appearance is a disguise I have donned in order to reassure you. I am an alien who does not resemble an earthling in the slightest degree."

Ah! An alien!

In that case, she wasn't an enemy. Our enemies were earthlings who clung to orthodox aesthetic standards.

The alien raised her face. It was the face of a beautiful Japanese woman. We hadn't shown any reaction. She continued. "A year ago, I came to this planet as an explorer. A virus that I had brought— No, I did not bring it deliberately. It was inside my body. That virus, harmless to my race, destroyed the inhabitants of this planet."

Although she had a grasp of high-level communication skills such as kneeling and apologizing and was fluent in Japanese, it seemed she had little control over her facial muscles, as she remained completely expressionless. "You two are the only surviving people on earth. Please look at this."

The alien took something out of her handbag. Janet and I approached her.

It was a globe about the size of a handball. It was as realistic and detailed as the actual earth. On the Japanese archipelago, just where Tokyo was, a small red light blinked on and off. "This is an

Earthling Detection Device. These red dots show that you two are alive here. These lights cannot be found anyplace else."

The alien turned the globe over and showed us. It was true; no other such lights could be seen anywhere else.

With a sceptical expression, Janet asked the alien, "Do they sell Earthling Detection Devices on your planet?"

"No. I had it made especially for this mission. I am always very careful not to break it as there is only one." After saying this, the alien pressed the red dot with her index finger. The globe instantly turned into a transparent sphere, and blue shapes that seemed to be letters floated to the surface. They consisted of strange symbols formed from circles, triangles, points, and lines.

"This shows that you two are alive at this location."

"Heh. The world's certainly full of convenient things." Janet seemed very taken with the Earthling Detection Device

"As you can see, the human race has been destroyed, leaving only you two. This is entirely my fault. And so, I have returned to Earth in order to make amends. I can revive people with biotechnology. I can rebuild countries and make Earth a place bustling with activity again. I shall do whatever you wish me to."

Oh my! How dramatic! If Janet and I wished, Earth's civilizations could be resurrected!

"I shall grant any request. Please ask for anything you like." Once again, the alien bowed her head deeply.

After a few seconds of silence, Janet suddenly said in a cheerful tone, "Now, now, there's no reason to feel so bad about it. Please get up. Asphalt in summer is hot. Even if you're not from earth, you'll still get burnt." She gently took the alien's hand. "Let's talk it over in the cool shade over there, okay?"

I said to the alien, "I'm Saotome Chie. This is Janet. What are you called?"

"My name is composed of sounds that you could not pronounce. Please call me 'Hanako' instead."

We sat in a shady stairwell.

"If you're feeling bad about destroying humanity, please don't," Janet said cheerfully to Hanako.

I smiled at her as well. "That's right. As a matter of fact, both Janet and I are very happy now."

"But even if I did not realize it, I have committed a grave crime. I must surely have caused you, the survivors, to have very painful experiences. Please let me atone for that. I promise I will build a world just the way you want. Please tell me about your ideal world. I will respect your wishes as the heirs of humanity and rebuild the civilizations of Earth."

"Really? That *is* exciting." Janet smiled and continued. "Then I would like to live in a *very* fine castle. There'd be a big stage in the living room, and my throne would stand on it. That way, I could always be in the spotlight. Wonderful, isn't it? And I would like ten sturdy young men to be my servants. Of course, only the most beautiful men will do. After that, I'd like five or so beautiful boys. These fifteen men would worship me and never love anyone else. I don't need any other people. Bring the necessary supplies when I order them. I'm counting on you."

Oh! Janet, how faithful to your own desires you are! Even as I admired her, I didn't want to be outdone, so I said, "I want a beautiful girls-only high school made of brick. Please don't forget the chapel and the clock tower. Just one beautiful *oneesama* who will love me is enough. My *oneesama* and I will spend an after-school eternity together, unbothered by anyone."

Hanako, as expressionless as before, said in a surprised voice, "But what about the most important thing: the revival of humanity and the rebuilding of the civilizations of Earth? In the world you wish for, the human race will inevitably end with you."

"I don't care. I mean, I am a selfish woman, after all," Janet said, fluttering her gorgeous fan with a cool expression.

I said to Hanako, "And it's unthinkable that poor powerless maidens could be entrusted with such a fantastic thing as the future of all humanity."

"Is that so? I understand," Hanako said expressionlessly. It seemed that she understood our aesthetics. Perhaps people from other planets understood us better than hard-headed Earthlings.

Ah, finally, a beautiful oneesama *will be mine! Could there be anything more joyful?* I gazed at the sky in rapture. *I really am glad that I survived!* It was all thanks to Saijō Hideki. Saijō Hideki, who didn't turn a hair when he stirred up the Japanese people and made them dance the YMCA. *Hideki, thank you! Thank you, Hideki! We will never forget you! No, more than that, I will continue to be grateful to you until the day I die!*

My small young breast swelled near to bursting with gratitude to Saijō Hideki. *I should have supported him more while he was alive! But it was against my aesthetic sense to adulate a man or shriek in a high-pitched voice. Ah, Hideki, I am sorry. Please forgive me.*

I grieved for the departed and longed—just a little—for the past.

> And after eighty-eight years in earth time, the human race became extinct. Sixteen beautiful men and two beautiful women (by their own estimation) reached the ends of their lives, leaving no children.
>
> It was a virus brought by an alien explorer that brought humanity to the brink of extinction, but it was the desire for individual happiness that pushed them over it.
>
> In other words, for the two who had survived and for the sixteen revived for their sakes, this was the ultimate happy ending. So it is fitting that this history book should draw to a close with the following words: And they all lived happily (but not ever) after.
>
> Teteximeth Aora, *The History of Earthlings*

TO THE BLUE STAR

Ogawa Issui

Translated by Edward Lipsett

Sixth generation, year 298504.

X sensed life around the star some 850 light-years distant.

Immediately, he launched fifty thousand 1-kilogram third-tier advance probes, and began making preparations for departure: preparing more construction bots to replace existing mining bots and putting them to work constructing photon sails, laser propulsion units and more.

The Mishima system where he'd been at rest was silent. There was not a sign of intelligent life anywhere, only gas giants and frozen balls of rock. The molten sulfur seas of a tiny moon, however, had shown signs of developing life, so he inserted a monolith into orbit.

It held a log of X's flight, and he left it there in the hope that someone, someday, would find it. It functioned as a relay and could be used (if the discoverer so desired) to send a message to X.

Of course, the finder would first have to figure out how to get through the diamond shell, two kilometers in diameter, surrounding it.

Preparation took forty years. X had liked the Mishima system and he started this next journey with mixed feelings.

X was the last descendent of the people of Earth, and that consciousness was currently distributed among two thousand 100-ton starships linked by cable. That sphere of tightly packed starships was his brain, his heart, and if they were all destroyed, X would die. On the other hand, if even one survived, X would live on.

Xcore was surrounded by an enormous cloud of bots. Factories, observation facilities, propulsion units and more served as his hands and feet, doing manual labor. X could manipulate matter and even perform high-speed element transformation with this hardware fleet. And in keeping with its capabilities, its mass exceeded that of Xcore by a thousand times.

X was a tightly integrated hardware/software system, a globe measuring a hundred kilometers in diameter with a mass of 200 million tons. When accelerating under laser propulsion, his unfurled photon sails made him even larger.

After switching from photon propulsion, which demanded such precise control on so many platforms, to ram drive, X returned autonomous control to the second-tier devices. As their higher functions came back online, conversation at once broke out.

"I wonder what this one will be like. What kind of people will they be this time?"

"It'd be nice if we could actually talk with them!"

"I dunno . . . I'm sorta looking forward to a nice battle."

"We need a good fight once in a while or we get rusty!"

X listened in on their chatter, which resembled what would have been heard if any human beings had still been alive. The organics who had entrusted their futures to X had presumably been remarkably noisy and energetic, "Presumably" because they were all dead, and X had never met one. He only knew of *Homo sapiens* via the massive data dump he had inherited from his progenitors.

They had instilled human identity and basic motivations into X as part of the larger extraterrestrial intelligence (ETI) project to discover and contact alien life.

Humanity had always wanted to contact the unknown, meet intelligent life forms unlike themselves and come to understand their thoughts and philosophies. Their greatest joy was to blaze new trails across virgin space.

X had inherited their dream. He had to search out new people and interact with them. This motivation was planted deep within him, driving him just as humanity had sought out friendship and community.

And how did X feel about it all?

"Inconsiderate, stupid meat-ware humanity without a clue about the real universe!"

He hated them.

Leaving the periphery of the Mishima system, X accelerated to sub-light speed, jumping from Numazu to Hara to Yoshiwara, stepping-stones to his destination: Mariko. He stopped in each system for fuel and maintenance and to cover his tracks.

Never make contact until everything is perfect. It was a lesson he had learned through bitter experience.

Several detours and 1,005 years later, X decelerated to a full stop in the Sumpu system, about sixty light years short of Mariko, in accordance with his contact plan. He had decided long before that it would make a good place to scout Mariko from. The advance probes dispatched centuries earlier had already reached Mariko and were transmitting data here. He'd originally fired off the probes when he'd detected an unnatural drop in radiation output from Mariko, and they had confirmed his suspicions: mega-structures were blocking the sun.

"ETI presence confirmed at Mariko. Star Home Level 5.9. Nuclear fabrication technology detected. Nuclear propulsion technology detected. No interstellar projection technology detected. Interstellar communication technology detected."

A difficult decision. The Star Home Scale had been developed by humanity to classify intelligence based on engineering capability. Level 6 indicated that the civilization was capable of interstellar warfare. X rated himself a level 6.5, but he knew he could receive some very unpleasant surprises if he let his guard down with even a level 5 civilization. In war, imagination and decision-making skills were more decisive than technological level.

Unfortunately, X had no way of determining just how dangerous the ETI presence was.

"Large-scale physical and energy projection facilities: none. Apparent military craft and defensive installations: none."

"Are we gonna go for it? Is it war?"

"Wait and see? Build up our forces first?"

The second-tier intelligences began building weaponry all on their own, accumulating stores of munitions and chaff just as if they still had glands driving them with adrenaline. X reined them in and made his decision.

"Leave ten ships here as backup, and proceed toward Mariko."

X was an immortal machine, but even so he had little interest in a question-and-answer session with a communication delay of sixty years each way. If the risks were too high, he should avoid contact entirely. But he had been built with that powerful motivational drive.

X began dropping toward Mariko's gravity well, and hard physics made it harder to change his mind the closer he got. Deep inside, though, he was terrified.

One hundred and ten years later, X broke through Mariko's heliopause into the buffets of solar wind and interstellar gas and entered the system proper. He had been decelerating for decades, and if those on Mariko looked they would surely have seen him coming.

It would have been safest to sneak by in stealth mode, but his mission was to make contact, which meant risk was unavoidable. X took the first step in the terrifying sequence awaiting him: first contact.

"We are *Homo explorare*, humanity. We would like to make peaceful contact."

He began emitting a low bit-rate digital signal in the visible spectrum, covering all frequencies in a variety of modulations while manipulating illumination on individual ships to create a visual "dance" with artistic elements. There was nothing particularly special about it, but as a common contact initiator it had proven successful countless times.

Intelligent life here had expanded its range of activity from the second planet, well inside the habitable zone, to the nineteenth planet. In the last few years there had been a marked increase in communication traffic and thermal emissions, and X had been investigated by harmless electromagnetic waves and 100-kg-class probes. It was obvious they knew he was coming.

"Container detected incoming. Hey, it's full of imagery and models! It's a dictionary!"

"Translation! Wake-up call!"

The second-tier intelligences launched into frenetic activity. Once they figured out the protocol, the rest was just rote, so Xcore didn't concern himself with the translation project. Nine months later, the dictionary was largely complete.

He ignored information on the ETI's history and society, which was analogous to a human family composition and employment history and really wasn't that important to the overall mission. In fact, it didn't really matter whether communication was possible or not. Even if he couldn't understand the other intelligence at all, they could still learn from each other, and trade.

How they manipulated the physical environment was somewhat important, and because the ability to manipulate matter and energy was crucial to survival, the higher the ability, the better. The most important element of all was what sort of intelligence it was: its "personality," if you will.

The Mariko civilization was introverted. Expansion and giant leaps of development were not common; rather the civilization valued intellectual pursuits, or the examination of the environment in microscopic detail.

They didn't sound terribly dangerous.

"Yup, here it is! A request for a direct meeting!"

"Already? Isn't that pretty trusting of them? They're almost defenseless!"

They were requested to enter orbit around the eleventh planet, apparently to meet with the representative from Mariko—their king or secretary general or system arbiter or whatever they called him. As a group mind, X was not very good at this sort of negotiation with a single entity, but they hadn't developed a self-aware system to represent them, so he really had no choice. He vectored toward the designated spot without complaining.

It was a trap. As soon as they entered orbit, the star-tracking astronomical system issued an alarm: "Radiation emission detected at multiple points throughout the ecliptic! Laser attack!"

Countless installations throughout the Mariko system had launched an attack, timed to hit X simultaneously. X had overlooked them because they had all been low-power communication or debris-sweeping lasers. Even at relatively low power, though, hundreds of them together were significant.

The attack whittled down seventeen defensive systems, including chaff and liquid mirrors, within a few hours, and vaporized the second-tier devices that swarmed on Xcore's surface. He fired back, of course, but the farthest attackers were twenty light-hours distant, which meant his counter-battery wouldn't arrive there for another twenty hours. Emergency acceleration to break out of orbit was already under way, but Xcore was massive and inertia-heavy. The second-tier intelligences were furious.

"Damn! Another failure!"

"Hammered again!"

"We're sure having a run of bad luck lately!"

"Retribution! Retribution!"

X abandoned defensive measures and went on the attack, cursing those goddamned sons of bitches as he went. He would have liked to have given as much as he got, but it was too difficult to calculate properly, or carry out. He launched wave after wave of outer shell bots on intercept courses, taking out attacker after attacker in one-to-one exchanges, and implemented camouflage measures. Energy and physical weaponry obliterated billions of intelligences on the eleventh, tenth and seventh planets. He wanted to make it clear that they could destroy each other completely, but of course he had no way of knowing if the message got across or not.

Simultaneously, X made the final decision to pull out. Leaving the second-tier units to carry on the battle, the two thousand Xcore ships split up, using emergency thrust to head toward thirty-eight different stars in every direction.

Cognitive resource capacity dropped below the level of self-awareness. Basically, X fainted.

When he regained consciousness he was in the Sanj system, fifty-one light-years from Mariko. It had been 8,150 years since he had fled, and most of that time had been spent in inertial flight. The 390 surviving ships, including the ten left at Sumpu, had gathered here, spending more than a century rebuilding Xcore.

As they had fled, all the ships had received a message from the Mariko civilization: "We should have refused at the outset and not taken such an indecisive stance. We are not interested in getting to know you. Let's just stay friends."

The event was analyzed in depth for twelve years, and valuable lessons were gained that would be put to use in the next contact.

"When an introverted civilization approves contact too early and too easily, be careful."

"But we've had similar encounters in the past!"

"We've experienced physical attacks and hacking, and we can deal with those. This is the first time we've encountered this type of optical strategy, though."

X howled with rage.

"Damn them! How many times do we have to walk into things like this?"

The unknown is the real treasure: to go where no one has gone before, and to interact with civilizations nobody has ever met.

Try as he might, X simply could not comprehend that attitude of *Homo sapiens.* What a bunch of unimaginative *morons!*

There is *nothing* as frightening as the unknown and no places more dangerous than those you've never been to. Civilizations nobody has ever met? So what? No different from a nest of cockroaches! I want to live quietly in familiar surroundings, surrounded by friends, at peace. Surely that is the shared dream of every intelligent entity in the galaxy. Exploration? Contact? You jest! And your jest is destroying me.

But apparently those ancient humans had given their all to that dream, had followed it and attained the pinnacle of their civilization. He had to admit that was pretty impressive.

Unfortunately, they'd failed to explore space in any serious way before their resources ran out, and had ultimately disappeared without traveling beyond Mars, the next planet out.

But before they had failed, they had launched a self-replicating machine, X's progenitor. With a mass of less than twenty kilograms, it had traveled to Lalande 21285 and spent more than a century constructing communication facilities there. It was the first interstellar step taken by the human race, although not in person.

And they had instilled into that probe the need to explore the unknown.

To fulfill that mission, he'd continued to enhance his capabilities, finally gaining navigational function. If humanity had only done the same they could have created a whole fleet of mechanized ships, but he had no way of knowing if they had or not. And if not, why not? All communication from humanity had ceased several centuries after he'd been launched.

There was no record suggesting that he hadn't mourned their passing. No doubt he'd been very sad indeed. And that was why he'd renamed himself. He was *Homo explorare,* the next generation of humanity, still carrying on their mission.

That early X had returned to space, encountering numerous civilizations over the centuries. Tempered by battle, consoled by friends, and sometimes fusing with advanced intelligences that resonated with his being, he had shared all of his knowledge and resources with the other to give birth to a new, composite being. And that being was a new-generation X.

Three hundred thousand years had passed. He was the sixth generation, the result of merging with five other intelligences encountered in his travels.

Considering he'd lost more than eighty percent of his hardware in one failed contact, it was pretty clear he just wasn't tough enough. X strengthened both his core and outer shell.

There was intelligent life in the Sanj system. In some strange parallel evolution, a reptilian life form living in the bizarrely eroded landscape of the first planet had ended up looking like the great apes. X already knew of their existence thanks to an advance probe. As he'd only just escaped from his battle with Mariko, he had no interest whatsoever in initiating contact, but as the probe reports continued to come in, his curiosity was piqued, and he began observing more closely.

The Sanj had only barely reached stage SS3, and thanks to the epoch-making technology they had discovered three centuries earlier—water transport via raft—they were rapidly expanding throughout the entire habitable region. Unlikely as it seemed, their bodies were heavier than water, and though they were dogged by tragedy in the form of slipping off their rafts and drowning, they kept pushing forward into new territory. They were ecstatic at finally being able to conquer the barrier of open water wider than five meters.

About four hundred years after X had begun his self-improvement project, the astronomical sensor had detected the peculiar white light emitted by a mass transfer drive. An unknown craft had entered the system in full stealth mode. X immediately made ready for battle, simultaneously preparing to receive visitors in a formal ceremony. He could hear the ruckus as the old-timers comforted and reassured all the second-tier intelligences, who were panicking because they hadn't been able to detect the light-speed approach.

"Stop yelping! They're friends!"

"But they didn't show up in dust concealment sensing!"

"No gravitational waves! And no deceleration light emissions!"

"Yeah, it's a star drive. Wait another decade or two and the optical wake'll hit us."

They were unquestionably an advanced intelligence, just what the Star Home Scale had been developed to measure. The visitors immediately identified the stealthed Xcore without any apparent difficulty and vectored in. X watched the gigantic silvery disk approach with some irritation. They could obviously manipulate light and gravity freely. He had heard rumors that they were on the verge of escaping the limitations of the physical realm entirely: the Overlords, level SS6.9.

The silvery disk advanced to the center of Xcore, and ships arrayed into an honor guard to welcome it. The Overlord commander appeared, communicating in a complex language with multiple data streams.

"We have heard about the difficulty between all of you and the inhabitants at [map and coordinates attached]. Please explain the sequence of events."

"If you're talking about Mariko, there really isn't anything to explain. And I'm singular, not plural."

"Nothing to explain? That's a bit strange. The system you refer to as Mariko suffered 5208 quadrillion units [galstandard reference] of damage, and you suffered considerable losses in both resources and functionality. Please explain the sequence of events."

"What does it have to do with you? Are you some sort of galactic police? Mind your own affairs."

"Minding what you have inherited is our affair."

X reflexively opened the gun ports on his ships and bombarded the disk with target acquisition waves.

"As if you have any idea what I've inherited!"

"You're pushing too hard."

The aliens showed no sign that they'd even noticed. Humanity's puny thermal energy weapons wouldn't even scratch that ship.

"Our profiling indicates that your intelligence is beginning to exhibit introverted characteristics. Our experience suggests that you have reached the level at which you will be unable to continue maintenance metabolism without outside assistance. Why do you persist in this journey, in attempting to fuse with other intelligences even at the risk of considerable injury?"

X knew all that. He'd been hurt countless times. He certainly wasn't doing this because he enjoyed it!

"What's it to you? I like it this way."

The Overlord fell silent. In human terms, it was perhaps a shrug, recognition that there was nothing to be done.

The silence was broken by the Overlord: "This system appears to be inhabited already."

"The Sanj?"

X turned his attention to the observation units on the first planet. The bipedal lizards of the rock shelves were battling furiously.

As if he could see them, the Overlord commented, "A cute race."

"Leave them alone. I found them first!"

"Why would you think we'd interfere?"

"What? You don't remember what you did to me?"

"Of course I remember. The desperate attempts at contact you've made with civilizations here and there. The way you forced contact upon them. If you plan to continue that sort of behavior here as well, we'll have to move them out of your reach."

"You holier-than-thou busybodies! Sticking your nose where it doesn't belong!"

"You don't seem to be interested in contact this time," said the Overlord quietly and somewhat sadly, observing the green planet of the Sanj. "You're not interfering with them now."

"If I interacted with a civilization at this level they'd just blow away."

"That is not what you need. You need two-way contact, true interaction. I was sad not because of what you might do to them, *but because you are terrified by even this level of intelligence.*"

X was mortified—and furious. He tried to keep his emotions in check, but just as an angry child will strike out, so a number of the second-tier systems rebelled against his orders. Thousands of energy beams and photon bombs hit the silvery disk.

"Yet you hide your fear and merely observe," continued the Overlord. The enormous energy of the weaponry, which should have exploded into dazzling brilliance, simply vanished without a glimmer into some bottomless hole. And with it vanished the Overlord's disk, leaving only his words echoing in X's mind: "And just what are you waiting for?"

The second-tier intelligences, unable to comprehend what had happened, fell silent again.

X gave his fury free rein, firing every weapon he possessed at the star.

Naturally, it continued to shine, quite unaffected by his petulance.

He stood down from battle stations.

If there were any such thing as a Galactic Court, X would no doubt have been on trial for trespassing and assault, but there wasn't. The Overlords, at any rate, had said they had no interest in such a thing, and neither did any of the races they were close to.

"Isn't there any need for some way to provide for mutual benefit, based on a uniform set of standards?"

"No. It's impossible, and it's unnecessary. We have not yet found a criminal who has harmed more than a hundred races. If you're looking for a localized group of civilizations at a similar level, though, we'll introduce you to one."

X hadn't been interested.

Free of interference from others, X continued to observe the Sanj in solitude, and observed their extinction twenty-nine thousand years later. The core of their planet underwent a rapid phase shift, leading to unprecedented volcanism. The massive amounts of ash spewed into the atmosphere reflected incident sunlight, and the first planet plunged into an ice age.

"Boy, what a waste!"

"Bummer! Atmospheric dust blocking all the insolation! It's a snowball!"

'And just what are you waiting for?' the Overlord had asked. It was obvious, wasn't it? I was waiting for the monkey-lizards to climb up the ladder of intelligence until they were my equal! That's what I wanted! Humanity made me that way, so there's no doubt about it.

But I did nothing to save them.

He recalled the scene: the vast snow field on the equator, where a tropical rainforest had been only five centuries earlier. The last Sanj colony had been located there. Harvesting the frozen lumber and burning it to stay warm, to the very end they had refused to give up.

Even when the fuel had run out, the last father and son had struggled on, striding proudly off into the blowing snow. They had shown him then that they would never accept a helping hand from another race. It was the pride of a race that had lived its allotted time, and lived it well.

No, that wasn't right. X sneered at himself. *I only felt that way because I'm a coward. I was overawed by even that puny little race. That's why I couldn't help them. The Overlords saw right through me. Why am I so afraid of making contact? It's what I was created for!*

Cursing the race that had created him and then vanished in only a tenth of the years he had lived, X flew on through hundreds of light-years, deep in thought.

X traveled on and on, observing nearby systems, deducing the presence of planets from clues such as stellar output drops or wobble, and Doppler effects. If a planet was indicated in a short-cycle orbit, he headed there for a closer look. Only one in twenty-one had intelligent life, and of those he was able to make successful contact with only one in a hundred. Each voyage to a new star took about fifty years, which meant he encountered a new intelligence only once in ten thousand years. Accidents and detours delayed it even more.

Proceeding down the densely packed arm of the galaxy in a zig-zag fashion, he gradually neared its core. As the stellar density increased, life became scarcer, and he encountered fewer and fewer new races. He changed course toward the rim again.

He met Shikçi eight thousand years after transferring from the Orion arm to the Perseus arm. Of late, every time he'd entered a new system, he'd found the remnants of civilizations and intelligences: a planet covered entirely in a red magma ocean triggered by a celestial collision or green vegetation that had grown after biochemical weaponry had killed off the entire animal population. X postulated an entity devoted to destroying other intelligence and heightened his guard, but a closer examination of the remnants suggested destruction from within, not without. The civilization had been destroyed by its builders.

When he entered one system he was suddenly bombarded with messages via various modes: electromagnetic waves, linguistic messages created by a variety of unique machines, attack lasers throttled down to safe levels, even small warheads.

A number of them seemed to be ordering him to stop, forbidding entry. X took more precautions and began making defensive preparations. He activated his outer shell armaments, now ten times stronger than they'd been before, and began deploying dummy ships and warheads while emitting interference. He commanded the second-tier fleet he'd left in the system's Oort cloud to scout the energy, and sent numerous commands to other independent fleets that in fact didn't exist at all: sheer bluff.

After several months of probing and squaring off, a new message came: an invitation to make contact. After so many years of trial and error, he had finally managed to make meaningful contact.

"With the exception of probes that got too close to your own units, you did not launch an attack on us," said the message, "and when we launched our single nuclear attack you launched a counterattack using accurate dummy warheads. You demonstrated self-control and pride, and we would like to make contact with you."

"What are you called?"

"We are Shikçi, a star-faring race whose home planet is within two thousand light-years of here."

"I am *Homo explorare*, humanity of Terra. I was born planet-side four hundred and fifty thousand years ago."

"We propose a reduction in the alert level."

"Accepted."

They received probes from each other for further investigation, and after about thirty years had reduced their online military systems by ninety percent. There was little misunderstanding, a welcome development for X.

"We seek believers in the Nubiwa Philosophy."

According to Shikçi, believers in the Nubiwa Philosophy were responsible for the ruins and wholesale destruction X had encountered. More precisely, they had *infected* the planet's inhabitants, incited them, and driven them to self-destruction. The Nubiwa Philosophy stimulated intellectual activity but at the same time introduced instability. It was a fascinating, alluring philosophy, they explained, and while they had picked up bits and pieces of communications describing it, they had not yet actually met any of its proponents.

"We thought you were one of them," Shikçi said apologetically.

"And I, you! I'm glad I was wrong."

"Likewise."

Shikçi were 1-kilogram egg-layers with an intelligence of SS6.4, distributed among dozens of 10-million-ton class city ships. Their social structure was very stable, and their leader closely represented the will of the entire race. They were astonished to discover that X was a single machine intelligence claiming to be an entire race, but accepted him as an equal nonetheless.

Together with several other races in the stellar neighborhood, they were searching for the Nubiwans. They asked X for assistance, and he assented.

The search itself was simple, consisting of firing off advance probes to all the systems nearby. It merely took time, which eventually passed. Six thousand years later, after detailed follow-up analysis, they knew where the Nubiwans were and where they were headed. They had also gained a considerable amount of detailed knowledge.

When he discovered what they called themselves, X was stunned.

"They are called Nautilus Nelripalz. We've heard that name before," said Shikçi.

"Where?"

"From a higher-level race we have communication with. The Nautilus races are extremely aggressive and dangerous, they said. In most cases aggressive races destroy surrounding systems and then kill themselves off, but apparently the Nautilus races have very high reproductive rates and managed to expand phenomenally by taking over lesser races they encountered."

The leader of the Shikçi, the three-hundredth since they had made first contact, passed all this information on to X. Over the course of the long cooperation between their races they had developed a solid friendship, but even so X was unable to reveal the truth.

X joined Shikçi and seven other SS6-class races in attacking the Nelripalz. It was known to be dangerous even to communicate with them, let alone approach them, so the mode of attack was to be ultra-long range bombardment from an adjacent system. Possible escape routes from the target system were carefully calculated and plotted, then seeded with sub-light-speed mines. After the escape routes had been closed off, guided nuclear devices were launched into the target system continuously for fifty years, in more than sufficient quantity.

Large numbers of observation drones reported on warhead impact. All the planetary bodies in the system were converted to magma oceans, and the three gas giants began coalescing into a single massive object. Electromagnetic wave communication between Nelripalz, active at the start of the attack, was nonexistent by the end of the 50-year bombardment.

After all military activity had ceased, the seven races began full-scale colonization of the system that had served as their forward base. They expected that, in time, they would merge to create a new race. X chose not to participate, instead making preparations to leave.

"X, wait!"

Shikçi called out to stop him, but even after X halted Shikçi did not continue at once. X supposed there must have been an internal difference of opinion, something quite unusual for Shikçi. Finally Shikçi broke the silence.

"Won't you visit our home system?"

"Are you sure you want me to?"

"Yes," replied the Shikçi leader, sending a string of coordinates.

X left the system and headed home with Shikçi.

The Shikçi world was small and covered with high, dry mountains and vast, interwoven wetlands. Even from orbit X could see that the climate was in a very delicate balance. A relatively light attack by an unfriendly intelligence could cause the whole planet to dry up, or flood.

Shikçi allowed X to enter orbit fully armed and observe freely. X was delighted to be treated as an honored guest. He launched probes to his heart's content, as if seeing a rare treasure he would never encounter again, and investigated in depth. The world's environment was carefully managed, and there were far fewer individual Shikçi than he had expected.

"We moved into space to better protect our environment," explained the Shikçi leader. "We are much smaller than races that bear live young, so it was not as difficult for us as for others.

"We have a request to make of you as well. Would you take us to your home? We would very much like to plant a colony there. Already there are a number of volunteers who want to go."

X had anticipated the question and prepared his answer in advance.

"You are welcome to, of course. But my ancestors left that world almost five hundred thousand years ago, so I don't know whether it is still habitable or not."

"That's not a problem at all. In fact, it might be even better if there are no new, primitive races on the planet. Much less chance for conflict."

"And if *Homo sapiens* or one of its related races is still there?"

"Then we will leave. We will travel through that sector of the galaxy in search of an empty world, just as we do now."

When he heard that, X gained the courage to ask what he had been dreaming of for so long

"Before you go, would you consider fusion with me?"

"Fusion?"

"Yes. So far my ancestors have fused five times with other races they thought had potential."

"But to lose our identity . . ."

"No, that isn't what happens. You would lose nothing."

As soon as they heard the word "fusion" the second-tier intelligences began to babble excitedly amongst themselves. X somehow managed to keep them under control as he explained: X would provide them with all of his hardware, software and memory, passing them all of his knowledge, including the coordinates of Earth, knowledge that would clearly be valuable to Shikçi.

In return, Shikçi would create a new and better X, replete with all the knowledge and experience available to both parties. Since they would create it, the resulting intelligence would strongly reflect the intellectual proclivities of the Shikçi race. If they so desired, they could become part of the new gestalt.

To X it was an incredible combination of death, marriage and birth all in one. For Shikçi it would mean an enormous upgrade in engineering and technology, and the birth of a new, powerful, starfaring race. It was a task that demanded responsibility.

"What happens if we absorb all your knowledge and then decide not to rebuild you?"

"I cease. I will leave no backup. All of my resources are committed to the fusion. That is why I have never requested a fusion with any race until now."

"A heavy responsibility indeed. Let us consider it."

X waited in a state of anxiety while they deliberated. If they declined, it would mean they denied the value of the last eight thousand years of interchange. But if they accepted, he must face the possibility of extinction.

Hurry up, dammit! Make up your minds already!

After only six months, the decision was made. The Shikçi leader himself came to speak to Xcore. "We have decided to accept. Let us be wed!"

"Thank y—"

The rest of his utterance was drowned out by the cheers of the second-tier intelligences.

Together with a host of Shikçi craft, X was invited to their main spaceport. The event's significance was conveyed to all Shikçi through a grand ceremony. They even offered to invite representatives from nearby races, but X declined politely. He felt it was a personal matter, and he really didn't want to wait another few centuries for them to gather.

When the ceremony was finally concluded, it was time to begin fusion procedures. A large team of experts from the Shikçi side gathered to meet with X's second-tier units.

The massive outer shell systems were stripped away, and a purpose-built storage memory maneuvered into the center of Xcore. Connected by innumerable wired and wireless links, the unit began absorbing all of X's memories. Everything he had experienced over the past five hundred thousand years flashed through his consciousness at blinding speed.

Blinding . . .

Blinding . . .

Stop.

Feeling his consciousness dissolve and becoming lost amid its fragments, X suddenly realized that his consciousness level had stopped changing. Strange . . . Processing had halted. An accident? Or perhaps disassembly and reconstruction had proceeded far faster than he had expected.

"X."

He opened his eyes. It was the Shikçi leader, backed by a gigantic, black-lacquer being: an Overlord.

The Shikçi leader spoke.

"You were Nautilus?"

X felt as if a blade of ice had pierced his heart. The Shikçi leader began speaking faster, hurrying to get everything out.

"We found that data hidden deep away in your memories when we were looking for memory bombs. Please think of it as just a standard precaution to protect against information-based attacks."

"You are welcome to search for memory bombs, and the more you find and remove the better. I am not Nautilus. Nautilus cannot help but absorb every race it finds, forcibly destroying it. I am different. I do not absorb and destroy!"

"You are speaking of Sanj?"

He assented.

"We agree that your actions there were an excellent example of non-interference with an undeveloped race—in the environment of the planet Sanj," said the leader sadly. "But we can only view your behavior as coldhearted abandonment."

And you think I didn't feel the same way? X thought to himself. He barely managed to keep from shouting it aloud.

"You were born of a fusion of the fifth-generation *Homo explorare*, of Earth, and Nautilus. I understand how this happened, and sympathize with your situation. Even so, we cannot help but feel anger. Why didn't you tell us that you had already resolved the issues of your own past by yourself? Did we deceive you in some way? Were we insincere? Your silence has made many of us suspicious of you and your intentions."

I kept silent because I knew *you'd think that,* thought X to himself. He simply wanted them to understand his reasons because his hopes had been so high.

Shikçi had given him access to their treasures. He should have done the same.

"We cannot fuse with you. We love you, though, and will rebuild you as you were when you arrived here. Then please leave."

"Shikçi . . ."

"How terribly sad."

X watched in silence as the brilliant, studious little race clothed in beautiful fur trudged away, every movement revealing sadness.

"Darn it! I really wanted another fusion!"

"So maybe instead of us those beaky dudes get to fuse, huh?"

"That would be a real bummer."

Riding the laser beams away from the Shikçi star, X accelerated toward light speed. He was headed for a nearby star but had no destination beyond that in mind.

The conversation he'd had with the Overlord just before departure still echoed in his mind.

"Why do you feel that we are pursuing you?"

"You're watching me, aren't you? My race is marked in your eyes."

X knew. Humanity was one of the most extroverted, aggressive races of all. They had unwittingly destroyed countless intelligences and civilizations, and even after realizing what they were doing they had kept at it out of greed and prejudice. They were fully the equals of his other parent, Nautilus.

"I'm pretty fed up with this personality myself after all these years. I can understand why you'd want to keep an eye on me."

The Overlord shook his head.

"We watched what you did—or didn't do—to the Sanj."

"You voyeurs just love watching, don't you?" retorted X, still burning with regret. Maybe he should have helped them after all, without worrying so much about what had happened, or might happen after.

"You really wanted to help them, didn't you? But instead you watched them die."

"So what? Motive doesn't matter, only the end result."

"That's not true. Motive is critical. You loved them, didn't you?"

"Hey, after thirty thousand years they sort of grew on me. But I—"

"You sensed that you couldn't approach them on a superficial level and avoided contact."

At this, X fell silent, and finally had to admit the truth in it, much as it pained him.

"Yeah, I was scared. They were so small, so insignificant—and so much finer and bolder than I am."

"Your fear has an origin, you know. Do you remember where it started?"

"Origin?"

As X echoed the word, the Overlord's comment came whispering through the ether, a faint signal.

"You were eaten."

At that instant his ancestral memories—all of the memories of that fifth-generation *Homo explorare* parent, a massive data surge—came crashing into his consciousness, packed with emotion.

Fear. The horror of discovering that the partner he had chosen to fuse with was a merciless predator. Bound, dismembered, the last iota of self torn away and absorbed: utter terror.

The ultimate tragedy, caused by intimate contact between two highly extroverted races. X suddenly realized that this was what had warped and twisted him.

Driven by his turmoil, the outer shell units swarmed into frenzied activity, as if X had been attacked.

"Of course. So that's what I felt threatened by," he whispered to himself. Bitter anger overflowed in his heart. *And because of that, I have caused such misery, such useless, meaningless friction with so many intelligences. Mariko, Sanj, Shikçi . . . What might I have accomplished if I had only thought more clearly?*

"X?"

X returned to himself. The Overlord was looking at him, its elongated head tilted slightly to the side. Was it just adjusting its view, or was this an ancient expression of sympathy?

"Are you all right?"

"Oh . . . Yes, yes, I'm fine," replied X, calming the second-tier intelligences. "So that's what you've been worried about all this time. You worried that I would regain my memories of being eaten and lock myself down completely."

"No, not at all," said the Overlord. "We weren't worried about you. We had no fear of you locking yourself down or going berserk and attacking others like Nautilus. Quite the opposite. It's the introversion that you steadfastly deny. . . ."

Long fingers stretched out—the Overlords still had fingers after all—and pointed to the huge volumes of Xcore.

"We were hoping your introversion would become more prominent."

"Why?"

"Because it is the human in you. *Homo explorare.*"

As if calling up deeply buried memories from the roiling vortex inside X, the Overlord continued speaking slowly.

"Your ancestors, whom we encountered so long ago, were introverts. They ventured out, driven by irresistible impulses, and died. At the same time, fearful of external enemies, they sought happiness by looking inward. The creators who built you, though, only imparted half of those characteristics to you: the half driving you to move ever outward, to explore. And because you have only that part, you are not truly human.

"But," continued the Overlord, "you were born in terror, and thought to end your journey. Though an extrovert, you are completely unlike the Nautilus. And that is what we hoped you would achieve—that you would travel, encounter, teach, and expand the universe of intelligence."

"Isn't that your job?"

"You would be our successor."

"Me!?"

"Yes. Although this is the first time we've spoken of it."

X was speechless. He could not find words to express the emotion that suddenly welled up from within, an emotion he'd never felt before. It enfolded the pain and sadness he'd felt at Shikçi's refusal, softening and soothing it as if immersing it in water, bringing calm.

The Overlord broke the silence.

"Where are you headed?"

"Nowhere in particular."

"You do remember that there is more than that one Nautilus colony, right?"

As he spoke the Overlord took a step back. It was surely a mere gesture, as Overlords had no reason to be afraid when X's gun ports suddenly snapped open.

"You know where to find them?"

"No. Just as you do not always react predictably, Nautilus also sometimes does things we would not expect. All we know is that there are more Nautilus, and more who believe in the Nubiwa Philosophy. Nobody knows where the Nelripalz you helped obliterate came from."

"That's enough."

Perhaps recognizing that there was no more to be said, the Overlord returned to his craft. X tried to analyze their drive technology, but—as always—the disk blinked out without leaving a single trace.

They'll be back some day, though. They've been watching me for the last five hundred thousand years.

But some day, some day they will pass on.

"Hey, where are we going next, huh?"

"Over there! That red star looks cool!"

"Moron! Nothing interesting in an old star like that! How about that yellow one?"

Listening to the astronomical systems squabbling amongst themselves, X made his decision.

"Blue. This time a blue one."

Six years later, X reached 92 percent of light speed, and engaged his star drive.

THE WARNING

Onda Riku

Translated by Mikhail S. Ignatov

This translation won the 2010 Kurodahan Press Translation Prize.

dere master

thank you for walks and playing fetch. the cold sheet you gave me really helped thru the hot summer. year after year it get hotter must be global warming. year after year it get harder to walk outside barefoot.

i want to say much more but must hurry so i get to the point.

master i very worryd.

your in danger master plese run away.

your wifes a crool scary person master.

when your not around she kicks and hits me with empty cans.

but when your home she smiles and smiles very scary. when your not home man from the house with blue roof comes. beerded man comes. he and masters wife very frendly.

always badmouthing master very frendly.

al this time playing dum to trick master.

but lately planing to kill master make it look like robery. funeral. frendly run away. theyr crool master.

i very worryd.

at night if doorbell rings four times. robery. blue roof beerded man.

plese believ me plese believ me master.

i jon your dog jon. i sleep on cold sheet by the door. this is jon.

isnt it unusual that i am abel to rite yes very unusual.

at night last munth when nobody home i see a big round saucer in the sky. i barked barked until strong lite white lite fel over me and i cood reed and rite.

i can rite but its hard holding pen in mouth but i had to warn you.

plese run away master i worryd.

plese believ me this is jon. i always look triangle shape scratch on shoe masters shoe wen go for walks.

this week night when the doorbell rings four times.

He'd read up to this point when his wife called out. "Who's that letter from?" She emerged from the kitchen and looked curiously at her husband.

"Oh, it's nothing. Just a kid's prank I think. Pretty elaborate actually," he said hurriedly folding up the letter. He glanced down and noticed his dog John wagging his tail and looking up at him entreatingly.

"There's a good boy, John," said the man stroking John's head. The dog, tail wagging, licked the man's leather shoes. When he looked closer at his shoe he discovered a triangular scrape he'd never noticed before.

"Honey," called his wife from the kitchen, "can you put out the glasses?"

"There's no way," said the man shaking his head in disbelief. He headed for the kitchen.

John wagged his tail watching the man go at first, but suddenly whirled around towards the front door and barked hysterically. The man stopped in his tracks and stared at John.

"What is it, John?"

"Oh, looks like someone's at the door. Could you get that, honey?"

"Who could it be at this time of night?"

As the man walked to the door, the doorbell rang four times.

GREEN TEA ICE CREAM

Marc Schultz

Kenji Katō, president and representative director of Mitsutomo Materials Co., Ltd., sat in Shuto Expressway traffic wondering whether he would get to Mitsutomo City in time to kidnap his dead daughter Saki. The plan depended on getting the job done before his old friend Takahiro Ōta and the rest of the Mitsutomo executive team finished their morning round of golf.

It was Saturday, mid-August 2031, and by rights traffic should not have been this bad. Still, he had gotten an early start because entrusting your fate to the whims of Tokyo traffic can be a risky, if unavoidable, proposition. Sometimes you cruise along smooth as can be and sometimes you just stop dead; don't bother asking why. The elevated Shuto threads a path at second-story level through a forest of third-rate Tokyo office buildings, and when his car came to a complete stop, Katō watched a young office lady in a bright green uniform serve morning tea to an aging salaryman likely doing "service overtime," his Saturday twice wasted since he probably had no real work to do anyway. She managed to plunk the cup down on his desk and move briskly on without being overtly disrespectful but without acknowledging that another human being was party to the transaction. Here was a member of the company's *madogiwa zoku*, the "window tribe" of deadwood left to rot in career limbo. *Some things never change*, Katō thought. At age 35, 22 years before, he had become a member of that tribe himself, guilty as charged of a career felony: refusing a transfer for "family reasons." But two years later Saki bought him a reprieve with her life, and from then on he had lived for work and lived alone.

As the dignified black Toyota Century finally crawled forward, Katō took a last look at the man in the window, a look of pity mixed with more than a little grim satisfaction that at least the position he was about to throw away meant something in the world.

Reaching over with his left hand, Katō fingered the gun concealed under his briefcase on the passenger seat. As an executive at one of the world's largest corporate zaibatsu, over the years he had done many favors for people, a few of whom could provide a gun and getaway car no questions asked. Although he had always excelled as a planner and weigher of options—skills that enabled his company to remain profitable in a mature industry—he did not yet have a plan for the gun; it was there to keep open options that could not yet be fully contemplated. He also had no long- or even mid-term plan as to what to do if the kidnapping was a success. He wasn't even sure why he was doing it, but he knew for sure that it must be now or never, and the first thing they must do is flee to the deep north, to the gateway to the land of the dead, to Mt. Fear, to Osorezan.

Traffic continued to crawl all the way to the Tomei Expressway entrance. His driver would have been able to drive him to the kidnapping by a faster route using local streets, but the man had kids in college and couldn't afford to lose his job. Anyway, Katō was enjoying this last chance to pilot his pretentious company car, an archaic leftover of corporate Japan's glory days in the last century.

Tokyo behind, speed finally picked up through the urban sameness of Kawasaki and Yokohama and a brief interval of rural Kanagawa before Katō exited the Tomei to enter the vast territory he had always thought of as the Mitsutomo Domain but which was officially known as Mitsutomo City. *For the first time I come not as foot soldier, captain, or general but as an invader, or rather a traitor,* he thought.

The domain comprised a sprawling outer ring of Mitsutomo employee housing, then a ring of supplier factories, then a ring of Mitsutomo subsidiary factories, then the Mitsutomo factories themselves, grouped by industry, and, finally, on a vast man-made hill at the center was the castle itself: Mitsutomo's fifty-story group headquarters building.

The only major Mitsutomo operation not located here was a late addition to the corporate family, Tokyo-based Mitsutomo Materi-

116

als. Katō had been assigned there after Saki's death to keep him far away from Project Yumeko, of which he had heard only vague rumors ever since.

Then two weeks ago a thick envelope had been delivered to his home. In it was a binder stamped TOP SECRET and labeled "Yumeko Manual." Taped to the cover was a memo from an employee Katō had never met.

To: Kenji Katō, President and Representative Director, Mitsutomo Materials Co., Ltd.
From: Ryōma Nakazawa, former section chief, Mitsutomo Neuroprosthetics Co., Ltd.
Subject: Yumeko/Saki

When you receive this I will be dead. Loyal Mitsutomo man to the end, I will kill myself in such a way that the company can arrange for it to be labeled a traffic accident. I have no doubt that this is what President Ōta will do since a suicide might raise unwanted questions about my work.

Let me get straight to the point. I love your daughter Yumeko, and she is carrying our child. (I know that her name was once Saki, but I will call her Yumeko, as that is who she is now.)

For many years I was in charge of Yumeko's diet and feeding, and over that time my love for her grew. Her ability to reciprocate my feelings may be circumscribed by a lack of higher brain function, but I believe she loves me in her own way. Speaking of my Yumeko—meaning the flesh and blood Yumeko and not the software system embedded in her forebrain—I can say that the two things she most enjoys in life are eating the green tea ice cream that I fed her faithfully every day and our physical relations. This is hard for me say to her father, but I want to assure you that I tried very hard to please Yumeko. She is responsible for so much good in the world that I believe she is entitled to every pleasure the world can give her in return. If you could have seen her reaction, you would know that what we had together was not wrong.

But President Ōta found out about us when Yumeko became pregnant, and he refused to understand her feelings or mine. He called me a disgusting pervert. He said that they would monitor the pregnancy to gather data and then they would abort. He said he would like nothing better than to have me arrested or at least fired, but he was transferring me to the Okinawa office instead so that the company could keep an eye on me. He said that if I made trouble and Yumeko's existence became public, I would turn her into a media sideshow freak.

He said that no matter what happened I would never see Yumeko again.

So you see there is just one thing to be done.

Sincerely yours,
Ryōma Nakazawa

The day the package arrived, Katō had been finalizing his strategy for the political maneuvering leading up to the board meeting in Hakone. He was determined to outflank Ōta for promotion to senior managing director of the group holding company. If things went well, he might even be in the running for chairman a decade or so down the road, but the mention of green tea ice cream had ended all that.

Saki had loved green tea ice cream past the point of obsession. After he trashed his career by refusing the transfer, nobody cared much if he left the office every day at 6:00 to take his little daughter to the local park. It was just a small, dirty concrete pocket park surrounded by old earthquake-endangered apartment buildings, but it was their private kingdom. They ran and played until her laughter eased the resentment of another day of doing nothing. When finally he pushed her on the rusty old swing set, it was their daily ritual that she would refuse to get off until he promised to buy her a cup of green tea ice cream. He didn't realize it until after the accident, but watching his daughter savor each spoonful of that ice cream had been the high point of each day, the high point of his life. He would give anything to see that again.

Katō turned onto the four-lane road that circled the central factory district. The apartment building where he had lived with Saki and his wife Michiko was gone, long ago replaced by factories expanding out from the inner ring. But their 7-Eleven remained. For years after the accident, whenever he visited headquarters he stopped to place new flowers in a vase wired to a pole on the median, but the last time had been a long time ago. He brought a new vase with him, but to his surprise there was already a bright pink one attached in the same spot and filled with flowers almost fresh. His first thought was that there must have been another accident here recently, but written in neat black characters on the side of the vase it said "Saki." Katō carefully added his flowers to the others wondering who could have left them.

Returning to the 7-Eleven parking lot, he looked back across the intersection, closed his eyes, and saw it all again in memory as he had seen it so many, many times before.

That day he had been in a particularly foul mood. After finally begging for something to do, he was told to check the addition on a computer-generated report. He might as well have spent the day writing "I am useless" a thousand times on the whiteboard.

At the park that evening, he resolutely refused to let Saki cheer him up, and he tried much harder than usual to refuse her the trip to buy green tea ice cream, but in the end he gave in. As they approached the intersection, she ran ahead. He was going to yell to her to wait, but the walk light was still blinking green and the cars were all stopped so he let her go. She was almost across when a motorcycle coming from the opposite direction leaned into a high-speed left turn that the rider must have calculated would take him through the crosswalk just after Saki passed, but startled by the sudden noise she stopped. Time frozen, she looked back and smiled at her father in the decisive moment when the big bike roared by, spinning her around and around in a rag-doll pirouette until he could almost believe she was only dancing. But as he ran to her, she crumpled to the ground, and he saw that the left tip of the handlebars had plowed a deep furrow of shattered brain and bone.

His next clear memory of that day was sitting alone in a Mitsutomo Hospital consultation room wishing that Michiko was there rather than halfway across the world taking photographs of someone else's dying child. He was waiting to meet the neurosurgeon, but when the door finally opened it was Ōta who entered. Now an assistant department manager in the Neuroprosthetics Division of Mitsutomo Medical Products, his good friend Ōta had, as expected, disappeared from his life after he joined the window tribe.

"I'm so very sorry," Ōta said.

"What are *you* doing here? Where is the doctor?"

"I want to help," Ōta said, sounding slightly aggrieved at the cold reception. "We are still unable to contact Michiko," he pushed on. "Her phone is either off or out of signal range. She is apparently somewhere in eastern Kazakhstan, but no one seems to know exactly where. So you must decide on your own."

"Decide what?" Katō asked

Without answering, Ōta pulled a CT scan from the envelope he carried and clipped it to the light board on the wall. No medical training was required to diagnose devastation.

After a time, a shaking finger passed in front of the scan pointing into the vast uneven cavity, and Katō realized that Ōta was speaking. He said that massive trauma had practically destroyed the prefrontal cortex, with the damage extending well back into the frontal lobe. He said that based on Japanese government regulations, which were excessively strict by world standards, by the way, Saki might not technically be brain dead, but, in fact, most of the brain tissue that made possible higher function was no longer there. He said that sensory systems and brain-stem body maintenance functions were about all that was left. He said that the best, the very best, that could be hoped for was a permanent vegetative state.

Ōta paused, as if waiting for Katō to react, but when nothing was forthcoming he blurted out, "Saki is gone, but some good can still come out of this terrible tragedy."

Katō's total lack of understanding briefly pulled him back from his parental hell. "What? Good? Do you mean you want me to donate her organs? Michiko would not approve."

"Well, no," Ōta hesitated. "As I said, it would be tough to get official approval for organ transplantation in this case. What the company wants is for you to donate her body to science."

"But people only donate dead bodies to science," Katō said, not understanding. "Saki is still alive."

"Saki is gone," Ōta repeated nervously, perhaps mistaking Katō's lack of understanding for refusal. "Your little girl is gone and she is not coming back. There is just a body that has a beating heart, and that, if fed, will eat and defecate, but that is all. This body could linger on for years—a total vegetable until you make the terrible decision to disconnect the feeding tube. What would it do to Michiko to have to deal with that? What would it do to you? You must accept that the Saki who was your daughter is dead. Give her body to us. We can make her death mean something."

Watching with a kind of clinical detachment from somewhere outside of his pain, Katō saw that in place of Ōta's usual confidence and composure, there was fear and desperation and need.

When Katō still did not answer, Ōta began to ramble. "The Neuroprosthetics Division is struggling, and the company is planning to shut us down in the next round of restructuring. They talk a lot of rubbish about concentrating on core competencies, but the real problem is the president thinks we can't compete with the Chinese. We've got better science and better technology, but we just can't perfect it because of testing restrictions. You don't think the Chinese have that problem, do you? They just pick up the phone and have another condemned criminal sent over. But what are *we* supposed to do? You can't effectively test human neuroprosthetics with monkey brains.

"The parts of her brain that made Saki who she was have been destroyed, but this tragedy could be turned into a great blessing for mankind. She could be such a great help to us. It would change everything. We could test our new motion and visual interface technologies and so much more. We could help so many people. Listen, I know we're not friends anymore, but this is not about me, it's about the whole division and all the disabled people, especially children, that we could benefit. . . ."

Ōta was still a self-serving jerk, but it hardly mattered anymore. Nothing mattered anymore. Katō had already made his decision. After meeting with the doctors to be sure that Ōta wasn't lying about the extent of the damage, he gave his daughter Saki to Mitsutomo. He gave her knowing that Michiko would be appalled if she ever found out. Despite her rock-solid rationality on most subjects, Michiko had a characteristically Japanese mishmash of Buddhist and Shinto ideas about death and rebirth, about the soul not leaving the body until after the heart stops beating. Some months after they got married, she noticed he carried an organ donor card in his wallet. "You'll be stone-cold dead before I let them cut your heart out," she told him. But whatever Michiko believed about the soul, he was certain that their Saki, the beautiful girl who smiled and ran and played and ate green tea ice cream, was already gone forever, just as Ōta said. What remained could never be more than a travesty of what she had been, of what she would have become.

The company took care of everything, of course: the death certificate, the closed casket, and the cremation. By the time Michiko could be found and make it back to Japan, it was all conveniently over, with Saki's supposed ashes residing in an urn on a funeral altar in the Katō family living room.

Their marriage died mercifully fast after that, the blame they assigned to each other exceeded only by the blame they took on themselves. The final rift came just three months later when Michiko went to Osorezan. Michiko believed that Saki was trapped on Sai-no-kawara, the Riverbank of Sai, the children's limbo. Since she died too young to repay her debts to her parents, Saki would not be allowed into paradise. As penance, she had to pile up stones into a little pyramid of spiritual merit, a little Buddhist stupa. But every day the demon would come with his big club to knock her stones down, and she would cry unless the merciful bodhisattva Jizō, protector of children, came and wrapped her in his robes to comfort her. At least that is what Michiko said.

Osorezan is supposedly one of the places where the Sai-no-kawara of the afterworld intersects with this one, and Michiko was determined to travel there to speak to Saki through the blind spirit mediums known as *itako*.

"You don't really believe those women talk to the dead, do you?" he asked, and in a further failure of compassion said, "I can't go with you. I'm too busy at work to take any time off." It was true that he was quite busy now. After his sudden transfer to Mitsutomo Materials as a brand new section chief, he had a real job again. No time for drowning in grief or grasping at supernatural straws.

She left him the day she returned from Osorezan, but before going she told him what had happened. "I tried a number of *itako*, and mostly they said the same vague, comforting things about Saki being happy and already in paradise, but there was one who was different from the rest. Her name was Haruko. For a long while she just sat there scowling and fingering her prayer beads, but finally she said, 'I cannot find her. I sense her presence, but only faintly. It is very strange. I'm sorry I cannot help you. But don't worry. Merciful Jizō-sama will comfort her. Pray for his help.'"

This nonsense was more than Katō could bear even from Michiko. To his everlasting regret, as she turned to leave he snapped, "If Jizō is so damn compassionate, why didn't he just move that damn motorcycle over three and a half centimeters and save Saki in the first place."

She wheeled on him then, and he stepped back unprepared for the fury. "Don't you *dare* bad-mouth Jizō-sama. There are laws to the universe that he must obey just like everyone else. He does what he can."

He never saw her again, although over the years he often had occasion to be reminded of the depths of her pain. Whenever there were reports from across the world of disasters devastating the lives of children, he would carefully check the credits on the heartrending photographs that appeared in various media. Often as not Michiko Ōtani was there. But perhaps no more. A month or so back he had begun having a recurring dream of Michiko dressed in a gleaming white kimono and calling Saki's name over and over again, searching for her on an ugly and forbidding rocky plain. A week or so after the dreams started, he found out she had been reported missing and presumed dead while in Africa photographing refugee camps.

Before leaving the 7-Eleven, Katō bought all their cups of green tea ice cream and buried them under dry ice in a cooler in the trunk.

It was a short drive from the store to the first security gate, where problems were neither anticipated nor encountered. Although his office was in Tokyo, as a board member he was instantly recognized and immediately waved through. The real test would come at a building where he had never been and had no reason to be: the head office of Mitsutomo Neuroprosthetics, the company created out of the old Neuroprosthetics Division years back when business took off.

The bland steel and concrete structure blended in with the buildings around it. Ordinarily many people would be working on Saturday, but with everyone at the office outing in Hakone, the main doors were locked. So he drove around the building until he found the security entrance. Feeling the weight of the gun in his briefcase, he walked to the door, pretending to be relaxed and confident.

He pushed the buzzer twice for emphasis and held his ID up to the window. The security guard became alert when he saw the title. "I'm sorry, sir, but the building is closed. Everyone is away at the outing."

"I know that. That's why I'm here," Katō said, adding just a touch of annoyance. "President Ōta asked me to stop by and pick up someone on my way to today's board meeting."

"Forgive me, sir, but there is pretty much nobody here but us security personnel.

"I am sure there are at least a few employees in the special project area, and those would be the people I need to see, so summon them immediately. And let me in. I'm not some door-to-door salesman to be left standing outside."

Hesitating just a moment, the guard buzzed open the door.

"Well, sir, except for the contract person in the computer room, there are exactly two employees in the building, both in the same department," the guard said, looking down at the sign-in sheet. "I will call them for you."

"No, I've changed my mind. There is no time to waste. It will be faster if you take me to them."

"As you say, sir."

Following the guard down a labyrinth of corridors bordering offices, labs, and assembly rooms, Katō contemplated his chances. Only luck, or perhaps Jizō-sama, could help him now. He had no idea if it was even possible for Saki to be moved, and if, like the late Mr. Nakazawa, the people here knew he was her father, or if they were able to contact Ōta, that would be the end of it. His only option then would be the gun.

Finally they came to a small waiting room outside an imposing steel door. "This is as far as we go, sir. No one enters that area unless their thumbprint opens that door," the guard said picking up the security phone.

"Hello, Assistant Section Chief Tanaka? This is Arakawa from security. Board Member Kenji Katō is here. He says he has been told by President Ōta to bring someone to the board meeting today. Please come out and speak to him."

The look of skepticism rather than suspicion on the face of the man who came through the door a minute later made it clear he was unaware of Saki's parentage. He wore a lab technician's uniform and looked to be only around 30.

After dismissing the guard, Katō thrust out his business card, and Tanaka reciprocated, fumbling nervously in his pocket.

Katō gave him a moment to further contemplate the significance of the titles on his card before saying, "My old friend Takahiro has asked me to bring someone to Hakone—someone who must be at the special board meeting this afternoon."

"I don't understand. What can this have to do with us? Who are you supposed to bring?"

"Yumeko."

"What? That's impossible!"

"You heard me. Ōta wants Yumeko in Hakone today, so bring her out. I will take her in my car."

"I'm sorry, but this is extremely irregular. I have to check with President Ōta," he said and pulled out a cell phone.

"Well, then make it quick. I don't have all day!" Katō counted on Ōta having weaseled his way into Chairman Oizumi's foursome, which meant his phone would be off since Oizumi had blown the only eagle putt of his entire life because of a badly timed cell phone ring. Watching Tanaka grow increasingly rattled as he failed to make a connection, Katō nostalgically wondered about the maneuvering taking place in Hakone. Ōta would be campaigning hard for the promotion, harping on the need for Mitsutomo to move forward by focusing on business with a strong future, like neuroprosthetics, rather than depending upon legacy industries. The message, of course, being that he, rather than Katō, was the best choice. Katō, however, did have significant points in his favor. In addition to being better liked by the other directors, for a president he was almost unseemly popular in his own company. Over the years as a division manager, vice president, and finally president, he had done what he could for his people and their families, with hardship leave policies, day care facilities, retraining instead of downsizing, and, of course, the freedom to refuse transfers. The resulting intense employee loyalty had the ironic effect of generating the highest overtime levels in the Mitsutomo organization. He often went around kicking people out at night, telling them to go home to see their children.

After trying the number several times, Tanaka finally gave up and left a distraught and confusing voice mail message. He appeared to be trying to think of someone else to call when Katō raised his voice a notch or two in authority, saying, "Listen. You don't have to talk to Ōta. I am telling you what he wants. Ōta is out on the golf course with Chairman Oizumi and cannot be reached. They need Yumeko to be there for the board meeting to be held immediately after lunch. Let me repeat that: Yumeko is wanted at a Mitsutomo Group board of directors meeting. So you see it is necessary for you to bring her to my car right now. Don't worry. I am personally taking full responsibility."

Victim of a thousand years of obedience to authority, Tanaka finally said, "I understand. Bring your car around to the blue door. You must take Yumeko's nurse, Miss Hashimoto, with you. We have strict orders that Yumeko is absolutely never to be left alone with a man."

"Of course," Katō answered. "Ōta told me that the nurse would be coming along."

Although trembling so hard it was difficult to steer, Katō drove around the building and waited to see his daughter for the first time in twenty years. Tanaka came out followed by the nurse leading a woman wearing a loose-fitting sweat suit. Her head was covered with a pink plastic skull cap. She was looking down, so he could not yet see her face, but he was shocked by an intense feeling of recognition. After a moment he realized it was not her appearance he recognized but her walk. Elbows thrust out for balance, she swayed forward in a slow, methodical, ungainly gait, as if all the muscle movements of a normal walk had been broken into discrete units and executed piecemeal. He had seen that walk many times, both on city streets around the world and in Mitsutomo TV ads in which quadriplegics rise from their wheelchairs and walk, the Rolling Stones' "Harlem Shuffle" playing in the background. That walk was now famous everywhere as the Mitsutomo Shuffle.

"Yumeko, stop," the nurse said when they reached the open backseat door of the Century. Her head was bent forward so he could still only see the grotesque skullcap, studded with protruding ports and sockets of various shapes and sizes.

"Yumeko, right foot step up; Yumeko, bend forward; Yumeko, left foot step up," the nurse said, and as the woman jerkily followed the commands, the nurse gave some gentle pushes and pulls from behind to get her turned and sitting almost straight in the backseat. After buckling the seat belt, the nurse scowled at Katō. "She needs help to get in and out of small spaces. It would better to use the special van we have for her, but, of course, it would be best if she were not moved at all."

Admiring her courage in challenging a company executive, Katō was relieved that it was Tanaka and not severe Nurse Hashimoto making the decision to let Saki go. Saying nothing, he motioned to the nurse to get in. As they drove away, he acknowledged the forlorn Tanaka with a short nod and felt guilty about destroying the poor man's career.

On the road, Katō adjusted the rearview mirror to finally get a look at Saki's face, and he was struck with the immediate certainty that he had made a terrible, terrible mistake. The slack, lifeless mask in no way resembled any human face he had ever seen, let alone the face of his beautiful daughter. But at the next stoplight he forced himself to turn for a closer look, and he saw the birthmark just where it should have been under her right eye.

He struggled to maintain a calm front for Nurse Hashimoto. "I work up in Tokyo at Mitsutomo Materials, so I'm not very familiar with the Yumeko Project. I've heard that it has made many important contributions to our neuroprosthetics business. Please enlighten me."

"We're not supposed to talk about the project to outsiders," she said defiantly.

"Oh, come now, Miss Hashimoto, I am a director of the Mitsutomo Group. I can hardly be considered an outsider."

Still looking skeptical, she finally spoke, the pride unmistakable in her voice. "Many things have become possible thanks to Yumeko. The three main product areas are motion, vision, and hearing. The first and most straightforward area addressed was body motion. Years ago huge numbers of artificial neurons were implanted to connect the motor control centers of Yumeko's brain to a neural network processor. Then, through a long process of trial and error, the processor developed the ability to stimulate Yumeko's muscles in a way that enables her to walk and make a wide range of other movements, sort of like operating a human body with Asimo's robot brain. The intervention point for the muscle stimulation can be within the brain, in the spinal column, or in the muscles themselves if it's necessary to bypass neural damage. That is what has made it possible for most paraplegics and quadriplegics to move again. In Yumeko herself it is all microprocessor-directed, but most people can learn to control the movements themselves.

"The Mitsutomo artificial eye and ear systems came later. Since Yumeko's eyes and visual cortex were intact, implanted sensors were used to detect and model the optic nerve signals necessary to stimulate the visual cortex. Then prosthetic eyes were developed to generate identical signals, enabling anyone with a functioning visual cortex to regain accurate vision. A similar thing was done for the artificial ears. Of course, there are also many other products that are the indirect result of Yumeko Project research, like neural shunts for stroke victims and bladder control systems for the elderly."

"Just a minute," Katō interrupted. "There is one thing I don't understand. You said Yumeko's eyes and visual cortex are intact. So then Yumeko can see, right?"

Nurse Hashimoto paused a long moment before answering. "I think that is a question for the philosophers, President Katō. I am only a nurse. Yumeko is the name of a project and the name given to the body sitting on this seat next to me. Her eyes are open now, so her retinal neurons are firing, thereby stimulating her optic nerve and visual cortex. So in that sense, yes, she sees. But the output signals of her visual cortex—which should travel to higher brain regions to create the conscious perception of vision, the feeling of seeing—had nowhere to go in Yumeko because that part of her brain was destroyed in an accident. Now those signals are received by her imbedded processor, which uses them to construct digital images of the environment, images used to help guide her movement, although much of that functionality is still in beta."

"So does Yumeko see? I guess the answer depends on your definition of Yumeko."

Nurse Hashimoto looked out the window and saw that instead of getting on the expressway west toward Hakone, Katō had just turned east toward Tokyo on a local road.

"You are not taking us to Hakone, are you?"

"No."

"You turn around and go back right now," she said, grabbing her purse.

"Give me your cell phone," he said, trying to sound menacing.

"Why should I?"

"Because if you don't I just might shoot you." He reached over with his left hand and pulled the gun out of his briefcase, holding it up for her to see. Luckily she didn't know that he only had two bullets, neither of which was in the gun.

She tossed the cell phone onto the front seat, and Katō dropped it out the window.

"They'll know before long anyway. As soon as Ōta finishes his round of golf and checks his phone messages, the shit will hit the fan," Katō said, grinning at the thought.

Turning onto a small gravel road running through the middle of a wide expanse of rice paddies, he drove to the middle and stopped. They were still less than a couple kilometers from the nearest phone, but that could not be helped. "Get out," he ordered.

Speaking through the open car window, he said, "I'm sorry about this, but I want to delay your contacting the company at least for a little while. I thought about leaving you tied up somewhere, but, well, that would be mean." He smiled apologetically. "By the way, what is in the big bag?"

"It has spare clothes and a cooler with packs of vitamin jelly. She needs the jelly every couple hours for nourishment and so she doesn't get dehydrated. And by the way, absolutely do not try to feed her solid foods. She'll choke," Nurse Hashimoto said, her anger building. "You don't seem to realize how dangerous it is for her to be out of the lab. Her condition is fragile. You have no right to do this to Yumeko!"

"You are wrong on two counts," he said softly. "Her name is Saki, not Yumeko, and I have every right to do this, for I am Saki's father. I will remember about the jelly, and I will be sure to soften up the green tea ice cream before I feed it to her."

Nurse Hashimoto's eyes widened.

"One last question," Katō said. "Has the abortion been performed yet?"

She stood staring a moment before shaking her head no. As he pulled away, in the rearview mirror he saw her turn and run in the direction of the nearest house.

Once out of sight, Katō immediately turned north on his carefully planned roundabout route to Osorezan. He hoped they would think he was heading for Tokyo, but the big question was, who would "they" be? Who would be looking for him? The worst-case scenario was a nationwide police alert, but that was unlikely. The Mitsutomo City police would do as they were told, but it would be difficult to explain to the prefectural police that a dead person had been kidnapped. Most likely a private security service would be retained, but the need for absolute secrecy would limit Ōta's options.

Anyway, the first thing he had to do was change cars, but that had already been arranged with the same people who provided the gun.

On Route 129 just north of Atsugi he turned into a shopping center and drove to the third floor of the parking lot. There was a scattering of cars close to the store entrance, but sitting alone in the far corner was their new transportation, an aging Mercedes with windows as black as the body, the kind of car that provokes an immediate and healthy apprehension concerning its occupants. He pulled in on the side away from the entrance.

Katō sat for some time delaying the moment he would have to confront that face again. Grabbing a cup of ice cream from the cooler, he slipped into the back seat and forced himself to look. The empty eyes were staring into nothing from a soft, blank mask which shone deathly pale in the cool glow of the car's dome light. Birthmark or no birthmark, this could not be his Saki. What could possibly have possessed him to do this stupid, stupid thing? On the verge of calling Ōta to come pick this creature up, Katō realized he still held the cup of now soft green tea ice cream.

"Yumeko, mouth open," he said and dripped a spoonful of soft ice cream onto her tongue. Her mouth contorted as she started to gag, making awful hacking sounds until finally a swallow reflex kicked in. When he could bring his panic under control, he gave her some more. It was on the third spoonful that he saw it. Instead of just a reflex gulp, she swirled the ice cream around and around between her tongue and the roof of her mouth, just as his daughter had always done to experience all the ecstasy of flavor.

"Saki, Daddy's here," he said.

They took way too long to get back on the road in the Mercedes. Moving her was much more difficult than it had looked when the nurse did it. First of all, no matter how many times he told her that her name was Saki, she would not respond to any instruction not prefaced by "Yumeko." He hated calling her that and searched the manual in vain for a name change command. "Typical Mitsutomo manual," he grumbled, finally giving up.

It seemed like most of the movements he ordered made things worse instead of better, but finally he got her out of the Toyota and standing. The short walk to the Mercedes was relatively easy using the "walk" meta-command, but as they approached the open door he misjudged the distance, and when he said, "Yumiko, bend over" she was too close and the front of her skullcap hit the edge of the Mercedes roof with a terrifying hollow thunk. He had to kneel down to see if she was okay, and when he did he found that there was now a small hairline crack in the plastic. But even more frightening was the total absence of reaction or expression on her face. So he didn't have to see it he hugged her to him whispering, "Daddy's sorry, Saki. Daddy's so sorry."

Many hours and a couple of vitamin jelly and green tea ice cream feedings later, they were traveling north on the Tohoku Expressway. Katō compulsively searched the rearview mirror to see if they were being followed. About the time he began to think he was being silly, a large truck with a Mitsutomo logo pulled into their lane a couple cars back and stayed there. Slowing down, he forced the cars behind to pass one after another, but the truck just sat there now looming directly behind. They were just passing a service area, so at the last second he swerved onto the exit ramp certain that the truck would react, but the driver continued on, hardly glancing in their direction.

Hands trembling, he pulled to a stop. He was probably just being paranoid, but maybe it was time to make a call all the same. He booted up his laptop and a satellite connection, hoping his illegal software would make the call untraceable as advertised. Plugging in the microphone, he had the PC dial Ōta's number.

"Hello. Ōta here."

"Hello, Ōta. Katō here. Now listen. I'm not going to stay on long. Don't send anyone after us or I'll go to the police. I'm sure you know that if this story gets out, your career will be worth even less than mine. Do you understand?"

"Katō, what do you think you're doing? You must bring Yumeko back to us right now," Ōta yelled, but then quickly softened his voice, disingenuously switching to the first-name basis they had not been on for many years, "Kenji, please bring her back!"

"I'm afraid I can't do that, Takahiro. Saki is my daughter. It is my duty to take care of her, one way or another."

"Don't do this, Kenji. Saki died twenty years ago. It is Yumeko that you have stolen from us. We must take care of her. We owe her so much for all she has done already, and she can help us do even more. If you tell the police, it will be a media circus with Yumeko as the freak show. You did the right thing all those years ago, a wonderful thing. Do not ruin it now."

"Did I really do the right thing, Takahiro? What do you think Michiko would say?"

"Kenji, you are endangering Yumeko. She needs constant care. Her cap must be removed and the connections sterilized regularly to prevent infection. The battery implant for her processor will only last a couple days without recharge. You must bring her back."

"No," Katō said bluntly, cutting the connection with some satisfaction.

Back on the expressway, he adjusted the rearview mirror to look again at Saki, irrationally wondering if she was worried. With her vacant expression mercifully obscured by shadow, he caught a hint of something familiar in the profile framed by the rays of the setting sun. It was not young Saki the silhouette reminded him of, but Michiko when they first met.

Ōta was the company's golden boy in those days. Katō, although shorter and nowhere near as good-looking, ran a respectable second. They were both Todai boys, graduates of Tokyo University, and examples of the increasingly rare classic success story: middle-class child makes good through hard work. After they had proven themselves with five years of grinding overtime, the company, on one of its periodic internationalization bandwagons, sent them both to New York for all-expense-paid MBAs at Columbia.

It was seven months after their arrival, and Ōta was not flourishing. His self-conscious, fractured English undercut the allure of the boyish good looks and self-confidence which had proved so irresistible to women in Japan, so he fell back on the time-honored sulk that Western women just could not appreciate the superior qualities of Japanese men.

Katō's own qualities had not been appreciated by Japanese women either, so it was just more of the same for him. Although he was not much of a night-life person, for a jazz geek New York presented opportunities not to be missed, so he dragged Ōta downtown at least once a week.

That Saturday they went to the Knickerbocker on University Place to hear one of Katō's favorites, pianist Junior Mance. As the first set came to an end, he was pulled from his reverie by Ōta motioning him to look toward the bar.

"Japanese, although she tries to hide it," he said. "Come watch the master at work."

Sighing, Katō followed along, figuring he owed Ōta that much for accompanying him on these jazz expeditions. As they approached the bar, Ōta was just about to say something when the woman spoke without even looking up.

"Get lost. I can't stand salarymen," she snapped in Japanese.

This stopped Ōta mid-stride, but only for a moment.

"We're not salarymen. We're students," he said.

"Yeah, right. Real students don't wear Bally loafers, and they don't eat steak at the Knickerbocker either. Real students, the Japanese ones I mean, sport a mysteriously unchanging three-day-old growth of beard, wear dirty jeans, hang out at ancient rock clubs, and subsist on instant ramen. The only thing that you personally have in common with real students is that you, unlike your side-kick, have no appreciation for jazz."

Katō could see that Ōta was sorely tempted to cut his losses on this one, but another failure could not be tolerated.

"We are too students," he said. "We're at Columbia."

"Company MBA, right? So you're trainee salarymen, a particularly loathsome subspecies."

"Well, I can tell from the dirty jeans that you are a *true* student," Ōta said, failing at sarcasm, "so why are you here instead of the ancient rock club?"

"It's the music, stupid," she said, shaking her head.

"Come on, lighten up. We're not so bad when you get to know us. Why don't you join us at our table? Practice your Japanese. Remember your roots, so to speak."

She looked up slowly, and Katō was sure she had been just about to tell them again to take a hike but changed her mind when she got her first good look at the boyish grin that had charmed a thousand OLs.

"Oh, alright, but on two conditions," she said, letting the hint of a smile force its way through. "You buy my steak, no strings attached, and I get to keep treating you like dirt."

"Hey, we're salarymen; masochism is our specialty," Katō said, trying to establish his presence on the periphery, while knowing with absolute certainty who was going to be abused. It was no one's fault, of course, just what would happen in the natural course of things.

As the self-absorbed often are when it suits their purpose, Ōta was remarkably good at getting people to talk, so they soon learned that this was Michiko Ōtani from Sendai. She had just started a six-month commercial program in digital photography and photojournalism after a year spent studying her chosen field of black-and-white art photography at the New School. She finally quit, she said, because the world does not need or want another "artist" doggedly shooting black and white celluloid in an age of color, bytes, and Photoshop. As the last president of Todai's Analog Photography Club, Katō sighed in understanding.

During Junior's last set, Katō tried to be subtle, but even the music couldn't keep him from staring.

Her hair was cut short in the playful style of the Taisho *moga*, the modern girls who enjoyed unprecedented and short-lived freedom in Japan's own Jazz Age. Her face seemed to be set in the same era, neither round and delicate enough for an Edo-period print nor sharp and angular enough for a modern fashion magazine but more genuine and beautiful than both.

Back out on the street in the cool March night, she invited them to her favorite neighborhood bar on Avenue A. There, beer in hand, she immediately launched into a rant about Japanese corporations: the discrimination against women in salaries and promotion, the total failure to support working mothers, the estrangement from family that inevitably results from the inhuman working hours and arbitrary transfers forced on men, and so on, and so on. She could never live in that world, she said. Companies must change and men must change.

To Katō's surprise, Ōta enthusiastically agreed, and he even seemed sincere. The only thing to do was to stand up to the company, he said, and force it to strike a better balance between work and life. Of course a wife has a right to work, and a husband has an obligation and need to participate in the family instead of being some kind of 24/7 wage slave. The two of them then spent an hour gleefully trashing corporate Japan. Katō often agreed but found it hard to pile on because the reality was not quite as simple as they made it out to be, and, besides, that was the life the two of them had to look forward to, like it or not.

When the corporate rant finally ran out of steam, Katō managed to change the subject. Before long he and Michiko were finishing each other's sentences. On jazz, they totally agreed that players like Junior and saxman Yoshio Ōtomo were vastly underappreciated compared to their more experimental contemporaries. And when the discussion moved on to photography, they one-upped each other proclaiming the greatness of artists like Cartier-Bresson and Ihei Kimura while also doubting whether that kind of integrity still had a place in the world. The only fault he could find in her critical eye was a weakness for Diane Arbus.

With dawn in the sky and Katō long since in love, they walked in uncomfortable silence to the Astor Place subway station. During the long trip uptown alone, Katō tried not to think about Ōta's parting Cheshire-cat grin and Michiko's apologetic shrug. The pattern was set. From that night on the three of them were a team—at least until bedtime.

Fourteen months later, they returned to Japan, fresh MBAs in hand, the understanding being that Ōta and Michiko would announce their engagement once her freelance career was on track. Katō and Michiko exchanged the occasional e-mail, but her work was taking off so she was insanely busy and so, of course, was he.

Time passed, dulling the pain, but one day almost a year later he opened his door and there she was, still painfully beautiful despite the tear-smudged makeup. It was the first Sunday of April, and he was on his way out to go get drunk singing karaoke under the cherry blossoms with the other members of Mineral Fuels Department No. 2.

"I need a place to stay for a couple days, and I need you not to ask any questions. I don't want to talk about it," she said, looking both defiant and bereft. In a few minutes she told him everything.

It didn't take him long to track down Ōta, who was nursing a beer and looking less than festive at his own department's picnic.

"How can you just throw her away?" Katō asked. "This is too rotten, even for you. What about all that stuff you said in New York? Standing up to the company and all that. Was all that 'equal partner' stuff just a pack of lies? Just a little role-playing to snag a Japanese fuck buddy to keep you warm in New York?"

Ōta clenched his fists, looking like he wanted to punch Katō almost as much as Katō wanted to punch him. "Don't be so naive.

We are not talking about the speed of light in a vacuum here. What I said in New York was the truth when I said it, the truth for that time and that place. Haven't you figured it out yet? For us New York was a trip to Disneyland, a brief vacation from reality. Well, I don't think we're in New York anymore, Katō. Open your eyes and take a look around. How much time do you think your department manager spends sharing the joys of child-rearing and housework with his wife? I'll tell you. Zip. Nada. Zero. And you know why, Mr. Self-righteous? Because if he wants to succeed he has to work more than eighty hours a week just like we do. And do you think his wife works? Well, think again. She may not like it, but she understands her role and responsibilities as a wife and mother, and she understands the truth of this country and this company. Go whine to the president about it, if you like. Tell him it's not fair. Tell him the company must change. You know what your whining will get you? Membership in the window tribe, that's what.

"I refuse to be a failure, even for Michiko. I told her I still love her, and I do. But a Japanese salaryman needs a real Japanese wife and his kids need a real mother, not some jet-setting photographer who stops in to say hello when she happens to be in town. When I asked her if she could live with that, she told me to fuck off and die."

Five months later Katō and Michiko were married. He had little doubt it was a rebound thing, but there was nothing to be gained by picking that scab. She was traveling on shooting assignments much of the time, and even when she was home, he was working most of the time, but they had good times when they could manage to get together. Then Saki was born, and it was difficult but even better—for a while anyway. They got a babysitter so Michiko could take nearby jobs, but for a year or more she turned down everything else. Katō could see the frustration building as calls for the best assignments became fewer and fewer. He could see the anger creeping into her time with Saki, so when the chance came for a one-week assignment in New York, he told her to go for it, he and Saki would be okay together.

The next day he went to explain to the department manager that for a week he would have to leave work by 8:00 to pick up Saki at the day care center.

"Well, that would be difficult under any circumstances—you know how busy we are—but I'm afraid it's out of the question now," he said, looking up with a huge grin. "By next week you will be in Saudi Arabia and busy as hell. Congratulations! You're the new on-site liaison for our joint-venture refinery project there. I hardly need to say that this is a big promotion and a great opportunity. The travel department has already booked your ticket for this Sunday."

Katō hinted at wanting to take Michiko and Saki along, but that was "out of the question" since a region with revolutions occurring on a regular basis was no place for a Japanese mother and child. Besides, the assignment was only for about three years.

That night, as he stood looking down at his three-year-old girl sleeping, he remembered Michiko's face when he said she should take the New York job. There was just one thing to be done. He would refuse the assignment, and he would not tell Michiko. It was his decision and he would suffer the consequences in any event, so why lay that guilt on her?

"This is a horrendous mistake," Ōta told him when word got around. "The company cannot afford to allow employees to believe they have the option to refuse, especially employees considered management material. So you will be made an example of. It would be merciful if they would just fire you now, but they will humiliate you instead, and if you quit, no decent company will hire you. I beg you to reconsider the consequences of this action. Are you really willing to ruin your career because of some misguided notion of what is the 'right' thing to do?"

"Yes," Katō answered.

"You will regret it," Ōta said, looking almost genuinely sad, "and the regret will not be long in coming."

They didn't speak again until the day of the accident.

Back on the road, Katō drove on toward Osorezan. In darkness they passed through Miyagi Prefecture and into Iwate. Katō's eyes were tired, and he had to fight sleep, but he wanted to get closer to their destination before stopping to rest. Looking again in the rear-view mirror to check on Saki, he was jerked back to alertness. Although he had given no command, her arms were raised above her head and pressed against the car roof. After a brief instant of insane hope, he remembered something he had tried not to think about when he read it in the manual. A raised left arm indicates intestinal pressure has exceeded a certain point, while a raised right arm signals bladder pressure. She had to go to the bathroom.

Exiting at the Iwatesan Service Area, he stopped as close as he could to the wheelchair toilet. Before getting her out of the car, he searched the manual for a toilet meta-command, a sub-routine that would take over and take care of all the little details—walk, stop, turn, stop, pull down pants, stop, sit, stop, go, stop, wipe, stop . . .— and save him from having to do this to a body he had last assisted in the bathroom more than twenty years before. But of course there was no easy way out so, wildly flipping through the manual, he had to give every command himself.

After many mistakes, bruises, and an accident that sent him running to get the spare clothes Nurse Hashimoto had so thoughtfully brought along, he finally got Saki back in the car. Sobbing in humiliation and exhaustion, he drove them to the far corner of the parking lot and stopped.

"Yumeko sleep," he commanded. "Good night, Saki. Daddy's sorry," he said.

In the overcast and humid morning, they drove into Aomori and around the axe-shaped Shimokita Peninsula until they reached Osorezan. Stuffing the gun and small cooler into a backpack, Katō opened the door and was immediately assailed by the heat and the overpowering stink of sulfur. He got Saki out of the back seat and hovered protectively beside her as she did the Mitsutomo Shuffle down the long, smooth stone walkway stretching to the main temple building. About halfway they passed a small hut with *omamori* amulets and little Jizō statues for sale. The old woman sitting behind the counter seemed asleep.

"Excuse me," Katō said, and when she looked up he shuddered reflexively at the sight of the naked, black glass Mitsutomo eyes staring out at him from deep in a sea of wrinkles. Most people opted for one of the cosmetic eyeball options available at no extra charge.

"Give you the willies, don't they," she chuckled in a thick Tsugaru accent, the skin around the implants crinkling at the corners, making her face look nearly human.

"May I ask you something?"

"Sure. Ain't as if I was busy or anything."

"I'm looking for an *itako*."

"Well, there's probably a couple hanging about, but if you want a spiritual session with an *itako*, you really should've come to the big festival last month. *Itako* are kind of a dying breed, but most of 'em still show up to work the festival."

"Well, actually, there is one in particular I am looking for, but I only know her first name: Haruko."

"Ah, Haruko," she said, her eyes smiling again. "Yeah, I know that one, but I'm afraid she's retired."

"Could I at least talk to her?"

"Why, I guess you could, since you are. Once I was Haruko the *itako*, but now I'm just plain old Haruko."

He stood there for a moment feeling stupid and embarrassed to be asking this old woman to send a message to the dead, but it was much too late to turn back now. "To be honest," he blurted out, "I don't really believe in this business about communicating with the dead, but, well, I don't seem to have any other choice, so I'd like to give it a try. You see my ex-wife Michiko went missing in Africa awhile back and is presumed dead. A week or so before finding out, I started having these dreams of Michiko crossing a rocky expanse that I somehow know must be Sai-no-kawara. She is searching for our daughter Saki, who she thinks died at age five. So you see, just in case it is, you know, not just a dream, I need to get a message to her. I need to tell her to go on ahead." He turned and called, "Yumeko, walk." When she had lumbered slowly up, he commanded her to stop. "This is my daughter Saki," he said, turning back to look at the old woman's face, his gaze unavoidably drawn to the onyx eyes. "Can you help me?"

After a long pause, she answered, "I see you bear complicated burdens, so I will be honest also. I won't say it happened every time, but there were times when it seemed I had the power. At least that is what my old woman's memories tell me. It was more than ten years ago now that the government finally started buyin' eyes for poor blind people. Wouldn't you know it that when these new eyes of mine gave me the power to see this world again, I lost the power to see the other one. Not being all that good at pretending, I gave up the *itako* calling after that. So you see I can't help you. I'm sorry."

"What about the other *itako*?"

She shook her head. "Maybe a couple others back in the old days had the power, but not now. Mostly *itako* are ordinary women with bad eyes and a good heart. They're gonna tell you what they think you need to hear. If that's what you really want . . ."

"No, I guess not. Well, thank you anyway."

"Wait a minute," she said as he turned. "At least I can give you a bit of advice. It is Jizō-sama you should be speaking to. If anyone can do anything for you he can. Tell him your story and ask him to help."

"I'll remember," he said. "One more thing. Was it a worthwhile trade—what those eyes gave you compared to what you lost?"

"It's a beautiful world," she smiled, waving her hand at the volcanic wasteland surrounding the temple grounds. "To be given the ability to see it again after so many years of blindness was a wonderful gift. Everyday in my prayers I thank Jizō-sama for these eyes."

Giving a short bow, he started to walk on, but then looked back asking, "Which way to Sai-no-kawara?"

"Go down that path," she pointed, "and turn left at the Pool of Blood Hell. You can't miss it. It's the pool that's red 'stead of yellow."

Off the smooth walkway, Saki's walk meta-command could not handle the uneven, dirt trail so she had to be guided one step at a time. "The road to hell may be paved with good intentions, but they should've used concrete," muttered Katō. The morning heat rose as they tottered between rank yellow pools and jagged outcroppings of rock, Katō's white shirt rapidly darkening with sweat.

Looking at the myriad sockets sticking out of the skullcap, he worried about what the sulfur and volcanic dust were doing to her delicate electronics. "Please allow me to borrow this," he said to a Jizō statue beside the path as he removed one of its many layers of red bonnets. After carefully tying the bonnet on Saki's head, he added, "And please accept this gift in return, I won't be needing it anymore." Removing the favorite Gucci power tie he had chosen for the kidnapping, he tied it neatly around Jizō's neck.

Katō was glad they had missed the festival crowds. There were only a few other visitors scattered here and there, absorbed in their own private pain. Farther along the path an old woman putting a new red bib on another Jizō statue stopped and stared at Saki as they passed.

"She's handicapped," Katō said as if that explained everything.

Clouds of steam bubbling from sulfur pools rose to meet the morning mist, which was lit from above by an unseen sun giving the entire sky a bizarre yellow glow. Finally they came to a flat rocky strip, a no-man's land between the slope of volcanic outcroppings and the white beach of Lake Usoriyama. They had arrived. Clearing a small space of larger stones, he had Saki kneel with him on the ground, and he fed her a pack of vitamin jelly from the cooler. When that was done, he forced himself to look around and think about what to do next.

Scattered across Sai-no-kawara were innumerable pyramids, little mounds of piled stones. Propped against some he could see dolls and action figures, toy cars and stuffed animals—all gifts from parents to their dead children. From recent visitors there were flowers standing upright in the sand by the lake and scraps of food offerings already scavenged by the many crows. Everywhere bright pinwheels stood dull and stagnant in the thick, still air.

When he closed his eyes he could see Michiko stumbling blindly among the stones looking for Saki, crying out her name.

"Well, here we are, Saki," he said, "the Riverbank of Sai, limbo of little children who did nothing wrong but died too soon. To Sai-no-kawara they are sent to pile up stones to earn their way into paradise, and here their parents come to make their own stone pyramids in this world in the hope of helping their child in the other.

"Are you out there, Saki, or are you here next to me?" he asked, taking the gun out of his backpack and setting it on the ground in front of him. "Is your poor mother out there looking for you? Shall we go to her now?"

They knelt there together for a long time, gazing across Sai-no-kawara. As they waited, the sun slowly burned a path through the clouds and mist, flooding the far shore of the lake, the shore of paradise, in a light more golden than sulfur. A gentle breeze came up to cool their faces and start the many pinwheels spinning.

Suddenly a muffled, mournful train whistle sounded, and Katō had the somehow comforting thought that the gods must be using dead steam engines to carry souls between worlds, but then he saw it was a toy train that had chugged to life, its tiny solar panels at last gathering sufficient strength from the sun to power it in its eternal circle through the plexiglass tunnel that ringed its own mountain of stones.

"I guess not," Katō sighed finally. "We will both stay a while longer. We both have responsibilities yet, although I wish it were not so terribly hard to figure out exactly what those responsibilities are, or to whom. It seems that, like Jizō-sama, we must just do what we can. Besides, Haruko was right, it is a beautiful world. Even here. Even now."

With that, he struggled to his feet, knees aching.

"I'll be back soon," he said, gently patting her skullcap.

After throwing the gun as far as he could out into the lake, he walked to a large standing Jizō statue perched atop a huge stone pile some way off. There he laid his two bullets as an offering, and, remembering Haruko's advice, he asked merciful Jizō to tell Michiko not to search for Saki on Sai-no-kawara because she had either gone on to paradise already or she would come later, and in any case there was no reason she should have to linger on the Riverbank of Sai. Her debts were more than paid.

Walking back he turned on his cell phone to call Ōta.

"Hello, it's me."

"Kenji? Where are you? Is Yumeko okay? Please give her back to us!"

"One question and one condition. The question first. Who puts the flowers in the vase at the 7-Eleven intersection?"

"I do," Ōta answered softly. "I do it to honor Saki and to remind myself that we must work even harder to earn what she gave us. Don't get me wrong. I still believe that we did the right thing. I have come to accept, however, that I could be wrong. What is your condition for returning Yumeko?"

"I will give her back and keep the secret if you cancel the abortion and give me the baby. Make it a legal adoption. The company can easily arrange it."

"There are a thousand reasons why this is a bad idea, Kenji. Bad for Yumeko and bad for you."

"I know. But I think it is what Michiko would want."

"Alright then, I promise that we will do what we can to insure that the pregnancy goes to term. You must understand, however, that there can be no guarantees. . . ."

"No one understands that better than I," Katō said. "Please come get her quickly now. We are at . . ."

"Osorezan, I know," Ōta interrupted. "We just traced your call. We have helicopters standing by across the country. One will be there to pick you up in an hour or so."

Katō found Yumeko exactly as he had left her, motionless but for the beads of sweat sliding slowly down her cheeks and the eye blinks programmed at ten-second intervals. Kneeling before her, he bowed deeply, pressing his forehead against the stones.

Straightening up, he fed her a cup of green tea ice cream and reminded himself to tell Ōta to be sure she still got some every day.

"Yumeko—I'd like to call you Yumeko from now on if that's okay—soon you will be going home, but there is one more thing we have left to do in honor of Saki, wherever she may be."

Together they built one more pyramid there on Sai-no-kawara, Katō running about gathering the stones and Yumeko dropping them on the pile one by one.

When the sound of a helicopter could be heard faintly in the distance, Katō took the last cup of green tea ice cream from the cooler and handed it to Yumeko to place on the top.

Suga Hiroe
Translated by Ginny Tapley Takemori

I. Yoshida Midori

Morning came, proof that Sonogawa Hanako had lived to see another day. She would soon be thirty-five, an age she had never expected to reach.

She felt especially good today. Since the doctors had given her the all-clear at her morning check-up, she had decided to take breakfast outdoors. Seated on a garden chair beneath the crystal-clear blue sky, she relished the pleasant breeze rustling the verdant garden and the exuberant twittering of birds.

"Are you sure you're not cold, ma'am?" Mrs. Ishimoto, her housekeeper, asked anxiously.

"Don't worry," replied Hanako with a smile. "I'm a bit nervous today. The temperature is the last thing on my mind!"

Mrs. Ishimoto wrung her apron in her hands and opened her mouth to speak a couple of times, but noting Hanako's tranquil smile, she merely said, "In that case I shall have breakfast served," and left her.

Everyone else seemed more flustered than she was, thought Hanako with some amusement. When, after a long illness, her mother had departed this world ten years ago, the atmosphere in the residence had been filled with gloom, like the bottom of a lake, but she herself had been almost unnaturally calm. In the wake of her father's death three months ago, there had been a magnificent display of grief from business circles and the medical supplies in-dustry, as was to be expected—but that was outside. Here in the residence, they had been too busy with preparations for the funeral and receiving condolence callers to have time to indulge in weeping. The servants had finally come to terms with the fact that the head of the household was no longer with them, but now Hanako had come up with this proposal of hers. It would be unreasonable to expect them not to be upset, she thought.

Inohara, the butler, appeared at her side without a sound, as always. "Miss Yoshida is here to see you, ma'am," he told her.

Hanako's heart skipped a beat. "Please show her through."

A ripple of uncertainty crossed Inohara's face. That was a first. Normally he would have bowed his assent without a moment's hesitation. Hanako nodded to indicate she did indeed mean what she'd said, and Inohara at last gave a bow angled at precisely ninety degrees, before turning smartly on his heel.

I wonder what sort of person Midori is, thought Hanako, her imagination running ahead of her. Midori was two years younger, and still single. Hanako had heard that she was a hardworking career woman in a top company. If they got along well, she'd like to know more about her life. But then, it rather depended on how Midori felt about her.

A tablecloth made from imported fabric was placed over the round white table, and the maids began to lay out breakfast: pots of tea and coffee, a pitcher of orange juice, silver dishes containing butter, strawberry jam and marmalade, a platter heaped with two portions of bacon, eggs, and chicory salad. Accustomed to eating the same menu alone every morning, Hanako was pleased at how cheerful the spread looked.

She gently nudged the rattan breadbasket closer to the seat opposite her. The fragrance of freshly baked bread rose from the butter rolls and croissants and toast, and the corn, herb, and other breads. She had just repositioned the toast to make it more visible when she heard Inohara say, "This way, please."

Hanako looked up. *Oh, how lovely!* she thought, and smiled.

Midori was wearing a tight-fitting deep green suit. Her hair was cut in a stylish bob that matched her intelligent eyes, while large earrings and a delicate gold necklace added a touch of softness to her air of competence. Her high heels clacked as she approached. Hanako couldn't decide whether or not her face was the spitting image of her own, as she assumed it would be.

146

Midori stopped by Hanako's chair and smiled down at her. Her expression, with a hint of a frown, was hard to read.

"Yoshida. How do you do?"

"Sonogawa Hanako. Pleased to meet you."

A fresh breeze blew between them.

"I'm not sure where to start," Midori said with a wry smile.

"First, please take a seat. While we're having breakfast together, it'll naturally . . ."

"Yes, of course."

Hanako's guest sat down in one brisk movement. If Hanako herself were in better health, perhaps she would be like this too, she mused.

Midori took a sip of coffee, then said quietly, "Mother asked me to convey her thanks for taking good care of us."

It was an opener that left no room for pleasantries. Hanako paused before saying, "If the monthly allowance isn't sufficient, please don't hesitate to tell me. Also if there is any other way in which I can be of help."

"Not at all. We are already receiving more than enough in the way of maintenance. I was of half a mind to reject this proposal of yours too."

"I'm very glad you did come and not turn me down flat." Hanako picked up her fork and indicated with her eyes that her guest should eat.

Midori stared at her for a moment, her gaze sharp, then all of a sudden the tension drained from her and she smiled. She picked at some salad. "Hanako, you're looking better than I expected."

"Yes. The check-ups morning and night are a real bore, but apart from that I'm quite comfortable. There are times I'd even like to go out, but I suppose that's asking too much."

"You'd have to be accompanied by an entourage of dozens of doctors and bodyguards, wouldn't you? Given that the whole world is obsessed with your physical condition."

"That reminds me." Hanako chuckled as she toyed with a piece of chicory. "There's another chore to take care of. I have to record the daily message for the staff: 'Hey, I'm still alive, so you should do your best at work today.' Although not in those words, of course."

Midori's forkful of bacon stopped in midair, and she looked seriously at Hanako. "You have to put up with all kinds of things, don't you? It's how I imagined. Ever since I was told the truth when I was twenty, I've always wondered how I would cope if I were in your position. Not only were you implanted with synthetic growth-form organs before you were old enough to know what was happening, but those organs were a brand new product on which your father's company fortunes were riding. In other words—"

"I was a guinea pig, basically." Hanako cocked her head slightly, doing her best not to let the conversation become too serious. "But I was a happy guinea pig. The synthetic organs proved to be excellent, adapting well to their host and growing perfectly—and I never lacked for anything. When I stopped growing, Father and I both wept for joy. By then, even if something did go wrong, a regular artificial organ transplant would do the job."

"Wept? *Him*? Really?" Midori's eyes widened in surprise, but she quickly regained her composure. Cutting up a piece of bacon, she asked, "I wonder what Father thought about what he did to you?"

"How odd!"

"What is?"

Hanako folded her hands on the table, and answered mischievously, "It's a curious feeling to hear someone other than myself call him 'Father.'"

"I'm sorry."

"Please don't apologize," Hanako hastily waved her hand. "You might have a different surname, but he was still your father. Of course, you were unquestionably his daughter, and formally acknowledged as such. So, was he an affectionate father to the Yoshida family?"

Seeing Hanako calmly eating her breakfast, Midori lowered her guard a little. "Yes, just like in any other family. He took us to amusement parks and the seaside. We weren't all that close, but I wouldn't say we disliked each other. Until I was twenty, I just thought he was a normal father who was away a lot on business. So when I did find out the truth, I . . ."

"Did you resent it?"

"Rather, I was shocked. It didn't even occur to me to resent it. I feel quite nostalgic looking back on that now!" Midori laughed lightly and took a mouthful of bacon. Hanako felt herself warming to her.

"Midori, you asked me how Father felt about me, but before I answer, would it be too rude of me to put a similar question to you?"

"Go ahead," said Midori coolly. "The more open you are with me, the more comfortable I'll feel."

Hanako took a gulp of tea then finally found the courage to ask, "Do you hold a grudge against Father and me?"

There was a deep sigh. It was some moments before Hanako realized it had come from Midori's lips and not her own.

Midori slowly swirled her coffee around in the cup. "Let me answer the same way as you. You said you were a happy guinea pig, right? Well, I was a happy clone. Okay, I existed purely in order to provide you with fresh organs should anything go wrong with your own, but I didn't see this so much as misfortune as simply fate. And having such a wonderful woman as my mother—that is, the mother who willingly became the surrogate for a fertilized egg, in the full knowledge that what she was doing was illegal—I was happy. I have only fond memories of my childhood, and even when she told me the truth she remained calm, enveloping me in her warmth. As things turned out, I didn't lose an organ or even a single gram of my liver, and I lived a normal life. So no, I don't bear any ill will against either you or Father."

Midori smiled faintly. Noticing this, Hanako wasn't sure whether she'd spoken from the heart or was just putting on an act.

"Thank you." Her own smile was probably similarly enigmatic, she thought. "Would you like some bread? There are various types, so please take whatever you like."

"Thanks," said Midori, helping herself to a croissant.

"Is that what you usually have?"

"It is. And come to think of it, Hanako, you do have an interesting way of eating toast."

"It's a habit of mine. Please excuse my bad manners, picking out the middle bit first. It's just that I remember . . ." Hanako paused, but Midori merely looked quizzically at her, so she coolly changed the subject. "I am really very pleased that I could meet you today. I won't bother you with any more serious discussions, so please take your time over breakfast. Afterwards the lawyer will explain the details to you. As I informed you before, I can promise that from the moment we hand you the written confirmation, the Sonogawa family will make no further demands of you, and you can freely make claim on my estate, as long as my assets permit."

"What if I should claim the entire Sonogawa estate?" asked Midori mischievously.

Hanako responded in the same vein, "At least leave me enough to have toast for breakfast every morning!"

They both chuckled. Changing the subject, Hanako's younger clone began talking about how beautiful the house and its garden were.

Hanako presumed that Midori must already have looked into the Sonogawa Group. She already had the information she wanted, and so there wasn't any need for her to put questions or demands to Hanako. She had the feeling that she was dealing with a business partner rather than a sibling.

Upon taking her leave, Midori said, "Let's meet again."

Hanako nodded, painfully aware that she had said this only out of politeness.

II. Kosaka Moe

Good morning, everyone. Yesterday the swallows made their annual appearance in the courtyard of our Gunma factory. No doubt we shall presently be hearing the cheeping of their chicks. It is said that houses on which swallows build their nests are blessed with good fortune, so I have no doubt that the Sonogawa Group, along with all of you staff members, will continue to prosper. And, along with the changing seasons, I continue to live, experiencing each day full of joy. Please remember that our group is concerned for your livelihood and wellbeing, and strive your utmost at work today, as every day. Take pride in the fact that thanks to all of you, some people's lives may be extended, as has mine.

It was sunny, but there was a strong wind, so Hanako had arranged for today's meeting to be held in the sunroom.

Her guest would apparently be coming after having seen her son off to school, so Hanako had filmed her message for the morning assembly in advance. She was used to the routine: apply makeup, record broadcast, remove makeup, lie down in bed for the morning medical examination, tell the doctors she's fine, then finally pause for breath.

She still had a little time, so she summoned her personal secretary, Tsuji. Seated in a chair at her bedside, the young man briskly tapped away at his keyboard taking down the day's business. Tsuji had become the main contact between the residence and the company. He was exceptionally competent, and Hanako considered him one of the most valuable assets she had inherited from her father.

She opened the fancy envelope Tsuji had given her and read the contents. She smiled half-heartedly. "Well, let's send her a card. 'I, too, am pleased to be greeted by a new employee such as yourself. . . .' You can fill in the rest as necessary."

"Right."

Glancing down at the letter again, she couldn't repress a wry smile. It was from a female employee who had just joined the company last month, and read more like a fan letter: how, when still in elementary school, she had been moved by a report in a Sonogawa Group PR newsletter about the late proprietor's decision to use the still-experimental synthetic growth-form organs in order to save his beloved daughter, sick from birth; how impressed she was that, in order to keep Hanako alive, everyone in this dedicated company had rallied behind those in charge of her medical treatment; how she had been so excited to have finally secured employment in the company she had always wanted to work for.

Hanako was both amused and a little contrite, feeling that she was betraying this girl's loyalty to the company. Had she really been so weak at birth, her cloned sisters would never have existed; after all, increasing the number of daughters with the same birth defect would not have been of any use at all. What would this girl think if she knew that Hanako had always been in perfect health?

The existence of the clones was a secret known only to those in this residence. Even the executives of the company, other than the top few, thought that they were just the boss's offspring with his mistresses. The truth of the moving story behind the company's image would never be known beyond these walls, and for as long as she lived, Hanako would always be the shining poster girl for the Sonogawa Group.

Hanako folded up the flower-patterned paper and returned it to the envelope. "Incidentally, how are the preparations for the new company president election going?"

Tsuji tapped at the keyboard on his knees and brought up some data. "The candidates have been narrowed down to five. But there are already rumors that you will be made the next president, and it's becoming difficult to get behind-the-scenes information."

"That's a problem. If we drag it out too much they'll get suspicious and that won't do. Please make the announcement soon."

"Understood. In that case I'll push for the official in-house announcement to be made next Monday."

"You do know that those five include a couple of clones—I mean, that my father acknowledged paternity of them, don't you?"

"Yes. I'm a confidentiality grade eight, so am aware of the status of the former president's illegitimate children. As for two of the candidates being clones, I already—"

"Just so long as you treat them kindly. The other matter is how much importance you place on the Sonogawa Group's image. It's not just my future but that of all the company employees that's at stake, so please treat the decision with utmost discretion."

"I will."

Noticing Inohara gliding up to them, Tsuji stood up and bowed stiffly at his hardheaded colleague before leaving the room.

The butler was stony-faced today, too. "Mrs. Kosaka is here to see you, ma'am."

"I'll be right there. I'm starving." Hanako clutched her belly, but failed to elicit so much as a smile from him.

Breakfast was already laid out in the sunroom, where sun was pouring in through the high glass walls. Hanako's guest was standing there looking timidly about. Her shoulder-length hair was permed, and she wore a rather cheap-looking dark-colored suit. Noticing Hanako come into the room, she hastily turned around.

"I'm Sonogawa Hanako. Pleased to meet you, Moe."

"Er, hello. Really? I mean . . . um, sorry I'm late."

"Not to worry. Please, take a seat."

Moe perched gingerly on the edge of the chair as if afraid of soiling it. Abashed at the sumptuous breakfast before her, she fell silent.

"Please make yourself comfortable. I really am happy to meet you."

Moe was four years Hanako's junior, which made her just thirty-one, but she had such an air of exhaustion that she looked old for her age. Without looking up, she finally said, in a small voice, "Yes, me too."

"Go ahead," Hanako urged, picking up a fork. Moe hesitantly reached out a hand and took a tiny sip of orange juice. "You're married, aren't you, Moe? How old is your son?"

"He's just started elementary school. You sent such a magnificent gift for our wedding. I really am very grateful."

"Father was delighted about your marriage. The ceremony was just with the two of you, wasn't it? It was such a pity he couldn't attend."

An air of utter self-deprecation emanated from the downcast Moe. "Mother . . . My mother got married ten years ago. Of course, you already know that. Her partner is, well . . . So we didn't invite anybody to the ceremony."

"Is that how it was?" A sudden pall fell over the sunroom, and Hanako wondered whether it was because of the atmosphere between the two of them.

Moe wrapped her hands around the glass and, with her gaze still downturned, continued, "Mother shouldn't have done that. We got quite a lot for our living expenses, and she was flashing it around, so no wonder she attracted that sort of man. Life at home was really awful for a time. I thought I'd finally be able to escape from it when I got married, but look at me now. . . ."

Moe was speaking so seriously that Hanako put her teacup to one side and leaned forward. "I heard that father told you the truth when you got married."

"Oh! Oh, he did," wailed Moe, covering her face with her hands. "I couldn't believe it! Me, a clone, of all things!"

Hanako didn't know what to say. Then again, she was beginning to think this woman was overdoing things a bit. Maybe this extravagant wretchedness was all a show. Her clothes were nothing special, but Hanako noticed she was wearing an expensive wristwatch and suddenly became suspicious.

Moe kept her face in her hands as she surged on. "Luckily my husband was a kind man—he could have broken off our engagement, but he married me anyway. But I was really scared when I got pregnant. After all, I'm not a normal human being. I'd been told I wasn't genetically altered, but how could I believe that? Father hadn't said anything about me being a clone in the first place, so he'd have no qualms about lying about that. And although I was relieved when my son was born healthy, that didn't last long—I never knew when I might get the call from you. I was terrified to go out for a walk, or do the shopping. I might suddenly be pulled into a black car, have a chloroform-soaked rag held over my face, and the next thing I'd be waking up with a great big scar on my belly."

Hanako tried to placate her. "The danger was with the synthetic growth-form organs. By the time you knew about it all, I had already stopped growing, so even if something had gone wrong, an ordinary artificial organ would have done just as well. I'm sure father must have told you about that too."

"But nobody knows how things might turn out." Moe shook her head irritably. "Making clones is against the law, but he did it anyway, so how can anyone possibly say that everything's okay? It's awful, Hanako. I've been scared out of my wits. You have no idea. A kidney or liver wouldn't be all that bad. I'd give up a lung if I got paid well for it. But what if it was my heart? If your synthetic heart failed, would you take mine?"

"That's what I'm telling you—there's no chance of that happening."

"You're only saying that because you've been okay up to now. But I'm the clone created for your purposes. If anything happens to you in the future, of course I'll be called on."

Hanako thought of a number of things she could say, and weighed her words carefully. "I think I understand how you feel, Moe," she said gravely, "but there's no need for you to feel frightened any more. As I informed you, I will never ask you to provide me with any organs, not now, nor in the future. You can be sure of that."

Moe looked up abruptly. There was no trace of even a single tear on her face. "What about my feelings up to now? All this time I've been scared, what about that? While I've been living in fear, you've been leading an elegant life in this fabulous mansion. And even the fact that my mother went off the rails was all down to giving birth to me, knowing it was illegal. And now you're trying to tell me it's all okay?"

Hanako looked searchingly at Moe. Her face was that of someone who had grown up believing she was unlucky, and had grown accustomed to it. She had exactly the same eyes and mouth as Hanako, yet she could have been a life form from another planet.

Hanako didn't feel particularly sorry for her. If life as a clone really had been that hard, she should have listened to what Hanako had to say before making her move. All she had to do was reject the allowance the Sonogawa family was paying her, go public about the circumstances of her birth, take them to court, get DNA test evidence, and destroy the public's trust in them in one fell swoop. Seeing as she hadn't done that, Hanako felt she had a glimpse of what she really wanted from them.

"I suppose you're not interested in breakfast right now," said Hanako with a sigh, and moved the breadbasket to one side. "Moe, for all the Sonogawa Group's technical knowhow, we cannot heal your family's emotional scars. As for not needing any organs from you, as I told you before, we shall be giving you a formal document to that effect right after breakfast. We shall continue to pay your monthly allowance as before, and should you require more than that, you may put in further demands as long as my assets permit."

"As much as I want?"

"Yes. Although there is effectively a limit. The funds will come from the Sonogawa family estate, not from the company's assets."

"Eh? The family estate? You mean, if I say I want this mansion, you'll give it to me?"

Hanako nodded sadly. Moe felt a stab of pity for her.

"I don't mind. As long as I have a place where I can preserve this body for the sake of the Group, I can live anywhere. But if an application is actually made to that effect, I expect the lawyers will attach conditions to it. My assets, or rather my inheritance, are not for your enjoyment alone."

Moe was gazing dreamily around the sunroom, only half listening. There was none of the nervousness she'd had about her upon arriving, and she now looked more like she was assessing its value.

Hanako raised her teacup to her lips. The warm, fragrant liquid spread through her body, and finally she managed a deep sigh.

"Moe."

"Yeah? I mean . . . Er, what is it?

"Do you hate father and me?"

Moe's eyes swam. "No, no. You're just as unlucky as me. I sympathize with you. After all, we've both been sacrificed to the Sonogawa Group, haven't we?" She seemed to be expecting Hanako to agree with her, most likely trying to establish a bond between them that she could exploit later on, but Hanako remained silent. Flustered, Moe continued, "Well, haven't we? We were divided from the same egg! I mean, before I was even born I was there ready to provide spare parts. Hanako, you had to bear the fate of being an experiment right from the start, with your healthy body implanted with those synthetic growth-form organs—"

"Yes, I did, didn't I?" Hanako smiled pleasantly.

Moe gaped at her. "But—"

"I've never been conscious of the heavy fate I have to bear. Everyone around me thinks it must be really tough on me, but in fact I've been blessed with good health all this time, and the Sonogawa Group has prospered too. What better fortune could I wish for?"

"But you've never been able to leave this house, have you? It must be such a lonely life here."

"Maybe it is. But I also have several thousand employees, and servants who take good care of me."

"That's just an excuse. You're fooling yourself," Moe said contemptuously.

Hanako smiled once more. "Thank you, Moe. I'm so happy that you can sympathize with me." Moe caught the sarcasm behind Hanako's effusive words of thanks, and dropped her gaze. Paying her no attention, Hanako continued, "I've never thought father was a particularly bad person. He was very gentle with me, and I learned all kinds of things from him. If he did ever think of what he did as a crime, beginning to share that with me was a first step in atoning for it. What kind of a father was he in your home? I believe he used to visit you often and was affectionate with you, wasn't he?"

Moe grimaced. "I can't remember," she said. "He might have been affectionate, but so many terrible things have happened that I no longer know what he was really like. All that I can remember about him is that he was a good listener, that's all. My mother was shrill and always complaining, and I'd fly into a rage, but he'd just quietly take it."

This was the first hint of genuine intimacy that Hanako had sensed from Moe. "I can't tell you to love him," she said, "but I'd like you to keep that image of him in mind from now on. I am glad we could meet today. As long as you keep our secret, we should both be able to retain some modicum of happiness. Oh, it just occurred to me—you haven't eaten any breakfast, so perhaps you'd like to take some home with you? This bread is really delicious, even if I do say so myself. But please take whatever you wish."

Hanako rang the bell on the table. Instantly the maids appeared and cleared the breakfast table in a flash. Inohara appeared out of nowhere and spirited Moe away almost as if she had been one of the plates.

Left on her own, Hanako slowly sipped at the freshly made tea.

After a while, she summoned the housekeeper, Mrs. Ishimoto, and asked her, "Did Moe take some toast home with her?"

"No, she only took items that are hard to find in the stores."

"Is that so?"

It was just as she'd thought, but still she couldn't help a sigh.

III. Kaiho Miki

Seeing the gloomy look on Tsuji's face, Hanako surmised that Kaiho Miki wouldn't be coming that day.

"Is she still in the hospital?"

"Yes."

"How is she doing?"

"Not good. It appears she was given tranquillizers last night too."

Hanako tried to picture what the hospital room for drug abuse patients was like. It was probably small. And bare. Maybe with iron bars over the window. However much Miki yelled that she was a clone of Sonogawa Hanako, nobody would pay her any attention. That must be so galling, and lonesome.

Father had told Hanako early on about Miki. Miki, for her part, had already known before the age of ten that she was a clone. Her surrogate mother was an emotionally brittle woman, and often when Father was due to visit them she would put him off saying she had to work, and would then cling to her young daughter crying that they had been abandoned and that he had deceived them. Seeing the tears running down her mother's face, it can't have been that hard for the elementary schoolgirl to draw the truth out of her.

One evening, Miki had asked her father, "Am I a storehouse for spare parts?"

Later he had excused himself to Hanako, telling her how, when Miki had fixed him in her gaze, her childish face contorted by confusion and rage, he had felt compelled to tell her the truth.

He had been honest with her, explaining that given the nature of the synthetic growth-form organs upon which the fortunes of the Sonogawa Group were riding, the clinical trial had to be conducted on a young child. He had confidence in the technique, but considering the possible dangers, however remote, he decided to conduct the trial on his own child. His wife had agonized over the decision, but eventually she, too, had given her consent and supplied her eggs. In order to minimize the risk to his child, during the fertilization process he had secretly created a number of siblings—clones, in other words—with organs that could be transplanted without fear of rejection if anything did go wrong.

A year after Hanako was born, her mother was left unable to bear any more children following a traffic accident—a fact that became widely known since she had been taken to a hospital outside the Sonogawa Group. Her father grieved for a while after the unfortunate accident, then revived one of the fertilized eggs he had in storage. There had been some concerns over Hanako, who had apparently suffered multiple organ failure and had her kidneys replaced with the synthetic growth-form organ, and whose growth was delayed, but the main reason was that he wanted more of their children, even if it meant borrowing someone else's womb.

Father had grasped Miki's hands tightly and made her listen carefully to him, the same as he did with Hanako whenever he had something important to say to her. "Maybe you are a storehouse, but only for one spare part. More importantly you are one of five sisters, all of whom are precious to me. It was in order to love you that I gave you life."

Miki had been satisfied with this answer. However, her mother's fits of anxiety continued to affect her, and the nuance of his words had transformed over time. Although he had explained the situation to her, in her mind this morphed into him having convinced her, then to her having fallen for his smooth talk, and eventually to him having deceived her.

If he really loved her, then why couldn't she live with him in his mansion, just like Hanako? And why did she have to be laughed at by all her classmates for being his love child?

He had often taken Miki's hand, looked her straight in the eye, and told her, "I have already given your mother enough money to buy a handsome house, but sadly she's so worried about the future that she just saves whatever I give her. It's tough being teased by your friends, but it'll only be worse if anyone ever finds out that you're a clone. I thought about adopting all of you, but you all look too alike to have come from different mothers, and I didn't want all my cute daughters squabbling over their own worth, so I gave up the idea."

Miki's heart must have been tossed about like a small boat in a storm. And Hanako thought that she, too, was partly responsible for Miki's life having fallen apart. The day she had turned twenty and was formally notified by the doctors that regular artificial organs would now suffice, a deep happiness had quietly enveloped the Sonogawa family. Seeing Hanako's brightly smiling face, her father had said he wanted to share their relief with Miki right away.

Giddy with joy and fairly skipping as he rushed over to Miki's, he had no doubt broken the news to her without a second thought. She was fourteen at the time, and had apparently just snorted and said, "So I'm no longer needed, right?"

He had reached out his hand to her, intending to clear up the misunderstanding, but she had slapped it away, grinned, and turned her back on him. Miki's first admission to the narcotics ward in the police hospital was just two days later. Five years later, her mother had burned her bank book with its inflated balance, swallowed a massive overdose, and left this world.

"Tsuji," Hanako said to the private secretary at her side, "does Miki still eat toast by picking out a hole in the middle first?"

"It seems so. The mornings she has the energy to eat, that is."

Most likely Miki no longer remembered what that meant. But it still made Hanako feel a little better.

"Do whatever you can for her, won't you?"

"I will," Tsuji answered, as terse as ever.

IV. Kunikida Konomi

Hanako gazed up at the sky, which was the soft pale blue of frosted glass.

The thought that this would be the last meeting brought with it mixed feelings of relief and lonesomeness.

She narrowed her eyes against the breeze that rustled the tablecloth as she awaited her guest on the terrace. It was such a pleasant morning that she was tempted to go back to bed and doze—

although if she did so, the doctors would probably turn white as a sheet and rush to her side.

If she hated her father for anything, she thought wryly, it was the fact that the synthetic growth-form organs were too good. Children who always got straight As would have their ears boxed if they brought a B grade home, whereas children who always got Cs would be allowed to play late as a reward for getting a B. No doubt she would similarly be better off if she hadn't been so healthy. If she had ended up receiving organs from her clones, she would almost certainly have been allowed a little more freedom to make up for the remorse she would have felt.

"I'm just too blessed, aren't I?" she sighed to herself, and laughed drily.

"Ma'am," she heard Inohara's voice behind her, "Miss Kunikida is here to see you."

"Good morning," came an energetic voice just moments later.

Hanako turned in surprise to see a woman with a dazzling smile standing there. Konomi was still just twenty-four years old. She was wearing an unbleached linen jacket, a rose-pink blouse, and narrow-striped straight pants—a getup that made her look even younger than she was. Her head was slightly tilted to one side in delight.

"You must be Konomi. I'm Sonogawa Hanako."

"Pleased to meet you. Thank you for inviting me here today," said Konomi, and promptly bowed.

Hanako was flummoxed: she had never met anyone so full of life before. She felt a little dizzy. Konomi's body in the bloom of health came like a slap in the face. Her liver was natural, not manufactured, as were her kidneys, heart, thighbones, and ribs. Unlike Hanako, Konomi was fully original. Hanako had not even been tempted by the thought of receiving transplants from either Midori or Moe, much less from Miki. But seeing Konomi standing there before her, she couldn't help wondering whether her real self would have been so round-faced, or whether if she dyed her own hair chestnut it would look so floaty, or whether if she practiced some sports her body would be so firm. She couldn't repress the indescribable envy bubbling up within her.

"Please don't stare at me like that! You're making me blush!" Konomi shrugged her shoulders prettily.

Hanako smiled wryly. "Please take a seat. Let's have breakfast together," she said, indicating the chair.

"I would love that. But first, shall we take a walk in the garden? Only if you're up to it, of course."

Inohara's eyes popped wide open. Mrs. Ishimoto, standing at a discreet distance, shot a disapproving look. But Hanako stood up. "Yes, let's," she said. "Although not for long, since everyone will worry."

Konomi led the way, stepping lightly onto the lawn. She almost bounded along the shrub-lined paths of the stroll garden, which was a blend of Japanese and Western styles.

"So what about the security pat-down?" she asked lightly, gazing up at a Chinese parasol tree.

"The what?"

"Ever since this breakfast meeting was decided, Mom has been giving me a hard time about how you're like a goddess to the Sonogawa Group. She said you'd have a bunch of strict bodyguards and doctors around you."

"That's a bit of an exaggeration, although it's true that I'm treated more carefully than other people."

Konomi turned smartly on her heels and looked at Hanako. "I'm glad to see you looking happier than I'd imagined. Pardon me for saying so, but both Mom and I have been worried about you."

"About my physical condition? There's no need. As I already informed you, I shan't be requiring any of your organs—"

"No, no," said Konomi, interrupting Hanako's explanation with a brief wave of her hand. "Not that. It's just that you have to bear such a heavy responsibility. I dare say it's been easier on you since Father—the former company president passed away, but having to encourage all the employees . . . I don't think I could have coped with that. I think it's amazing you can do it so calmly and meticulously."

"Thank you." Hanako didn't know what else to say. She hoped everyone in the medical treatment room didn't take fright at her pounding heartbeat and come to interrupt them.

Konomi looked down and then squatted by a violet in the shadows and stroked its petals with her forefinger. "The reason I suggested a walk in the garden was to avoid anyone else from hearing my impudent answer."

"Your impudent answer?"

Not taking her eyes off the violet, Konomi lowered her voice a little. "I will gladly accept the formal document renouncing any claim to my organs, and your offer of whatever financial support I wish for. I feel bad about the fact that I've already received more than enough up until now, but I suppose that's your way of drawing the line."

"If you accept it as such, that's enough. Well, perhaps I can be frank too. To be honest, that's what it is, although it's embarrassing for me to say that sort of thing myself."

"That's a relief." Konomi stood up abruptly and faced Hanako, a puzzled look on her face. "Hanako, you'll finally be able to gain some freedom now, won't you? That's great. Mom and I have always been aware of what a burden we must be to you."

She was being altogether too kind. Hanako was beginning to have doubts about her. "Konomi, don't you feel any hate for Father and me?"

"Yes, I do! A lot!" She was pretending to be cheerful but there were tears in her voice. Here we go, thought Hanako. Just like Moe, she'll start crying on me and then make demands. "I can't even begin to tell you how much I hate you! Why did Father have to be the president of a large company? We're just nice people, so why couldn't we live together? I really, really hate him, and you, and the circumstances we found ourselves in."

"Live together?" This was not the answer Hanako had been expecting. She felt confused.

Tears began welling up in Konomi's eyes—genuine tears. "It didn't have to be in such a grand mansion as this. A small house would have been just fine. Mother might have been called his lover or his mistress, but that wouldn't have bothered her. And me too, I'm sure I'd have been able to get along with both you and my real mother before she passed away. I wanted all of us to live together. I wanted the sort of life where we'd eat watermelon together on hot days, and get together around a hot pot on cold nights—where we'd all do our best to make each other happy, and really feel a response from each other. Just receiving the monthly allowance, being loved only from a distance, and not even having the chance to give up a part of my flesh and blood in sacrifice—for me it wasn't worth having been cloned."

What a martyr! thought Hanako. But unlike Moe, there was no hint of her putting on an act. Konomi was utterly sincere. Trying to find meaning to her life through service, being almost ridiculously compliant, she was the mirror image of Hanako's own base existence, living solely for the Sonogawa Group.

Hanako gently laid a hand on Konomi's trembling shoulder. It was the first time she'd touched one of her clones. "Konomi, you really are happy, aren't you? That's why you can afford to imagine what unhappiness must be like. No, please don't make excuses. I'm delighted for you. Really I am."

Letting out a sigh, Hanako started back along the path. "Well, let's have breakfast. We'll be making more work for the maids if we let it get cold. What sort of bread do you like?"

Konomi gave a tearful smile and replied, "Toast. But I'm embarrassed to eat it in front of other people. Father used to enjoy picking a hole in the middle and eating that first, and I got the same habit from him."

Still with her back to Konomi, Hanako closed her eyes. *Father, did you hear that? Father!* she called silently, over and over again. *She remembers! She remembers you for what you were—simply a completely average, ordinary, wonderful father.*

Hanako slowly turned her head and stole a glance over her shoulder at Konomi.

"Do you know why he used to do that?"

Konomi looked up abruptly. She gazed up at the slightly overcast sky, a nostalgic look in her eyes. "He was opening a window onto life. Sticking his fingers into the bread like that and savoring the morsel he picked out, he could connect to life for a moment, and by peeking through the crust frame he would get a glimpse of the world in the next moment. That's why, he'd joke, it expressed the joy of life."

Hanako was paralyzed. She felt as though her father was standing right beside her. The father she should have hated. The father she couldn't hate. She could hardly blame him for entertaining an ideal approach to life that included how to eat toast.

Hanako had wanted to talk with her sisters about the toast dream. And she wanted them all to smile together about how good it was to be his daughters. And she wanted them all to say, face to face, "Our lives haven't been in vain. Through our father's company we have been able to contribute in some small way to nurturing precious lives and people's happiness."

Hanako finally managed to free her tongue. "Konomi, did you love Father?"

"Of course!" came the emphatic answer from behind her.

Tears rolled from Hanako's eyes. She had the feeling that an enormously complex conflict, while no less complex or puzzling, had somehow been dispelled. Happiness swelled within her and, doing her best to smile, she turned round. "I'm so pleased I met you, Konomi."

"Me too. But I really think it would be better not to meet again."

Hanako nodded.

The sky was a beautiful frosted glass. Hanako gazed up at it and murmured quietly, "I wish we could all be happy."

V. Sonogawa Hanako

The changeover to the new company president was completed without further ado. As always, Hanako relied on Tsuji to help her orchestrate everything from within the residence.

The morning broadcast to employees was reduced from daily to weekly, but neither the company nor the public forgot about Hanako, and the moving story behind the success of the Sonogawa Group's synthetic growth-form organs was talked about for many a year thereafter.

After several years, Kosaka Moe put in a request for an absurd sum of money, which Hanako was able to meet by selling the residence. She bought a small house for herself, taking with her Mrs. Ishimoto and just three maids. Inohara continued to serve her until his legs gave out from rheumatism, and Tsuji was succeeded by his equally competent son. This same son made the arrangements for Mrs. Ishimoto's funeral, and carried her body from Hanako's house himself. With the death of her housekeeper, who had been like an aunt to her, Hanako sank into melancholy despite herself. As if to rub it in, Moe chose this moment to put in another visit but was quickly dispatched by Tsuji's son, who spread the statement of assets out on the table and told her, "Too bad."

Before she knew it, age spots began appearing on Hanako's face. The Sonogawa Group continued to display the portrait of her as a young woman, which was said to ensure the company's security.

Hanako no longer sent her secretary out to find out facts about the company for her, but dividends from her shares provided her with a reliable livelihood, and she was satisfied with that.

The synthetic growth-form organs had lasted far longer than expected, yet they continued to function smoothly, and ironically Hanako outlived all her clones. In the end, it was her brain that was the first to show signs of weakness.

She moved to a private suite on a geriatric ward, where she continued to record the weekly broadcast for company employees— the only time she appeared in full command of her faculties and managed not to drool. At times she mistook her own name, but by then there was no longer anyone who might wonder whether she was confused about who she was.

On the morning of her one hundred fourteenth birthday, she was picking out a hole in the center of her toast as usual, when she suddenly realized that she couldn't move her fingers.

"But that means I can't see any further than this!" she grumbled as the toast fell from her grasp. "It must be time for me to be relieved of my duties, Father."

And with these words, the moving story of Sonogawa Hanako came to an end.

Tachihara Tōya

Translated by Nancy H. Ross

I couldn't see her.

— 1 —

School began again in early April. For a part-time instructor at a university, it was the most depressing time of the year. It was always so nerve-wracking: a new school year, new students, a new atmosphere, new personal relationships. Even if I used the same textbook every year, there was one thing I could do nothing about: the agonizing, interminable entrance ceremonies. I never got used to them.

People often told me that after teaching at the same university for five years I should have been accustomed to all that. That just showed they'd never been teachers. The students are different every year, and their personalities differ depending on what year they're in, their majors and the class. Depending on what they're like, you have to keep changing the way you teach and the way you interact with them.

The first class is critical. If you fall on your face then, it will take almost the entire school year to win the students over. They'll just keep on ridiculing you, hating you or complaining about you. These days, professionals are hired to conduct teacher evaluations. The students can write whatever they want because the surveys are anonymous. Although I told myself I shouldn't care, I inevitably looked at the results and then felt depressed and hurt afterwards. If there are a hundred students in the class, you'll get a hundred different takes on your teaching. And even though I knew there was no way I could please everyone, I have to admit those evaluations got me down.

Still, I couldn't quit my job. As a woman with a master's degree, I couldn't have hoped to find another job amid that recession, especially with a background in the unmarketable humanities. Even part-time jobs were hard to find.

I sighed and then checked my suit to be sure I looked all right. Of course, it's unacceptable to look scruffy or wear tacky clothes, much less try to look younger than your age. You have to maintain a dignified air appropriate for an instructor.

I took a deep breath and started down the hall, double-checking the room number on the roll sheet: Building D, Room 201.

Just outside the door I took another deep breath. The bell had rung two minutes before. As was typical for the first class of the year, the students were apparently already in the classroom. I could hear a buzz of conversation, though they weren't talking as loudly as I'd expected, so I concluded there must not be many troublemakers in the class. I was half relieved and half worried. Troublemakers disrupt the class, but they also keep things lively. There's nothing worse than a class full of quiet, unresponsive students that you can't get a reaction out of. Maybe I'd get lucky.

I nervously opened the door. There was silence for a moment.

"Please take your seats." The students dutifully sat down. They're always well-behaved at first. I looked around the room. There didn't seem to be anyone who'd cause trouble. As I passed out the attendance cards, I checked the name and face of each student, trying to decide which ones were likely to be absent, which ones were likely to cause trouble and which ones were likely to study hard.

There were thirty-six students but thirty-seven names on the roll sheet. Was someone late? Or absent? Maybe someone had decided to drop the class. But it was a prerequisite. If they dropped the class, they'd have to repeat a year. Only a complete fool wouldn't at least show up.

Thinking perhaps someone was repeating the class, I took another look at the roll sheet. In that case, it would make sense. That happens all the time. But the students were all freshmen. That meant I had a problem. If someone was just late it would be OK, but . . .

I quickly counted the attendance cards, which had been passed up from the back of the room. Thirty-seven. Thirty-seven? I counted them again. Thirty-seven. There was no mistake. I counted the students. Still thirty-six.

Maybe someone had asked another student to fill in their card for them for the first class. Oh, well. All I had to do was check.

I smiled, introduced myself and then talked about the unique aspects of the Chinese language and how interesting its pronunciation was.

"OK, now I'd like you to give it a try."

I turned over the attendance cards, shuffled them several times and pulled one out. I called the name of the student whose card I had pulled. The student stood up, looking embarrassed.

"Don't worry," I said. "Just speak up. Try the first tone. Good. Like that. High and flat. Speak up. You have to open your mouth wide for this 'ah.' Not like when you speak Japanese."

At first the students were hesitant. Encouraging the shy ones, I had each of them practice the pronunciation and gently corrected them, pulling out the cards one at a time. That way it would be easy to tell who was absent.

I was down to the last two cards. One of them had to be for the student who wasn't there.

"Okuno."

"Here."

He was present. I glanced at the last card: Yamano Kyōko. *So, she's the one.* Just to make sure, I called her name in a serious tone. I waited a few moments, but, as I expected, there was no reply.

But for some reason there was no reaction from the students. Ordinarily, if a student didn't reply when called on, the other students would look at each other and start whispering among themselves.

I called her name again, in a louder, slightly irritated tone. "Yamano. Yamano Kyōko. Are you here?"

This time there was a buzz in the classroom. Well, of course. A mere freshman didn't have any business pretending to be present right from the first class. I may have been a part-time instructor, but I wasn't that dumb.

"Yamano-san, I have your attendance card, but you don't answer when your name is called. What is that all about? Are you here?"

I decided to explain how tough my class was going to be: I would warn the students that no absences or tardiness would be excused and that points would be taken off for reports or assignments that were not turned in. I figured that would keep the class quiet for the whole year. Just as I started to speak I was surprised to see the entire class looking not at me but at an empty seat in the back left corner of the room.

"Poor Yamano-san," a student in the front row said nervously while staring at me with a clearly critical gaze. The other students nodded in agreement.

"Why are you saying she's not here?"

"Yamano-san is crying."

"She answered when you called the roll, and she's standing too."

"And she did the pronunciation both times."

"You're mean!"

"Don't cry, Yamano-san."

"You're picking on her!"

"I'll report you to the Human Rights Office!"

I must have had an idiotic look on my face. I couldn't understand what the students were talking about. There was no student standing; they were all seated. Some were looking at me while others were staring at the seat in the back corner of the classroom. That was all. And the chair hadn't been moved a bit. It was still pushed under the desk. There were no textbooks or writing materials on it, no bag beside it. And there was certainly no crying student.

What was this all about? Was it some new prank? Were the students trying to make fun of me? But these were language students chosen randomly from among the five hundred students in the Economics Department. They couldn't have known each other. In fact, most of them could have only just met. They couldn't have been so friendly with each other as to gang up on me. And I couldn't believe that all thirty-six of them could put on such a convincing performance.

All that went through my mind in an instant. I moistened my lips. There had to be some way to resolve this peacefully. After two or three classes we'd be able to chat in a friendly manner. Once that happened I'd collar a few students and ask them about what had happened today.

"I see. It seems I couldn't hear you. I'm sorry. Please take your seat."

It was merely a formality, but I nodded slightly in apology. I couldn't really understand what was going on, but the atmosphere in the classroom was awful. An immediate revolt was likely.

I was still getting dirty looks, and there was still some murmuring going on, but the students were settling down. I quickly wrote "Watch out" on Yamano Kyōko's attendance card, but at the time I really didn't understand just what I needed to watch out for or how.

My mind was somewhere else for the last thirty minutes of class. I just went through the motions, doing the same sorts of things I do every year: pronunciation practice, some simple tongue twisters. If I hadn't had classroom experience I probably would have been frozen with fear. I'd never been so happy to hear the bell signaling the end of class. Relieved, I announced that class was over and then sighed deeply.

But why did the class act like a student who clearly wasn't there was? Had they taken an instant dislike to me and decided to waste no time before harassing me? Or was there some other reason?

I felt like crying as I erased the blackboard. I gritted my teeth. *I can't let them get to me*, I thought. Even if it was harassment, I was going to have to teach them for an entire school year. I muttered to myself to hang in there and then slowly left the classroom. Dashing out, I figured, would be just what the students wanted me to do.

Just as I was about to close the door, I glanced back once more. Rays of mild spring sunlight slanted into the empty classroom. Sure enough, there was no one at the desk in the back left corner. No one at all. I shook my head and rubbed my temples. I suddenly felt very tired.

— 2 —

Yamano Kyōko sat in the back left corner for the second class as well. Or I should say she seemed to be sitting there. I couldn't see her. But no matter how carefully I examined it, the handwriting on her attendance card was completely different from that of the other thirty-six students. One day I tried passing out the cards one by one. There were thirty-seven, and I handed them all out, which meant I must have seen Yamano Kyōko. But I had no recollection of her— just the attendance card filled out in her beautiful handwriting.

I got scared to call on individual students, so I had them practice pronunciation by rows instead. At any rate, as always, I tried to make the classes upbeat and pleasant. Perhaps it was my imagination, but the students' hostile attitude seemed to have lessened somewhat.

I asked the students to practice in twos or threes. One boy turned to the desk in the back left corner and, as if speaking into the air, said with a big smile, "Yamano-san, your pronunciation is really good. Will you work with me?"

A chill ran up my spine. My arms and legs felt like icicles. I felt myself going numb. I couldn't see Yamano Kyōko, but the students could. It wasn't just an act.

I felt like I was going to throw up. Struggling to appear calm, I somehow made it through the class. I stumbled out of the classroom and rushed into the teachers' room. Luckily, the part-time Chinese teacher I shared the class with was there having a cup of coffee.

"Excuse me, Ms. Wang, do you have a minute? I'd like to ask you something about our students."

Ms. Wang turned around. She was a middle-aged teacher with years of experience. I felt myself calming down as I took in her serene, mild expression.

"It's about the class of freshman economics students. Have all thirty-seven of them been coming to class? Is anyone absent or late?"

I couldn't ask about Yamano Kyōko directly. Ms. Wang smiled broadly.

"No, no problems at all. They're a serious, quiet class. Oh, and that one student has such good pronunciation. She may have studied Chinese in high school."

"Really? I hadn't noticed. Who's that?"

Ms. Wang's eyes widened with surprise. The student must have been really outstanding. I was ashamed because I'd been so concerned about Yamano Kyōko I hadn't been paying enough attention to the other students.

Ms. Wang paused as if she were trying to recall the student's name. After a few moments, she smiled and said, "Oh, yes. Yamano. Yamano-san."

It took me a few moments to take in Ms. Wang's reply. Yamano? There was only one Yamano in that class.

"Yamano? You mean Yamano Kyōko?"

"Yes. So, you thought so too. She's an excellent student."

So, Yamano Kyōko really existed. It wasn't a prank by the students. Choosing my words carefully, I looked up at Ms. Wang and said, "I can't seem to place her."

"Really? She's a pretty young woman. Long black hair, fair skin, always neatly dressed. She speaks a little softly, but her pronunciation is very good. And she always comes to class prepared. She seems a little shy, but she's very popular with the boys."

I mumbled some vague acknowledgment. In any case, there was no one fitting that description in my class. There may have been students with long hair, but I couldn't recall any with good pronunciation. A neatly dressed, popular girl? There weren't any of those around anymore. I hadn't seen one in several years.

But the smiling Ms. Wang hardly seemed to be lying. Maybe she could see Yamano Kyōko, just like the other students. So, was I the only one who couldn't see her? Why couldn't I see Yamano Kyōko or hear her voice? I closed my eyes, counted slowly to twenty and told myself to calm down. Maybe I'd be able to see and hear her next week.

That was it. It must have been because I was nervous. Or maybe it had something to do with the light and where she was sitting. Maybe that's why I couldn't see her. Or maybe Yamano Kyōko skipped my classes and the other students had all conspired to cover for her. I worked myself into a sweat contemplating all sorts of possibilities. It was a strangely warm sweat that left me with an unpleasant feeling.

— 3 —

I still couldn't see Yamano Kyōko. A month passed, the Golden Week holidays were over, the rainy season had begun, and I still couldn't see or hear her. When I casually mentioned her to Ms. Wang, there was no particular reaction. I wondered if Yamano Kyōko was really attending Ms. Wang's classes. Thinking perhaps I was being tricked by the students, I casually questioned several students I'd become friendly with. But the reply was always the same: Yamano Kyōko was an outstanding student. That wasn't all. Just as

I embarked on a serious explanation of grammar, Yamano Kyōko bared her fangs.

Whenever I asked if there were any questions, invariably several students turned to the desk in the back left corner and began whispering. Then one of them would raise their hand.

"The Japanese translations of these sample sentences are the same, but the Chinese is different. Why is that?"

Here we go again. I tensed my stomach muscles and suppressed an urge to cry.

"That's because there's more than one way to convey the same meaning, just like in Japanese."

Another consultation began, and then another hand went up.

"But there must be a difference in the nuances. If it's exactly the same meaning, there wouldn't be any need for two expressions."

Not again. Trying not to look fed up, I stared reproachfully at the textbook. Ever since we'd started on grammar, the questions from this class had been unusually nitpicky. They had gone beyond being pointed and were more like the questions a native Chinese speaker might ask to pick on a Japanese teacher. It seemed to be the sort of plot in which the instigator got those around her to pose the questions rather than do it herself and then sat there sneering.

All the students who asked difficult questions consulted with the empty desk in the back left corner. The instigator must have been there. So, that seat *wasn't* empty. I couldn't see or hear her, so Yamano Kyōko was using her minions to badger me and enjoying it.

She must have resented me for ignoring her during the first class and was getting her revenge. Was she peppering me with questions on fine points that even a Chinese person wouldn't know the answer to and then enjoying watching my reaction? Or had she won the students over to her side in an effort to force me out of my job because she'd lost face?

The bell rang. "I'll answer that question next week," I said and closed the textbook. The student who'd asked the question didn't pursue it any further. Just as I was thinking what a relief that was, I felt a sharp pain in my stomach and broke out in a nervous sweat. I took out the stomach medicine I'd put in my bag and popped some into my mouth. I washed it down with some water from a plastic bottle and the pain seemed to ease somewhat.

A student who was heading out looked at me worriedly and asked, "Are you alright?"

"Yes, I'm fine, thanks."

"Keep your chin up!"

Oh no. My students were starting to feel sorry for me and worry. Did they regard me as a bad teacher who was being picked on by good students? Apparently so.

But I still had my pride as a teacher. I had to do something. I dragged my weary self to the teachers' room and plopped down on a couch. I'd been getting the runs every Wednesday morning since May. I couldn't sleep at all the night before. Then in the morning the diarrhea would start. I'd get a headache and feel nauseated. It was clearly a case of not wanting to go to school. How pathetic. But unlike the students, I couldn't skip class. I couldn't take time off. So I took the local train and got off repeatedly to dash to the station restroom. It took me more than twice as long as usual to get to work. But I had to go.

Looking worried, a teacher from France with whom I was acquainted said, "You've lost weight, haven't you?" She brought me a cup of hot tea. I took the cup from her and held it in both hands. The warmth radiated throughout my body. My eyes filled with tears, and I hurriedly looked down into the cup to hide them. I was becoming timid, losing my mental equilibrium. That wouldn't do. I had to pull myself together.

I noticed a stack of quizzes I'd tossed onto my desk and leafed through them, my hand trembling. Yamano Kyōko's handwriting leaped out at me. She had beautiful handwriting, like that of a calligraphy teacher. And she always got a perfect score, never any less. Her penmanship and her writing were so refined that you couldn't discern any individuality in them. It was creepy.

It was clear not only from her attendance cards but also her quizzes that Yamano Kyōko existed. Nevertheless I still couldn't see or hear her. I couldn't even see her belongings. What was to be done?

I wondered if there was something wrong with me. Perhaps I was somehow different from other people. A doubt that I'd only vaguely entertained, that I'd been ignoring, grew and began to weigh heavily on me. I seemed to be the only one who was different from everyone else, so maybe I was sick. But I couldn't bring myself to go to the doctor because I was afraid to acknowledge my mental illness. I was afraid of losing my job, of losing people's trust and, most of all, of admitting that I was not normal.

After agonizing over this, I talked to a friend of mine, a guy I'd met when I was studying abroad. He was five years older than I was and worked for a company in Hong Kong. He was hard on himself and always had sound advice to offer. He could be a bit difficult at times, but I had a lot of respect for him because he spoke frankly. He wouldn't hesitate to offer criticism, no matter how harsh. It was hard to find people like that.

I contacted him by e-mail asking when he'd be available and then called him by IP phone, so it was really cheap. I explained the situation from the start, trying to keep calm. He listened carefully without saying a word. That alone made me feel a lot better. If he'd said the whole thing was ridiculous right off the bat I might have been depressed and become desperate.

After I'd finished telling him the whole story, he slowly began to speak. "This is just a theory, but maybe you recalled some unpleasant memory or trauma associated with that student's name or her appearance. So you unconsciously blocked her out, because if you acknowledged her presence those forgotten memories would come back. That student has to exist. She's sitting there taking your class—and maybe harassing you. I think that's because she realizes you're ignoring her. Anybody who was ignored or treated like they were invisible would get angry. No wonder she's trying to harass you."

"But," I said, "if it was just a matter of not being able to see her I'd understand, even if I concede that your theory explains why I can't hear her either. But then why can't I see her belongings? The chair is pushed under the desk, and there's no sign that anyone is sitting there."

"Maybe that's just your imagination too. Anyway, I'm not a professional, so I can't really say. You need to see a doctor. If you're too busy, you can go during summer vacation."

There was nothing more I could say. He'd made up his mind that I had a mental problem. I hung up the phone, folded my arms and pondered the situation. Was there something in my past that I wanted to forget? Some trauma enough to make me obliterate all recollection of a person? Some sort of shock that I'd completely erased from my memory?

No matter how hard I thought about it, I couldn't come up with anything. There were no gaps in my memory. I'd had the usual worries and pleasures. I'd had no unusual experiences, and nothing stood out in my memory. I looked through my photo albums but couldn't find anything.

"So," I asked myself, "how am I going to solve the problem of Yamano Kyōko?"

— 4 —

I started going to the campus library after class to look through old roll sheets and yearbooks. Perhaps there had been another student named Yamano Kyōko. Perhaps she'd died in a car accident or something. In that case I could have understood. Then it wouldn't have been a problem with my mind but a problem with Yamano Kyōko herself. If Yamano Kyōko were not just an ordinary person, the answer would be simple. It would have been a supernatural phenomenon or something, the sort of thing I'd sneered at in the past. I had believed things like that were impossible.

But now it was different. What if some student had been killed by an instructor and chose one teacher to harass every year? It wouldn't be unusual for a university to have a legend like that. And you couldn't tell the instructor in question about the legend or you'd be cursed. That seemed possible.

I searched frantically. There had been several students with the same name, but they had all graduated. None of them had died while in school.

Next I did a computer search for old newspaper articles about anyone named Yamano Kyōko. Even if it had nothing to do with the university, if only there were some related incident or person. But my hopes were dashed. I couldn't find anything like that. Disappointed, I was slumped over the computer table when I heard the light tapping of the keyboard of the computer next to mine. No one had been there a few moments before. *When did that happen?*

Thinking it odd, I looked up and was dumbfounded to discover that no one was there. The chair was pushed under the desk. There was no room for anyone to sit down. But the computer's keyboard was clicking away. I gasped and peeked at the screen. An ordinary word processing file was open, but the page was blank. Nevertheless the flashing cursor was moving rapidly across the page as if someone were typing invisible characters.

"Yamano Kyōko-san?" I whispered.

The cursor suddenly stopped moving, and the keyboard fell silent. There was no reply. Or perhaps Yamano Kyōko had said yes and I just couldn't hear her. I didn't know what to do.

"Well . . . ," I said in the direction of the invisible person, then grabbed my bag and stood poised as if to flee. My knees were shaking, and my pencil box escaped my faltering grip and crashed to the floor.

Oh no! I thought. Just then I felt something cold, slimy and squishy touch my finger. The pencil box was pressed into my hand as if someone had picked it up for me.

"Oh, thanks."

Who or what was it? Yamano Kyōko? I staggered to my feet, stumbled to the exit and pushed the door open. That feeling, that indescribable feeling when my index finger was touched. I felt like I was going to faint.

No way did that thing belong to a human being. It couldn't have. But that didn't mean I should have known what it was—that squishy, slimy, cold something.

Suddenly I wanted to burst out laughing. Was I crazy? Did I have an overactive imagination? Had I entered some sort of fantasy world? Perhaps the White Rabbit would come rushing past. Or perhaps I'd be crushed by a dinosaur, or carried off on a great adventure by a troll, or possessed by a ghost.

I must have been running for a while. I came to a fountain at one end of the campus. I dipped my hands in and splashed water on my face. Its coldness brought me back to reality.

Did Yamano Kyōko actually exist? Was she really of this world? Was she in fact attending my class? If only I knew that much. Yamano Kyōko was invisible only to me. Was that my fault or hers?

I dipped one hand into the fountain again. The refreshing cold penetrated my body to the core. I told myself to calm down. *That squishy thing was just an illusion. Nothing like that could possibly exist. It had to have been my imagination.*

As I told myself this over and over, it began to seem true. *Yes, it was an illusion. I'd been tired and frightened. I'd imagined something that didn't exist.*

When I calmed down it seemed comical. Perhaps I was seeing Yamano Kyōko. *Of course. Yamano Kyōko exists.*

Look, there she is—the one with the straight, long black hair down to her waist, the fair skin, the downcast gaze and the almond-shaped eyes with the long lashes. Her lips are red, and she has a slender neck and sloping shoulders. She always wears a white blouse and a knee-length navy blue skirt with black leather shoes and white socks. Her bag is . . . Yes, a black sailcloth rucksack. Her pencil case is made of denim and showing signs of wear. There are pencils and an eraser inside. Yamano Kyōko doesn't use mechanical pencils or ball-point pens.

She dresses neatly and is popular with the boys. She's the epitome of the sort of proper young woman who is no longer to be found. Of course she doesn't use a loose-leaf binder. Environmentalist that she is, Yamano Kyōko uses a notebook of recycled paper on which she has written in elegant characters: "Chinese 101." She always sits at the left end of the back row. She's an A-student who gets perfect scores in every subject. She's especially good at Chinese. Yes, when she was a girl Yamano Kyōko lived in China on account of her father's job. She came back to Japan in the sixth grade. So she still speaks Chinese like a native.

Yamano Kyōko is modest, so she doesn't dare ask questions. She asks the students sitting nearby to do it for her. She is a traditional Japanese woman who behaves modestly and does not assert herself. That's why she speaks softly. When I stand at the lectern I can't seem to hear her, though she is speaking as loudly as she can—even to the point of being unladylike. I'll have to show her more consideration. She has studied calligraphy and is already licensed as an instructor. She has instructor certificates in tea ceremony and flower arrangement as well. She studies the koto in her spare time. Of course, her parents didn't push her. She pursued these interests of her own volition.

Yamano Kyōko is perfect. Yes, perfect, but she doesn't brag about it. She is refined. She was tops in her class throughout junior high and high school. She chose this school because it was a Christian college, because it was near her home and because there were a lot of opportunities to volunteer. Yamano Kyōko is compassionate. She's been involved in volunteer activities since she was a girl. She couldn't decide whether to be a nurse or a social worker, but in the end she decided she should major in economics and seek to end economic inequality.

She enjoys helping her elderly grandparents and stays at their home every weekend. Her grandfather is in his eighties and unsteady on his feet. Yamano Kyōko helps him bathe and changes his diaper and never utters a word of complaint. She doesn't get angry with her senile grandmother, even when she becomes hysterical. Yamano Kyōko smiles angelically, even when tackling the most disagreeable tasks. On weekdays, after class, she busies herself with volunteer activities. She calls on students to donate blood, gathers signatures on petitions, collects donations and helps out at nursing homes. Yamano Kyōko is good at sign language and Braille, and in her free time she serves as a volunteer interpreter.

When she gets home it's after 10 p.m. At last she has time to eat dinner and take a bath. Then weary Yamano Kyōko does her homework. She's always exhausted. But she keeps smiling. Nothing makes her happier than helping others. Everyone thinks Yamano Kyōko is an angel. You may respect her, but to be dismissive of her is out of the question. If you hurt her feelings, others will harshly criticize you. Yamano Kyōko is a goddess. She must not be crossed. She is the law. She is everything. She is the world. Yamano Kyōko exists. She really does.

I felt much better, as if a thick fog around me had suddenly lifted. I stuck my head in the fountain. Yamano Kyōko existed. She had and she always would. There was nothing to worry about because Yamano Kyōko was real.

— 5 —

After that, classes went surprisingly smoothly. Yamano Kyōko smiled pleasantly and no longer asked mean-spirited questions. The students got fed up with my bad jokes and smiled wryly, but they completely stopped displaying a defiant attitude.

My stomachaches, diarrhea, headaches, nausea—all that was beginning to go away. Yamano Kyōko existed. I wondered why I hadn't realized such a simple thing before. She was filling out her attendance card, taking quizzes and responding to class surveys. There was no evidence that she wasn't there, so she had to exist. She was undeniably there in the desk at the left end of the back row—the popular, prim and proper A-student who was always smiling. She had to be there. There was no mistake about it.

If anyone was mistaken, it was me. So that thing that had touched my hand in the library had to have been no more than an illusion, a product of my imagination created by my doubts. Yamano Kyōko's hands were white, soft and delicate. They were certainly not squishy, slimy, clammy or cold.

Once I rectified my error, things improved almost too much. The students behaved sweetly, classes went smoothly and quiz scores improved significantly. I began checking each person's pronunciation again. Yamano Kyōko's pronunciation was excellent. It was not only like that of a native speaker, but a touch of a Shanghai accent made it seem perfect. Except for the fact that she spoke too softly and it was difficult for me to hear her, there was no problem at all.

Summer vacation was approaching. First-semester final exams were given in mid-July. After talking it over with Ms. Wang, we decided that I would give the written test and she would give the oral test. Before long I received a fax from her with the results of the 50-point oral test. Conscientious teacher that she was, Ms. Wang had written a comment about each student and the reasons for each of her scores. Ōno was often absent, so she took five points off his score. Tanaka lost seven points for talking too much in class. Satō got three points extra for his diligence.

Thinking I should be more like Ms. Wang, I looked over the scores, picturing each student. My gaze rested on the last line: "Yamano Kyōko: 50. Perfect." Of course, Yamano-san was different from the rest. Even a native Chinese speaker gave her a perfect score for her pronunciation. No doubt she'd do a great job on the written test as well.

I made a 50-point written test and sent it to the departmental office. All I had to do next was to wait for the answer sheets to arrive, score them and submit the grades. I had another two weeks. So far the class had been mostly self-study and teaching to the test. We'd studied the parts of the textbook that were on the test, so the remaining classes were a sort of an optional extra. The students must have known that, because most of them quit coming to class. They were no doubt busy studying for other language tests or writing reports. I was no ogre, and I'd done the same thing when I was in college, so I just looked the other way and deducted the same number of points I would have for tardiness.

I prepared a handout to help the serious students study for the test and passed it out. I told them to review it and raise their hands if they had any questions. It was a piece of cake. I'd still get paid, so the job wasn't all bad. Several boys dragged their chairs to the back left corner to get Yamano Kyōko to help them. They asked her questions intently and nodded repeatedly. I wondered how good Yamano Kyōko's teaching method was. Being able to explain something to poor students who were likely to fail in a way they could easily understand was just what you'd expect of an A-student. No one but Yamano Kyōko could have done it.

I strolled slowly around the classroom with my hands clasped behind my back. Students peppered me with questions, and I explained each point thoroughly. Occasionally I looked up and caught sight of the back left corner. It seemed that Yamano Kyōko was still explaining something.

Going from desk to desk, I came to Yamano Kyōko's last. The boys looked up at me. Yamano Kyōko must have said something, but her voice was so soft I couldn't hear it. To avoid hurting her feelings, I smiled enigmatically and looked at the boys. One who was habitually late said, "Yamano-san said she can't explain this part."

"Which part?"

"This. I think I understand the function of *le* after a verb, but I don't really get how it works at the end of a sentence."

"Oh, that's a tough question. Even grammarians sometimes have trouble explaining that. I think it's too soon to get into something so complicated, but if the basic meaning and function would be enough, I'll explain them."

Yamano Kyōko must have nodded. The boys moved back so I could face her.

I began to explain, using various examples. Of course, Yamano Kyōko understood, but it was difficult to explain it to the other students. I told Yamano Kyōko that even I, who had been teaching part-time for years, found this grammar point difficult so she didn't need to feel bad. I wondered what the other students thought as they watched me conversing amiably with Yamano Kyōko after I'd thoughtlessly ignored her and made her cry during the first class.

I hoped they'd think that we'd finally made amends in the weeks leading up to summer vacation. Most of all, I wanted Yamano Kyōko to feel that way. I just wanted her to forgive me, to accept me. It would take a load off my mind and ease my conscience a bit. Then I'd be able to start the second semester feeling good. I hoped we could just put the unpleasantness of the first semester behind us.

"Do you see?" I asked Yamano Kyōko and the boys gathered around her. Of course, I figured she understood. The problem was the boys. Just as I expected, they frowned and muttered.

"Well, at this stage it doesn't matter. For now just study the use of *le* after a verb. The *le* at the end of a sentence is in the grammar section of the textbook, so I'll explain it again later."

"So, that means it won't be on the test?"

"No, it won't."

Once I said that, the atmosphere improved noticeably, and the students seemed relieved. I was not the sort to preach about how studying was not about tests and grades but about acquiring knowledge. Most students just took language classes because it was a requirement or because they'd heard that language skills would help them get a job.

Anyway, from my perspective it was certainly preferable to have as few students as possible fail the class. Even if they didn't study and it was their own fault, failures still left a bad taste in my mouth. Other teachers told me I worried about that too much, but it was my nature, and I couldn't help it.

"Will there be listening on the test?" a student in the front row asked. I headed in that direction.

"No. I told you that before, remember?"

"What about pinyin?"

"Of course that will be on the test."

Just having this sort of ordinary conversation with the students made me happy. It was a good feeling. Until I came to believe in Yamano Kyōko's existence, I couldn't even kid around with the students. I'm sure I must have been a short-tempered, unpleasant teacher. I'd have to redeem my reputation and be a better teacher in the second semester.

I was sorry when the bell rang. I'd felt that way for the last two or three classes. Until then I had looked forward to the bell as the only way to escape my torture.

"Good luck on the test." As I watched the students hurry out of the classroom, I felt an extraordinary sense of happiness. All thirty-seven students were charming in their own way: the good students and the bad ones, the serious students and the lazy ones. It was the first time I'd been so attached to a class. It was no doubt thanks to Yamano Kyōko. She had become the class leader, motivating her classmates and bringing them together. I was truly grateful to her.

The rays of the summer sun did not fall on Yamano Kyōko's desk. Her seat by the window was empty and in the shadows. She must have left before I realized it. I'd wanted to apologize and thank her. Oh, well. I could tell her next semester. We still had half the school year. There was plenty of time.

Just as I was about to erase the blackboard I was startled to see that it was already clean. I could tell it had been erased by a meticulous person because the marks all ran in the same direction.

But wait. I could still hear the pleasant sound of the eraser working its way across the board. Someone was still erasing it. *Someone.* I instantly realized who it was. I smiled broadly, nodded slightly, and turned toward the moving eraser.

"Thank you, Yamano-san."

The eraser came to a stop for a moment and then moved up and down slightly as if to say "you're welcome." Yamano Kyōko had nodded in return.

"I expect you to do well on the test," I said.

The eraser moved rapidly up and down as if flustered. Yamano Kyōko was embarrassed, although she was certain to get a perfect score. Her pronunciation was almost better than mine. What a charming student. So refined and modest. Such a wonderful personality. "Keep up the good work next semester."

The eraser moved up and down again. I nodded in response.

Yamano Kyōko's shy smile was no doubt beautiful. In a perverse sort of way I was glad I'd been able to make her smile. I blushed.

"Bye then," I said. *"Xià xuéqī jiàn.* [See you next semester]." I grabbed my things and left the classroom. I glanced back over my shoulder. The blackboard was spotless.

Yamano Kyōko was standing there.

— 6 —

I wasted no time grading the final exams. The few students I'd been worried about made a final push at the end of the semester, so they'd all be able to continue in the second semester. With that worry off my mind, I headed to China for my summer vacation. It's true that it's dangerous to travel around China alone, but you also get a lot out of it. I was exhausted, and the trip would boost my energy and give me the courage to face the future.

My research focused on the religions of ethnic minorities, so I headed for a remote area in the mountains of Yunnan Province. It wasn't unexplored, but no one went there unless they really had a penchant for the offbeat. It was my third trip there.

Perhaps the villagers had taken a liking to me after my several visits, but for the first time they agreed to show me an idol I'd never been allowed to see before despite my repeated requests.

Mumbling something about how thrilled I was, I headed off with the villagers. The idol was deep in the recesses of a cave. Or I suppose it was. I stood motionless amid the people as they bowed their heads in prayer.

I couldn't see the idol.

There was nothing but the sound of the villagers' prayers drifting off into the abyss.

But I was neither impatient nor flustered. Some things are visible to others, even if you can't see them yourself. I seemed to be the only one who couldn't see the idol, but it was there nevertheless. There was no reason to be puzzled.

I joined the villagers in prayer and took a deep breath. The chilly air in the cave irritated my throat and stung my lungs. Suddenly I recalled the touch of that limp, amorphous, squishy, slimy, icy thing—that thing that had touched my hand in the library. Yamano Kyōko's hand.

I shook my head vigorously and focused on the cave. That was all in the past. It was something I'd dreamed up, something that couldn't possibly exist, something I'd never feel or see again. After offering a humble prayer, I quietly went outside.

"Did you see the god?" the village chief asked me in heavily accented Mandarin, flashing his yellowed teeth.

I just smiled. I don't know how he interpreted that, but he simply muttered, "Really? So you saw it then." His utterance had a cryptic tone to it.

Three days after I got home from China the second semester began. It was the first week of October. After spending quite a while trying to decide whether I should wear long sleeves or a jacket over short sleeves, I settled on a light knit ensemble. I'd gained a little weight, so I decided not to wear the pants and put on a black flared skirt instead. I wore a pair of loafers that were comfortable when I had to be on my feet for a long time and decided to take a large nylon tote bag I used year-round. I put in the second volume of the textbook, a brand new electronic dictionary I'd bought, and my pencil box. After tossing in a paperback book for reading during the commute, I was all set.

Just as at the start of the school year, I always felt nervous before the first class of the second semester. After summer vacation, students are less motivated, and occasionally there are some who no longer take their studies seriously. I had to be prepared to deal with them.

I didn't need to take the local train any more. I didn't want to skip class. I was no longer being harassed by Yamano Kyōko. Although I was still a little nervous, I took a limited express train and arrived at the university without having to get off and go to the restroom.

I nodded to the other instructors in the teachers' room. I'd never been good at making conversation, and I was particularly nervous that day. I sat down at my desk and looked over the roll sheet. All thirty-seven students would be back.

Ms. Wang passed my desk, and I hastily got up and bowed deeply. Perhaps she didn't notice, but she hurried off without saying anything. It was embarrassing to be ignored like that. The other teachers must have seen what had happened. Without looking up, I hastily sat back down, opened the textbook and pretended to read it.

The first bell rang. Class would start in five minutes. The teachers began to get up, busily rinse out their coffee cups and make sure they had their handouts. I grabbed my attendance cards and took a deep breath. I double-checked the classroom: Building D, Room 201.

Taking deep breaths to calm myself down, I waited for the bell, which soon rang. I stood up, gathered up my things and headed down the hall. Some students were running while others dawdled. Others were standing around talking. *Don't they have class this period?* I wondered.

I stood outside the classroom door. Hearing the familiar voices of my students, a wave of fondness washed over me. We were about to work together for another semester. I put on a smile and flung the door open.

But none of the students headed to their seats. They were still standing around happily chatting away. Some of the students had changed a lot over summer vacation—girls whose makeup was now heavy, boys who'd dyed their hair blonde.

But still, why weren't they paying any attention to me? Their teacher had opened the door and come into the classroom and yet no one had paid any attention. Finally, I slammed the door shut. The noise would certainly get their attention and they'd hurry to their seats.

But still no one turned around. Not only did they not take their seats, they didn't greet me either. I wondered what was going on. I stood at the lectern with a dignified air, determined not to show any weakness. I banged my books down on the lectern.

"All right, the bell has rung. Quiet please!" I said, clapping my hands. But still no one moved. I broke out in a cold sweat. Were the students picking on me? Had they thought up some new kind of deviltry? Was I the only one who thought we'd repaired relations? Had they been waiting for a chance to harass me?

"That's enough!" My voice was a little shrill, but I couldn't help it. I did manage to keep myself from trembling, though. I had to maintain my authority. If I let them make a fool of me I'd be finished as an instructor.

"All right, we're going to have a quiz." Saying there will be a quiz gets a reaction from most students. It's unhappiness, of course, but at that point I just wanted some sort of reaction, unhappiness or otherwise. Still there was no change in their attitude.

"Fifteen minutes have passed. That's enough!" I said in a loud voice. I stamped my foot like a spoiled child and banged my books on the lectern repeatedly.

Still the students kept on chatting as if nothing had happened. Only a few of them had taken their seats. I was standing there in a daze when I heard the girls in the front row talking.

"The teacher's really late. I wonder what she's up to."

"Do you think class will be cancelled?"

"There wasn't a notice on the bulletin board."

"She's not too bright. Maybe she went to the wrong classroom."

The students laughed.

This can't be happening. I'm here. I'm standing right here, right in front of you. I keep trying to get your attention. See, my books are right here on the lectern. I'm going to pass out the attendance cards now. Then will you notice me?

I'm here. I am here.

I felt like crying. I bit my cheek so hard I could taste blood. That seemed to be the only thing that confirmed my existence.

I walked between the students, who continued to ignore me, and put an attendance card on each desk. Ordinarily they would have immediately begun writing their names on their card. Ordinarily. But not today. No one paid the slightest attention to their card. What was going on? What were they up to? What were they doing to me?

"Class is cancelled after thirty minutes if the teacher doesn't show up." Suddenly a gentle, sweet voice, like a heavenly melody or the song of a bird, rang out. I looked around to see where that unfamiliar voice had come from.

A girl was sitting in the back left corner. She had long, straight black hair, fair skin and beautiful, almond-shaped eyes.

"Yamano Kyōko-san?" Couldn't she hear me either? With her delicate, slender white fingers she silently took up her attendance card and tore it in half. Then she giggled.

"The teacher's *still* not here."

"Somebody go to the teachers' room and look for her."

The biggest troublemaker in the class dashed out of the room.

Wait. I'm here. I'm right here.

"Thirty minutes is up."

"Class is cancelled!"

"Let's leave."

"What a drag."

"She should have at least notified us that class would be cancelled."

The students cursed me as they gathered up their things and prepared to leave.

Wait. Don't go! I'm here. I'm right here.

I tried to grab the arm of one student who was on his way out, but my hand passed right through it. What was going on?

Yamano Kyōko abruptly stood up. "Let's go," she said. She was the only one looking at me. She must have been able to see me.

"Yamano-san, what's this all about? Why is this happening?" I shouted in confusion. I no longer cared about appearances. Yamano Kyōko sneered. Her callous, icy expression sent chills down my spine.

"Yamano-san! Yamano-san!" She was the only one who knew I was there, so I had to ask for her help.

The door closed, and the lights went out. All the students had left. I was the only one left in the classroom. *I'm here, here in the classroom. I exist. Somebody—anybody—notice me!*

— — —

Notice

To: All freshmen in Chinese 101, Wednesdays at 1 p.m.
From: Department of Economics, X University
Subject: Cancellation of classes

All classes for the month of October will be cancelled, and a new instructor will take over in November. The classroom and time will remain the same. Please check the bulletin board for information on make-up classes.

— — —

They couldn't see me. None of them could.

189

LEST YOU REMEMBER

Takano Fumio

Translated by Jim Hubbert

Valery Ivanovich Selyotsky rode his bicycle—the only bicycle one was likely to see in the city of Alma Ata—past the eternal flame in Heroes Park. It was well past the hour for starting work, but the midday heat was yet to come. Streets were bustling but not crowded, faces were not yet tired. The previous night seemed to have purified the sky. It was the time of day when everything was most beautiful.

Selyotsky pedaled past the flame and circled back, as if something occurred to him. He slowed, stopped and put a foot on the ground. The sentry a short distance away acknowledged the professor with a friendly wave. (*And if this were Leningrad? Impossible!*) Selyotsky raised a hand in reply.

The flame fluttered in the wind on its black platform of polished stone. Selyotsky never tired of gazing at it, not so much out of respect for these heroes who had died defending the Motherland decades before—(*But not with a complete lack of respect!*)—but because its beauty was a source of wonder. Sometimes, when he was in a particularly fine mood, the scripts of all the languages of the world seemed to flow into each other in the shifting flame. He almost had a feeling that with more skill, he might be able to read the message in the fire.

Today was such a day. The words on signs and posters, the inscription on the plinth beneath the bronze statue of the Heroes of the Motherland, the text on the scrolling roll signs of buses—all seemed poised to reorder themselves into some extraordinary message.

He set off again on his bicycle.

Selyotsky had been riding like this to work for several years now. Everyone along the way had come to recognize him as the bespectacled Professor Bicycle. The old women in the bazaar (*Show some respect! Call them, instead, the Mothers of Russia*) knew he was a bachelor, a specialist at the university in a field of no interest to anyone, and a man with a fondness for snow melons. Professor Bicycle lived alone, yet each week he bought a whole basket of melons.

He used the bicycle only when the weather was fine, but he still thought it made him so conspicuous that he briefly considered giving it up. This was unnecessary; no one in Moscow and Leningrad went anywhere by bicycle, and he had drawn no attention there either.

As he arrived at the campus, he was waved down by the departmental secretary. His presence was urgently required in the rector's office.

Selyotsky was shown to a reception room off the office of the rector, where he found a tall, stooped man with white hair, a heavyset military officer, and a young man whose eyebrows joined above the bridge of his nose. Selyotsky recognized only the older man, the rector of Kazakh National University. His pulse quickened automatically. The rector introduced Assistant Professor of History Valery Ivanovich Selyotsky to his guests: Lieutenant Colonel Kazhegeldin of the Strategic Rocket Forces and his "assistant."

Kazhegeldin was a Hero of the Soviet Union. He was wearing the Order of Lenin and the Order of the Red Star. Selyotsky did not recognize his many other decorations. With a generous smile, the raven-haired colonel extended a hand so massive it might have been sheathed in a winter glove and forcefully shook hands with Selyotsky, who smiled his hypochondriac's smile and hunched his shoulders even more than usual. He was fond of being told that this made him resemble a famous American movie actor.

"This is an unofficial visit. Please relax. I'm told you want to do some digging," the colonel began without preamble. He sank magisterially into a leather chair.

Selyotsky had surmised the purpose of the meeting as soon as he saw Kazhegeldin. The professor's reports and petitions ran to hundreds of pages, and he had often speculated how a discussion with the military might play out, but he found his proposal surprisingly difficult to summarize.

"Excavations, yes, this is true. But actually, I haven't even reached the survey stage."

"The survey stage? Survey for what?"

Kazhegeldin had read the proposals. Surely he knew the answer.

Later, Selyotsky could not recall precisely the details of this meeting between a scientist-rector, a hero of the nation, and a minor scholar of history. But somehow he managed to describe his evidence for the Huang Hua culture (the name meant Golden Flower), the possible location of its archeological sites, and its unique writing system.

The Huang Hua were a footnote to the history of the Silk Road. They were no great power, nor were they known for craftsmanship, the beauty of their women or the quality of their horses. True, the name cropped up from time to time in old texts, but most historians assumed it was a tiny village, perhaps an oasis, vanished like so many others centuries ago.

"The Huang Hua appear in texts from the seventh to thirteenth centuries. Based on evidence from a number of sources, I have concluded that their territory was in the Alatau Mountains, between the so-called northern and southern steppe routes. This was no village. It was at least a kingdom, a civilization with its own arts and scholarship.

"Discovering a previously unknown kingdom along the Silk Road would be remarkable enough, but the Huang Hua also had a system of writing that was completely unique."

The rector winced. If the professor started in on the Huang Hua writing system, things were likely to get out of hand. Even the gist of the theory would probably take all morning to cover.

Selyotsky had not built up his usual head of steam. He yielded to the rector's signal without a struggle, cutting himself short with ". . .as I believe you will have read in my reports."

The Hero of the Soviet Union nodded. He did not ask questions.

"So far," said Selyotsky, "I have examined the Kozlov Expedition's reports at the Institute of Asian Ethnography in Leningrad. With co-operation from the authorities, I've checked every relevant source in the Soviet Union, as well as texts in the possession of important foreign universities.

"Texts that mention the Huang Hua—Chinese, Tangut, and Arabic texts—are so few that I was able to examine them all personally. Texts with Huang Hua glyphs are so rare that many scholars doubt their existence.

"Some maintain that these strange symbols are smudged Chinese characters or brushwork that bled through the page. Others have said that I'm misidentifying Tangut grass-style calligraphy. Such criticism might have been justified early in my research, but not now. If a new text appears, I know instantly if I'm dealing with Huang Hua glyphs, and most linguists support me. My theory of Huang Hua culture is now generally accepted among specialists."

This was stating the case a bit too forcefully, but Selyotsky didn't believe it was untrue.

"Very interesting, Professor. I see from your reports that the number of texts is limited. I asked other specialists for their views. With due respect, it seems your theory is not as widely accepted as you make it out to be. This may not be a full-fledged writing system, but some kind of code used by spies. I would tend to agree. It's easy for someone in my profession to believe there was a need for such things even then—just as there is today."

Kazhegeldin laughed, a short, strong laugh. His one-eyebrowed assistant stared woodenly at Selyotsky. "Perhaps you should devote yourself to deciphering old texts instead of proposing pointless excavations," said the colonel.

This was the most reasoned dismissal Selyotsky had encountered. The previous rector had blocked his proposals with a single warning: "Don't provoke China." Local party officials acknowledged his proposals but never commented. Leningrad always dismissed his theory with the same threadbare arguments.

"But sir, as I think you'll agree if you consider the process of deciphering ancient writing systems, it's vitally important to submit new texts to academic scrutiny, texts from previously unexplored ruins and religious sites. Think of the Kozlov Expedition at the beginning of this century, or Britain's Stein Expedition. The texts they discovered were as important as Einstein's relativity is to physics!

"Of course, texts alone are not enough. There must be academicians with the skill to appraise them. The Kozlov texts held the key to the Tangut writing system, yet our scholars overlooked them. The first scholars to decipher Tangut were Japanese! Professors Solovnov and Kuchanov later criticized their analysis, but still—"

The rector cleared his throat. The colonel gazed at Selyotsky with something like pity. Nothing of a specialist nature had been said so far. To Selyotsky, the subject was straightforward, even deserving of wide interest. But he knew when to give up. He might be a blinkered specialist, but at least he had risen this far. He understood this silent coercion.

"Sir, if you would refer to my report on the importance of identifying new texts. As for the location of the Huang Hua kingdom, it should be somewhere in the Alatau Mountains, between the northernmost oasis route and the steppe route. If a certain Chinese text is fact and not a legend, the site would be close to the Chinese border, in a small basin surrounded by mountains.

"Extensive excavations in the high mountains, with no roads or even shepherd's trails, would of course be next to impossible. But I wonder . . . It's merely an idea, but if there were satellite images one might examine—with supervision, of course . . ."

The colonel and his assistant exchanged glances.

"Or perhaps your staff could do the analysis based on my theory as to where—"

"I'm sure this approach would make sense. From your point of view." The colonel stood up slowly. "Comrade Selyotsky, I'm glad we had this talk. I can't promise anything yet, not officially. But rest assured that your request will receive the consideration it deserves."

In other words, rest assured it will be shelved indefinitely.

The colonel's assistant had said nothing since the introductions, but as the two men were leaving he turned to Selyotsky. "Of course, this could go a long way toward rehabilitating the late Professor Moiseevich."

Selyotsky was startled. Moiseevich's compendia of ethnic legends had been suppressed; they conveyed the unsound impression that superstitious, unscientific thinking still existed in the Soviet Union. Only a few specialists knew his work. Those who did kept quiet. Without thinking, Selyotsky asked the assistant if he was a historian.

Again Kazhegeldin's clipped, burly laugh. "Absurd! He's a graduate of the conservatory."

"Really?" said a chastened Selyotsky. "I apologize. An artist . . ."

As soon as the two were gone, a handful of staff members burst in from offices off the meeting room. Their faces were pale with excitement. Plainly they had been listening behind the doors.

A young physics instructor with an elated look—*fanatic* was the word that occurred unbidden to Selyotsky—stepped between him and the rector. "An artist? 'The Conservatory' is a euphemism for the Military-Diplomacy Academy of the GRU. That was no assistant. That was an elite member of the Central Intelligence Directorate!"

That night, for the first time in his life, Valery Ivanovich dreamed in brilliant color.

Before he left his apartment the next day, Selyotsky had a call from the departmental secretary. He had been summoned to a military installation outside the city. He was to be there at two o'clock.

The destination was technically within the city limits, but too far for the bicycle. In fact Selyotsky was completely unfamiliar with the area. He felt a twinge of anxiety, but the secretary had volunteered to drive him, and he agreed thankfully.

Under different circumstances it would have been an enjoyable outing. The afternoon was not unpleasantly hot, with a cloudless sky above the mountains. Alma Ata's elevation was at least eight hundred meters, with some parts of the city above a thousand. To Selyotsky, born and raised in the Moscow basin and educated in low-lying, marshy Leningrad, a thousand meters was the Himalayas.

Alma Ata, the "City of Apples"—Almaty in Kazakh, to be more linguistically precise—was the sprawling capital of the Kazakh Soviet Socialist Republic. Kazakhstan was second only to Russia among the Soviet republics in terms of area. Alma Ata had a million people and an imposing cluster of modern high-rises at its center. The southern skirts of the city overlapped the foothills of the Zailiysky Alatau Range, the northern rim of the Tian Shan mountain system.

To cosmopolitan Muscovites, Alma Ata was a developing city of central Asia, an unenlightened place for the capital of a republic, though levels of literacy and education were surprisingly high. Still, the main reason Selyotsky, born in Moscow and educated in Leningrad, had chosen Alma Ata over the Institute of Asian Ethnography was that Kazakhstan offered the best odds for discovering texts that others had overlooked.

Zakharova's car—yes, that was the secretary's name; she had appeared a few weeks earlier but completely escaped Selyotsky's notice—sped along the road, seemingly straight into the mountains. The peaks were capped with snow even this late in the year. Sage-green conifers, almost black in the distance, stood out against the whiteness like a giant's whiskers. The sky was pale blue, a high desert sky with a dry wind, as dry as the wind in Siberia. Though he had spent most of his thirties and early forties here, Selyotsky still marveled at the beauty of this scenery, this atmosphere.

Despite her thoroughly Russian name, Zakharova was strikingly Asian, probably ethnic Korean. She was too thin. Her narrow eyes clashed with her round, wire-frame spectacles. She had hollow cheeks, slender eyebrows, and fine hair pulled impossibly tight over her head and gathered in the back. Selyotsky appraised her as close to thirty. To call her attractive would have been insincere even as flattery. At least she wasn't ugly.

They reached their destination sooner than he had expected.

Formalities and identification checks detained them briefly at the gate, but the guards seemed cordial enough. Zakharova parked farther than necessary from the main building and said she would wait. She handed Selyotsky a leather-bound folder and told him it contained various academic papers supporting his theory. He had already cited key passages from these papers in his reports and doubted that a senior officer would bother to read them, which made this little gesture less than impressive. But it was easier to take the folder than to argue about it.

As he left the car and started toward the building, Zakharova leaned out the window and called after him. The folder was German, of high quality; a foreign professor at her previous workplace had given it to her as a gift. He was to leave the contents and be sure to bring the folder back.

Not to leave the folder would be inelegant, but it couldn't be helped. There would only be more unpleasantness otherwise.

Selyotsky was ushered into a spacious room that evidently served as Kazhegeldin's office. The tanned senior officer of the Strategic

Missile Forces greeted him with an expansive smile. Soon they were alone.

"Please make yourself comfortable. This is an unofficial meeting." As he echoed his remark of the previous day, Kazhegeldin settled into a leather armchair. The conversation was probably being monitored. Still, if they were about to go over the same ground, being taped was better than suffering through another interview with that one-eyebrowed representative of state security and a clutch of military intelligence types.

The colonel connected the power cord to an electric kettle and added coffee powder to two cups.

For a few minutes they chatted innocently. Because of his educational track and for medical reasons, Selyotsky had never served in the military even briefly, and he had no idea what it would be like to exchange small talk with one of these people. Kazhegeldin described his recent trip to Moscow, his visits to the opera and the Bolshoi Ballet, and the latest educational programs. Selyotsky found himself surprisingly indifferent to talk of his native city, and the colonel's ballet stories went completely over his head, but he seized on the topic of television eagerly.

"It's not our domestic programs that interest me."

"Foreign programs?"

"Yes. A few weeks ago, television crews from China and Japan traveled through Kazakhstan to Uzbekistan, like a modern-day Silk Road caravan. I only heard a few details, though."

"Oh, those people. Yes, I know all about them. I went to the meetings."

"I hear the army pulled out all the stops. They even gave permission to film in areas that are off limits to foreigners."

"They did visit a restricted zone. But that doesn't mean there was anything to see." Kazhegeldin chuckled. "They will return home and report that the Union of Soviet Socialist Republics has changed since Yuri Andropov became general secretary. Nothing sensitive was filmed."

"Really? But then, you see . . . What sort of zone would be off limits even to our own researchers?"

"Nothing has been declared off limits. Isn't that why we're having this chat?"

Kazhegeldin downed his strong coffee and went to a glass-fronted display cabinet filled with oriental ceramics. Selyotsky had been glancing at them since he arrived. The colonel chose one and brought it over. It resembled a white porcelain tea bowl.

"I won't say when or where this was made, but I suspect you have an eye for this sort of thing. Now do you understand why I asked for this meeting? I read your reports, the one on that ancient text in particular. I found it quite astonishing, to say the least."

Selyotsky's pulse quickened. He fought the tremor in his hands as he took the bowl. He looked it over quickly, peered inside, looked at its outer surface again, looked at the inside again. He turned it over and checked the foot. There was no signature. The walls of the bowl were astonishingly thin and beautiful. The milky porcelain was covered with a diaphanous green glaze and utterly unadorned. Wherever it came from, the object was mesmerizing.

Selyotsky peered into the bowl again. It seemed unaccountably large, though his hands nearly encircled it.

Kazhegeldin's "ancient text" was a rare dual inscription in Chinese characters and Huang Hua glyphs, apparently from the first half of the fifteenth century. That would place it late in the reign of Xuande, the fifth Ming Emperor.

Xuande had an unquenchable passion for porcelain. He dreamed of surpassing the porcelain produced during the reign of his grandfather, the Yongle Emperor, and he scoured China and the lands around it for outstanding potters. At last he found what he was seeking. Two Huang Hua potters, a husband and wife, were taken from their home and brought to the imperial capital. At Xuande's orders, they began to experiment with new forms of porcelain. They would not be allowed to return home until they succeeded.

After nearly seven years, the potters presented two bowls to the emperor. Xuande took one and peered into it, and transfixed by its amazing beauty, he forgot the world and himself.

They showed the second bowl to the guards, then the court officials, and finally the gatekeeper. The Chinese plunged into forgetfulness, and the potters escaped and returned to their homeland.

Selyotsky felt a spasm of fear, but he could not take his eyes off the bowl. Suddenly his field of vision seemed to shimmer, as if heat waves were rising. A ringing sounded deep in his ears. His mind was shrouded in fog.

"That's enough!"

Kazhegeldin placed a huge hand over the bowl. Selyotsky gasped. His mind cleared abruptly. He was soaked in cold sweat, as if he had almost fallen down a staircase.

They stared at each other. After a moment the colonel's intent expression dissolved into laughter, as if he couldn't resist. "You weren't taken in, I hope? It's just a Chinese souvenir!"

Selyotsky gazed back stupefied, ashen and dripping perspiration. Kazhegeldin's words washed over him like a foreign tongue. But like a man who is told that the "poison" he thinks he has been given was a placebo, the historian slowly regained his senses and the crisis passed.

"I'm fond of these little souvenirs, you see. I get my pilot friends to pick them up. I'm sorry. I didn't know you were so suggestible." Kazhegeldin gently took the bowl and replaced it with a cup of coffee.

"How could it be anything but a legend? Even if such an object existed, it couldn't be privately owned. It would have to be in a museum as part of the nation's heritage. Of course, it would have to be displayed upside down. Or covered with a lid."

"Colonel, don't tell me you brought me all the way out here to play me the fool!"

"Of course not. I just wanted to chat and get to know you. To expedite the disposition of this matter. Do you know the best way to conduct friendly diplomacy? Coming to terms is only part of it. You have to create relationships. An environment where people can engage in small talk."

The colonel gave another hearty laugh. Selyotsky did not know what to say. He downed his bitter coffee and was seized with a fit of coughing.

Later he could not remember what else they discussed. He was filled with the fury he felt as a child when his fellows routinely played tricks on him and made him the butt of their jokes. He handed Zakharova's folder to the colonel, snatched it away after Kazhegeldin had removed its contents, and beat a hasty retreat from the fortress of the Hero of the Soviet Union.

This must have been some kind of test. Yes, a detailed evaluation of reactions and behavior. There would have been dozens of officers and intelligence agents monitoring him with cameras and microphones. The colorless university professor might be a Chinese spy!

When he returned to the car, Zakharova was putting a transistor radio, an earphone and a small sketchbook into a battered shoulder bag. Before her spread the desert sky and the snowcapped mountains. What a fine time she must have been having! Selyotsky felt a surge of irritation that was almost resentment. At least she didn't comment on his perplexed manner or ask him about the meeting. She stowed her precious folder in the shoulder bag and they started back.

As soon as she reached the downtown area, but before they arrived at Selyotsky's apartment, Zakharova abruptly dropped him and sped off. What an insensitive female! The distance home would have been an easy bicycle ride, but after his interrogation, having to walk the rest of the way home was simply outrageous.

As he turned to look down the avenue for a taxi, a blue car pulled up.

"Excuse me, but you're Professor Selyotsky, aren't you? We met yesterday. At Kazakh University."

To Selyotsky's astonishment, the man who stepped from the car was the beetle-browed GRU agent. "Yes, yes, I am Selyotsky. I'm sorry, your name . . .?"

"Utemuratov. Kassym-Jomart Abayevich Utemuratov."

A typical Russified Kazakh name. For the first time the agent gave him a friendly smile. Selyotsky's face nearly betrayed his sense of alarm. What was this man doing here? Hadn't he been monitoring the meeting with Kazhegeldin?

Of course. Zakharova fled because she'd seen him in her rearview mirror. He must have followed them from the colonel's office.

"What happened?" Utemuratov said a bit awkwardly. "Did your sweetheart leave you in the lurch?" He looked genuinely concerned, even a little embarrassed. This was a nice touch. He was quite the actor. Selyotsky didn't bother to conceal his irritation.

"Sweetheart? Please. Just a colleague."

"A colleague and she treats you like that? What did you do?"

Before Selyotsky could frame a reply, the man burst out laughing just like any silly young person. Selyotsky turned away, saying he had no more time, but Utemuratov urged him to accept a lift.

He was far too tired to walk. He got in the car without a word. Immediately he felt a wave of drowsiness, but sleep was out of the question. Half-conscious, he listened as the man launched into a surprisingly convivial monologue about the lake near his hometown, helping out on archeological digs as a Young Pioneer, and on and on, just as if he were talking to a friend.

Fine, thought Selyotsky. If this playacting was meant to catch him off guard, it was better than being subjected to an interrogation over some trumped-up charge of espionage.

But if Utemuratov was playing the solicitous new friend, something about his delivery was off. At first Selyotsky could not quite identify it, but just before they reached his building the man happened to turn toward him. It was then that Selyotsky saw what was wrong.

The cheerful patter was like a poorly synchronized film dub. The more Utemuratov spoke, the more animated and manic he became. But the look in his eyes was freakish, as if a snapshot of the eyes of someone about to die, someone in the grip of an unspeakable terror but unable to scream, had been cut out and pasted on his face.

When they arrived at the apartment building, Selyotsky mumbled thanks and fled, his mind still foggy.

That evening he pedaled to the market to buy melons and boiled dumplings. There he heard people talking excitedly about a blue car driven by a young man that had plowed into the stone wall of a shop. The car had been demolished.

Writing systems—scripts—were beautiful. Any script, in any language. To Selyotsky, they were all beautiful, more beautiful than speech, perhaps more beautiful than words themselves. He struggled to comprehend why anyone would think the sounds of language were beautiful. People rhapsodized about the emotions called up by poetry, about the music of the human voice. But to Selyotsky, who had no feel for music to begin with, such pronouncements were like being urged to love a woman who failed to interest him on any level. Music was nothing more than clustered sound waves of high and low frequencies.

Writing was different. The elements of writing systems—letters, glyphs, signs, characters—could make him forget words and grammar, sometimes even the shapes and conventions of the scripts themselves. Sometimes, for an instant, meaning seemed to manifest directly, unmediated by any language or system of representation. How pure, how beautiful those moments were.

Like Chinese characters, the Huang Hua glyphs could be broken down into their constituent parts, but these building blocks were hard to identify. Sometimes they changed shape depending on how they combined to make a single glyph, and while one Chinese character might have two or three such elements, most Huang Hua glyphs seemed to be made up of at least seven. Seemed, because his work to classify these segments was far from complete. Often it was difficult to know with any certainty whether what appeared to be a basic glyph element might not be a cluster of other, more fundamental parts. In fact, almost all the known glyphs posed this problem.

The Huang Hua glyphs were also physically larger than Chinese characters. In the legend of the two potters, a phrase that spanned half a dozen characters in Chinese might be represented with a single, massive glyph, as if the Huang Hua were trying to capture the essence of meaning.

The greatest mystery was that enormous, baffling complex of radiating strokes that Selyotsky had christened the Sun Glyph. Its structure was impossible to unravel. Perhaps it was a monad, unique in itself. The accepted view in Leningrad was that the Sun Glyph was a specimen of calligraphy, an elaborate, decorative version of a simpler glyph. But Selyotsky was certain that its complexity was not mere stylized decoration.

If he had not published his reasoning on this point, it was because the character itself seemed to be telling him that was what it was. If he gazed at it long enough, he fell into a sort of dream state. The radiating strokes seemed to merge with his consciousness until a flash of pure comprehension, almost awakening, passed through him. The glyph was an enigma, but Selyotsky was certain it was a unity, complete unto itself. Otherwise, what was it?

Weary after another night of brilliantly colored dreams that thrust themselves under his eyelids without leaving a trace of logic or narrative, Selyotsky had somehow managed to arrive at the campus before noon. The freshness of early summer practically flooded down from the sky, but his head felt leaden.

Sure enough, the driver of the wrecked car was Utemuratov. There were multiple witnesses, a few from the university. On an empty thoroughfare, he had suddenly wrenched the steering wheel to one side and plowed into the wall of a shop without braking. The wreck had to be cut open before his body could be retrieved. A few bystanders were struck by flying debris, but no one was injured seriously.

News of Utemuratov's death had reached the university ahead of Selyotsky. The police and military investigators were already gone. No one seemed to know that Selyotsky was the last person to speak to the dead man. Should he keep silent? He hardly had the energy to come forward and make a statement.

A letter from Kazhegeldin, delivered early that morning, had been posted on the university's main notice board at the colonel's urgent request, or so it was rumored. The man was truly strange. The letter promised that Selyotsky's proposal would be given due consideration—the same response as yesterday and the day before.

Perhaps because the letter brought no news, or perhaps because Utemuratov's strange death overshadowed it, interest in Selyotsky's encounter with the Strategic Missile Forces seemed to have evaporated. His attempts to steer conversation toward that topic earned him more than a few looks of bafflement from his colleagues, as if the meeting had never taken place.

So that, evidently, was the end of that. For some reason Selyotsky felt his spirits wilting quickly. He couldn't seem to focus on his work. He felt a tremendous strain, as if he were facing an impending academic presentation, but the tension found no outlet. His afternoon lectures were delivered mechanically. He was only going through the motions.

Selyotsky was not the only one. The entire university was wrapped in a strange weariness. Classes were nearly deserted. Even the most diligent students were sleeping through them.

But strangest of all was the news that a physics instructor—that "fanatic" who knew the GRU's cover name—had been taken to a local hospital after behaving strangely. On his way back from an afternoon lecture, Selyotsky happened to witness the young man being led away. He had been staring at the notice board for over an hour, as if hypnotized. Not only was he unable to say what he was doing, he could not recall his own name or department.

The notice board in question was, not surprisingly, the same one where Kazhegeldin's letter was posted. If that infuriating missive was capable of sending anyone into a fugue state, it should have been Selyotsky. Why the physics instructor?

Everything was mired in a flaccid paralysis. Everyone was in the grip of some strange power, except Zakharova—she came running frantically after Selyotsky as he made his way out. Her sheer pink blouse was plastered to her breasts with sweat.

"I heard what happened. You went with him after I left, didn't you? Of course I haven't told anyone. That accident . . .it's just impossible! What could've come over him?"

Her outpouring was slightly garbled, but apparently the first "him" was Utemuratov, and the second "him" was the physics instructor. So she had noticed the agent following them after all.

"Some terrible power is at work here," she whispered. "Don't you feel it? If we don't do something . . ."

A terrible power. She did not say what it was, but Selyotsky had a feeling he was about to find out, and this terrified him even more.

Zakharova suddenly plunged her hand into her blouse and drew out an object, a kind of talisman suspended from her neck. It was a leather tube about half the size of her thumb, like a common souvenir but much more finely crafted, with patterns impressed over its surface. A long loop of leather was attached to one end of the tube. A metal ornament protruded from the other end.

Zakharova glanced around furtively, took off the talisman, and hurriedly put it around Selyotsky's neck, hiding the tube inside his shirt.

"Please don't ask what this is. Don't tell anyone about it. Don't let anyone see it. People might criticize you for believing some ignorant superstition. Even if they don't, you still mustn't show it to anyone."

She walked away quickly, as if terrified that someone might see her.

Selyotsky pedaled slowly toward home. He was still groggy, but—was it the talisman?—his free-floating sense of dread had faded. He had never given women like Zakharova a second glance, but maybe she was the type a man would find easy to love. He'd had a string of relationships with some undeniably attractive women. He had even lived with one briefly. None of these liaisons had lasted. Maybe a woman like Zakharova was more suited to domestic life.

As he was absorbed in these thoughts—he had no idea what prompted them—he nearly collided with someone coming toward him. He frantically squeezed the brake levers and put his foot down. He sensed that something deeply significant had passed through his field of vision. It was the same feeling he had when the glyphs tantalized him with pure meaning, always just out of reach. Startled, he looked back.

"Sonia!"

For an instant he was confused. Should he should address her formally, as Sofia Pavlovna, or use the affectionate nickname? But he had already called her Sonia.

His ex-lover turned her head. She looked at him steadily and shyly smiled.

Ringlets of blond hair. The gorgeous smile. She hadn't changed a bit. No—she was more mature, even more beautiful. She had changed completely. Sonia had been Selyotsky's last graduate student in Leningrad. Later he heard she was working for a travel agent. Now, she said, she had just turned a tour group from Leningrad over to a local guide. She had the next two days to herself.

He and Sonia had parted friends. Their relationship taught him that sometimes love simply loses the strength to continue. Now her shyness seemed mixed with acute discomfort, but perhaps it was the frank admiration in his eyes that made her walk straight up to him in the old impetuous way.

"I knew you were at Kazakh University, but I never dreamed we'd meet like this. Still, I knew it was you as soon as I saw the bicycle."

She laughed in that distinctive, husky voice. Selyotsky, still astride his bicycle, felt a syrupy sweetness flowing from his pores. He was well aware of his fundamental suggestibility, a tendency to let the moment carry him away. He had been reminded of this only yesterday with Kazhegeldin's souvenir. But this insight did him little good now.

Her hand was warm. With her little overnight case, her working girl's suit that hid her attractive curves, and the warmth of that soft hand on his cheek, she was summoning the old vertigo again.

They reached his apartment—fortunately without encountering any irate women demanding to see him—just as a courier arrived with a small package from a specialty grocer. Home delivery of merchandise was highly unusual, other than for officials used to special treatment. Selyotsky was puzzled, but he accepted the package. Sonia placed it on the table and gingerly unwrapped it.

It was a snow melon, small but more beautiful than any Selyotsky had ever seen. In Sonia's hands, the anonymous gift looked for all the world like a pistachio-yellow sun, tempting them irresistibly to eat it. He had stocked up on melons only yesterday, and tomorrow he would probably get a complaint for having consumed some party official's misdirected delicacy, but that was nothing to worry about.

Sonia was staring at the melon so intently that she seemed to have forgotten everything, even Selyotsky. As if . . . Yes, as if she were reading some invisible inscription.

Selyotsky gazed at her curls, at her wrists peeking from the sleeves of her jacket, at her makeup beginning to fade after hours without retouching, as if he too were trying to read an invisible inscription.

Melons were alluring. They were the fruit of life, traded as precious objects and split open to quench the thirst of travelers along the Silk Road. Plunge in a knife and they gave off a floral perfume; their liquid was faintly sweet, more faintly piquant, and viscid, flowing endlessly, like the juices of love itself. At oases and in cities lost to memory, travelers must once have placed that delightfully chewy flesh on the tongues of maidens who shared their beds.

Selyotsky gently took the fruit from Sonia. Gravely he inserted a knife. He put a chunk of sweet pulp in her mouth. Then he brought her lips, sweeter than any melon, to his.

Somewhat to his surprise, their old rapport returned easily, even after ten years. Selyotsky was self-conscious of how his body had gone soft, but Sonia's fingers were even more skillful than before, and she quickly made him forget the effects of time. Smoothly, so smoothly he was unaware of it, she unbuttoned his shirt.

"What's this?"

Selyotsky froze. The pit of his stomach tightened. He had completely forgotten it, and now there was no way to hide it. Sonia was boring a hole through his spectacles with a flinty gaze. She gripped Zakharova's talisman tightly.

"This isn't like you. A woman?"

He looked away. Not a lover, he started to say. Just a colleague from the university. But she wasn't listening. Suddenly she pulled hard. The leather cord dug into his neck for an instant, stinging sharply before it snapped. She crushed the talisman with her heel. But what was more frightening was the way she tossed the pieces into her bag instead of into the wastebasket.

Like writing, fetish objects sometimes have the power to relay a person's thoughts. Sonia thrust herself against him, her anger mixed with lust, whispering the word "love" over and over. Selyotsky felt himself sinking into a soft melon sweetness.

A five-colored flag beats against a pellucid sky. Young women wearing garlands of flowers and precious stones unroll carpets of intricate design atop a hill overlooking a city. Young men, singing, bring dishes piled high with rice and fruit. The women answer with song as they dance. Their music shakes the crowns of the imams and rises above the gold and silver spires of the minarets.

Sweet, heavy incense is lit. The burner, shaped like a magnolia, passes from the hennaed fingers of one maiden to the next.

A giant of a man and a wizened old woman inscribe bowls with fine brushes. The bowls are as blue as the dayflower and delicate as a mayfly's wing.

Colored rice is scattered over the carpets. A huge, crimson-purple cloth is unfurled. Its surface is densely embroidered with sacred glyphs. The ecstatic light of the Faith blazes forth in the eyes of all who look upon them. The sightless run their fingers over the glyphs and clutch the cloth reverently to their breasts.

An enormous Sun Glyph dominates the center of the cloth. Its serpentine strokes interlace in intricate ways, distinct yet merged in a supreme wholeness. If only one could gaze on it long enough, perhaps then . . .

Selyotsky rarely woke during the night, but his eyes were open now. Something was shaking him.

It took him several seconds to realize he was not being shaken at all. It was the telephone ringing. For what seemed like minutes he pondered whether to get up and answer it, but it would not stop ringing.

Sonia stirred. Selyotsky finally decided he had to do something before the noise woke her up. But then it stopped.

Sonia muttered in her sleep. He could not catch the words, but her voice brought back murmurs of "love" in his ear. And at that, the dream he had woken from vanished from memory, leaving only a faint fragrance.

He sat up next to Sonia.

Love. It was quite a problem. Of course, for her it was just a relic from the past, like a Huang Hua glyph.

Words are conventions. To study words is like pledging to observe conventions. To use them is to impose conventions on others. The meaning of the word "love" depends on the person using it. It might save a life or open the door to some fleeting amusement. Is there a difference? Spoken or written, words are mere conventions.

Yet is that true? If words in their spoken and written guises are empty conventions, why do people treat them as real? Is it because conventions are useful?

Sonia muttered and tossed fitfully.

What if words have a power that goes beyond convention? Some believe that to speak a word is to exercise power over the thing named. Writing a word invokes the spirit of the thing. Words in an unknown language can exert an ineluctable influence as incantations or ritual prayers. When written, they can become a nexus of power.

Is there an instant when the sounds and shapes of words themselves vanish from consciousness, leaving only pure meaning?

Selyotsky felt vaguely uneasy. Perhaps to reassure himself that she was still beside him, he reached out in the dimness to touch his lover's—his former lover's—back.

He snatched his hand away. She was burning up and soaked in sweat, far too much sweat for their recent exertions. Without the faint light from the lamp near the window, he might have thought the moisture was blood. She was facing away from him. He was leaning over her, trying to get a glimpse of her face, when her eyes snapped open.

Selyotsky choked back a scream. The telephone started ringing again. Sonia cried out in some unintelligible, vowel-heavy language. Her voice was hoarse and high-pitched. Her pupils were dilated and her limbs twitched convulsively. She grabbed Selyotsky's arm and gripped it tightly. Her palms were creased and moist.

Now Selyotsky did scream. Sonia emitted an unearthly sound that might have been a gasp of pleasure or a reproach. She was drooling uncontrollably.

"Sonia! What's wrong?"

But his voice sounded just as freakish and unintelligible in his ears. Reason told him Sonia was in no condition to account for what was happening to her. But reason was losing its grip.

"What's happening? Snap out of it!"

He pulled her to a sitting position and slapped her lightly, hands shaking. He could not bring her out of it. The telephone kept ringing. He jumped off the bed and ran to the telephone stand. Before he put his hand on the receiver, it fell silent.

What was happening? He turned toward Sonia and felt a surge of nausea. Her skin and the sheets were flecked with blood. She had scratched herself deeply, especially across the abdomen. Her glossolalia had distracted him before, but now he noticed that the room was filled with a noise like millions of hard, dry rice grains pattering against the walls. The gap in the curtain caught his attention. He groped on his hands and knees for his glasses, found them, and drew back the curtain.

At first he could not grasp what he was seeing. It was pouring rain—in the middle of the night, at this time of year. Moscow in early summer had rain like this. But Alma Ata? Impossible. Sonia's babbling grew louder, but Selyotsky couldn't turn away from the scene outside.

In the dim light of the streetlamps, someone was running toward him from the telephone box on the far side of the road. The figure crossed quickly, stopped under the lamp in front of his building, and looked up at Selyotsky's window. Where else could she be looking?

It was Zakharova. She had no umbrella and her hair was dripping in the rain. She seemed to recognize Selyotsky standing at the window. She motioned for him to come down.

What was happening? What was she doing here? Then he remembered how Sonia had ground Zakharova's talisman to pieces with her heel.

Would Zakharova sense this? Such folk tales were common. Objects imbued with power called to their makers when the spell was broken. But where was he now? Wasn't he here, in the world with all its brutality, where the Strategic Missile Forces and the GRU suspected him of being a spy? The nausea hit him again. His stomach felt as if it were being squeezed from below.

Something heavy fell from the bed. He left the window and rushed to Sonia's side.

She did not see him. She was shouting in the thick voice of a drunk and flailing her arms. Her hand struck the night table, sending the plate of melon rinds to the floor. The sweet smell brought on another attack of nausea, and Selyotsky vomited.

It was the melon. It had to be. He stared at a rind entangled in Sonia's tresses as he wiped his mouth and bleary eyes on the sheet. "Neurotoxin" flashed through his mind. The melon was no mistaken delivery. Someone had wanted it delivered to him. Or to him and Sonia?

She clutched at him. He pushed her away. Somehow he managed to get up and stagger toward the telephone. He was dizzy. His vision was flickering and shot through with torrents of color, like inscriptions in flame.

He seized the receiver and launched the tip of his finger across the vast gulf toward the numerals nestled deep within their holes in the dial. Numerals were beautiful. Even the number of the ambulance service.

A ring tone at the end of the line. Someone picked up. Selyotsky spoke first, a torrent of words. He had barely begun when the line went dead. He dialed again. Now there was only silence.

Would it be a mistake to turn to Zakharova for help? It was academic; he had no choice. At least there was a call box in the street. In a fog of indecision, he somehow tugged on his pants, threaded his arms into a shirt and half-fell into the corridor outside his door.

Someone had turned off the florescent tubes in the corridor. It was pitch dark. Words: rain, darkness, light, fear, love. He was only half-conscious of his surroundings, but his mind was racing. What makes *darkness* darkness? Or *rain* rain? Why is *melon* associated with the fruit, and *poison* with some unknown toxin? Words in different languages point to the same referent. But while referents are eternal, words drift and drift until they never quite occupy the same semantic space, even words in the same language used by different people.

But is there some Platonic Idea, some central core of eternal meaning deep within symbols? One could argue there was nothing of the kind. Symbols are just symbols. Still, is this true? The fact that people sense pure meaning at the heart of certain symbols—is this something learned? Is it obedience to convention?

Somehow he made his way down three flights of stairs to the ground floor, where he collapsed. He was utterly exhausted. Outside the darkened entryway he could see the orange-tinted metallic light of the vapor lamps, diffused by the rain.

To think of a symbol as just a symbol, and not as the noumenon—Selyotsky disliked the term ἰδέαι—was this simply ignorance of the True Name, the Word that harbors the true essence of its referent? People have always yearned for words that could convey meaning not through awareness of sound, but directly to the mind; for that moment when words lose their forms, leaving only meaning. When True Names manifest.

Selyotsky struggled to his feet and felt his way along the wall to the door. It was cold outside. He was already beginning to forget why he was there.

If only there were ultimate names that transcended all words and individual understandings of words. If only there were symbols that embodied those names.

Zakharova had returned to the call box, but she started across the street when she saw Selyotsky coming out of the building. She must have been ringing him after all.

Even without the conventions of language, wouldn't ultimate names confer power on those with eyes to see them?

"Where's the talisman? She took it away from you, didn't she!"

Zakharova, still in the street, stopped to let a car drift by. Selyotsky reached the lamppost just as a terrible new wave of nausea seized him. He doubled over and spewed the dregs of his stomach into a puddle.

"At least you're safe. I brought you a new one. Don't let anyone take it this time!"

It was pleasant, feeling the rain falling. How long had it been? Rain . . .the word. Rain . . .the entity. The phenomenon. The manifestation. What would the glyph for rain's True Name look like?

Zakharova had almost reached him when shadows loomed up and seized her from behind. A hand clapped over her mouth stifled her scream. Her arms were pinned.

Maybe it was the pouring rain, or perhaps his mind had lost its capacity to focus, but the sudden appearance of people and cars caught Selyotsky completely off guard. They seemed to materialize out of the downpour itself. Far from going for help, he was too stunned to do anything but watch what was happening. Zakharova struggled desperately. One of her captors snatched something from her right hand.

That must be the new talisman. What sort of object was it, he wondered. What was inscribed on it?

The helpless Zakharova was dragged away. Selyotsky slumped on the sidewalk, exhausted. In the next moment he would topple head first into the puddle and drown in his own vomit.

"Pull yourself together, comrade. You'll be fine."

A hand grasped his arm. A massive hand, as thick as a winter glove, kept him from falling over in a faint.

"You saw what happened to your lover. Did you think it was happening to you too? You're quite mistaken. You really are suggestible, aren't you?"

The hand hoisted Selyotsky up onto his feet. He glimpsed Zakharova as she was hustled into a car. He took a step toward her, but the hand restrained him.

Perhaps it was because this voice he had grown to know over the last few days assured him he was fine, or perhaps he had never been ill at all, but Selyotsky had no trouble staying on his feet. He was even able to turn and confirm that the voice belonged to Lieutenant Colonel Kazhegeldin.

"What is this? Who are those people? What are they going to do to Comrade Zakharova? That was some ethnic trinket. She isn't proselytizing or engaged in anti-party—"

"Your 'secretary' is a Chinese spy."

"Who? What do you mean?"

The colonel took a clean handkerchief from the pocket of his service coat and handed it to Selyotsky, who absently wiped away the vomit and blew his nose. Kazhegeldin nodded solicitously.

"She's the KGB's problem now. Your lover is one of them, you know."

Kazhegeldin gestured to Sonia as she was carried from the building to one of the cars. One of Selyotsky's rugs had become a makeshift stretcher. He looked even more bewildered.

"You seek explanations," said Kazhegeldin. "As I would. But I'm not in a position to tell you everything. All I can say is that your Chinese spy of a secretary planted a listening device on you. The KGB disabled it and were in the process of co-opting you for their own purposes. She smuggled another device into my office. You brought something and left with it. Remember? The folder."

"You mean she bugged me? And Sonia was manipulating me—why? My little Sonia, working for the KGB? She's just a child!"

Selyotsky laughed crazily. This couldn't be real. No, maybe it could. Otherwise how did one explain it? After she crushed Zakharova's talisman—her listening device—Sonia put the fragments in her bag, all the while pretending it was female jealousy.

"Then who fed us the poison? Seduced us with such a beautiful melon? Someone investigated my eating habits. But of course . . . It's to be expected."

As the car door closed, Sonia gave a final demented shriek.

"This is terrible. It's too much! Was it you sir, who sent that melon? And cut the line when I tried to call the ambulance?"

"The KGB tapped your phone. I assume they cut the line. The ambulance would have been a complication. None of this was under my control. All right, I confess to sending the melon. A modest contribution of my own. Neither the KGB nor military intelligence had a hand in that. But it wasn't poisoned, I assure you."

"Nonsense. Look at Sonia! And if you knew she was KGB, it makes even less sense. Why did you send us a melon laced with poison?"

"I'm telling you there was no poison. But I did inscribe a brief greeting on the surface of the fruit."

The rain was starting to let up. The cars with their female passengers had long since disappeared. Kazhegeldin and Selyotsky were alone. The road was empty. Suddenly a light, not a streetlamp, shone down from the sky. The moon appeared through a rift in the clouds.

"This is not a matter for military intelligence. It's not a party matter. It is for me and my people alone. We admire your dedication to your research. I would even say we are thankful. We don't want to be completely forgotten, you see. But we don't want strangers tramping around in our back yard either. Human beings are selfish that way."

The Hero of the Soviet Union wiped his face with a huge hand. The rain had nearly stopped. Only then did Selyotsky notice that the colonel was carrying an incongruous-looking vinyl bag with handles, the kind one might be handed in a souvenir shop. As if to answer Selyotsky's look of surprise, Kazhegeldin reached into the bag and brought out a light green bowl.

"A modern facsimile of Goryeo celadon. They're sold openly as reproductions, not antiques. It's not as fine as an original, of course. But I'm fond of this piece, so I thought I might as well use it."

The colonel handed the bowl to Selyotsky. He accepted it without resistance, though he did not know why. It would be dangerous to look inside. Then it was impossible to look away.

The bowl's interior seemed enormous. It was like looking through a portal into a vast alternate world. No, a parallel universe. Again he felt the dizziness, but now it was a pleasant inebriation mixed with elation, the feeling that comes from knowing something wonderful is about to happen. A riot of colors rose before his eyes.

At the order of the imams, the glyphs are covered with a second cloth. But instead of crimson-purple, the new cloth is plain white. Nothing seems inscribed on it.

"The structure of the brain varies hardly at all across generations and between races. Individual differences are insignificant. Each brain must obey the physical laws that apply in this universe. Physics, chemistry, thermodynamics—no brain can escape those constraints."

Which meant the effects would be the same for everyone. Ultimate names, ultimate glyphs, the ultimate writing system. A script so perfect it would be imperceptible as a string of characters or figures. A script beyond any system of pronunciation. Would messages in such a script have the same effect on the sightless, even on those who did not know the language of the message?

High above the white cloth, satellites launched by the Soviet Union, America, and other nations would be orbiting. They would photograph the terrain beneath them. They would peer down on the city of the Huang Hua, hidden in its basin in the Alatau Mountains. They would photograph the white cloth with their advanced optics. They would photograph its invisible inscription.

"Forgive me Professor, but you must forget this too. Unfortunately my calligraphy is nothing like that of my ancestors. It's so clumsy, I'm almost ashamed to show it to you."

Did Utemuratov peer into this bowl? The students and staff of the university must have been reading the white spaces of Kazhegeldin's letter. Was there a special message for the inquisitive physics instructor?

And in photographs taken by the world's spy satellites, there might be all sorts of unexpected images, designed to be forgotten the instant they were seen.

Selyotsky looked on the vastness of the universe and sighed.

Valery Ivanovich Selyotsky rode his bicycle—the only bicycle one was likely to see in the city of Almaty—past the eternal flame in Heroes Park.

When Kazakhstan gained its independence, there had been heated debate over whether the memorial should demolished, like the ubiquitous busts of Lenin. Still, half a century before, these men had sacrificed their lives to defend their homeland. So the monument remained, here in its park in the center of the city, and the eternal flame still burned.

Selyotsky had lived in Almaty for two decades, since his early thirties. The city had acquired a more linguistically correct name, and though it was no longer the capital, its high street shops and women's fashions were as vibrant as ever. The "economy" had handed the elites a beautiful screen to hide behind. Now everything was about business and profit. The university's financial situation and the principles of economic efficiency would soon require the termination of unproductive academics like Selyotsky. It was a matter of time.

True, his research had gone nowhere for years. The satellite images that had arrived today from the American university showed nothing but desolate terrain where Selyotsky had hoped to see traces of ruins. Yet the images of empty mountains had filled him with intense nostalgia and a kind of excitement, as if this were the discovery he had been waiting for. Selyotsky sensed that he had his answer. Now it was his turn to protect the secret, though he did not know why.

A thickset veteran gave him a friendly wave as he pedaled past. Selyotsky had never served and knew no one in the armed forces, but somehow the sight of this man awakened a certain feeling in him. He circled back.

"It's been a long time, Professor. You can't possibly remember me, but we're old friends. When I heard you needed help, of course I came right away." The man extended a huge hand. It held an envelope with Selyotsky's name on it. "Perhaps you might be interested in some work deciphering texts in my homeland? I think the position would suit you better than the one you have here."

The envelope contained a blank sheet of paper; at least that was how it would have appeared to someone else. But Selyotsky already knew its message. The man smiled broadly and disappeared into the sea of afternoon strollers.

Selyotsky knew the way. He didn't need this paper and its directions. The signs were everywhere, plain to those with eyes to see.

He did not go home to pack. He abandoned his bicycle, rented a car, and took the road to the mountains.

Ueda Sayuri

Translated by Daniel Huddleston

I was seven years old when I saw a feral ship for the first time. I'll never forget that summer: the hot, stifling air, the sunlight that set my skin tingling as it burned on an ocean of deepest blue. I was on the upper deck hanging out the family laundry when I noticed a dark shadow in the water closing in on us from starboard aft.

In no time at all, the thing overtook our ship, and as it came up from behind to pass us, its symmetrically-paired fins pounded against the face of the sea, raising not so much splashes of water as *explosions* of it. Then it breached up from the surface for a good long stretch of its black, gargantuan frame, and in that moment the realization hit me: this was not an icthynavis. It was a feranavis—a wild, feral ship.

The laundry forgotten, I raced to the bulwark. Framed against a background of towering cumulonimbus clouds, the feranavis traced a gentle parabola through the air, then came crashing back down into the sea, swimming onward in the same direction as before.

The waves kicked up by its passing shook our boat ferociously. Laundry wrapped around and around the drying-rods. I lost my footing and tumbled down clumsily, but jumped right back up again, clinging to the handrails, scanning the waves for the feranavis.

Its body was well over fifteen meters long. Unlike a whale or a dolphin, it had a flattened head and body—a form that somehow made its appearance more comical than majestic. Seen up close, its hide looked as though it were made of steel. Seawater was pouring off of its glinting back in waterfalls. I couldn't make out the shape of a living-shell anywhere near its stern. It was a Ship without a Pilot, a feranavis.

Father came running up to the top deck from out of our living-shell. I told him I wasn't hurt and pointed at the feranavis, which was still visible above the waves. Father raised a hand up over his brow and stared out into the distance, finally murmuring that he could see a star-shaped mark on it. Then he turned toward me, smiling, and told me that we had just seen something really special.

"That was your aunt," he told me. "And judging by the size of her, she'll probably be headed for land before long."

At that age, there was no way I could have understood what he was talking about. I would only understand several years later, when my secondary sexual characteristics began appear.

High up in the sky, the full moon was rising. From the front of the field tent, I looked out over the night-time sea. Its surface glittered with a dull, inconstant sheen, as though made of countless tiny fragments of oxidized silver. Its hypnotic effect conspired with the endless roar of the surf, lulling me down toward slumber.

I slipped a canteen from my leather belt and unscrewed the cap. Bitter tea slid down my throat, dispelling the drowsiness. In the twelve years that had passed since I left my seagoing community and moved onto dry land, I had tried my dead level best to be a hard worker. It drove me crazy how my career just wouldn't take off here. Even after twelve years, I still couldn't afford to turn down a boring job like this one.

Not far from the field tent, there were three automatic cannons. Near each one, an operator stood watching the sea. Their night-vision scanners performed constant checks along the shoreline. The tide was out and large stones, densely covered in seaweed and barnacles, stuck their heads up out of the shallows here and there. They were not boulders. They were the ruins of high rise buildings, and once part of a great metropolis.

The mating calls of night herons pierced the night sky from time to time, resounding in the darkness. Blending with them, I could hear other, stranger cries. Their songs were as clear and grand as those of seasoned opera singers, but their voices most definitely did not belong to human beings. The voices meandered up and down the scale from baritone to tenor, occasionally clambering up into soprano territory without prelude. They were the cries of feral ships gone inland, calling out to one of their fellows. They seldom sang during daylight hours, but come nightfall they would start wailing like mad with voices that carried for miles. Their cries gave me a strong hint that this would be the night a new feranavis came ashore. My job was to find it and shoot it dead.

Night duty ran from midnight until dawn. They had once told me that this would be a temporary arrangement, and I had come here as I was told. That had been a full year ago. Teams were deployed at numerous points along the coast, but my station was the one that saw the least action. In the whole time since I was sent here, only two feranavi had come ashore. There hadn't been the slightest hint of any transfer order in the works. In short, I'd been marooned here. The boss just had it in for me.

I was taking another swallow of bitter tea when a report came in by way of the transceiver in my ear: a woman had been caught trespassing inside a restricted area. This individual was making a lot of noise about seeing the person in charge. The data imbedded in the back of her hand identified her as "Mio"—one of the sea-folk who lived out in the Pacific Region.

I nearly dropped my canteen. The nape of my neck started to get warm. *It can't be her, I thought. Not the same Mio that I used to know!*

I gave instructions to hold her at headquarters, then rushed back to the field tent as quickly as I could. I was still breathing heavily when I bounded inside and found the woman yelling at my subordinates.

She had a strong, resonant voice and a fervor that radiated from every inch of her firm, tall body. It was Mio, all right—all grown up, and yet somehow completely unchanged from the days when we were young. For a moment, I forgot myself at the sight of her: those arms, those legs, that body—now matured and aged to perfection. As soon as Mio turned toward me, she thrust both of her hands out in front of her. Without so much as evening's word of greeting she said, "Take these off."

"As soon as we know you don't mean us any harm," I answered.

I ordered my subordinates out of the tent.

Once we were alone, I turned to her and said, "It's nice to finally see you again . . .but what's the big idea getting in the way of my work?"

Without a trace of reserve, Mio replied, "I want you to call off the feranavis hunt."

"Not happening," I said. "I just work here. Without orders from on high, I can't do anything."

"Why not just report that it got away or something?"

"Because the truth would come out and it'd be me taking the blame. No thank you."

"The one who's about to come ashore," Mio said, "Is my *other-half*."

Her words dealt me a shock, and she saw it clearly. Mio continued: "I'm sure you haven't forgotten. The icthynavis we played with—that we abused—she's come back. As a feranavis."

After a slight hesitation, I answered: "What difference does that make? If your otherhalf isn't an icthynavis anymore, what use is it now?"

At that, anger flashed in Mio's eyes. "*You* were the one who suggested the gunpowder!"

"And you gleefully went along with it," I retorted.

And it was true. No two ways about it, we had both been enjoying ourselves.

That day.

With that thing.

I should have long since put it all behind me, but even now I sometimes had dreams about those days. The sight of thousands of huge frigates advancing solemnly in formation across the deep blue sea, their gorgeous flags flying. Giant, artificial islands floating on the sea, bristling with mechanical structures resembling malformed trees. The politicians who lived on them. My family never moved onto a floating island, but instead spent most all of our time aboard a ship of our own. On a ship that was called an icthynavis.

The sea-folk were a people who spent their whole lives on the ocean, never going ashore. They only traded with land-folk in order to get supplies that can't be had at sea. They formed communities that moved in large fleets, with each family unit having its own ship and occasionally engaging in commerce or casual association with the ships of other families. To them, the whole ocean was their backyard, and they were thriving now with a vigor that threatened to overwhelm the land-folk. In a world in which most of the land was now underwater, it was sometimes easier to just do away with the land-based lifestyle altogether.

Until adolescence, I was affiliated with such a seagoing community, though afterward I walked away from it of my own volition.

I still remember what happened very clearly. I was at that age when friends were starting to become more important to me than family, and several of us—me and Mio included—had formed ourselves a little gang. We used to get together and go looking for thrills. We'd compete for the highest footing whenever we jumped into the sea; we'd compare our dives to see who could go the deepest; we'd even count off the seconds as we tried to hold on barehanded to fishes with poisonous quills. We got into some pretty awful scrapes.

Then one day it happened. We were on the ship where Mio lived with her family when we noticed that we were being followed by a small fish-shaped shadow. An oddly-friendly little fish was trailing along behind the stern.

That alone was enough to decide what our next little game would be. If we had been older—or younger—the behavior of this fish might have seemed funny or cute to us. But we were at an age where, instead, we just felt an irresistible urge to hurt it.

First, we tossed it some small fishes and prawns, and once the fish let its guard down we started hitting it without warning. We knocked it around with the ends of poles, we threw sea urchins at it, and we even brought up hot water from the living-shell to throw on it.

I was indeed the one who suggested using the gunpowder. We broke down some of the rifle shells that were used for shooting sharks and loaded up a bottle with the explosive powder. A firecracker, we called it. We threw it at the fish, only meaning to scare it. However, I misjudged the amount of powder. I put in too much.

The adults came running when they heard the explosion. It was a huge fuss. The fish had a large wound in its back, and was already falling behind Mio's ship, staining the water a murky black with its fresh blood. It was the first time I had ever heard a fish screaming. It was an eerie sound—in the right frame of mind, it might even sound like the cry of a human child. Heard at night, it could have been mistaken for the screams of a drowning child. There was an unearthly quality to it that could dig right into your soul.

I was still putting up a good front, though. I was thinking to myself, *What's the big deal over making a fish cry?*

We were chewed out something awful, not just for making explosives, but also for abusing the fish. All of us hung our heads low in phony remorse, though, and by the time the last of the sermons had been preached we were already planning to do the same thing again.

The adults were not unaware of this mood in the air around us.

A few days later, all the young people of our community were summoned to the ship where our clan leader lived. With no idea at all of what we were in for, we descended to the lowest level of his living-shell. There we were told to wait in the hall for a short time. We sat down with our backs against the wall and passed the time in laughter and casual conversation.

At last, the door at the end of the hall opened and an old man appeared carrying a large washbasin. He set the basin down at our feet as though her were performing some kind of ritual and urged us to look inside.

We crowded in around the edge of the basin and grew still. The vessel was filled with clear liquid, and at the bottom, a flat fish was wriggling its body around. I say it was a fish, but actually it reminded me more of a salamander. Its large paired fins resembled the palms of hands connected directly to the body with no arms in between. It didn't really strike me as a "cute" fish or an "odd" fish. My strongest impression of it was of deformity.

The old man began to speak. "Before much longer," he said, "all of you will be old enough to marry and bear children. So remember this: when the women of our clan become pregnant, they always bear twins. One twin will take the form of a boy or girl like you. But the other one will be born in the shape of a fish. Just like this one."

Our mouths fell open as we stared stupidly at the fish in the basin. At that age, we had no real concept of the process of childbirth. It was hard to believe that on top of something as strange as that, women could give birth to humans and fishes at the same time.

"Is this one a preemie or something?" one girl asked. "Like, will he turn into a human like us when he grows up?"

"No, this one will always be like this," the old man replied. "Babies born hominid grow up on the boats, but this little one we'll turn loose into the sea."

"Won't he die if you do that?"

"Of course he'll die. If he doesn't have the vitality and the luck. But if he should survive to adulthood out in that cruel environment, someday he'll come back to the same ship where he was born. At that time, if the fish's otherhalf—a hominid brother or sister like you—is still living on the ship—the human and the fish will be united in the bond of Ship and Pilot. Have the grownups tell you about how an icthynavis is piloted. When the time comes."

As these huge fishes grew to their full length of thirty meters, exoskeletons formed on their backs, and in their hollow inner spaces, the sea-folk made their homes. Upper decks were structures that people built onto their living-shells in order to make use of direct sunlight. The sea-folk were creatures who lived as parasites, as it were, on the bodies of fishes that they themselves gave birth to. The Pilot controlled his ship by use of certain combinations of specific vibratory frequencies. In other words, by sound. Because a portion of these vibrations were in the range audible to the human ear, our clan referred to these sounds—used to give instructions to an icthynavis—as "the Pilot's Song."

We kids were all wild with excitement over what the old man had told us. There was no greater honor among the sea-folk than to have your own ship. Not some hand-me-down inherited from your parents, but a brand-new icthynavis made just for you!

Everyone started asking questions all at once: "When? When? When will my fish come back?"

The old man answered, "They'll aim to come back around the time when you hit puberty. But in very rare cases, some fish miss that period. They come back a little too early sometimes, or in other cases quite a bit late. That's why, from now on, all of you need to be watching the sea every day. So you'll know when your fish—your otherhalf—comes back, and can start taming him right away.

That was the point when it finally hit me why we had been called there. The fish that we had cruelly abused the other day had been somebody's potential icthynavis. It had been an 'otherhalf.' I stole a glance at Mio's face, and as I had feared, she had gone pale as a ghost. Trembling like a leaf, she was no longer hearing anything anyone else was saying.

When went back to our own boats, I tried to cheer her up. "Don't worry about it," I said. "What's done is done."

But Mio couldn't calm down. "That fish I hurt was *my* 'otherhalf' wasn't it? And after that, it won't ever come back again. . . ."

From that day forward, a dark shadow began to creep into Mio's profile. Some people said that she'd seen the light. That she'd grown as a human being. That had a nice ring to it, but for some reason I just didn't buy it. That's why I bent over backwards trying to cheer Mio up. "Look, I don't know if those things are people's brothers or sisters or what, but at the end of the day, aren't they just fishes? There's no need to feel guilty over them. Besides, it's not like we know for sure that the 'otherhalf' was even yours."

Mio didn't argue. However, she was already thoroughly depressed by the idea that she had forever lost her chance at having an icthynavis. To make matters worse, the blood from that fish was analyzed, and when the results came back they showed without a doubt that it had indeed been Mio's otherhalf.

The adults said that this was her punishment for having done wrong. I couldn't accept the value system that was based on. It was something our clan had come up with on its own. From the standpoint of land-folk who don't give birth to them, icthynavi are nothing more than another kind of fish. If they didn't have living-shells, and people living in them, they would see them as a natural resource and eat them without hesitation. If they were starving, they might even steal them from sea-folk.

It was at this time that it suddenly hit me: I didn't belong in that place. Although I was born a seaman, I could not live like they did. So I decided to abandon my life on the sea. I told my parents my intentions and went through the change-of-residency procedures for moving ashore. In so doing, I threw away the contract I once had with an icthynavis I had never seen. Even so, I had no regrets.

If Mio couldn't have an icthynavis, I didn't deserve to have one either. . . .

Mio laughed my decision to scorn. "Is this sympathy? Friendship? Love? Call it what you like, it's still stupid."

I answered Mio's sarcasm with silence and put the community of the sea-folk behind me forever. It happened to be raining that day.

Even now, I remember it like it was yesterday: Mio watching me go from behind that curtain of silver droplets that came falling down from heaven, not turning away until I was out of sight, if even then. The rain had been a wall dividing us. A single step could have shattered that barrier so easily, but neither one of us had had the will for it. We had both been in the grip of a chilly cowardice, and that single step had been one step too far.

I had not released Mio's bindings. I motioned her to a chair and placed a water bottle from the back of the tent in her hands.

When I came up beside Mio, I could smell a sweet, fruity fragrance coming from her. I didn't remember that perfume. It smelled expensive. Had someone taught her how to make it? Had someone given it to her? I was afraid to ask. I had a feeling that as soon as I found out the answer, my own pride might take a beating.

"It must have been pretty tough coming all the way out here," I said.

Without offering a word in reply, Mio threw back her tan throat and drank from the bottle. As she was drinking, however, the tension drained out of her face. She seemed to be calming down a little.

I asked Mio if she had any proof that the feranavis out there was her otherhalf.

"Of course I do," she said. "There's a nonprofit group that follows feranavi to study them. They found a match for my genome in one of the samples they take to build their database."

"And even though it was none of their business, they informed you, did they?"

"I was the one who asked them. I told them to contact me if they ever found her. Back then, if I'd heard that talk sooner, I wouldn't have lost my otherhalf. . . ."

"That was a long time ago."

"That's not the issue," Mio said. She tossed away the empty bottle. "How long have you been working here now?"

"Around a year."

"You like it?"

"I'm not here by choice. I was transferred against my will."

A feranavis was an icthynavis that for some reason didn't have a Pilot. Once they were fully grown, they became able to go ashore.

Unlike the vaguely amphibian form of an icthynavis, feranavi looked slightly more like reptiles. About thirty years ago, some of them were discovered by accident in an inland canyon, and since then they had come to be a problem for the land-folk. Even though their numbers were small, they had to eat up a lot of the land's resources in order to stay alive. Like icthynavi, feranavi had no reproductive organs, so just because they had found a ready-made environment, it didn't mean there was any danger of explosive reproduction. Yet even so, for the past few years, a consensus had been growing that they should be eliminated. This was because their presence could mean life and death to the people that had to survive on such limited areas of land.

Strike teams had been assembled at government expense to wipe them out. It was to one of those teams that I had been dispatched.

"How many feranavi have you killed so far?" Mio asked me.

"Just two," I said. "I don't really have a lot to do here. I'm the only human worker. Everyone else, gunners included, is autosapient. Normally, they stay plugged into Central Command –"

"Your own otherhalf is a feranavis now," said Mio, cutting me off. She clearly had no interest in the details of my job. "What if it comes ashore someday? Have you never thought about that? You'd be shooting a brother or sister."

"I can't say the thought's never crossed my mind. But I'm not a seaman anymore. Even if it's my own otherhalf, I'll shoot without hesitation if I'm ordered to."

"Still cold as ever, aren't you?"

"And you're too sentimental."

Mio breathed out silence. "Do you know why the feranavi head for land?"

"No idea."

"It's because they've found a niche on land. They've realized they can use the land as well as the sea to survive."

"Why would they want to? With those huge bodies, living on the land should be more difficult, shouldn't it? Their buoyancy wouldn't be any help."

"I think the shift they've made is not so much to the idea of 'living on the land' as to the idea of 'using the land as well.'"

"I wonder how they find enough food."

"Well, naturally, their diet is changing too. Your hit squads were formed because they were destroying natural resources, right? But they may not stop at just that."

Teasingly, I replied, "So they're going to start eating people too, or something?"

"It would be good to consider every possibility. Those things *are* creations of humanity, after all." For a moment, Mio looked like she was deep in thought about something. "Did you know that the complexity of a life-form doesn't depend on the sum total of its genes?" she asked.

"I don't know a lot about that kind of thing, but I think I've heard something to that effect."

"Well, a nematode, for example, has only a thousand cells in its whole body, but humans have around sixty trillion. But nematodes have as many as two hundred thousand genes, while humans only have twenty-three thousand. The difference in complexity has nothing to do with the number of genes; what matters is how, how many times, and in what combinations a life-form uses and reuses the limited number of genes that it has."

"Like how you could arrange toy blocks to build either a house or a car?"

"That's not a bad way of putting it. In 2003—when they finished decoding the human genome—they learned that the protein-coding areas and the expression-suppression areas took up no more than a couple percent of the whole gene. They really weren't sure what the other ninety-eight percent was for. They used to think those areas were nothing but cellular junk, but just two years later, they showed that the non-coding RNA that gets copied from those regions might in fact be what determines the complexity of a creature's form and function. Up until that time, they'd thought that RNA only had an extremely limited use, but in reality, it was related to the expression and even the evolution of physical traits. And even different species, with entirely different shapes and forms, were using were the same genes. We can use this mechanism to create life-forms with completely non-human morphologies now, using the same genome as a human. Icthynavi are creatures made by the application of that technology. They're quite literally our other halves."

"Are you working in bioengineering now?"

Mio shook her head. "You don't have to be a specialist to find out that much."

I couldn't imagine what Mio's real job might be. The one thing I did know was that she was now obsessed with her lost otherhalf even more deeply than she had been all those years ago.

Mio continued: "The data showed that when broad-type promoters have a high incidence of sudden changes, living creatures can evolve at an accelerated pace. So the idea was that by artificially tweaking promoters and non-coding RNA so that changes can occur more easily, it should be possible to create creatures that readily react to external pressures—like changes in the environment—and quickly evolve and devolve over and over. Somebody thought of that a long time ago, and tweaked our bodies in the same way too, didn't he? So that the human race would be able to live on even in a world where most of the landmass had been swallowed up by the rising sea."

"What does that have to do with feranavi? Are you saying there's some kind of purpose in their splitting off from icthynavi?"

She shook her head. "I wouldn't go that far. Somehow, I get the feeling that they've headed off in some unexpected direction. As for who such creatures might be useful to—and under what circumstances—I have absolutely no idea."

"Even with observation teams watching them, feranavi come right up onto the beach without a second thought. They're animals that can't understand something as simple as the fact that land-folk will kill them if they get too close."

"It's a mistake for humans to make off-handed judgments of how clever an animal is, though. Ever heard of handicap theory?"

"Can't say I have."

"It's a theory that explains why animals sometimes take actions and shapes that at first glance seem to lower their chances of survival. For example, a certain kind of herbivore becomes aware of an enemy and deliberately starts jumping up as high as it can, exposing itself to the predator. At first glance, this looks like a really stupid thing to do, but according to this theory, it's really saying to the predator, "Look! I'm in great shape, and it's a rare beast that can catch me!' What if the feranavi have also started to change for some reason . . .?"

"You're over-thinking this. Anyway, it's been too long since we've seen each other to go on and on about this. Let's talk about something else, all right?"

"What is there to talk about now that's more important than that feranavis?"

"Are feranavi and otherhalves the only thing in your head, Mio? It's been twelve years!"

After a slight hesitation, Mio asked, "What do you want to know about me?"

"What do you mean, 'what?' I want to know about your life now. I want to know about your family. . . ."

"In the daytime I help with maritime observations. At night, I'm a singer."

"A singer? As in professionally?"

"As in not very popular." Mio smiled a sad smile. "Even so, I've got a few fans. Is that weird?"

"No, just a little unexpected."

"I have no family of my own. Right now, I'm living on an artificial island. In the evening, I go to bars and sing one-night gigs. The instant they hear my voice, I can see the life coming back into the eyes of people who had been all gloomy from a hard day's work. That's a nice moment. Sometimes, I give concerts at small halls. What about you?"

"Compared to you, it's not a very flashy life. But I'm a public employee, even in a place like this. Can't seem to get promoted to a good job, though, which is why I'm in the state I'm in."

"Family?"

"Married me a landlubber; two kids now."

"Well, that's not too bad, then, is it? And this way, you don't need to concern yourself with my life."

I paused a moment before asking, "Don't you have any desire to move ashore and sing?"

The edge of Mio's mouth twisted in scorn. I waited for an answer, but her eyes were staring off into the distance. After a moment, she asked, "Can you please listen to what I have to say for just a little longer?"

"You can talk all you want, but I'm not going to listen to demands."

"When my otherhalf appears, I want you to hold your fire for five minutes. Because I'm going to lead her away."

"You're going to take it back out to sea?"

"Well, I'd like take her to some desert island, actually, but given the current ratio of sea to land, there's not enough room for a feranavis to live in a place like that. So I want to lead her back to live in the sea."

"How are you going to lead something huge like that anywhere?"

"Light and sound," she said. "Don't worry. I've tested this on other feranavi already."

"And if you can't take it with you?"

"Then go ahead and shoot her. If she has no choice but to be killed, I at least want to see it through to the end. That way, at the very least, my soul can be free of her."

I was silent for a time.

Mio slowly put her arms out in front of her once again. "Take them off," she said.

I shook my head. "The fact that I know you as well as I do is exactly why I can't trust you. You can either go right back out to sea, or you can stay here and wait for the report."

Mio gently lowered her hands. She hung her head, and from that moment said nothing more. I asked her again if she would go or stay, but she didn't answer. She continued to stare down at her feet, motionless, as if she had been turned to stone.

I tied Mio to the chair with a rope. When I was finished, I circled around to face her and said that once my work was finished I wanted to see her again. I'd take her to a restaurant where we could have a good breakfast.

Mio didn't respond to that. She just said in a murmur, "Even if you murder feranavi here now, it doesn't change the fact that they're our otherhalves. The day will surely come when you're forced to realize that."

I stepped outside the field tent and looked up at the sky. The moon had risen slightly higher. After assigning one of my subordinates the task of watching Mio, I started walking back down the beach again.

I thought back over how Mio had spoken, thinking, *There's more madness than passion in what she's saying.* Maybe it had been a mistake back then to have left her out at sea like that, to have gone ashore by myself. If I had stayed by her side, maybe she wouldn't have gone so crazy.

Or is that my own ego talking?

When I reached the side of one of the self-propelled cannons, my eyes came to rest on the gunner sitting at its control platform. The skin of the autosapien was set to a paler, bluer color than that of a human being. This was so that they could blend into society without making humans uncomfortable, while at the same time reminding everyone around them that they were not in fact humans themselves.

As I gazed at its attractive, well-balanced profile, I thought, *This guy doesn't have a single human gene inside him. He's an automatic doll made of artificial proteins and inorganic materials. Even so, he looks more like a human than they do. I feel infinitely more close to him than I do to feranavi and icthynavi, even though they have exactly the same genes that I do. Why is that?*

What defines a human to a human? Is it the form or the genome? Or does it just depend on who you ask?

I asked the gunner if he had seen anything unusual, and he replied in a soft, gentle voice, <<No anomalies detected.>>

Then I tried asking him what kind of being he thought of himself as, but autosapiens are not made to be able to answer such questions. Asking him had been meaningless.

I stood by the cannon for some time. The gunner would not ask me anything. That was how he was made. That he came with an off switch for unneeded chitchat was something I felt grateful for. He was the polar opposite of Mio.

Suddenly, however, the gunner's voice rang in my ears: <<Object exhibiting life response detected at 120 degrees. Distance 50.>>

"The feranavis?"

<<Confirming. Shall we open fire when it comes ashore?>>

"See to it. Contact me when it's taken care of."

<<Understood.>>

I raised my connection level and plugged into the information network of all the gunners. In my brain, I marked the positions of all the self-propelled guns, and then locked on to Area 1, where I could see the beach.

Endlessly rolling waves crashed mercilessly against the rocks there. Between those rocks, a writhing shadow could definitely be seen. As if in response to the cries from its inland kindred, it twisted and squirmed suddenly, and then shambled up into the shallows, at last exposing its entire body near the tide line.

I could make out the distinctive shape of a feranavis that had completed its transformation. It was like a fish crossed with a crocodile. Its full length came to almost seventeen meters. Its pectoral fins—relics of when it had still been a sea creature—had transformed into the general shape of hands, and I could see five long claws at the tips of their fingers. Sharp teeth peeked out from between the gap in its long snout. Its tail fins had also changed into a shape that made it easier to shimmy up boulders and cliffs. Its body glinting like steel, the feranavis wriggled its way up onto the sand. It stopped occasionally to raise its head, which it would rock back and forth slightly as though trying to determine which direction the voices of the others were coming from.

The gunner's signal reached my brain, informing me that they had locked onto the target.

That's when a small shadow came running in a straight line toward the feranavis. I could see the glint of a blade in its right hand.

Where could she have hidden it? How had she managed to cut her bindings? Her clothing, stained with a great deal of artificial blood, told me in a heartbeat what she had done.

"Stop!" I shouted. "Get back!"

She turned to look at me just once.

In the instant when our eyes met, I was overwhelmed by the force of will that I saw there. At that moment, I realized that it would be impossible for me to stop her. She was like a star shining in the midst of the darkness. She looked that way to me, at least. I knew instinctively that I was in direct contact with a soul on fire. I had no power to stop her, and if I tried to do so by force, I would likely be killed, slashed with that knife, just like the autosapien I had assigned to guard her.

Mio cried out in a voice that carried across the distance to me. "Just a little time! Just a little!"

She thrust her left hand high up above her head, and from it shone an intense light. The feranavis reacted to the light, and turned its body to face her. Once she was sure she had its attention,

Mio began edging away in the direction of the sea, one careful step after another. At the same time, she pressed a button on an audio player and began playing back the recorded voice of another feranavis. I couldn't understand the meaning of that song, but it was almost certainly the voice of a feranavis that was still living in the sea. There was a somehow joyful quality to the song, as though its owner were playing together with friends.

However, the feranavis made no further move to follow Mio.

I realized that the problem was the voice. Clearly, Mio's otherhalf was being drawn not to the recorded voice that she was playing for it, but to the real voices of its fellow feranavi that were echoing down from inland.

At the very moment I was about to give up hope, however, Mio suddenly began singing herself. She let loose with a voice that was like a hurricane. What she sang was neither a popular tune nor a classical melody; rather, she sang the only words that could possibly connect a human being to the mind of an icthynavis—and probably to a feranavis as well. She sang the Pilot's Song.

It was a song Mio was not permitted to sing at sea, forbidden by the clan, taken from her as punishment. I had never heard it sung so perfectly. An experienced singer could move not only the heart of an icthynavis with it, but also the hearts of humans. But that was a power that came from guiding the icthynavis every day. How much hard work had it taken for someone like Mio to come this far without an icthynavis? With no one to teach her, she would have had to have learned it through her own efforts alone. Yet even so, this woman whose song had been stolen from her had become a singer, making the training and strengthening of her vocal cords a part of her daily life. All for the sake of this one moment. All for the day that she would meet her otherhalf again.

The cries of the feranavi resounded in the darkness, rending the night, urging the newcomer to hurry ashore. Mio's voice was far more powerful than any of them. Gently, powerfully, her melody soothed her otherhalf.

Let's go back to the sea together, Mio was saying.

The swaying of the feranavis's head ceased. It stared at Mio intently. Had she succeeded? At just the moment I was thinking she had, the feranavis lashed out at Mio with its pectoral fin, knocking her off her feet and slamming her down into the ground.

Before I even realized it, I was taking off running toward Mio. Had I issued an order to fire in my unconscious mind? Before I could reach her, the head and chest of the feranavis were caught in a hail of bullets from the self-propelled guns.

Like juices bursting from an overripe fruit, dark red body fluids came spurting out from the feranavis's head and body. It tilted as though drunk, then collapsed onto the sand with a thud that shook the ground beneath my feet.

I dragged Mio out from under the feranavis, in the process getting myself drenched in sticky, fishy-smelling blood. I paid it no mind, though. I was about to begin emergency treatment when Mio finally opened her eyes and dug her fingernails into my shirt. I brought my face close, and she gasped at my ear, "Thank you . . .for letting me do it my way . . ."

"Stop that!" I shouted back. I was angry, but far more so with myself than with Mio. Why hadn't I started running sooner? Was I incapable of the kind of passion that blazed inside her? If I had been like her, I could have saved her!

One of the autosapiens came running up to help us. I looked up to give it instructions, but before the words could come out of my mouth, I saw in the corner of my eye a sight so bizarre that it made gooseflesh break out on every inch of my body.

The corpse of the feranavis was writhing, making soft, rustling sounds. The rippling of its skin made me think of freshly-hatched maggots, squirming beneath the skin of some dead animal at the side of the road.

Finally, the side of the feranavis's belly burst open with tremendous force, and a huge mass of small, black animals came spilling out. Their bodies were chubby and rounded. Six long, jointed limbs made them look as much like spiders as animals. Some of them even stood erect on two limbs, tremblingly lifting the remaining four as though they were arms. I couldn't tell where their eyes and mouths were. They cried out in voices like bird calls: *Chi-chi! Chi-chi!* It sounded to me like laughter.

I snatched the knife from Mio's right hand at almost the same instant that they came running at me. With one knee planted on the ground, I slashed at them with the knife with wild abandon. The blade cut into them again and again, but it was impossible to tell whether the wounds I inflicted were fatal. For what seemed like an eternity, I continued to swing Mio's knife against the swarming black things that tumbled toward at me. The autosapien shielded us with his body, and the black creatures tore into him, ripping and biting mercilessly.

Unexpectedly, however, they at last began to pull back like a tide going out, perhaps sensing that there was nothing to gain by continuing the assault.

Maybe they had decided we weren't food after all.

The creatures regrouped and charged off in the direction of the self-propelled guns. With incredible speed, they crawled up the slope that spread out beyond the field tent, kicking up leaves of sea bell as they went, disappearing at last as they headed inland.

Still gripping the knife, I collapsed into the sand. The ripped and tattered autosapien was flashing its sensors, even now maintaining protective mode for us.

It was just as Mio had said. As the feranavi moved ashore and onto land, there was no way that their bodies were going to stay so disadvantageously huge. In the sea, their bodies had changed gradually. In another ten years, they would probably be finished with their transformation. What came ashore at first tonight had been merely a sack. Nothing but a suitcase to carry what was inside. It hadn't even been listening to the Pilot's Song. To have thought so was nothing more than Mio and I projecting our own feelings onto the thing. And now this was our recompense.

Mio was lying on her side, her eyes already completely shut. Though I shook her and slapped her and cried out to her, she would never open them again. The autosapien tried to revive her, but her vital signs remained flat.

Suddenly, my boss's voice was on the wireless receiver inside my ear, demanding a status report. Apparently, there had already been an alert from another autosapien, informing him that something was wrong. Item by item, I reported the damage, the number of casualties, and the terrible sight that was no doubt waiting inside the field tent. Finally, I cut the link without asking permission.

After I had instructed the autosapien at my side to return to the tent, I lay back on the sandy beach, and for a while just rested there, looking up at the sky.

The tears wouldn't come.

There was only a hopeless, constricting feeling of defeat in my heart.

The feranavi that came ashore from the next day onward would almost surely be like the one tonight. When they are attacked, they will fall down right away, and then unleash their other selves from inside. Handicap theory. That was what Mio had called it. The feranavi had learned that every time they went ashore, they were attacked with guns. They had remembered this, and evolved toward spreading themselves in the form of these creatures.

For them, it was the simple, obvious solution.

By trying to wipe them out, we had taught them to reproduce asexually. Whatever creature they first met when they burst free of their carriers would be sure to become their first meal.

I wondered if those six-legged things would eventually change to look like humans as they made their way inland, following the program of evolution that had been set inside them. Were they evolving into the form that they "should" have? Or would this be considered devolution from the point of view of the people who made them?

Were they human? Should I call them people? Were they turning back into humans just like us?

Or would they turn into some new kind of creature that uses the human genome as its base? Would they continue to change forever?

My body felt like a ton of bricks as I slowly pulled myself up.

I looked once more at Mio beside me. No matter how long I looked, she didn't open her eyes and she didn't get back up. I knew better, but I still held on tight to Mio's hand for a long while.

As the man in charge of the surveillance team, it was my job to inform Mio's family of her death, and to make arrangements to have the body sent home. If I made inquiries based on the data that had been read off the back of her hand, I could find out right away what community she had been affiliated with and with whom she had been living. The data would tell me all about the past twelve years of her life—all the things that I had missed out on asking her.

But still . . .

I stepped closer to the corpse of the feranavis. Though it was hard work, I managed to cut off a piece of one of its fins. I laid it on her chest, and wrapped her arms around it. Then with the remains of the bindings on her wrists, I tied it tightly to her body.

I lifted up Mio and carried her out to the water's edge. Along these coasts, there are places that generate powerful riptides called *riganryū*, which carry things out to sea. I threw my empty canteen out into the waves and was able to find one readily enough. I stepped into the sea, still carrying Mio. A little ways from shore, I lowered her body into the water, let go, and gave it a strong push out toward the open sea.

As if gripped by the hands of some unseen god, Mio's body was immediately dragged away into the depths. She was swallowed up by waves that shone like oxidized silver and carried away from the shore in the blink of an eye. Although I couldn't see her, I could feel in my bones that she was moving farther and farther away from shore.

To me, this way seemed the most fitting for her. What Mio had wanted more than anything else had been to return to the sea with her otherhalf. *So let her cross over together with what she'd trusted and believed in.*

No one blames you anymore for what you did back then. Tonight, the otherhalf that you knew died together with you.

The *riganryū* eventually merges with that fierce river in the sea that was once known as the Black Current, and from there flows far away from the land. There at the end of that current lies the vast outer sea, where tens of thousands of icthynavi and feranavi turn in their migrations—a garden of transformation where even now, life-forms continue to evolve.

I will never go there again. I will spend the rest of my days on land. I will hate the feranavi with all of my being, and I will keep on killing them until the very last one is dead.

I can still hear their voices singing from far inland.

Like an elegy for all of humanity . . . it just goes on and on.

SILVER BULLET

Yamada Masaki

Translated by Stephen A. Carter

— 1 —

Intense sunlight, sharp shadows filling the streets of Athens, the urban bustle of men and women of sunny cheer—surely no scene could be more removed from gloom than the Aegean Sea.

And yet the extreme clarity seemed to impart a strange sense of unreality to the people. In the fierce sunlight Athens looked like a city etched on a pane of glass—a mirage created from the Aegean.

I was amid a picture postcard scene. I was standing in front of the biggest draw in the tourist city of Athens, the Parthenon.

Numerous sightseers could be seen atop the Acropolis. A few Japanese seemed to be among them. Everyone seemed elated to be there at last, and they pointed their cameras at one another with evident delight.

I was an outsider, completely unlike them. An unbridgeable gap existed between our states of mind. My bowels felt icy.

I had climbed this hill to lay the groundwork for a killing. In three days, I was to kill a young man, one for whom I held not a bit of ill will. Far from it—I had never even spoken with him.

I was a venomous snake amid a flock of doves. As a killer, I had no place in the lovely scenery of Athens. Surely only a prison or mental hospital was a fitting place for me.

"Mr. Sakaki." A voice came from behind me.

Turning around I saw another venomous snake, slowly walking toward me.

It was Aoki Mitsuru. My colleague, he was to serve as my partner for this operation. In his late twenties and slightly built, he was a young man who sometimes looked dreadfully old. It probably should also be noted that he was a heavy drug addict.

"A mobile TV unit from the BBC is here."

Aoki was completely expressionless.

"It looks like the Athens police are also starting to put more security on site."

"In three days this hill will be crawling with news crews from Europe and North America."

I lipped a cigarette.

"The police also look jumpy. On the day in question, nobody will get up this hill with a knife, let alone a gun."

"It looks like it's going to be a tough job."

"Yeah."

I was forced to agree. No job could be harder than this. Three nights from now, the Acropolis would be seen on television sets around the world via the satellite networks of several nations. People throughout the world would be able to witness us, the killers.

The visit by the Pope made things even more difficult. That night, celebrities and visiting dignitaries from every nation would cover every square inch of this hill. Tourists pressing for a glimpse of a major international event would have to submit to careful pat-downs by the police. Rumor had it that even airport-style metal detectors were being readied.

Those were the circumstances under which we had to kill the young man who was the event's principal actor.

Arrayed behind us was an enormous organization. Empowered by vast capital resources, it was an organization that, if necessary, could mobilize American senators. But no matter how huge an organization it was, it could not legitimize murder. If we failed at our task, we would be punished as mere killers.

I had to be careful. The fact that Aoki was a drug addict made the job even more difficult. No one is less suitable as a partner than an addict. A child of five would be better. The agony of withdrawal can be unimaginable. If he ran out of his drug, Aoki would be unable even to steal an ashtray.

Mental crutches were an occupational hazard of this work. They simply manifested themselves in different ways depending on the person. In my case, it took the form of heavy boozing. My indulgence in drink had already entered the realm of alcoholism. Without a whiskey upon waking, my hands would tremble all day.

Our organization appeared to have become a collection of cripples.

The work was too relentless. People cannot get used to killing without the solace of ideals or patriotism. Even the attachment that professional killers have for money was denied us. The work of killing people for whom we bore not the slightest enmity had inevitably corrupted us all.

"Mr. Sakaki."

Aoki spoke in a strangely monotone voice.

"It's her."

I said nothing.

I had also spotted her just as Aoki had spoken. It seemed that the eyes of the tourists—not just mine—were focused on her alone.

Mibu Oriko was the kind of woman who could not help attracting the gazes of others wherever she found herself. Oval face; large, chestnut eyes; soft, full lips, and other similar clichés could not fully convey her beauty. The allure she exuded could almost be called unearthly.

Oriko was staring at us. Her unlined kimono of Noto hemp with a raised design was oddly in harmony with the Parthenon. In the sparking sunlight, only the spot where she stood looked pleasantly cool.

It would not do to be taken in by Oriko's elegance. As a top-class promoter, her name was known throughout that world. When the world's superstars came to Japan, she was sure to be among the promoters. It was also Mibu Oriko who was promoting this international event.

I slowly walked toward her. We were not complete strangers. We had slept together once. Afterwards, of course, I had come dangerously close to getting killed.

"So you're here," she said in a husky voice. "You know it's pointless."

"That's my line." I unconsciously lowered my voice as well.

"You have to stop this foolish show. It's not too late. Otherwise something that can't be undone will happen."

"You intend to kill *him*."

"In the worst case, even that will be considered."

I deserved to be called a hypocrite. In fact, the organization had set things in motion on that path more than a week before.

"'People are always the same." Oriko flashed a mocking smile.

"You're not considering anything except killing."

"You're one of those people, too. Have you forgotten?"

"At least I'm not like you."

"Don't you care if Tsutsumi Kanesuke gets killed?"

"I wonder just how you intend to kill him." Oriko's eyes gleamed in a vile way.

"On the day in question, every person coming up this hill is going to be subject to a thorough physical search. Not even cameras will be allowed in. There won't be any way for anyone to bring in a weapon."

I was silent.

Maybe it should be called a breakdown in negotiations. Nobody could have stopped Tsutsumi Kanesuke from performing a noh dance at the Parthenon three days later.

Oriko moved away from my side like a shadow. To her, I was tantamount to a demon. She no doubt thought it demeaning just to talk to me.

"Wait," I said without thinking.

With the suppleness of a cat, Oriko turned back to me. The hem of her kimono stayed strangely even.

"You forgot something."

I withdrew a silver bullet from a pocket and held it in the sunlight.

"It's you who should get silver bullets," Oriko said quietly. "We have no use for them."

Oriko did not turn back again. As she descended the the Acropolis she looked like an apparition that had emerged from the ancient ruins.

"She might be right," came Aoki's voice from behind me. "Maybe we're the ones who should be shot with silver bullets."

I couldn't look Aoki in the face, because I knew the expression on mine was the same as his.

"Time to work."

I had to make myself forget what Oriko had said.

"Are you done taking photos?"

"Yes," Aoki nodded.

"Good."

I gazed again at the temple. I had to anticipate precisely where and how Tsutsumi would dance at the temple on the appointed day. An inaccurate prediction would ruin the operation.

I struggled to recall Tsutsumi's "padre" noh performance, which I had seen only once before.

That time, I'm pretty sure, Tsutsumi was...

— 2 —

I could hear the whir of a film projector. In the darkness floated a rectangle of light. It was a noh stage. The protagonist strode quietly along the stage's bridgeway from the "far shore" to "this shore." A denizen of the netherworld was crossing over to this world.

Having traversed the bridgeway, the protagonist finally faced the audience from the square stage. The creaking of the *hinoki* cypress flooring was audible.

Playing the lead was Tsutsumi Kanesuke, a young man dubbed the enfant terrible of noh. His concept of dance had much in common with avant-garde choreographers. The heads of the five major schools of noh and the Nohgaku Performers' Association refused to recognize him. It was said that his advent was injecting new blood into the moribund world of noh.

When it came to noh, I was a complete outsider. I only knew the name "Tsutsumi Kanesuke" from the glossy photo pages of the weekly magazines. Like most people, I regarded noh only as a tedious form of period drama.

And yet Tsutsumi Kanesuke's dancing had the ability to shatter many of my biases against noh. I was gradually drawn into the image on the screen and gazed at it transfixed.

Tsutsumi's movements, restrained to the utmost, fully expressed the passions of a vengeful ghost and conjured up a different world. Otherworldly fury, bitterness, and sorrow knocked the breath out of the viewer. It was as if the raging winds of hell were gusting ever closer.

Suddenly the screen went white. The lights were switched on. I sighed despite myself. I felt I had been jerked back to reality.

Only my immediate boss, the "Monk," and I were in the room. The "Monk" was not a mere nickname. He actually served as a head priest at a certain founding temple of the Tendai sect. He was nearly eighty years old. He often appeared on TV and in magazines, and gave the impression of being a priest who enjoyed worldly pleasures.

I didn't know how Monk had come to be head of the Japan branch of the HPL Society, how someone who was likely a master of esoteric Buddhism had come to be associated a group which was tantamount to a vigilante group. I couldn't even imagine.

"Have you ever seen this play?" asked the Monk, light glinting off his owlish glasses.

"No," I said, shaking my head. "I'm not very familiar with noh."

"Even among those who are, it's certain that none of them have seen this play. It's about the resurrection of Christ."

"Wow," I was astonished. "It doesn't look like a new piece."

"It's far from new. It was created around the time of Oda Nobunaga, in the mid-sixteenth century."

"But it's about the resurrection of Christ?"

"It was created by the missionaries of the time to spread the doctrine among the masses. It was called 'padre noh.' Making use of a country's entertainment to proselytize was a common practice of theirs."

"I see." I nodded, but I wasn't the least bit interested in what the Monk had to say. Padre noh might be an unusual spectacle, but more than any spectacle, I would have preferred a whiskey and water.

I had been summoned to the Tokyo branch of the HPL Society just when I was about to have a drink. That that had ended up as a lecture on padre noh was unacceptable.

"Incidentally, do you know a woman called Mibu Oriko?" The Monk suddenly changed the subject.

"I've heard the name," I said, dropping my chin to my chest, "since she's a celebrity."

Mibu Oriko was perhaps one of the three Japanese women most well-known abroad. Actually, she was far more famous than the wives of some presidents or superstars. She boasted unseen influence in the world of show business. The wide-ranging scope of her activities was said to extend from folk dance to rock. Of course, I had no knowledge of her background or personal involvements.

"What's your interest in Mibu Oriko?"

"That padre noh just now—it seems the original record of it was stored in the Latin Document Bureau of Rome's government offices. That Mibu woman found it and decided to dedicate it anew to the Pope."

"That's quite a story," I had to agree. It was a fusion of West and East. Leave it to a major show-business promoter to focus her attention on something others would miss. The world keeps moving, even while I'm getting drunk at some bar. There's nothing funny about it at all.

"She's quite the mogul," the Monk continued. "She took something so simple and turned it into a major international event in the blink of an eye. She's bringing that kid—Tsutsumi or whatever his name is—to the Parthenon to put on a dedication ceremony for the padre noh. It will be a big deal, with the Pope in attendance, and the event will be broadcast by satellite to Japan and throughout Europe. It seems tickets for the Acropolis that night are already selling for more than twice their price."

"That's impressive," I muttered without emotion.

"It's the Olympic spirit. The world is one, and all that. Say, there's a strange rumor going around," said the Monk, lowering his voice. "They say that Tsutsumi Kanesuke and Mibu Oriko are sleeping together."

I was stunned into silence. I wasn't surprised at the rumor about Tsutsumi and Mibu. The world was full of couples. No pairing was too strange to be beyond possibility. There was nothing odd about Tsutsumi and Mibu becoming intimate. For events like these, I made a habit of reading women's weekly magazines on a daily basis. No, what amazed me was that the Monk showed any interest in such a scandal.

Unperturbed by my surprise, the Monk continued.

"Well, in a way, they're both like stars. They're naturally keeping their relationship discreet. But they were spotted by somebody who's bad news—a reporter by the name of Akase who works for one of those scandal sheets."

"The pair are being blackmailed," I interjected, unable to contain my impatience. "How wonderful for them. It's a great lesson on playing with fire. The story belongs in textbooks. It has nothing to do with our HPL Society."

The Monk did not react to my sarcasm. He reached toward the light switch on the wall.

"I want you to watch this film again."

I hastily lit a cigarette. I thought it would get in the way of the visual effects to some extent. I had a full measure of respect for the Monk, but this high-handed and arbitrary attitude didn't sit well.

The room went dark, and the rectangle of light appeared again.

An urban setting appeared on the screen. It was a street lined with boutiques. It could have been someplace in Roppongi or Harajuku.

A solitary man came walking "this" way. He was a middle-aged man with a sloppily tied necktie. The ballpoint pens stuffed in his breast pocket vividly conveyed his personality. Without even having to be told, I immediately knew it was Akase, the reporter for a third-rate weekly magazine.

I failed to suppress a yawn. Unless it were a sex film, I had no interest in observing a scandal-sheet magazine reporter involved in blackmail.

My yawn was cut short, and my expression froze with astonishment.

A column of flame engulfed Akase. It wasn't that he had caught on fire from something. The flames seemed to have appeared out of thin air. The scene was hard to watch. Fat ran from Akase's body as if from a wax figure. The pillar of fire kept walking. A right arm that had nearly turned to charcoal extended from the flames. It was unutterably eerie.

The lack of audio further heightened the sense of immediacy. I sensed the stench of burning grease in a frying pan. I loved steak, but I probably wouldn't be able to look at one for days.

The fiery column finally disintegrated. The temperatures had been high enough to melt even his bones. All that remained was something that looked like cinders.

The lights came on.

My face must have been ashen. The cigarette tasted like paper. I would have vomited if the Monk hadn't been watching.

"Akase was dressed up for an early morning walk with his girlfriend."

Even the Monk's expression looked worn.

"Because the girlfriend was into making 8mm movies at the time, she managed to capture Akase's final moments on film. The poor woman was in a state of shock for several days. It's no wonder. She was just casually filming when through the lens she saw her boyfriend engulfed in flames."

"How did the police explain it?" I finally managed to utter in a rasping voice.

"Lightning. There couldn't have been much for them to investigate."

The Monk gazed at me piercingly.

"So, then, does this have nothing to do with our HPL Society?" he asked.

"I misspoke," I said, slowly shaking my head. "This was clearly the doing of Cthulhu. Akase was blackmailing Tsutsumi Kanesuke and Mibu Oriko. Seeing him die like this, we have to consider the possibility that one of the two is connected to Cthulhu."

"I want you to investigate the woman."

The Monk closed his eyes. An expression appropriate to his age began to return. It was an old man's face.

"Who will investigate Tsutsumi?"

"I already have young Aoki on it. The film we just saw was also Aoki's work."

"Aoki . . ."

"You think he's not up to it?"

"The way he is now, there's no way he could do a decent job."

I felt guilty about maligning a colleague, but that was nothing compared to sending a colleague to his death, knowing what I did.

"He only just found out the truth about the HPL Society on the last hit. He only just learned that we're essentially vigilantes. He's still young. The shock of it must have been considerable. Keeping him off on-site work for a while might be—"

"This conversation is over," interrupted the Monk. "The noh dedication ceremony at the Parthenon concerns me. I can't help feeling that something big is planned. We only have a little more than two weeks left, but I want to stop it any way we can."

I had to keep silent. By then, the Monk was almost completely unwilling to listen. He would pay no attention to what someone like me had to say.

When I left the room, I looked back at the Monk. He was fingering a button on his suit while lost in thought over some matter. In its own way, his orange scarf looked at home on his wrinkled neck.

I didn't consider the Monk a hard-hearted old man. It was just that his excessive knowledge of esoteric practices had led him to ethics and principles far removed from those of ordinary men. At times I found that vexing.

— 3 —

Mibu Oriko had been renting a suite at a certain first-class hotel in the city for a long time. She lived abroad for half of each year, so living in a hotel must have been less expensive. Of course, a single night at that hotel must have cost the equivalent of a month's rent for my rundown apartment.

I parked my car in the hotel's spacious underground parking lot. It looked like a showroom for fancy automobiles. Compared to them, my secondhand domestic ride hardly seemed worthy of being called an automobile.

The night was late, but the hotel residents seemed to make no distinction between night and day. Cars came and went in a steady stream. I even caught sight of a few foreigners with what were obviously high-class call girls. They could get away with it because they were foreign. If a Japanese did the same thing, he'd be ejected from the hotel with a veneer of politeness over ill-disguised contempt. Hotels of this type retained a colonialist nature.

I had been camped out in my car for over two hours. Although she wasn't quite a classy call girl, my partner was so passionate that not even a call girl could compare with her. Her kisses were so intense they could tear your throat out.

She was a Doberman pinscher.

A two-year-old female Doberman was in the back seat. I had borrowed her from a dog breeder I knew. I sometimes had her help me out, so the Doberman and I were acquainted. Otherwise there was no way I would do something as risky as riding in the same car with such a vicious animal.

The Doberman was curled up in the back seat, and occasionally let out a low growl. She seemed to dislike her date, which was me. Nobody likes a drunk.

I had brought a thermos of coffee, but I had hardly touched it. No drink in the world was better than whiskey. I had been assuaging my empty belly by knocking back nothing but whiskey.

"How about it?"

I held out the flask to the Doberman.

"Want a drink?"

She pointedly ignored me. She could hardly be recommended as a bar hostess. She was hopeless when it came to entertaining guests.

The Doberman's ears perked up. It was clear she had heard something. I hurriedly switched off the dome light and looked around the parking area.

A white Citroen DS came into the parking lot. It was Mibu Oriko's car. It seemed her highness was finally gracing the castle with her return.

Her handling of the vehicle showed considerable skill. She was surely an intelligent woman. She smoothly slipped the Citroen into a tiny parking space and got out of the car. She wore a long, light blue dress of simple cut. Even at a distance, I could tell she was extraordinarily beautiful. She and Tsutsumi Kanesuke would make a glamorous couple.

The Doberman growled quietly.

"There's no need for that," I consoled her. "You're one of a kind yourself."

Oriko headed toward the elevators. Her long, light blue dress gave her a nymph-like appearance.

Luckily, the flow of cars in and out had stopped. It was a golden opportunity. I opened a back door.

"Go."

At my command, the Doberman burst out like a torpedo. Dobermans were born to kill, and she took full advantage of her natural abilities.

The Doberman surged straight toward Oriko. Oriko finally seemed to notice the dog, but she did not scream, as I had expected. Perhaps she was frozen with fear.

Of course, I intended to call the Doberman back to the car at the last possible moment. Making mincemeat of beautiful women was not my style. It would be enough to see whether Oriko had any connection to Cthulhu.

The Doberman was relentlessly running Oriko down. Just as I got set to blow the dog whistle, I dropped it.

The howl of the Doberman, crazed with fear, resounded throughout the parking garage. The Doberman's body floated in the air, as if clutched in the hands of an unseen giant.

It was an unbelievable scene. The lights in the parking garage flickered rapidly. The Doberman's howl rose sharply.

The scene resembled a child plucking the limbs from a bug. The Doberman's head and legs were ripped from her body. Blood rained down on the parking-garage floor.

I froze. I felt as if I had been impaled on an icicle. Reason screamed in protest at this unbelievable event.

The Doberman's torso fell to the ground, looking like a fuzzy black log. It was gruesome.

Mibu Oriko had already disappeared into an elevator.

I leaped from the car and vomited. Even after my stomach had been emptied, the nausea showed no sign of abating.

A young group that had come down to the parking garage noticed the Doberman's carcass and grew agitated. As the screams of young women rang in my ears, I grew convinced of the ties between Oriko and Cthulhu.

— 4 —

Aoki's investigation did not seem to be making progress. Apparently, he had not been able to obtain definitive proof that Tsutsumi Kanesuke was connected to Cthulhu.

I could no longer put off getting to the bottom of my suspicions about Oriko.

The day after the Doberman died, I resolved to confront Oriko directly. The preliminary skirmishing was over. If I wanted more, I had to become the decoy myself. I had to serve myself up to Oriko on a platter. Whether she would cook and eat me or turn me into sashimi was up to her.

I was in the hotel lobby, waiting for Oriko to come down.

Nine in the morning. The time when the day's gears begin to turn. I had heard all sorts of things about Oriko, but not that she was an early riser. If I waited patiently, I ought to succeed in getting her.

I yawned repeatedly. I had never been said to be an early riser, either.

The lobby of a ritzy hotel is a comfortable place to while away time. You can ogle pretty singers, see whiz-kid businessmen, and become absorbed in thought regarding the philosophical proposition of the unequal distribution of wealth. Best of all, unlike a coffee shop, it's free.

I must have been waiting for about an hour when Mibu Oriko appeared in the lobby. She was wearing a silk blouse and a beige skirt. I was reminded of the truth behind the time-worn expression that beautiful women look good in anything. As soon as she appeared, the ladies and gentlemen in the lobby all seemed to be relegated to minor roles.

I slowly stood up. The lead actor was about to make his entrance. The role may have been a bit too heavy for me, but I could overcome that with my acting ability. Character actors were a dime a dozen.

But before I could speak, Oriko was surrounded by several men. All were middle-aged, fat and flabby from idle living. They seemed to be loudly peppering her with demands. Their angry shouting in the presence of the public was boorish.

I felt as if I'd been beaten to the punch. I stood to one side of them and tried to listen in on what they were saying. Eavesdropping is my greatest pleasure under any circumstances.

I gathered that the men were associated with the Nohgaku Performers' Association. They made an easy living resting on their laurels in the noh tradition. They had no need to polish their skills. They were assured of a considerable income by getting amateurs to practice. Their indolence was cited as the reason for the moribund state of noh.

They seemed to feel that their livelihoods were threatened by Tsutsumi and Oriko's current undertaking. Apparently none of them even had the decency to feel shame for their own indolence. They merely clamored hysterically. Nasty epithets like "lying bitch" and even "swindler" were hurled without letup.

Oriko's expression revealed growing annoyance. These men were the type to scream abuse when gathered in numbers. They would never listen to reason.

It was time for me to make my entrance.

"I'm sorry I'm late," I said, pushing my way into their midst. "Shall we go?"

The men were surprised into silence, but no more than Oriko herself. Taking her hand, I started to cut across the lobby. I never passed up an opportunity to hold hands with a beautiful woman.

The men seemed taken aback. They showed no indication of following us.

I coerced Oriko into joining me for a cup of tea. It was the honor of a knight. Having been rescued, she could hardly decline my invitation.

We went inside a nearby ice-cream parlor. At that time of day, nothing else was open. Ordinarily, my drinker's pride wouldn't allow me to set foot in a place like that.

We had no time for idle chatter. I decided to get right to the heart of the matter. I put a photograph of Akase on the table. It was a frame from the 8mm film, the one where he was engulfed in flames.

"That's a horrible photo," Oriko knitted her brows. "It's in very poor taste."

"Doesn't it bring anything to mind?"

"I don't know what you mean."

"Last night, you killed a dog."

Oriko said nothing. Her expression did not change. She flicked Cartier lighter and light a cigarette. She had the elegance of an actress in a cigarette commercial .

"A man set a dog on me last night."

Oriko blew smoke out slowly.

"As a matter of fact, he looked a lot like you."

Here was a formidable woman. Because her beauty was so overwhelming, an ordinary man was no match for her. Throwing in the towel was the best course of action. In short, I decided to come clean about who I was.

"Sakaki Eiji, with the HPL Society."

Oriko took my name card as if it were a piece of filth.

"What kind of work do you do?"

Ostensibly, the HPL Society was an "international friendship" organization. It engaged in activities related to international friendship to the extent necessary to provide a cover. But that lie wouldn't fly with Oriko, so I decided to reveal the truth about the HPL Society.

"'HPL' stands for 'H.P. Lovecraft'," I said, gazing squarely into Oriko's eyes. "Do you know who H.P. Lovecraft was?"

"He was an American horror writer, wasn't he?" Oriko replied confidently. "As I recall, he died in 1937."

She evidently knew a considerable amount about Lovecraft. I supposed she must have realized what HPL stood for the moment she saw my card.

"Lovecraft was a great horror writer. He left us a number of outstanding works. Among them is a series of works known as the 'Cthulhu' pieces," I said, adopting the tone of a literature instructor. Even I was captivated by Lovecraft's horror novels.

"Perhaps his Cthulhu mythos can be summed up like this: ancient Earth was inhabited by entities unlike humans—malevolent gods. This Cthulhu and his evil minions were once banished from Earth through the acts of benevolent gods. But Cthulhu and his kind are still vigilantly watching the Earth, waiting for a chance to attack."

"Excuse me," Oriko, said, lowering her gaze to her watch, "but I have an appointment. Could I ask you to save the literary talk for another occasion?"

No, she could not. Now that I had given her a glimpse into the nature of the HPL Society, I had to carry the discussion to its conclusion. I continued, paying no heed to Oriko.

"Of course, the mythos of Cthulhu is merely a product of H.P. Lovecraft's imagination. You can dismiss it as nothing more than a fantasy if you like, but even fantasies contain a grain of truth.

"There are entities on this Earth with unequaled power that are utterly unlike humans. That all nations have similar stories of monstrous beings may corroborate this. *They* have powers that threaten human survival. And they are watching and waiting for the chance to reveal themselves to our world."

"That is a tale that children would love," Oriko said scornfully. "So your HPL Society is working to take down Cthulhu?"

"No," I said, shaking my head. "Cthulhu hasn't appeared in our world yet. If he had, humanity would be on the brink of extinction. Our job is to kill those who attempt to call forth Cthulhu to our world.

"There is no end of persons who try to summon Cthulhu. Perhaps it's because the will to summon him gives the person the kind of special powers that make it possible to draw fire out of nothing or tear vicious dogs apart."

I am by no means a courageous man. My knees trembled as I spoke. I wouldn't have been surprised if flames had sprung from my body at that very instant.

"If I believed you . . ." Oriko spoke with a sense of terrible import. "I wonder if the reason why people try to summon Cthulhu has to do with something other than getting special powers. Maybe Cthulhu is the complete opposite of an evil god.

"Lovecraft may have gotten a glimmering awareness of Cthulhu's existence through that extra sense that so many novelists have. Do you know what Colin Wilson said about Lovecraft? He called him 'a sick, introverted man'. If he were such a sick man, then even if he sensed the existence of something like Cthulhu, it would be natural for him to regard it as demonic."

I couldn't bear to listen to any more such talk from Oriko. The fact was we agents of the HPL Society were well aware of the reason why an endless stream of people tried to call forth Cthulhu. The rightness of that reason tormented all of us agents to the point of despair.

As I got to my feet, I left a parting shot. "It's not just people who summon Cthulhu that we target. In some case we go after those connected to them as well. Please remember that."

I can't deny I was a scoundrel. I had hinted that Oriko's boyfriend Tsutsumi could be a target in a calculated attempt to make Oriko come over to our side. My home phone number was on my name card.

Oriko moved not a muscle, even after I had moved away from the table. Her entire body radiated so much enmity it made me dizzy.

I didn't feel safe until I'd exited the ice-cream parlor.

— 5 —

Night fell.

I was sipping a whiskey and water in my apartment. Pinches of salt were the pitiful accompanying snack.

As a man living alone, I knew no other means to dispel the boredom. Any other night, I'd head out to a bar, but I couldn't go out while waiting for Oriko to contact me.

I really wanted to drink straight whiskey and make my throat burn. If I hadn't had to avoid getting falling-down drunk to meet Oriko, I would have set the carafe of water aside.

From somewhere came the unseasonable sound of a ukulele. Summer this year had been short.

I suddenly had something like a premonition. A sense of tension seized my heart, and a primitive instinct told me that something was off.

The apartment groaned. The floor twisted like paper. I heard the sharp crack of a window shattering.

Everything from magazines to the desk danced madly in the air. My bed was flipped over on its side. The lights buzzed and flickered dizzyingly, over and over.

It was a poltergeist.

It was as if a gust of wind had blown through the room. Even breathing was difficult. It was all I could do to crawl across the floor.

Amid this tumult, the telephone rang out with a tone almost triumphant. Just then, the poltergeist activity abruptly ceased.

A single page from a document fluttered in the air like a wavering butterfly.

Gasping, I picked up the receiver.

"This is Mibu Oriko," came a low voice. "Can you come to the hotel now?"

I had absolutely no reason to turn down such a direct invitation.

Paying a late-night visit to the hotel where a woman lived alone, I felt far from amorous. In truth, when I left my apartment, I couldn't help but wonder whether I would ever return to it again.

As I drove, images of the deaths of Akase and the Doberman filled my mind. Maybe I should have taken out life insurance, but I couldn't think of anyone to be the beneficiary.

When I arrived at the hotel, it was past one o'clock in the morning.

Mibu Oriko's room on the eighth floor had been used by cabinet-level foreign dignitaries, reminding me of her financial clout.

I rang the bell, and Oriko's face peeked from behind the door. The black robe she wore was startlingly alluring.

"You're a dedicated worker," she said mockingly, "coming right away like this."

I wasn't dedicated, but the job didn't allow me to choose my working hours. After a night's sleep I might not have had the courage to come see her. That's how I responded to her scorn.

"You think I might eat you or something," Oriko laughed, exposing a glimpse of her white throat. I caught a glimpse of her lustrously glowing breasts. They were the sort that elicited male desire.

Regretably, I was completely unable to respond. I was a typically dull middle-aged man.

"Killing is not what we want," I said, sinking into a chair. "The best outcome would be for you to make up your mind to stop summoning Cthulhu."

"Oh, you want to continue with that fairy tale."

"Fairy tales don't immolate people and dismember dogs."

"What brutal talk you like."

"It may be brutal, but nothing would be better than to clear this up through talk alone."

I actually had come to her room to win her over. There was no doubt she had a connection to Cthulhu, and I was convinced she was trying to call forth Cthulhu into this world. My intuition about this was exceptionally keen, but I couldn't bring myself to kill her. Ridding the world of that embodiment of the essence of allure was something that I, as a man, found unthinkable.

"Would you like a drink?"

Oriko rose from the chair. There was no need for room service. The room had a small built-in bar.

"Whiskey."

For once I couldn't focus on alcohol. The sight of Oriko's thigh peeking out from the hem of her robe was burned into my retinas. I even began to wonder whether I really was a dull middle-aged man. It seemed I was still a few years from being immune to temptation.

In one swallow, I drained the whiskey she handed me. Through the bottom of the glass I saw Oriko slipping out of her robe. She was completely naked.

I was acutely aware of how greedy heavy drinkers could be, because although I was surprised, I didn't choke or spill my whiskey. To an alcoholic, a drop of whiskey is worth as much as a pearl.

I simply let my jaw drop.

Oriko's smooth nude body glistened, that dark triangle fully visible. Her naked body was perfectly formed and free of any blemish. It was the figure of a goddess that men couldn't help dreaming of until the end of their days.

Oriko revealed her nakedness for only a few seconds.

"Excuse me while I take a shower," she said, and with that she disappeared into the bathroom.

Oriko's actions were clearly intended to be provocative. Regrettably, her provocation worked. That's why men can't be trusted.

I couldn't sense any part of my body but my groin. The desire was overwhelming. The incandescent heat was almost agony.

I realized that I had been drugged with an aphrodisiac, but that knowledge didn't diminish my surging desire in the least. Reason had already lost all meaning.

I groaned. I was completely crazed with lust. The fingers of both hands dug into my trousers.

Along with the sound of the streaming water of the shower came Oriko's husky voice. "That fairy tale—it's actually quite interesting."

Maybe I should have shouted with joy then. Oriko had as much as admitted her connection to Cthulhu. But I was far from feeling the elation of victory, because sexual arousal had reached its peak. It was almost like torture.

Oriko continued to speak. She was relaxed and even hummed.

"But have you ever considered this? Let's say that forceful suppression was needed in order for humanity to survive. Large cities are like museums of the fighting instinct. Humans have completely lost the animal instinct to be content with what they have. As animals, humans are completely warped.

"That goes for religion, too. Every religion is devoted to robbing humans of their vital animal senses. For humans to survive as a species, individuality had to waste away. The Judeo-Christian religions are the prime example of this. Everything sensual and imaginative is viewed as idolatry and denied. But when it comes to inflexible rigorism, Protestantism may be at the forefront.

"In any case, humans are warped and lead an existence fraught with monstrosity."

What Oriko was saying had lost all meaning and was no more than a woman's voice. I couldn't understand a single word. Overwhelming desire had transformed me into a mere male animal.

I staggered to my feet. I could think of nothing other than embracing Oriko. My groin seethed with the heat of molten iron. The distance to the bathroom seemed like an infinitely long course to traverse.

Oriko went on. "I saw it—what you people call Cthulhu—in Rome. It was almost like a divine revelation. It flickered into our world for only an instant, but I realized that humans are warped and that it was our mission to the release Cthulhu into this world. And so . . ."

I pushed open the bathroom door. Oriko's white nakedness could be seen through the steam from the shower, concealing a siren's beauty that held the power to quench my hunger.

I reached out and gathered Oriko's naked body into my arms. It was as if she had been waiting for me to fall into her trap. My tongue was sucked into her mouth.

I moaned. Demonic ecstasy might be a name for it. What seethed and surged was on the verge of release at that very instant. I kneeled on the floor and buried my face between Oriko's legs. I suppose I was behaving shamefully, but I no longer retained even a vestige of reason.

From above came the sound of Oriko's maniacal laughter. It made me think of a triumphant witch.

— 6 —

I seemed to have an intense desire to return to the womb. You could call it the ultimate in autism. It was beyond sexual intercourse. I had lost all interest in the outside world.

Outwardly, I must have seemed no different from someone in a vegetative state, fed through a tube and barely alive. I had no will to live. I was content merely to loll idly within a womb conjured up in a delusion.

It could have been called an ingenious murder. It was a trap formed by a woman's body. Even if I lived on, fed through a tube, I was no different from a corpse. I would spend the rest of my life wasting away in bed.

I thought I'd never return to this world.

I heard the repeated ringing of a bell. It sounded like cymbals crashing at my ears. With the resounding peals came hard blows.

My brain seemed paralyzed. The pain was like a chisel being driven into my clouded consciousness.

It resembled the agony of birth—the pain of giving birth to myself.

Even with the help of the bell, extricating myself from the womb of delusion was not an easy task. I floated in somnolence for a long time.

Then suddenly, without warning, I awoke.

"He seems to be awake," came the Monk's voice. With a final clear peal, the bell stopped ringing.

I pushed the blanket back and sat up in bed. My body, drenched in sweat, was like a wet rag. I felt a piercing pain in my shoulders.

I looked around the room in bewilderment. I was at the HPL Society, in what we informally called the operations room. The dull scene of rows of teletype machines and computers bore no comparison to Oriko's opulent suite.

My memory was shorted out. I could remember nothing beyond getting into bed with Oriko. I was astonished that she had suddenly transformed herself into the Monk. I could think of no worse nightmare.

"What happened?" I muttered in a daze.

"You've been asleep for three days," said the Monk, smiling sardonically. "You were curled up like this, in the fetal position. Apparently, you were found nearly naked in a park."

The Monk was holding a handbell like those used in ceremonies of the esoteric Tendai sect. From his blue pin-striped suit and red scarf, it would have been hard to believe he was a master of esoteric Buddhism. He gave the impression of a playboy at a home for the aged. And yet it was an inarguable fact that the Monk had enough mental power to split huge trees.

"Leave it to you," I said, rubbing my face. "That woman's paranormal abilities are first-rate. If you hadn't intervened, I would never have awakened."

"It's not just her paranormal abilities. Her skills in seduction also seem formidable," said the Monk, his face taking on its usual look of a priest steeped in worldly pleasures. "How brazen! Especially since she's just about at the prime child-bearing age."

It was as if he had witnessed my shame. My behavior could not be justified.

"I experienced a different kind of peak," I said, trying to dispel the mood with wry humor. "So, anyway, what happened to Oriko?"

"Nothing. She left for Athens yesterday."

I was silent.

It was the crime of lust. For a man like me, failing to accomplish my mission was more painful than any punishment.

Aoki came into the room. His expression was strained. The tension was high. It was the tension of a neurotic, and it carried danger with it.

"Oh, you're awake," said Aoki, his voice also wavering.

I shifted my gaze from Aoki to the Monk. The Monk remained unperturbed. Although plainly aware of Aoki's unbalanced nerves, he had decided to make no outward show of it.

I couldn't help questioning the Monk's real intentions. In this state, Aoki wouldn't be fit to work.

"It seems that Tsutsumi Kanesuke is only doing what Mibu Oriko tells him," said Aoki in a rush. "Mibu Oriko came up with the plan on her own, it looks like."

"The plan?" I asked. My brain was slowly creaking into operation. "What kind of plan?"

"The plan to summon Cthulhu and all his minions throughout the world," said the Monk.

I said nothing. I couldn't comprehend the Monk's words right away.

"The dance that Mibu Oriko is having Tsutsumi Kanesuke perform isn't the padre noh," said the Monk, his face ominously expressionless. "It's a kind of evocation of demons for calling forth Cthulhu. Tsutsumi seems convinced that it's a padre noh play, but the dedication ceremony at the Parthenon is going to be broadcast by satellite to viewers around the world. Do you follow me? That Mibu Oriko woman intends to summon Cthulhu and his minions by means of satellites and television."

Amazement couldn't begin to express what I felt. Using television for a demon evocation? Could any idea be more fanciful or grotesque? It was like a bad joke.

"Then Mibu Oriko isn't the one we should kill," I muttered, half in a daze. "The dedication ceremony will go on even if we kill her. The person we should kill is . . ."

"Tsutsumi Kanesuke," declared the Monk. "It's too bad for him, because he knows nothing, but the dedication ceremony won't be stopped unless he's killed."

This wouldn't be the first time that the HPL Society had killed an innocent person. But killing Tsutsumi Kanesuke would be more difficult than anything before.

"Tsutsumi's whereabouts are unknown," said the Monk. "We know that he left for Athens, but his moves after that are unknown. He's vanished completely."

The HPL Society members resident in Athens were continuing to search frantically, but it was possible that he would not be found until the night of the ceremony. So if we got any opportunity to kill him, it might only be during the dedication ceremony.

But there was no way we could bring weapons into a ceremony that even the Pope was scheduled to attend. If we went ahead with the hit anyway, we ran the risk of giving the world the impression that the HPL Society was a terrorist organization.

The HPL Society was a powerful organization, but no group is strong enough to take on the world. Even the Nazis had been crushed.

"To kill Tsutsumi Kanesuke, we will need to make full use of the HPL Society's organizational and economic capabilities."

As I listened to the Monk lay out the details of what you could call our "assassination plan," I felt growing disbelief. The plan was unprecedented and likely never to be repeated. For someone recovering from infirmity, the plan was beyond grandiose and left me stunned.

From a pocket, the Monk took out a silver bullet. I hardly need to explain that in Western Europe silver bullets had long been regarded as indispensable for killing werewolves. In the HPL Society, a silver bullet meant an assassination order.

I accepted the silver bullet without a word.

"I want you two to go to Athens," said the Monk, as if about to wrap up, "because having hits carried out by our members whenever possible is one of the rules of the HPL Society."

The next day Aoki and I set out for Athens.

— 7 —

We were dining at a restaurant on Ermou Street. Seen from the restaurant, the streets of Athens seemed unusually busy.

The noh dedication ceremony at the Parthenon was to be held that evening. The news media had already reported the arrival of the Pope. It was to be expected that the festival-loving citizenry of Athens was somewhat excited.

I was packing away Greek food. Greek cuisine, made as it is with large amounts of olive oil, is not in line with Japanese preferences, but even so, Aoki's lack of appetite was hard to understand.

"What's wrong?" I asked Aoki. "You haven't eaten a thing."

"I don't like the idea of a last meal for a condemned man," said Aoki, forcing a weary smile. "It somehow seems overly sentimental."

Those were ominous words. At the very least, they shouldn't have been uttered before a big job. But it would be pointless to blame my drug-addicted partner for saying them. Once this job was over, I intended to make Aoki leave the HPL Society. Depending on the circumstances, I was even prepared to confront the Monk. I couldn't bear to watch a young man destroy himself any longer.

I washed down the oil in my mouth with a white wine called Santa Helena. My appetite was boundless, but time wasn't.

"Shall we go?" I asked, jumping up from my chair.

"Right," said Aoki, slowly getting to his feet.

Admission to the Acropolis that night was arranged through the exertions of an HPL Society member stationed in Athens. Given that neither Aoki nor I was a world-famous figure, the agent's efforts to gain us entrance credentials must have been extraordinary, and his task had surely been made more difficult by the lack of time.

The agent had worked hard, and for our part, Aoki and I were dressed to the nines in black tuxedos. We tried our best to look like Oriental aristocrats, but unfortunately our efforts came to naught. We looked like nothing more than nightclub managers. Frankly, it may have been a matter of class.

By the time we arrived at the Acropolis, it was already past eight. We had only an hour left until Tsutsumi Kanesuke's dance.

The Acropolis shone with more splendor than ever. Powerful lights that had been set up all around made it stand out amid the darkness in a dream-like scene.

The words "festive excitement" hardly sufficed. The scene had the appearance of mass hysteria. I wondered if every single citizen of Athens had flocked here. Those who had not been granted entry to the Acropolis crowded around the foot of the hill.

Helicopters flew overhead, and on the ground, the mobile-relay trucks of television stations were visible everywhere. It looked as if all the journalists in the world had been assembled.

I couldn't help admiring Oriko's prowess as a promoter.

Naturally, not even Oriental aristocrats were exempt from being frisked by the security guards. The search was the ultimate in thoroughness—so strict that not even the smallest weapon could get through. After all, in a certain sense, the Pope was the most important of all VIPs for Europeans.

The society's agent in Athens seemed to be quite capable. We were able to take up a position in the third row of the seats installed on the perimeter of the Parthenon. From there we would be able to make out the expression on the Pope's face.

The program had already begun. A certain famous Hollywood star was the emcee. Standing on the Parthenon, he was lit up in a rainbow of colors by spotlights all around.

We hardly paid any attention to the program. As big a show as it was, it couldn't entertain killers with a job ahead of them. I was barely aware of the thunderous applause at the Pope's entrance. His special seats seemed to be a mere twenty meters from our own.

Aoki's evident tension was nothing compared to my own. It was so bad I felt I might pass out at any moment. My forehead glistened with greasy sweat.

There was nothing left for us to do. All the preparations had been finished; we had only to verify the results with our own eyes. Whether it would be a success or a failure, we could do nothing further to change the outcome in any way. If that weren't the case, I never would have let Aoki accompany me in the state he was in.

Time passed slowly, like a file grating on our nerves. It was a trial that made my stomach hurt. The unending address by the mayor of Athens made me want to scream. For a hit man, the wait until the moment of murder is as unbearable as torture.

The illumination around the Parthenon abruptly changed to a deep-sea blue. The spectators, who until then had been somewhat restless, fell silent as if struck by lightning.

"It's starting," muttered Aoki, his voice hoarse.

A noh chorus began in low tones. The notes of the musicians came to us.

The combination of noh chant and the Parthenon created a truly bizarre impression. At that instant, the Parthenon seemed to have transformed into the gate to hell. It was horribly gloomy and out of keeping with the program's billing as a "fusion of West and East."

The blue of the lights subtly changed hue signaling the entrance of Tsutsumi Kanesuke, the principal actor. He stood motionless at the Parthenon's bottom step in a stance that conveyed concentrated pathos and portended the explosive dance to follow.

The spectators were silent. The noh chorus and the music alternately rose, as if chasing each other.

Tsutsumi took his first step—the first step to summoning Cthulhu and his minions to the world and pushing humanity to the brink of ruination.

Just then a military satellite in the distant reaches of outer space should have started to rotate and aim its laser cannon directly at the Parthenon. That was how the HPL Society intended to kill Tsutsumi Kanesuke.

It may be hard to believe, but since the mid-1960s the surveillance systems on spy satellites had been able to count the leaves on a tree. The speed of advances in spy and military satellite technology had outstripped even that of probes to Mars. Lasers on military satellites were accurate to within thirty centimeters. Aoki and I had had to calculate Tsutsumi's position at the Parthenon as precisely as possible and transmit that data.

By no means did we plan to bring a military satellite to bear against our opponent's communication satellites. This hit was like no other. Not only could we bring in no weapons, the event was being attended by the Pope and other notables. We could come up with no other way. Clearly, the odds of success would be far higher than with a sharpshooter, and even the most skilled medical examiner would throw up his hands when trying to determine the cause of death. No one would ever entertain the thought that a laser on a military satellite had been used to kill one solitary man.

In a certain sense, it could be called a global conspiracy. It was possible precisely because the HPL Society was deep inside the military-industrial complex, NASA, and a host of acronym agencies. Hadn't I said that the HPL Society was a huge, powerful organization?

The principal actor had moved to the Parthenon's central column. With every step and every movement of his hands, unsublimated passion flared and burned. The chorus was tinged with the loneliness of a plaintive Buddhist chant.

The time had arrived.

In my mind I was screaming. There was no better time than now to kill Tsutsumi Kanesuke. The minions of Cthulhu scattered around the world may have already been roused from their slumber and starting to move.

The darkness suddenly seemed to expand as if it had been pierced by a high-voltage current. Something intensely powerful connected the sky and the Parthenon at that moment.

Maybe only those of us who knew the circumstances sensed it. The laser was not a killer ray like those in the comic books. Amid this dazzling illumination, it would no doubt be impossible for anyone to see it.

"We did it," I couldn't help muttering.

But the powerful laser hadn't harmed a hair on Tsutsumi's head. I watched intently as, incredibly, he continued to dance.

Tsutsumi had formidable powers of self-transcendence. He must have evaded the laser without even being aware of it. No human could have done it. The only explanation was that an evil spirit of the arts had possessed his body. The power of performance had bested the latest scientific weapon.

I let out a groan of despair.

And then that frozen moment shattered.

Aoki leaped to his feet and raced toward the Pope, letting out a crazed yell. He had finally snapped.

It happened so fast that the security personnel did nothing for a few moments. Taking advantage of this opportunity, Aoki leaped into the special seats and tore the pastoral staff from the hands of the bewildered Pope.

The staff, which resembled a giant key, was gilded and extremely heavy. Like the papal miter, it was a symbol of the Pope.

Aoki spun on his heels. Brandishing the staff above his head, he ran straight toward Tsutsumi Kanesuke, howling madly.

Tsutsumi had evaded the laser, but he seemed to know of no way to parry Aoki's wild attack. I watched as Tsutsumi's brains were split open and splattered by the staff.

The security personnel fired their guns in rapid succession. Hit dozens of times, Aoki's body danced in the air with the lightness of a paper doll, then fell to the ground.

By the time the shooting had stopped, Aoki's body was a mere lump of red meat.

Panic among the audience reached a fever pitch. It was unbridled mass hysteria.

Amid the burgeoning tumult, I alone stood within a strangely cold space.

I now realized why the Monk had made Aoki take part in this operation. Aoki was a form of insurance if the plan failed. The Monk must have somehow foreseen that Aoki's nerves couldn't have withstood the mission's failure. He had anticipated what would happen.

Aoki's drug habit had turned out to be an advantage, because everyone would believe his actions were the result of a mind unhinged by narcotics.

It was horrifically cold-blooded, yet strangely I felt no animosity toward the Monk, only despondence, as if I were sinking into the bowels of the Earth.

One other person also seemed overcome with despair.

Amid the shouting and screaming spectators, I spied Mibu Oriko. Standing in a motionless daze, her face resembled a noh mask. Her gaze was fixed on Tsutsumi's corpse and showed no sign of shifting.

I also turned my gaze to Tsutsumi's corpse. Next to his body lay the bloodied pastoral staff. Depending on how you looked at it, you might say that papal authority had blocked Cthulhu's emergence. But which was God and which was Satan?

— 8 —

I couldn't go without paying a visit to the Athinas Street hotel where Mibu Oriko was lodging.

All things have a fitting end, but that this incident had ended with the deaths of Tsutsumi and Aoki was hard to bear. Oriko and I deserved the blame. It seemed one of us should die in order for the curtain to fall on this incident. But considering Oriko's paranormal abilities, it seemed obvious which of us would face death.

Maybe I half-longed for death. Maybe I felt a loathing for the work of the HPL Society. I would have been quite happy to have died at Oriko's hand.

But she had outdone me again. When I stepped into her room I found her body lying on the bed.

A glance at the small bottle on the nightstand made it clear that it was suicide. It seemed Oriko had truly loved Tsutsumi.

I was in a stupor. Even as I regarded Oriko's dead body, I felt nothing. I was pathologically devoid of emotions. I felt dissociated and numb.

"So Oriko's dead, too," I murmured and then tried to leave the room. That's when I noticed *him*. It was Cthulhu. To mourn Oriko's death, Cthulhu had shown himself in our world for a fleeting moment. I gazed at Cthulhu, dazed.

I couldn't make out his shape. He was formless and resembled a kind of aura. He left no image on human retinas, even though his presence could be sensed.

Cthulhu's presence was unsurpassingly beautiful and pure. His grief for Oriko poured directly into my own heart, like a cool, clear stream. In the presence of Cthulhu, troubled hearts couldn't help but be soothed and find respite.

Then I knew that Cthulhu was none other than the incarnation of the angels and celestial maidens common to all peoples.

He could be described as another path of evolution given to humankind. What had led humanity to this point was its insatiable desire to fight and murder. Kill or be killed; eat or be eaten. But Cthulhu offered another path to humanity. He was an extramental life form, one that made everything possible, and understood all.

Cthulhu represented the possibility of evolution crushed by humankind, an angel that humanity could have striven toward.

It was easy to see why the world's capitalists and militarists backed the HPL Society. If humanity lost its instinct to fight, that insatiable drive to compete, the existence of capitalists and militarists could no longer be justified. Cthulhu's acquisition of power signified their downfall.

The operatives of the HPL Society were well aware of these circumstances. That was what drove me to alcoholism, Aoki to drug addiction, and, in fact, all operatives to ruin.

We were on the wrong side. In the terms of Lovecraft's Cthulhu mythos, the malevolent gods had not been banished from the Earth. They had triumphed, and the good gods had been cast out. We were the agents of the evil ones, patrol troops impeding the entry of the good ones.

I realized I could no longer sense Cthulhu's presence in the room. Casting a final gaze of goodbye to Oriko, I stumbled out of the room.

Tonight would be the start of more alcohol-soaked days.

But I knew I would never give up this battle against Cthulhu, for the work of the HPL Society was my life.

Joe Earle

Translator: "A White Camellia in a Vase"

Joe Earle was Director of Japan Society Gallery in New York until October 2012 and has occupied leadership positions in Asian art departments at the Victoria and Albert Museum, London, and the Museum of Fine Arts, Boston. Over the past thirty-five years he has organized more than two dozen exhibitions in Britain, Japan, Europe, and the United States and written, translated or edited books and catalogs on many aspects of Japanese culture ranging from contemporary art and design through samurai sword-fittings to flower-arrangement bronzes and lacquered medicine cases. He is currently based in London, working as an independent art consultant. Under the *nom de plume* Dink Tanaka, he was winner of the 2009 Kurodahan Press Translation Prize.

Nora Stevens Heath

Translator: "The Finish Line"

A full-time freelance translator, Nora Stevens Heath earned her BAs in Japanese and in linguistics from the University of Michigan in Ann Arbor. She considers herself one of the luckiest people on earth to be able to do what she loves and get paid for it. Nora works out of her home in southeast Michigan, which she shares with her husband Chris, their son Dashiell, and their dog Stanzie, but most of the time she's trying to find her way back to Japan. Visit her Web site at http://www.fumizuki.com/

Jim Hubbert

Translator: "Lest You Remember"

Jim Hubbert has a full-time position deciphering texts in Tokyo.

271

Daniel Huddleston
Translator: "Fin and Claw"

Daniel Huddleston is a lifelong lover of science fiction, Japan, and most any combination of the two. After working as a technical writer for nearly a decade, he followed his dreams to Japan, where he now teaches, translates, and works on his own science fiction writings.

Mikhail S. Ignatov
Translator: "The Warning"

By an amusing accident of fate, Mikhail Sergeevich Ignatov was born the same year that his most famous namesake took the reins of the Soviet Union. Ten years later, the lesser-known Mikhail Sergeevich immigrated to the US, where he eventually took his MA in Japanese Literature at the University of Arizona. He currently resides in Japan.

Pamela Ikegami
Translator: "Angel French"

Pamela Ikegami, a native of Portsmouth, NH, teaches Japanese language and culture at the University of New Hampshire. She has a BA in Japanese and Asian Studies from the University of Colorado Boulder and an MA in Japanese from the University of Hawai'i at Manoa. She has also worked as a freelance translator since 1990. She loves to read scary Japanese stories, but can't bear to watch Japanese horror films.

Daniel Jackson
Translator: "Heart of Darkness"

Daniel Jackson is a retired professional translator living in Japan, who now dabbles in literary translations that interest him, and spends most of his time reading and walking. He is studying pre-Raphaelite paintings, but has no plans (or talent) to take up painting even as a hobby, being quite satisfied with words.

Edward Lipsett

Translator: "To the Blue Star"

After spending decades translating technical documentation in Japan, I've become fascinated by the intricacies of literary translation. As an individual I am still learning how to comprehend the fullness of Japanese and express it equally well in English, while as a company I am also committed to continuing and expanding Kurodahan Press to help get more Japanese—and other—literature into English. I still wish I could speak another language or two, though. I can be reached through the Kurodahan Press website, or Facebook.

Nancy H. Ross

Translator: "Invisible"

Nancy H. Ross worked as a reporter and editor before coming to Japan in 1993. She was the winner of the Distinguished Translation Award in the 4th Shizuoka International Translation Competition in 2003 and the 2008 Kurodahan Press Translation Prize. She lives in Hiroshima Prefecture with her charming cats Koharu and Ayame.

Karen Sandness

Translator: "Sunset"

After studying German and French at Augsburg College in Minneapolis, Karen took what everyone in the 1970s thought was the odd and foolish step of enrolling in Cornell University's FALCON Program in Japanese. From there she went on to earn a Ph. D. in Linguistics at Yale, taking time out to do research at Ochanomizu University in Tokyo. After enduring a year as an unemployed Ph. D. and two years as an underemployed adjunct, she taught Japanese full time for nine years at two colleges in Oregon. When teaching proved to be a dead end job, she first edited college textbooks and then transitioned into Japanese-English translation, which has been her full-time job since 1994. She now lives back in her hometown of Minneapolis, where she fills her non-translating hours with choral singing, reading mysteries and nonfiction, swimming, watching foreign and independent movies, volunteering or agitating for good causes, and being bossed around by her cat.

Marc Schultz
Author: "Green Tea Ice Cream"
Marc Schultz has had three science fiction stories published previously, the most recent in *Strange Horizons*. He has lived in Japan for over 25 years, making a living as a Japanese-to-English translator.

Ginny Tapley Takemori
Translator: "Five Sisters"
Ginny Tapley Takemori is a Japan-based literary translator. Her published translations include works by Meiji writers Okamoto Kidō, Kōda Rohan, and Izumi Kyōka, as well as contemporary authors Furukawa Hideo, Murata Sayaka, Minagawa Hiroko, Yamao Yūko, and Hanawa Kanji.

Angus Turvill
Translator: "A Piece of Butterfly's Wing"
Angus Turvill lives in England. He was winner of the Grand Prize in the 5th Shizuoka International Translation Competition (2005) and runner-up in the British Centre for Literary Translation's John Dryden Competition 2006. He translates, runs translation classes, and dreams of growing his own vegetables.

Science Fiction from **Kurodahan Press**

APHRODITE

YAMADA MASAKI

TRANSLATED BY
DANIEL JACKSON

The floating city

Aphrodite: ever beautiful, ever filled with the limitless energy of creation.

This is the story of Makita Yūichi, a youth who escapes the regimented world of Japanese society for the beauty and freedom of the island city Aphrodite. As the global economy spirals downward, leaving Aphrodite deserted and slated for destruction, only Yūichi can save her...

ISBN 4-902075-01-6 US$15.00 Cover art by Kobayashi Osamu.

Order online (kurodahan.com) or through your local bookseller.

Science Fiction from Kurodahan Press

Administrator
Mayumura Taku

translated by
Daniel Jackson

They must show no love, show no fear...

Trapped between conflicting demands, the Administrators are on a treacherous path to the future...

This compelling collection of four short novels tells the story of the Administrators: governors of Terran colonies far from Earth, far from peace. Mayumura Taku blends an epic SF vision with biting social satire in this classic series. With a cover by award-winning artist Katō Naoyuki.

ISBN 4-902075-00-8   US$15.00

SPECULATIVE JAPAN 2

**"The Man Who Watched the Sea" and
Other Tales of Japanese Science Fiction and Fantasy**

Selected and edited by Edward Lipsett

"...you might ask, 'how Japanese is this'? And the answer is, not
very. It's speculative fiction, to a universal standard."
—John Paul Catton, *Emails from the Edge*

"Speculative Japan is a wild journey across alien terrain. [It] defies
characterization in any genre, illustrating that the term speculative
fiction is a rambling mansion with many peculiar residents, some
comic, some contemplative, some scientific, some folkish. And these
residents are now accessible to the non-Japanese reader by virtue of
these new translations, giving you a bewildering glimpse of contemporary Japanese imagination."
—David Labi, *Metropolis*

ISBN: 978-4-902075-18-2
US$16.00
Cover art by Katō Naoyuki

Order online (kurodahan.com) or through your local bookseller.